SECOND COMING

BY GARY GENTILE

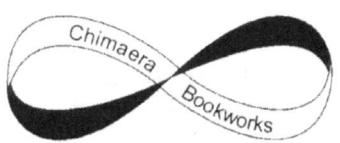
Chimaera Bookworks

Chimaera Bookworks
3 Lehigh Gorge Drive
Jim Thorpe, PA 18229

Additional copies of this book may be purchased from the same address by sending a check or money order in the amount of $20 U.S. for each copy (plus $4 postage per order, not per book, in the U.S. Inquire for shipping cost to foreign countries). Alternatively, copies may be ordered from the author's website and paid by credit card:

http://www.ggentile.com

Front cover picture credits
Top: *Christ Carrying the Cross* (circa 1516) painted by Hieronymous Bosch; middle right: courtesy of the Atomic Energy Commission; bottom: detail from *The Kiss of Judas* (circa 1305) painted by Giotto di Bondone.

International Standard Book Numbers (ISBN)
1-883056-44-6
978-1-883056-44-5

First Edition
Printed in U.S.A.

PROLOGUE

"I asked for this private meeting on the spur of the moment because we have a big problem – the Islamic Revolutionary Forces have developed a time machine."

Frank Marshall, President of the United States, stared without comment for several seconds – so many seconds that Chet Anderson, Director of the Central Intelligence Agency, began to feel decidedly uncomfortable. Anderson wondered if the President did not understand his statement, or if the concept of time travel was so difficult to accept that he didn't know how to respond.

President Marshall drew in a deep breath but otherwise appeared casual. He straightened a fold in his mauve pullover shirt. "Would you care to elaborate?"

Anderson drew a deeper breath. It was impossible for him to appear casual in a charcoal gray three-piece suit and pale blue matching tie, but at least he was able to overcome his trepidation and speak in a normal tone of voice. "Recent intelligence indicates that their machine is nearing completion, and that they intend to use it to alter the past in order to create chaos in the Christian world. . . . " At this point he faltered. He grasped for the words to express his consternation. "I – I can hardly believe myself that time travel is possible, but I assure you that our sources – "

Marshall cut him off in mid-sentence. "Do you consider the situation to be of the *utmost* potential threat to the security of the United States?"

Anderson stumbled awkwardly. "Well, that is, the credibility of such a report is naturally suspect – " This time he cut himself off in mid-sentence. He was so flustered that he failed to recognize immediately the President's operative string of words.

"I mean, yes, I do consider the situation to be of the utmost potential threat to the security of the country."

Marshall barely nodded. "I concur."

He swiveled his thickly padded leather chair so as to face a small control panel that was situated next to his antique wood desk. He flipped back a clear plastic cap that covered a red inset button that was labeled RECORDING FEED. He turned his head, looked across the plush Oval Office into the lens of the surveillance camera, and stated for the record:

"Due to the utmost potential threat that the afore-mentioned matter imposes upon the security of the United States of America, I hereby exercise Presidential prerogative to prevent a recording of a sensitive discussion to reach enemies of the state."

He pressed the button. The camera's green READY light blinked out. A message flashed on the control panel's monitor: RECORDING STOPPED.

Marshall glanced at his watch as he swiveled back to face the CIA director. "I can give you seventeen minutes, Chet."

"Sev – seventeen minutes?"

Marshall grinned. "Nixon was crucified for losing eighteen minutes of tape. I don't plan to exceed that number. Now tell me about this IRF time machine."

Anderson did not get to his current position by being slow on the uptake. He nodded in comprehension but did not grin. "Well, I don't necessarily believe the report, but it originated from sources that we have used in the past – " He paused momentarily at his usage of a time-travel oriented word. " – and that have provided accurate intelligence on a number of occasions. To be frank, if the sources had informed us up front about a time machine, we would have laughed it off as propaganda or misinformation, but that isn't how it came about.

"You see, we've been monitoring the construction of a large facility in the Iranian desert in the Kalmand Protected Area. Satellite imagery shows a circular structure in the shape of a doughnut but with a thin exterior wall that's more like a ring or bracelet than a doughnut, if you follow me."

Marshall nodded curtly.

"Our science experts identified the structure as a cyclotron; a particle accelerator. This is odd because the IRF doesn't conduct pure science experiments. There's a wealth of literature about the breakup of subatomic particles and their subsequent interactions, all freely available. Such experiments don't achieve any useful purpose, uh, that is, not that I have anything against pure science . . . In any case, satisfying scientific curiosity about the makeup of the atom or the structure of atomic particles is not what we expect the IRF to spend money on. Every rial they can steal they spend on weapons, not on scientific research.

"Then we started collating reports from other sources: the distillation of heavy water at one facility, the refinement of pitchblende at another . . . " Anderson spread his hands. "I don't have to draw you a picture of what this means. Every grade-schooler knows that heavy water plus uranium equals nuclear device."

Marshall grinned. "I prefer the term atomic bomb because it tells it like it is, but then I'm from the old school that deplores euphemistic expressions . . . except in political speeches, that is." He grinned again.

Anderson's face softened. "I can't disagree with you, but in my line of work we rely on vague nondescriptives as a means of inducing convenient misperceptions." Now it was his turn to grin at a common Company joke. "To continue – because of the implication of these reports, we changed the priorities of our covert operatives – "

"Spies."

" – who were working in the Middle East, shuffled our resources, recruited more local assets – "

"Informants."

" – augmented emoluments to favorable government officials – "

"Bribes."

" – to produce reliable intelligence. One official who has been in our pocket – "

"To fill his own."

" – for quite some ti – uh, for quite a while, confirmed our suspicions that the IRF was building a weapon of mass destruction to be used against the non-Muslim world: specifically Christianity, but perhaps later against Buddhism. Recently our spy-sats have spotted an increase in transportation activity. Large trucks are moving massive amounts of material in a puzzling pattern whose purpose, we suspect, is intended to confuse our collators. Then this certain official informed us that the cyclotron appearance was a disguise for the true nature of the facility: not to accelerate particles for scientific study, nor were the surrounding buildings constructed as an assembly plant for the fabrication of a nuclear, uh, an atomic bomb, but to create a disturbance in the space-time continuum that would enable the transmission of solid matter into the past. Put two and two together . . . "

Marshall stared silently at Anderson for a couple of seconds. "Smuggling an atomic bomb into the past? That's ingenious, when you think about it. I didn't think the IRF was that farseeing, if you will pardon a timely pun." He grinned at himself. "Okay, Chet, I apologize for my glib interruptions but please don't talk to me as if I were a member of the press. I want my information straight."

Anderson tilted his head forward in a single nod. "Point taken."

Without preamble, "When do you expect this time machine to become operational?"

Anderson hesitated. "Well, uh, excuse me, Frank, but before I go on, I'm astonished at your complete acceptance of the situation. You know I've never misled you in the past, uh, no pun intended . . . but this situation is so bizarre, so farfetched, that it stretches the bounds of credence."

Marshall exhaled loudly. "Permit me to be Ciceronian by saying that I won't mention the fact that nothing we discuss is to leave this room." He did not wait for Anderson's nod of acknowledgment. "I'm not astonished because we have already developed a time machine, and it has been in operation for a year and a half, although the Group is proceeding slowly and cautiously."

In the stunned silence that followed Marshall's blunt admission, the soft pattering of raindrops on the window panes was hauntingly loud. Neither one was distracted by the noise.

"The theoretical work was conducted by physicists in our Advanced Weapons Group. After they determined that the concept might be feasible, they were given the go-ahead to produce a small-scale model. Construction was authorized by my twice-removed predecessor. The project was funded under the Defense Appropriations Bill from a sequestered account that contained unallocated expense money. Final approval was given by my immediate predecessor. We now have a working model."

After a pause, "Who knows about this, uh, time travel machine?"

"It's code-named Project Stitch, but you won't find it in any administrative documents. The only people who know about it are those who are working on it. The project administrator reports only to the President. I didn't learn about the project until after my inauguration, when the Presidential Packet was passed on to me by my predecessor. Even the Vice and the Joint Chiefs aren't privy to this knowledge. Until now, no one else has had a need to know. Project Stitch is *the* – and I emphasize *the* – most highly guarded secret in the country."

Anderson breathed deeply. He never lost eye contact with the President.

"Despite my personal and political position that the public has the right to know everything about their government, and my campaign promise to close the egregious loopholes in the Freedom of Information Act, I have made an executive decision to endorse the secrecy of this project – not because I want to keep knowledge of its existence from the American people, but because we can't afford to let our enemies know about a weapon that is concealed in our arsenal.

"After all, during World War Two we didn't advertise that we were building an atomic bomb. The public was kept in the dark; so were our allies. Even Congress didn't learn about the bomb until it was dropped on Hiroshima. Today's war on terrorism is as real a threat to

American peace and security as both wars against Axis powers. Terrorism is as insidious as Nazism. It's a war against humanity fought in a different manner.

"Project Stitch is a card up the sleeve; an ace in the hole; a means to prevent a terrorist attack from occurring, or to plan a pre-emptive strike, or to undo an attack after it has occurred due to the failure of our intelligence gathering services to detect it in advance."

Anderson inhaled sharply, and opened his mouth to speak.

The President raised his left hand like a traffic cop signaling for a car to stop. "Don't take it personally, Chet. No disparagement was intended. You know better than anyone that gathering and interpreting intelligence isn't a precision discipline. Only in mathematics does A plus B always yield C. When you throw in the human factor, the answer becomes a probability factor that is open to interpretation and that is often biased by the interpreter's expectations.

"Okay, I'm off the soapbox. I thank you for a job well done. The only thing that astonishes me about your report is how the IRF possessed the imagination to conceive that time travel was possible. That has me worried. Be that as it may, instead of bemoaning a bad hand, let's play the cards we've been dealt and decide which ones to discard in the hope of drawing a better hand.

"I will not hog the show, and I will not try to second-guess the way you should proceed. I will facilitate communication between you and the administrator of Project Stitch, then slip out of the picture and let the two of you to decide on the best strategy to employ. Both of you will report directly to me: you about ongoing intelligence-gathering, the project administrator about utilizing *our* time machine to either stop or circumvent the actions of the IRF in the use of *their* time machine.

"I will need you to be available on a moment's notice. Appoint a liaison – someone you trust implicitly – to work with the people at Project Stitch, in whatever capacity you and the administrator deem most suitable. Now, to return to my question, when do you expect their time machine to become operational? Give me a ballpark figure."

Anderson spread his hands. "The heightened activity leads us to believe that commencement is imminent. What that means with regard to objective time is difficult to determine. I would estimate days or weeks rather than months. In any case, time is of the essence."

"Not when you have a time machine that enables you to choose your time of arrival." The President was no longer grinning. "How far back are they planning to go? What are they planning to do?"

Anderson pursed his lips. "Two thousand years, to the time of the Crucifixion."

"Jesus Christ!"

"Exactly. We believe that they are going to intervene with the onset of modern Christianity."

"Are they planning to kill the Savior?"

"On the contrary. They are planning to save Him."

Chapter 1

Laila Masterson plopped her minipurse and the extra-large Duncan Donuts coffee cup on her desk. She doffed her yellow rain slicker and turned around to hang it dripping on the coat tree. Her dark hair, twisted into an oversized bun, had been kept dry by the fold-out hood during her short sojourn from house to car in the driveway.

She dropped into her utilitarian office chair, rolled across the plastic mat, scooped up the coffee cup as she glided past her work station, dug her heels into the carpet in front of the microwave oven on the counter, and nuked the cup even though steam was still escaping through the sip hole. She liked her coffee super-hot, but ever since Stella Liebeck's ludicrous lawsuit against McDonald's, she was able to purchase coffee that was only lukewarm.

While the timer counted down from one minute, she rolled back to her work station. Besides drinking coffee, her first order of business for the day – for every weekday – was to download her email via the secure network server. Her desk computer was never switched off so she could access data remotely when she was home or on the road.

She entered codenames and passwords in order to access her account. After successfully negotiating three firewalls, she entered the final key-code:s a random six-digit nonrepeating number that was generated in an undisclosed or nonexistent facility somewhere in the country, transmitted to a satellite that was parked in a geosynchronous orbit, then telemetered to the display device that was attached to her keychain. The numerals changed every thirty seconds. If she did not type the digits and tap the ENTER key before the new sequence appeared, the system denied her entry, and she had to type the next sequence of digits.

As soon as the microwave timer beeped, she retrieved the cup and glided back to her computer console, sipping gratefully along the way.

If she was too late or mistyped the coded sequence three times consecutively, the system locked her out. In that case she had to call tech support, or, as she referred to it, the helpless desk: a pet name that reflected the "help desk's" lack of efficiency in an organization that was powerless to proceed without good and timely technical support that was all too often not forthcoming.

This is the CIA, for heaven's sake, she was often wont to state in a loud tone of voice as she idled at her desk while a nameless TSP, or technical support person, attempted to mollify her while he or she worked remotely to rectify a system problem or a computer malfunction.

In her more bitter moments she referred to the agency as the CIAO: a play on the Italian salutation that could mean either hello or goodbye: contradictory definitions that made her wonder sometimes whether the Company was coming or going.

Laila sighed deeply. It was too early in the morning to get into a huff over something that had not yet occurred. She sipped casually on the milky hot brew as the message center synchronized with her email account, downloaded files, and organized them into folders by means of security classifications.

Quickly she skimmed the subject headings in order to prioritize her workload. She automatically checked off all of Tim Clement's messages and moved them into a low-priority folder, despite the acronym ASAP in capital letters in the headings. He was a nervous turkey who gobbled that every one of his issues was a crisis situation, when in fact they were never anything more than ordinary interoffice communications that could be handled on a free-time basis.

On the other hand, General Lewis needed responses most immediately, but always prefaced his requests with "at your earliest convenience."

Laila's initial task was to separate the wheat from the chaff, bake the wheat, and dump the chaff on subordinates who held the appropriate security clearance for the matters at hand. Being chief collector, collator, and analyst in her unit had both perks and high pay, but with those benefits came the crush of responsibility. She hardly had any time to call her own. What spare time she did have she spent at home cuddling with Harvey. Sad to say, Harvey was a cat. She hadn't had a date with a man since her devastating divorce more than three years earlier, after learning that her husband was having multitudinous sexual relations . . . with other men.

The ringing desk phone interrupted her morning litany before she plunged into intense concentration by putting out fires before they spread to other forests.

She lifted the handset off the cradle. "Masterson."

"Hello, Bat."

"Hello, Brian."

Brian Halpert was her boss and currently her best friend. He was the only person since her childhood who made reference to the famous gunslinger and lawman. And he made the reference constantly. Despite his age – he was a grandfather twice over – the soul of a little boy resided inside his textured skin. And he was proud of it!

"I need to see you right away."

Although day to day operations were fairly informal, the CIA was neither a corporation nor a sitcom. No one argued or made snide remarks to the camera when a Section Chief issued an urgent request. Laila did not complain about her workload or the number of emails that stuffed her in-box to overflowing. Compliance with operational orders was an important part of her job.

"I'll be right there."

Despite her promise, she couldn't leave until she logged out of her secure networks. She opened General Lewis's email, quickly ascertained that it required an immediate reply, drafted a brief memo that forestalled a worsening situation, then logged out of her secure areas. Anyone who tried to hack into her computer without the proper access codes would literally fry the computer when a miniature incendiary device wiped the hard drive clean. All data and emails were backed up automatically on the mainframe in the basement vault.

Halpert's office was located on the same floor at the opposite end of the building. Laila removed the jogging shoes that she wore to and from work, and donned pale blue pumps that matched her outfit. She smoothed down her light blue blouse and skirt. She took her coffee with her. Halpert maintained an open door policy. Laila smiled at the secretarial staff as she swept past them into his office. In the CIA, secretaries, file clerks, maintenance workers and such were referred to euphemistically as non-defense support personnel.

"Hello, Boss."

Halpert looked up at her arrival. He wore a beige suit but the collar of his immaculate white shirt was unbuttoned, and his dull black and gray pinstripe tie lay stretched out on the side of the desk in front of him. "Thanks for coming, Laila. Please close the door." He made it sound like an invitation instead of an order.

Laila did as he asked. The asking meant that they had high level issues to discuss: issues that non-defense support personnel were not permitted to overhear; they had security clearance to enter the building and not much more. She sat without being asked and calmly sipped her coffee. It was up to Halpert to open the discussion.

"Anderson wants to see you."

"Anderson? Who Anderson?"

"Head honcho Anderson." Halpert affected a light-hearted mien among his employees because, he said, it helped to promote morale in a business that was fraught with too much seriousness. Little gambits like the one he had just opened on Laila were his stock in trade.

Laila was dumbstruck. After she processed and analyzed reports that were generated under her purview, her written summations were automatically forwarded up the chain of command if they were deemed of sufficient importance. "What does he want with me?"

Halpert shrugged. "That information is on a need-to-know basis, and I don't need to know."

Odd as it may sound, Laila's security clearance exceeded that of her boss's. She had the highest level of security – top secret, sensitive compartmented information, or TS/SCI – whereas he had only a top secret clearance. A Section Chief was basically an office manager; his job was to manage people, allocate resources, approve travel vouchers, authorize reimbursement, and so on. He was not privy to secrets that his subordinates possessed. He often dispatched Laila to high-level meetings with admirals and generals – meeting to which he was not invited –without ever ascertaining what was discussed at those meetings.

"Did you submit any reports that might have pissed him off?"

"No," Laila said absently. In the back of her mind she cogitated her most recent intel. It did not take much imagination to suspect which item of information could have triggered Anderson's interest. "There are some Middle East developments . . . "

"Be prepared for a full briefing in front of a select audience."

"Yes, of course. I'll get right on it."

"It's too late for that. Your meeting is scheduled for nine o'clock."

Laila erupted, *"This morning?"*

Halpert glanced at his watch. "Two hours and forty-five minutes from now."

"That's barely enough time to drive to Langley in commuter traffic." Technically this wasn't true because there wasn't that much of a rush hour in the backwoods of western Virginia, where her building was sequestered in order to avoid overmuch notice.

"I agree, but it wasn't my call to make. And it gets worse. Anderson said that you shouldn't expect to go home tonight because he is sending you on a special assignment that may last for a spell. I had the impression that you might be going overseas in time."

Laila rarely argued about orders from higher-up because she usually had time to adjust her schedule and find coverage for duties that fell under her purview. All of her work could be handled by co-workers who possessed the equivalent security clearances. Nor would this be the first time that she had been sent around the world in order to confer directly with agents in the field. But never had she been asked to do so on such short notice.

"But, I'll have to go home for some clothes – "

"I was told that everything you need will be provided for you, including underwear."

That was certainly different. "Is this an undercover job?"

Halpert shrugged. "I don't know." And if truth be known, he didn't really care all that much. To him, the CIA was not an adventurous career as a superspy; it was a job that paid well, had good benefits, and offered a respectable retirement plan. He possessed a managerial mindset that did not differ much from that of an office manager of any other company, with or without a capital C.

Laila adjusted to the new situation with professional aplomb. She would delegate her emails and the rest of her workload to co-workers and subordinates. She stood up, grabbed the Styrofoam coffee cup from which she had not taken so much as a sip after entering Halpert's office, and took a long draft, after which she nodded perfunctorily. Her job was important and she liked it that way.

"I'll collect my laptop on the way out of the building."

"Anderson is expecting you." Halpert gave her a quirky smile. "I'll hold down the desk while you have all the fun."

"I'll send you a postcard if my location isn't classified."

Back in her office, she reheated her coffee while she pulled her laptop and travel case out of a locked steel desk drawer. It contained secure satellite uplink software so she could communicate with her desktop via the Internet from anywhere in the world. She could also check her personal emails: the few and growing fewer that she received.

She had been gone long enough that, because no

keystrokes had been entered on her desktop computer, it had gone into sleep mode. She changed her shoes again. When she donned her slicker, she stuck her dress shoes into its side pockets. Then she grabbed her minipurse and vacated the premises. The elevator dropped her into the underground garage.

From the outside, the four-story brick-façade structure looked like an ordinary office building with some architectural motifs whose purpose was cleverly concealed. What appeared to be signboard extensions at each corner of the roof were in fact guard stations that were accessed from the floor below; all four stations were continuously manned (or womaned, as Halpert was wont to quip). The center space of the large letter O on the two outward facings was fabricated of one-way glass. The word OrthoDym was spelled vertically, twice on each corner; it was a meaningless name that disguised the true nature of the work that was conducted inside.

The nondescript building was surrounded by a concrete pad that was twice the size of a football field. Employees with a government pay scale of G-12 and above were assigned a parking spot underground, where their license plates could not be seen and photographed from passing aircraft or satellites; everyone else parked in the all-around parking area. Surveillance cameras were strategically located to monitor the entire compound inside the ten-foot-tall chain-link fence that was topped with strip-wire.

The surrounding forest of hardwoods appeared innocuous unless one examined it in detail. Rotatable security cameras were mounted on the stout limbs of birches, cedars, and scarlet oaks. Motion detectors were tucked into the base trunks of mountain laurel and rhododendron. Infrared heat detectors were buried in the ground and covered with naturally fallen leaves. The grounds were a virtual minefield of non-explosive devices.

OrthoDym was only one of an untold number of anonymous facilities that the CIA maintained across the country. Halpert joked that the building was more secure than the White House. In many ways, it was. In some ways, it was more important than the White House.

Laila entered a narrow driveway between twin rows of red pines whose needled branches created a tunnel that covered the guard shack and gate, masking them from above. She halted at the security check point where scanners worked over her vehicle.

Two non-uniformed soldiers manned the guard shack. They were armed with pistols and automatic weapons which were kept out of view. Civilian clothes – white shirt, black pants, and black broughams – avoided military connotations. Exit security was not as severe as entry security. Laila held up her identification badge. The male guard remained in the shack while the female guard examined her photo ID.

"Have a pleasant day, Ms. Masterson."

"You too, uh – " Laila glanced at the guard's nametag. The guards were constantly being rotated and shuffled from rooftop to guard shack. " – Ms. Daily."

The male guard activated the gate motor. After the gate swung open, Laila accelerated slowly through the opening. Fifty feet to the north, she saw the entry gate, complete with its own guards and guard shack.

The driveway wound through a deciduous forest for a quarter mile and passed another, smaller building, where low-level CIA communications were conducted. This building was gate free, and acted as a front for the secret facility from which Laila had just departed. The front building also sported fake OrthoDym signs.

Both buildings displayed bogus roof facades that were designed to fool flybys – from tropospheric to exospheric – that the black tarred flattops held nothing more than heat pumps and air-conditioning units, when in fact the cleverly designed fabric that was stretched across an intricate steel framework cloaked a vast network of antenna arrays that facilitated satellite communications.

Once on the open road, Laila programmed her GPS receiver for CIA headquarters at Langley. She drove there often enough that she knew the route by heart, but she liked to glance at the readouts and see how many miles remained to her destination. That way she would know if she had time for a pit stop, or, as she referred to it, a coffee exchange: let some out, pour more in. She sipped her now-tepid coffee, glad that she had squirted before leaving the building, because she was only going to have enough time for a drive-through.

Working at the foot of the Appalachian Mountains offered an environment that Laila found pleasant and relaxing. Thick forests traded space with rolling farmland to create a patchwork quilt of riotous color that reached its peak in October. The onset of autumn was already visible, from the tint of the leaves to the exposed earth in the harvested fields.

Laila called the Pet Your Pet Clinic and Kennel to arrange for an assistant to feed Harvey and empty his sandbox once a day. The clinic had a house key and knew the four-digit code for her security system – *if* the assistant they sent remembered to enter the numbers on the keypad within the prescribed thirty seconds, before the local police office were alerted of a potential break-in. Her travel per diem more than paid for the occasional pet service.

Traffic was light. The gentle rain of the previous night and early morning had stopped, and the overcast was already dissipating. During the drive, Laila mentally composed rough drafts of responses to the morning's emails whose subject headings provided sufficient information for her to determine the nature of the message. As soon as she was able to sit at her laptop – in an airport lounge or a hotel room – she could shoot off rapid-fire replies. Lost in thought with concentrated mental activity, she hardly noticed the scenery until the best of it was behind her, and she found herself passing through towns and suburban areas whose sprawl was harsh by comparison.

The security at Langley appeared casual, but the apparent informality was a cover for intense scrutiny. Inwardly she grinned at the time she parked in a nearby pullover to complete a phone conversation before entering the grounds. Within five minutes a deuce-and-a-half filled with heavily armed soldiers stopped alongside her. Fatigue-clad combatants dismounted and surrounded her vehicle while an officer in dress uniform politely requested that she identify herself.

The thought that flashed momentarily through her mind was to peer into the rearview mirror and announce, "Yep, that's me." But that fleeting wisecrack evaporated the moment she realized how many muzzles were aimed in her general direction. Instead, she was embarrassed and overly apologetic for causing so much trouble. She soberly presented her CIA identification card, along with an explanation for her stopping and her business in the building. Potential security breaches were serious threats that were treated as such – guilty until proven innocent in the eyes of the weapon wielders.

Back in the present, Laila and her nondescript vehicle passed through the gate without a hitch. She found a parking space where she was instructed to park. In the lobby she turned in her cell phone – which was not allowed on the premises – and tossed her minipurse on the X-ray conveyor belt. She passed through the metal detector without a beep. People in her business learned never to wear anything metallic, because it was so annoying to partially undress or remove such items on a daily basis. Fabric and plastic composed the apparel of choice.

The elevator whisked her to the appropriate floor. A secretary guided her to Anderson's outer office. Another secretary admitted her at once.

Anderson stood upon her entrance. "Good morning, Ms. Masterson. Thank you for coming on such short notice."

The secretary closed the door behind her.

Laila smiled curtly. "I barely made it in time."

"My apologies." Anderson walked around his massive deck and held out his hand.

Laila shook it.

"May I get you some coffee?"

Laila's usual composure felt lacking. She often spoke one-on-one with high ranking military officers, but Anderson was the "head honcho," as Halpert designated him. "Uh, sure," she said hesitantly. "I'd love some."

Anderson poured a cup of steaming brew from a commercial percolator. "Cream or sugar."

"Black. Uh, I'm watching my girlish figure."

In olden times, an innocent response might have been one that complimented her appearance. But in these days of abuse of sexual harassment laws, a smart boss declined from saying anything that could be intentionally misinterpreted. Such pleasantries and common courtesies went by the wayside due to the rash of gold-diggers who exploited legal process to achieve unethical goals.

Anderson merely nodded and pursed his lips in the semblance of a smile. He swept his hand toward one of the plush chairs in front of his desk. "Please, sit down."

Laila took the proffered cup and saucer. "Thank you." She sat and sipped. To her liking, the coffee was burning hot.

Anderson tried to be informal. He indicated a folder that lay on his desktop. "Ms. Anderson, I have read your report about the, um, temporal displacement apparatus, and I found it quite, um . . . "

Laila was suddenly flustered with such an unnerving grip of anxiety that she put her cup on the saucer with a clatter, held up her free hand, and interrupted before he found the word he was looking for, "Mr. Anderson, I – I must apologize for the information in the report. If you read my recommendation you know that I didn't give the intel full credibility. I felt duty bound to report what the foreign field agent described, and even met him in person in order to document his story, but I clearly concluded that he must have misconstrued the purpose of the particle accelerator, if that's truly what it is."

When she paused for a breath, Anderson flashed another grin. "Please, Ms. Masterson, there is no need to be defensive. I did not call you here to denigrate your report, but to praise you for having the courage to forward it along with your evaluation, despite the, um, unusual nature of the, um, so-called accelerator. Time travel is certainly an intriguing concept."

Once Anderson took charge of the conversation, it was not Laila's place to butt in with apologies. She slowly picked up her cup and took a soothing sip of coffee to calm her nerves.

"Many analysts in your position would have buried the intel out of hand instead of following the, um, rather bizarre lead, and submitting a cautious but honest appraisal. Despite your evident misgivings about the notion of transporting physical objects backward through time, once you tipped me off I ordered further investigations by other operatives. They confirmed the IRF belief in time travel, if not its actuality."

Laila smirked and sipped her coffee. "The Muslims believe a lot of things. That doesn't make them real."

"I agree. Nonetheless, we have to deal with their beliefs when those beliefs impose upon the freedom of the world; when Muslims invoke Allah as a way to justify their fanaticism. The IRF's present ambition of world domination is as real a threat as Hitler was in the 1930's, only then we did not recognize or appreciate the danger. We are not making the same mistake again."

"Hitler's belief in the occult was not very different from Muslim cultish beliefs."

Anderson laughed lightly. "A Muslim would slit your throat for saying that Islam is a cult – or even for thinking it if he could read your thoughts."

Laila shrugged. "The only difference between a cult and a religion is the number of adherents."

Anderson laughed lightly again.

Laila was feeling more comfortable in Anderson's presence, now that she understood that he did not intend to bawl her out. She switched to the advisory mode that she affected when dealing with military minds that were eager to hear the intel that she had to impart. "Mr. Anderson, you didn't invite me here to discuss Middle Eastern religious philosophy. About this particle accelerator . . . "

"Quite right."

She gulped down the rest of her coffee.

"Help yourself to more."

"Thank you. I will." Laila rose, refilled her cup, then resumed her seat. This time she leaned back and crossed her legs, making certain that her skirt covered her knees.

"I would like you to lead a task force to investigate the IRF temporal displacement apparatus. I will not force you to accept the assignment, nor will I penalize you if it interferes with your, um, personal life. The assignment will entail foreign travel for quite some time, and could potentially put you in harm's way overseas, so please take these considerations into account before making any decision. But in light of what you have already uncovered, and your level-headed assessment of the situation, I think that you are the best person for the job."

Laila was quite taken aback. "Well, I – "

"I understand your trepidation, yet I cannot stress enough how much faith, um, if you will pardon the expression, um, trust that I have in your ability. I *have* studied your dossier, so I am well aware of how you have already connected seemingly unconnected dots into patterns that might otherwise have gone unnoticed. More than one military officer has commended you for your intelligence – both innate and that which you have provided the forces in the field.

The head honcho had studied *her* dossier? "Well, I – I hardly know what to say."

"I will not mislead you. There are other agents who can do the job, just as there are others who can do *my* job. No one is indispensable. But I prefer to have you in charge."

Her coffee was all but forgotten. Her mind was atwirl and atwitter. She had gone overseas before; time was not a factor. Harvey was a house cat who lived quite happily in her absence. Her neighbors would never miss her: the only thing they had in common was proximity.

She seldom flew to California to spend time with her mother.

Laila's heart suddenly ached when she realized how empty her personal life had become since her divorce and subsequent move to another neighborhood that was located closer to her worksite. Her job had become a hectic career, and her career had become her life.

She stalled by asking, "What kind of support will I have?"

"Essentially the same as you have now. You will continue to collaborate with your informers and agents in the field, but from a different secure location. I will inform Halpert of your temporary duty assignment so that he can delegate your non-pertinent workload to other analysts. Additional personnel are being brought into the fold. The other operatives that I used to confirm your report will be transferred to your task force. They will answer to you. You will no longer answer to me but to the Defense Intelligence Agency, whose mission leader will have overall control, including but not limited to interdiction by force should that prove necessary in his or her estimation."

Laila took a draft that emptied her cup. "That's a bit more responsibility than I've been used to."

Anderson spread his hands. "A famous person once said 'you don't know what you can do until you try'."

Laila smiled. "I think that was a Tupperware saleswoman."

Anderson laughed out loud. "You are probably right." After the laughter calmed down, he donned a solemn mien. "I do not have to tell you that anything that the IRF contemplates is serious business; more serious than you might think unless you knew more of the situation. I cannot brief you further until, or unless, you accept the position."

Laila nodded slowly in acquiescence. The upward lilt in Anderson's penultimate sentence implied that he was waiting for her answer. The ultimate sentence informed her that he was withholding crucial information until she had the need to know. Her curiosity was aroused. "I don't doubt that this is serious business."

"So, do you want the job?"

She hesitated. "I appreciate the confidence you have in me . . . " She hesitated again. She wanted to say something besides "I do," so she didn't sound like a blushing bride giving her life away at the altar. " . . . and I hope that I can lead the task force to your satisfaction."

Chapter 2

The drive from Langley to the Pentagon was short and uneventful. Laila was ushered through the gate by a guard who directed her to park in a pickup space behind the guard shack. Only two minutes elapsed before a hatless guide wearing dress khakis approached the driver's side of her car. Laila rolled down the window.

The guide's tanned face was relaxed but his dark brown eyes shone with piercing intensity "Ms. Laila Masterson?"

"Yes."

"May I see your ID, please?"

Laila held up her CIA photo identification card.

"Thank you." His concentrated stare rose from the card to her bright hazel eyes. "I am to take you to General Cercopley's office. May I direct you from the passenger seat?"

"Of course."

The guide did not provide his name and was not wearing a nametag, so Laila didn't ask. She knew by the silver bar on each collar that he was a first lieutenant. In the military, rank was more important than name; anonymity was standard protocol in the undercover community. Laila knew several people in her line of work who went by different names, each name dependent upon the group to which he was being introduced. The lieutenant directed her to drive around the building to a parking lot that was reserved for visiting dignitaries.

The guide exited the vehicle. "Follow me, ma'am."

Laila followed the guide into the building and along a corridor that sliced through a warren of rooms whose doors were labeled with the names of the occupants. She had difficulty in keeping up with his long-legged pace. He led her to a waiting room in which she waited only long enough for him to tap on an inner door, lean in, and announce, "Ms. Masterson has arrived."

A gruff voice called out, "Send her in."

The guide pushed open the door and with a sweep

of the hand invited Laila to enter. She was understandably reluctant to meet the "head honcho's" head honcho, but she did her best to maintain a confident carriage. The guide closed the door behind her.

George Cercopley was the director of the Defense Intelligence Agency: the umbrella organization to which all other American intelligence agencies were subordinate. He was a three-star general whose grizzled features matched the gruffness of his voice. The left breast of his jacket was plastered with enough colorful campaign ribbons to decorate a small Christmas tree. He was walking toward her with an outstretched hand as she entered the room. His grip was firm but not crushing.

"Chet told me that you had accepted the position. It's my pleasure to welcome you to Project Stitch." The gruffness of Cercopley's voice belied his manner. His smile was broad and genuine. "How much did he tell you about it?"

Laila looked up at him. "Not a thing. He didn't even mention that the project had a name. He told me that you would brief me on my duties and responsibilities."

"Have a seat, Ms. Masterson." He indicated a high-backed leather chair across from the one in which he plunked himself with aplomb. "You'll be briefed in full after your arrival at project headquarters. The project is under my direct supervision, but I don't handle or interfere with day-to-day operations. Competent people are doing that already. Your participation will add materially to that competence."

Laila eased her slender form onto the pleated red cushion. "Why, thank you, sir."

He waved her off with a hand. "If Chet recommended you for the project, then you must be superbly qualified. Besides, I read your dossier. There's a very good reason why he didn't give you more information. He only learned about the existence of the project recently. He was told very little about it, so there is very little that he could have told you. And what little he knows I instructed him not to divulge. He has not – and *will* not – be informed about the project's conduct or missions. He is officially out of the loop. By that I mean that from this point forward you will submit your reports only to the mission leader. The two of you will work together at the project compound."

General Cercopley leaned back. He pushed gently on the arms of his chair, which turned out to be a recliner. The seatback stopped at a forty-five degree angle while the footrest rose parallel to the floor but slightly higher than the seat.

"Make yourself comfortable, Ms. Masterson. You're perched on the edge of that chair like a spinster school-marm. Relax. May I call you Laila?"

Laila realized that she *was* on edge, and not just on the edge of her seat. "Yes, sir, of course."

"Please call me George. I get enough 'sirs' around here." The general took a deep breath as he settled into the recliner and crossed one elevated leg over the other. "I'd like to say that I'm suffering from old combat wounds, but I can't. I've got phlebitis. I've had two operations already and another one is scheduled as soon as I can make the time. I guess it isn't really scheduled then, is it?"

Laila pushed herself all the way back into the chair.

Before she could respond to the general's rhetorical question, he continued, "I called you here instead of sending you directly to the compound because I like to meet my primary field commanders. In addition, I want to impress upon you the importance of this project with regard to national security. The world is in peril from the insanity of terrorism. We have to utilize every means at our disposal to stop it. Well, we can't utilize *every* weapon in our military arsenal, because of humanitarian reasons, to say nothing of the political ramifications. Drop an A-bomb on the Muslims and you wipe out a lot of supposedly innocent people – people who perhaps support Islamic goals if not the means to achieve them."

Laila was feeling sufficiently at ease to make an off-color comment. "Don't the marines have a saying that goes something like, 'Nuke 'em all. Let God sort 'em out.' "

The general guffawed. "Marines! Gotta love 'em for

being hardcore GI's whose fathers were bachelors. But we're not fighting on Guadalcanal or Iwo Jima anymore. Nowadays we have to use tactical precision to separate snipers and suicide bombers from not-necessarily-so-innocent civilians. Like goddamn surgeons slicing out malignant tumors. We're fighting with one hand tied behind our backs. Maybe both hands."

The general was on a roll. "Being a God-fearing man, I don't pretend to know how God might sort 'em out, but I can guarantee you how Allah's believers would do it. If they get the opportunity, they'll kill every Christian on the planet – and the Buddhists to boot. Our job is to see that they don't do it. They've already killed more of my boys and girls in uniform than the Romans fed to the lions. And the Twin Towers attack proves that they don't care about civilians or collateral damage."

He switched the way his legs were crossed. "The war on terrorism is an ugly war. The aggressors don't abide by humanitarian principles, but the Christian defenders are handcuffed by their faith. So we can't nuke 'em all. We are honor bound to identify discrete terrorist cells, then kill only those individuals who are armed when the cell is invaded. They can escape death by simply raising their hands – a tactic, I might add, that isn't offered in return. Muslims don't believe in turning the other cheek. Later they complain about being mistreated, even though prison conditions are better than those of our soldiers in the field. POW's are served hot meals, eat in heated or air-conditioned rooms, and sleep on cots; while our boys and girls in uniform eat cold MRE's in a dusty foxhole and sleep under the stars in desert heat and cold. Laila, are you prepared to storm the front lines with the troops?"

"What?" She was suddenly taken aback. "What do you mean?"

The general waved her off. "I don't mean with guns and grenades. One of the qualifications that you have for this job is that you speak, read, and write Farsi. How else could you communicate with local field agents or translate intercepted intelligence? If we have to interrogate enemy 'soldiers,' " – he made quote marks with his fingers – "I need your assurance that you're equal to the task. You'll be shielded, of course, by well-trained troops, but there's no such thing as guaranteed safety on the battlefield. What's your response?"

Laila didn't hesitate. "I am committed to this mission. I'll do whatever it takes."

"Good girl! I knew I could count on you. I had to make certain before I let the cat out of the bag, so to speak, meaning no disrespect to Harvey. Laila, prepare yourself. The TDA is real."

"The what?"

"The temporal displacement apparatus." The general did not pause long enough to let the concept sink in. "The IRF plans to use it to eradicate Christianity from the face of the Earth."

The concept was slowly sinking in. "You mean, you really believe that the IRF has a time machine? Sir, I specifically wrote in my report that I doubted the validity – "

The general waved his hand again. "And Chet duly informed the President of your doubt."

"Chet?" She didn't mean to shout. The chain of command went from Chet Anderson to George Cercopley to Frank Marshall. The President was her head honcho's head honcho's head honcho – the top head honcho. She managed to tone her voice down to a squeal. "You mean Anderson informed the President?"

"Now don't get your tit in a ringer. And call me George. Chet did his homework before he thought it was his responsibility to alert the Chief. He was pretty certain of his facts. The President then informed me, and I asked Chet to bring you onboard. Even now the IRF is building tactical nuclear weapons to unleash on the Christian world: either the Christian world of the present or the Christian world of the past. As yet we don't know everything about their plans for the bombs; they may be a diversionary tactic. But they most certainly intend to use the TDA to invade the past and make terrorist attacks against Christianity."

Even though she had not fully accepted the reality of the situation, Laila found herself leaning forward and nodding absently. She fumbled for adequate words: "How, uh, what are they – how do they plan – to do with it?"

General Cercopley raised both bushy brown eyebrows, and ran one hand through over his nearly bald pate. "At this point we can't be certain, but we believe they're going to kidnap Jesus of Nazareth before his Crucifixion."

Laila wanted to scream "What?" but she refrained herself from acting like a naïve schoolgirl.

"It's ingenious when you think about it. I know you went to *Bible* school, but I'll give you a recap of biblical history without the religious overlays. Whether Jesus was the son of God is in dispute. Whether he was born of Immaculate Conception is also in dispute. In fact, nearly everything about his life and times is in dispute. The image of Christ that's accepted today is based largely on group perception or the blind acceptance of Gospel rather than cold hard facts.

"That's not to say that Biblical history is hogwash, only that you have to take it with a grain of salt. The King James version was cobbled together long after the events that are depicted on its hallowed pages. How much of the *Bible* is history and how much is exaggeration or conjecture or pure fairytale has been argued by scholars for a thousand years. The Holy Scriptures undoubtedly contain kernels of truth, but those kernels are buried among reams of misleading information and oratorical platitudes that were designed to appeal to the masses – much like campaign rhetoric.

"I suspect that most of the incidents that are recounted in the *Bible* are based on real events, but that the factuality of those events has been garbled in the telling or intentionally embellished or lost in translation. Now don't get me wrong. I grew up on *Bible* study in Sunday school, followed by sermons as fervent as the one that Christ gave on the Mount. Those sermons were delivered by preachers who were every bit as devout as the Savior, and who possessed the oratorical skill to profess that devotion to zealous members of the church.

"For the sake of argument let's accept that there is truth in the *Bible* as well as allegory. Christ was a roving minister whose dedication was sincere. He didn't want to convert the world to Christianity as much as he wanted to preach Christian and humanitarian principles in opposition to the cruelty of Roman rule. He and his disciples drew large crowds in places such as Jordan, Jerusalem, and Galilee: outposts of the Roman Empire.

"Perhaps Jesus didn't claim to be the son of God, but only his prophet. Perhaps God was the moral paradigm for his teachings. And perhaps because of the zeal of his teachings, Jesus came to believe in his own divinity. History is replete with people who made themselves out to be something more than they were. Or, perhaps Jesus *didn't* have delusions of grandeur, but was deified by a gullible public, either contemporary or later."

The general spread his hands. "I don't have the answers. In any event, Jesus possessed that rare charisma that all great leaders possess – bad leaders as well as good leaders – he could control crowds with promises. Instead of lowering taxes, he promised everlasting life in the great hereafter. His followers were eager to believe his promises because the Romans made their existence on Earth so miserable.

"When the situation got out of hand, the Romans – fearful of an uprising – ordered his assassination. This was their way of proving to the people that Jesus was not the Son of God but a mortal human being who could die like everyone else. And the rest is either history or make believe. If Christ was *not* the son the God, his followers glorified his divinity by way of protest.

"The Romans sought to destroy Christianity by executing its loudest spokesperson in public. Much to their annoyance they martyred Him. Instead of dying out for lack of a pious and hypnotic leader, Christianity crystalized and grew stronger. If Rome had let Christianity run its course, it may have been only another passing fad or fancy, like many other religions that existed at the time.

"Mob psychology is a powerful force. Facts become irrelevant when a crowd takes control of a situation. What people believe to be true has a far greater effect on their conduct than actual truth. Christianity as we know it is based on the New Testament, which was written by Christ's disciples in honor of their Lord. Christianity rose to prominence when its followers started worshipping their martyr.

"The deification of the King of the Jews came about *because* of his Crucifixion."

Laila found herself nodding in understanding.

"I don't believe every word that's written in the *Bible*. In fact, I believe very few of the words. I ascribe to the principles of Christianity without taking the *Bible* literally. I suspect that the facts surrounding the birth and death of Christ are grossly in error. I suspect that the *Bible* consists of historical facts, figures, and time elements that were composed, contorted, and contrived to create a chronological presentation for its dramatic and didactic effect, the way a detective novel or murder mystery is written to lead to a satisfactory conclusion."

Laila shrugged. "The *Bible* as parable."

"I don't pretend that the idea is original with me. What I think is irrelevant. What *is* relevant is that the Muslims believe that Christ's Crucifixion represents the birth of Christianity, and that preventing his Crucifixion will abort its birth."

Laila absorbed the information as best she could. She didn't grow up on science fiction like a lot of teenagers, so she couldn't fathom the concept of time travel much less the possibility – or possibilities plural, as the case may be. "So – what? Are you're suggesting that the IRF is going to create a new present by altering the past? A present in which Christianity never gained a foothold?"

Again the general spread his hands. "I wouldn't be very good at my job if I accepted intel on blind faith. Part of what I do is to question my sources and the validity of their claims. But neither would I be doing the country service if I ignored a threat as serious as this. We know that the IRF is building or has built nuclear devices. We *hear* that they're building a time machine. Maybe the time machine intel is the diversion, and they intend to detonate the bombs in the present or near future. At this point we don't know, but we must find out. Whatever they plan to do, it is implicit in our Congressional directive that we have to stop them . . . by fair means or foul, the former being a humanitarian directive if not one that is implied by Congress."

Laila kept nodding in agreement but didn't know what to say.

General Cercopley didn't wait for her to reply. "There are those who believe in God and those who have faith in God. I have faith in God, but I believe that God helps those who help themselves. You and I and the folks at Project Stitch are going to work under the presumption that the IRF is planning some kind of dire offensive maneuver against a world in which religious tolerance is practiced by everyone but them."

Although Laila was confused about actual IRF directives, she knew one thing for certain: General Cercopley was as zealous about his commitment toward assuring world peace as the IRF was in taking it away.

"So you want me to continue collecting data about the, uh, putative time machine, but from a more secure venue?"

"I want a lot more than that. I want you moved from the middle of the heap in CIA intel gathering services to the top of the heap under my direct command. Consider it a promotion in position and pay scale. You're a sharp gal. No one else picked up the innuendoes concerning an IRF time machine. I don't blame you for not believing in time travel. Yet you had the nerve to write a report about it. A lesser person would have ignored the obvious and not called attention to such an absurd concept because it might have compromised his job. Her job.

"Well, I was just doing my job – "

"And doing it damn well. That's the kind of person I want in charge. And you still haven't called me George."

Laila could not suppress a grin. "Okay, George."

"That's my gal. That didn't hurt at all, did it, Laila?"

"Uh, no, George."

"Let me tell you something else that will make your job easier, while at the same time put another hat on your head. I think your intel about the TDA is accurate because we already have one."

Laila stifled a gasp but could not prevent her eyes from expanding.

"That's what Project Stitch is all about. The Group has already made tentative incursions into the past. They are treading lightly so as not to upset the universe, or God if there is one. Results so far have been paradoxical. There seem to be limitations on what can be achieved by visiting the past. Our theoretical physicists are not even certain that we *are* visiting the past. Perhaps, they theorize, we are visiting a different time stream or parallel dimension: a place where things are dissimilar and not connected at all to us or our past. The fabric that they have ruptured in the space-time continuum may have to do with space rather than time or perhaps with neither. It's all speculation.

"In any case, because of your report it now appears that whatever it is we have, they have, or claim to have. Unless they are perpetrating the biggest hoax since Moses parted the Red Sea, they're building the same kind of machinery that we've built to bridge the gap between alternate universes. We can't afford to let them proceed uncontested. Islam is like a metastasized cancer. It has already infected our time and space. We can't let them infect another time and space, or worse, our very own past. What's your response?"

Laila was no longer nodding. She didn't know what to think, what to believe. But if a lieutenant general believed that time travel was possible, and that the United States had already constructed a device for traveling into the past, then she had to take his information at face value, no matter how difficult a concept it was to accept.

She slipped into her best professional mode. "Let's

go on the premise that the IRF has a, uh, temporal displacement apparatus, because we know that such an apparatus is possible. Let's further presume – from intel that I haven't seen – that they can use it to kidnap Christ. We can respond to this crisis in several ways: destroy their TDA, keep tabs on their plans in case they change them, and – " Her pause was barely perceptible. " – go into the past ourselves and forestall the kidnapping by a show of force. I suggest that we work on multiple fronts."

"Cover all bases," rasped the general. "The best strategy. Your initial part in this multiphase mission is to take charge of the intelligence network. I want you to go to Bolling and get the network started. Then go to the project compound and confer with the mission leader. You will work from there until the mission is completed. Learn what you can about the IRF's apparatus: who did their theoretical work, where did they obtain the technical expertise, when they started construction, how close they are to completion, and how they plan to carry out their objective."

Laila took charge in accordance with her new description. "The DIA infrastructure already exists. All you have to do is redirect intel to my new location. Your people will continue to do the collecting, and I will handle collation and analysis."

General Cercopley pulled forward in his recliner. As the footrest dropped and the seatback moved upright, he stood up in one smooth motion as if he had been propelled out of the chair. "You have carte blanche to meet these objectives any way you see fit. Just send the bill to me."

Laila rose a moment behind the general. "I'll do that."

He thrust out his hand. "As much as I've enjoyed your company, I must bid you goodbye. The adjutant who brought you here will see to your transportation, for which arrangements have already been made.

Laila gripped the general's hand harder than he gripped hers. "Thanks for giving me the opportunity to work on this project, uh, George."

The general smiled. "We'll beard those Islamic rascals in their own den. I'm sure you'll make me proud, Laila."

Chapter 3

Monday mornings were always hectic as a result of the weekend buildup of reports and requests from field agents. Terrorist activities did not conform to a nine-to-five schedule. But Laila had never had a Monday morning like this one. When she got out of bed in the black pre-dawn hours, she had no inkling that her day would turn out to be so different from any other Monday morning – or *any* morning, for that matter.

She had seen her head honcho as well as *his* head honcho. Now she was on the way to Bolling Air Force Base with three escorts in an armored Humvee. Her own vehicle had been parked in a long-term garage at the Pentagon, not to be retrieved until her newly appointed mission was completed.

The High Mobility Multipurpose Wheeled Vehicle in which she found herself ensconced had been modified for domestic escort service: the left rear seat faced backward so that one of the two armed guards had a clear view to the left and rear of the vehicle. The other guard rode shotgun, with a clear view forward and right. Each guard wore fatigues and full body armor, and was cradling an MK-16-CQC 5.56-millimeter assault rifle that was fitted with a stubby ten-inch barrel for close-quarter handling in the confined seat arrangement. Each guard also sported an Glock 17 9-millimeter pistol that was fitted with a double-stack 17-round magazine. The olive drab frame was nearly invisible in its thigh holster because the color matched the fabric. Extra magazines for both weapons adorned their dress and lay on the floor.

The anonymous lieutenant drove through commuter traffic at five miles under the speed limit. He was now armed with an Glock 17 pistol that was concealed in a shoulder holster under his formal dress jacket. He also wore a hat.

Laila thought that the amount of security was excessive – she tried not to think of the word "overkill" because of its negative connotation – but was forced to admit that her unexpected promotion and newly acquired intel made her a valuable commodity in the counterterrorism community: a commodity that could be replaced, of course, but not without some difficulty. Yet in the back of her mind, she couldn't help but fear that her position was in some respects untenable: that is, that she was powerless to escape an agenda that the government might have in store for her.

Bolling Air Force Base was practically within shooting distance of the Pentagon. The roadway measured three times as far because of the circuitous route across the Potomac River into the District of Columbia, then across the Anacostia River to the left bank of the Potomac. Due to airspace congestion – less than one mile of water separated the base from National Airport – only low-flying rotary-wing aircraft flew into and out of Bolling.

The Air Force base housed the multidisciplinary Defense Intelligence Analysis Center – the guts of the DIA – where more than five thousand skilled personnel coordinated every aspect of military intelligence. Experts in all fields of science provided up-to-date intel on everything imaginable, from biochemical agents to political expertise to computer diagnoses. General Cercopley worked in an office there when he wasn't holding down a recliner in the Pentagon.

Laila's escorts had not uttered a word from the time they entered the vehicle. The lieutenant kept his eyes on the road and nearby cars and trucks. The gaze of each guard panned back and forth like the lens of a pivoting video camera. It was obvious to her that they took their jobs very seriously.

Having been forewarned of their arrival, the guard at Bolling's gate allowed the Humvee to enter the base without a hitch. The lieutenant stopped at the front door of the visitor's annex. A tall man with dark brown skin and black curly hair bent down by the driver's door. The lieutenant lowered the window.

The man showed his photo ID to the lieutenant. "My

name is Mark Clayton. I'm to take Laila Masterson from your custody."

The lieutenant scanned the card as if he were studying it for a final exam. "Thank you, Mr. Clayton." He looked diagonally over his right shoulder at Laila in the right back seat. "Mr. Clayton will take charge of you from here."

"Thanks for the ride." Laila smiled, but neither the lieutenant nor the guards changed their facial expressions. She opened the door, stepped out with her computer pack (whose zippered pouch held her minipurse), gently closed the door, and waved goodbye to her entourage. "Ta-ta."

She felt slightly foolish when neither of the three musketeers favored her with a word or so much as a quiver of the lip. The Humvee drove away.

Looking after the retreating vehicle, she said to no one in particular, "That's a gruesome bunch."

"Don't take it personally, Ms. Masterson."

"I don't, but do they have to take life so seriously?"

"It's part of their training. You'd be thankful for their attitude if a group of terrorists attacked you on the road."

"Yes, I suppose you're right." Laila flung the pack on her back and thrust out her right hand. "Call me Laila."

The new escort gripped her hand briefly. "I'm Mark Clayton."

"So I heard. Aren't you the section chief I'm superseding?"

"That's one way of putting it."

"Mark, I'm so sorry. I know how you must feel, but believe me, I had nothing to do with taking this position of superiority. It was pretty much thrust upon me, and out of the blue at that."

"Hey, don't feel bad about it. I've got a wife and three kids at home. The last thing I want is to go traipsing across the country – or out of the country – on TDA. I've done temporary duty assignments for a couple of days at a time and didn't care for them. I like to work behind a stationary desk. And this assignment is open ended.

No one knows when you'll be coming back."

Laila shrugged. "I guess I'm used to it. I go on briefing assignments all the time. It's part of my job description. But they could have warned me before I left home this morning. I don't even have a change of underwear."

"I don't know where you're going, but on this kind of last-minute assignment I expect that you'll be given a clothing allotment – although, you might be wearing desert duds until you have time and are in a place where you can buy some new clothes."

"MultiCam camouflage fatigues? Cammies are not my favorite pattern, and coyote brown doesn't compliment my complexion. Would you like to trade places with me?"

"Forgive me for saying this, but better you than me." Clayton was dressed casually with blue slacks and a white shirt whose top button was not in its hole. He rubbed both upper arms with his hands. "Hey, I'm shivering out here. Your transportation won't arrive until long after dark. Why don't we go inside?"

"Are you my bodyguard or baby sitter?"

Clayton laughed. "A little bit of both. Would you like some coffee while we wait?"

"I'd love some. Are there vending machines around where I can get some food? I've had nothing but a Duncan Donuts breakfast sandwich all day. I'm famished."

Clayton tilted his head toward the double glass doors. "Follow me. The cafeteria is open twenty-four seven and the food is quite good. I'll even join you. I've already called Jasika and told her that I'm working late, so she can go ahead and feed the kids. She's used to my late hours. Of course, I neglected to mention that I'm entertaining a lady."

Laila winked.

They entered the ultramodern building whose architectural design reflected light from an all-around full glass façade. The interior was sparkling clean and bereft of furniture, like the lobby of any new office building. They walked side by side along a broad corridor whose linoleum floor showed skid marks from shoes and tire tracks from pushcarts. A maintenance worker was operating a polishing machine at the far end of the corridor.

"As you know, our operations here are not much different from yours, except that we receive reports from multiple sources: CIA, FBI, JAG, military intelligence agencies, and so on. In theory that gives us a bigger picture of worldwide events, but in practice our own intel often merely duplicates intel from our subsidiary sources."

"I prefer to think of it as confirmation rather than duplication."

They turned down a perpendicular corridor whose floor had already been polished. A few men and women walked both ways; most of them were gazing at papers that they held in their hands, or were lost in thoughts that gave their eyes the appearance of dull marble. The DIA worked in three-shift mode so that each office always had someone on duty, although the nighttime work force was reduced. The DIA never rested from keeping a proverbial finger on the pulse of ongoing events, and from casting predictions about where those events might lead.

"Thanks for the vote of confidence. I wish the taxpayers and Congressional purse holders would see it that way."

"Budget restraints affect every intelligence agency. What Congress and the taxpayers fail to understand is the overwhelming value of detailed foreknowledge. An ounce of prevention is worth a pound of cure, as my granma used to say."

"Your grandmother was wise." Clayton indicated another offshoot corridor. "As I was saying, our biggest asset here is that we have experts in nearly every field of human endeavor. That plus intel from other agencies such as yours is supposed to give us an edge when it comes to providing the latest intel to the Joint Chiefs of Staff, as well as to field commanders in tactical situations. I have to give you credit for uncovering the IRF time machine. We missed it big time – no pun intended."

"Now wait a minute, Mark. I never said the IRF *had* a time machine. I only interpreted data that implied that going back in time could be an alternative way to destroy the Christian world. It might be purely coincidental that they are constructing a particle accelerator which our sources claim can break the time barrier. General Cercopley suggested, and I concur, that the synchrotron may have another purpose entirely, and that the IRF is using it as a means to disseminate misinformation, in order to make us divert our resources and waste our time."

Mark opened the door to the cafeteria. "No pun intended?"

Laila humphed with a smile. "Misdirection is the oldest trick in the magician's book." The aroma of food suddenly distracted Laila from continuing the conversation. Her salivary glands seeped in anticipation. "For right now, please direct me straight to the food and coffee. I can think better on a full stomach and loaded with caffeine."

Clayton led the way to the counter. He went first so he could show Laila by his actions where the trays, plates, and utensils were located. Although it was dinner time, only a few employees were scattered across the large room, and no one stood in line ahead of them. Employees who were going off shift ate later at home; those coming on shift ate before their arrival. The cafeteria did most of its business during daytime lunch and nighttime midshifts.

"I'm a simple meat and potatoes woman." Laila asked the server for meatloaf, mashed potatoes, and corn. The coffee cups were small so she purchased two of them. She paid with her expense account credit card.

"I hear that." Clayton asked for the same meal but with cauliflower instead of corn. He led Laila to a corner table that was isolated from the other diners. "We can talk here but keep your voice down. Not everyone in the room is cleared to our level of security, especially the kitchen help."

Laila put her tray on the table, doffed her pack and

placed it on the floor, pulled out a chair, and sat. "Can we talk about the time, uh, the temporal displacement apparatus?"

Clayton pursed his lips as he took a seat. "You're the boss."

"Now cut that out." Laila scowled and pinched her eyebrows. "Just think of me as the person on point. I'm not taking over your job."

"Fair enough."

They held their discussion between mouthfuls.

"My report didn't necessarily cause this, uh, didn't put this mission in motion."

"Maybe not, but it was the trigger. After your report was funneled up the channels it was tossed in my lap. I appreciated your cautions, but I was obligated nonetheless to follow up your leads. I put the majority of my group on the job. We didn't come up with all that much new intel. Mostly we reverse engineered your primary research.

"Laila, I don't know how you did it. The pieces of the puzzle were all there, but in so many disparate locations that none of us brought the complete picture into focus until you pointed it out. We confirmed everything in your report. Until then, we thought the synchrotron and support structures were a cover story: a disguised missile silo and assembly plant for their nuclear weapons program."

"A synchrotron doesn't look like a missile silo. Not from the air. It looks like a big circle."

"You're right. But taken with the other indicators – heavy water distillation, pitchblende imports, the number of large trucks that were transporting who knows what to the so-called particle accelerator – we thought the circular construction was camouflage. Sure, we had reports about time displacement, but we thought they referred to delays in assembling the nuclear device."

Laila chewed thoughtfully. "I'll bet you translated the Farsi text in the local agents' reports to mean device instead of apparatus. The two words are synonymous in English, but each can have a slightly different meaning when emphasized in another context. Our local agents were laborers, not scientists, so they didn't understand the concepts behind many of the words they overheard and reported to their handlers. They heard "time displacement" here, "device" or "apparatus" there, "nuclear" somewhere else. The way those terms are put together depends upon translation as well as interpretation."

"But, how – how did you put all that together and come up with "time machine," even if you thought the concept was fictitious: a local belief, a radical idea, a complicated diversion?"

Laila swallowed half a cup of lukewarm coffee before it lost all its heat. "I don't know."

"You don't know?" Clayton dropped his fork on his plate. "What do you mean you don't know?"

"It's – it's a subconscious thought process."

"You mean – a gut feeling?" Clayton rolled his eyes. He was aghast. "Do you mean to tell me that you submitted a report that was based on – emotion? A mood? Woman's intuition?"

"Not exactly." Laila sealed her lips for a moment, and bulged the muscles in her forehead. "No, not at all. I mean, yes and no."

Clayton rolled his eyes again. Without sarcasm: "That tells me a lot."

"Sorry."

Clayton breathed deeply. "Intelligence work is a science, not a sentimental attachment to an vague impression." He realized that he had raised his voice. He leaned across the table and spoke in almost a whisper. "Please tell me that you had more to go on than your intestinal tract. According to your dossier, you're a topnotch analyst with some very impressive deductions to your credit. One of which in particular embarrassed me considerably."

Laila scrunched her eyebrows. "Oh? Which one was that?"

"Last year's restaurant bombing in Baghdad."

"Oh." Laila was sympathetic. "That was unfortunate."

"It was unfortunate that I didn't give your report more credence – the credence that it ultimately deserved." Clayton sighed. "I had my people review your sources. They confirmed the facts but interpreted them differently. They – and I – thought the self-proclaimed suicide bomber was pretending to be a member of the IRF in order to impress his girlfriend. We – we thought he was just trying to get laid. We couldn't associate him with any terrorist cell.

"You know the result. Fourteen people killed, twenty-seven wounded, and my local asset hospitalized with serious cuts and bruises and concussions from bricks from a collapsing wall. I sent him there as an observer, just – just so I could discount your interpretation. Don't get me wrong. My action wasn't personal. It wasn't any macho thing because I was a man and you were a woman. I wanted to prove that our intel was more factual and our interpretation more accurate than what we got from a subordinate analyst. Call it interagency rivalry if you want. But a lot of people paid the price for my unwillingness to concede to your interpretation."

"I'm so sorry." Laila was even more sympathetic. "I was angry at first, when I heard about the bombing; when I learned that my report had been ignored. I was quite emphatic in making the point that the suicide bomber was serious about his intent. His ravings . . . "

"Please don't tell me that your conclusions were based on a hunch."

"No, not at all."

"Then tell me – how did you do it? How did you know that he was going to blow up that restaurant? How do you know that the IRF claimed to have developed a time machine, whether or not it's real?"

"It's difficult to explain."

"Try me."

"I can explain the process but it won't help you to apply it yourself."

"Give it a whirl."

Laila pondered about where and how to begin. "My earliest memories in this regard go back to my granma's house. My granpa died before I was born so she lived alone in the old family homestead in West Virginia. The property looked like a Paul Detlefsen painting. No waterwheels or covered bridges, but a mammoth barn behind an old-fashioned house complete with a hand-pumped well in the front yard. The well worked but it was mostly for show because the house had been renovated with indoor plumbing. The outhouse had been converted to a corn crib.

"Anyway, Granma, as I called her, was always losing things – mostly her reading glasses, but anything else she put down, except in the kitchen. She never lost a thing in the kitchen. She had dementia before memory impairment came to be called Alzheimer's disease. My biggest fear is that, because of inherited characteristics, someday I'll lose my ability to recall and process data.

"Anyway, when I was a tot I either knew or could remember where Granma put down her things. If I didn't already know from having seen them before, I could walk through the house and find her things as soon as I entered the room where she left them – unless they were hidden or had dropped behind the furniture. Granma called it my 'noticing aptitude.' I noticed things. I wasn't conscious of noticing things until she asked me if I knew where they were. It's as if I stored images in my mind but didn't look at those images closely until there was a reason to do so.

"No one thought this 'noticing aptitude' was anything more than the ability of a little girl to observe things that adults didn't pay attention to, because they were preoccupied with bigger matters.

"Then my mother gave me Nancy Drew books after I learned to read. They were such simplistic and amateurish mysteries that I quickly outgrew them. I started to read my daddy's mystery books. He was a police detective. I started with the oldest ones first: Sherlock Holmes."

Clayton interrupted with a smile. "Arthur Conan Doyle. I never read any of the originals but I've read some recent pastiches."

"I read all four novels and fifty-six short stories. I loved them! I ate them up. But I also knew the solution before the end of the story. Well, most of the time. Then I worked my way forward: Mary Roberts Rinehart and Agatha Christie. Christie was the best – ever. I found that I could distinguish her real clues from the red herrings. I nearly always figured out the ending before the climactic scene. Most modern mystery writers bore me. They are always pulling a rabbit out of the hat, or tacking a flashback into the final chapter, in order to achieve a believable resolution. I call them 'dishonest mysteries' because they withhold information from the reader, usually because the writer didn't know how the book was going to end until he contrived a semi-satisfactory solution.

"Anyway, I didn't pay none of this no never-mind, as my granma used to say. I thought of these abilities as nothing more than childhood gimmicks. In college I got interested in world politics and current events, especially in the Middle East. The more I read, the more it seemed to me that I had some kind of precognitive ability to know – and I mean *know* – what scenarios were most likely to occur. I took Farsi as my foreign language. That helped me get into the CIA after graduation, despite a largely useless degree in business management. I barely passed the Company aptitude test.

"Now it gets interesting . . . "

"You mean *more* interesting. I'm already fascinated by your background. I'm almost afraid to hear what's coming next."

Laila grinned broadly. "At the risk of sounding spooky, I don't consciously know where my analyses come from. I don't reason them out. It's more of a creative process – as if each fact is one of a vast assortment of puzzle pieces spread across a table: some are twisted sideways, some are upside down, some are irrelevant, and some are missing. But I remember the pertinent facts, discard the false leads, and usually put them together into a meaningful context. It's like finding my granma's reading glasses or recognizing clues in my daddy's mystery novels."

Clayton grimaced. "You'd be hell in a casino if you could remember cards that way. Remind me never to play blackjack with you."

Laila tilted her head. "I never tried my 'noticing aptitude' with cards. Hmmnn. . . . Anyway, to continue. My mind operates on three levels of complexity. If the puzzle is an easy one and doesn't have many pieces, I see it as a color chart in an optometrist's examination room. You know, the one they use to test people for color blindness? If you're not color blind, the colored word jumps out of the differently colored background as if it were black on white.

"If there are a lot of facts, then the picture doesn't come into focus right away. Some of the intel could be misleading, misunderstood, patently false, or irrelevant to this particular picture. In that case I'm a might confused, as my granma used to say. Simply reading and collating reports doesn't work for me – at least, not on the conscious level. I look at the facts from every angle until, voila, an image suddenly forms, as if it were turned on by a switch. The truth was there all the time, but I was looking at it the wrong way.

"I compare this level of analysis to one of those black and white pictures that looks like either a white ornate vase in the middle of a black background, or two black silhouettes on either side of a white middle ground."

Clayton smiled. "Sure, I know that one. It's an optical illusion that's used to test a person's imagination. Some people see the vase, others see the faces. Once you see one it's hard to see the other unless it's pointed out to you."

"Exactly. And even when you point out the other view, some people stare and stare and are never able to see it. Their minds are locked in on the first image they saw."

Clayton scowled. "I see where you're going with this. An analyst will study the facts until he forms an opinion about the intel's meaning. Once that opinion is formed, it's unalterable."

"That's why it's better to have more than one person analyzing data, and why multiple intelligence agencies produce better results than a single autonomous agency. Don't take this personally, but sometimes an agency adopts a mindset that is blind to alternative views. The trick in our work is to pick the right view but keep an open mind about the other views."

Clayton shook his head. "We certainly picked the wrong view of the Baghdad restaurant bombing."

"I didn't mean my analogy to be a criticism. I was only pointing out what you already know: there's always more than one interpretation of data. Often there are several."

Clayton shook his head again. "Please don't remind me."

"Mark, no one ever said that intelligence work is perfect. Sometimes you simply don't have enough pieces of the puzzle to see the picture that's forming."

"Then why didn't we see the picture that you saw?"

Laila shrugged. "I saw your picture, too. After switching my point of view back and forth a number of times, I discounted it."

Clayton was circumspect. "So what's your third level of complexity?"

"You're not going to like it."

Clayton raised his eyebrows and twisted his lips into a scowl.

"Okay. Do you know what a stereogram is?" When he returned a blank stare, she continued. "It's a computer generated image that from a distance looks like an ordinary flat or two-dimensional abstract painting of various colors, all without form. It looks like a riotous hodgepodge of hues and tints. As you get closer to the picture, the image resolves into a pattern of repeating dots or small indecipherable images. But if you stare at it long enough – either by crossing your eyes or by focusing on the plane and backing away, and concentrating – a hidden three-dimensional image is rendered: an image that has depth or relief and seems to grow out of the plane."

"Sure, I know what you mean!" Clayton grinned broadly and fluttered his hands. "Jasika bought some books like that for the kids a couple of years ago. Magic Eye, I think they're called."

Laila nodded. "That's one brand. There are other companies that generate stereograms for T-shirts, advertisements, corporate logos, and the like."

Clayton shook his head. "Once they learned the trick, the kids were able to see the hidden images right away. It took me and Jasika quite a while to do it. Sometimes I gave up. Crossing my eyes or adjusting my focus gave me a headache."

"You can tell when a first-timer sees the image when he gasps or shouts 'Oh, wow,' or something like it."

"Sure, that's exactly what I said the first time I saw it."

"Seeing the hidden feature in a stereogram is a matter of visual perception. I do something similar on a mental plane. I assimilate reports, I extract pertinent data, I discard irrelevancies, I gauge the reliability of sources, and I ponder over the information in the back of my mind. Sometimes this goes on for days as additional intel is acquired. Hazy images appear in my head but no clear picture emerges. The process continues subconsciously while I'm working on other projects, eating, sleeping, even talking with coworkers. Then suddenly, like a burst of light, the pieces of the puzzle come together and form a picture of events . . . and I know it's true."

"So it's a flash of insight and not soothsaying or clairvoyance?"

Laila tilted her head. "That's how I perceive it."

"Well, I feel a little better about how you do it. At least you don't use a divining rod." Clayton's cell phone jingled. He pulled it out of his pants pocket, glanced at the screen, pressed a button, and returned the phone to his pocket. "Your transportation will be here in fifteen minutes. Let's head for the helipad."

They disposed of their dinnerware. Laila purchased cup of coffee to go. She sipped the hot brew as Clayton led the way through the intersecting corridors.

"Do you know where I'm going?"

"That's a negative. This project is so hush-hush that my department has been taken off of it. All I know is that you are going to a most secure location. From this point forward, all intel relating to the synchrotron facility will be funneled directly to you, and only to you. Our local assets will continue to report to their handlers, but the handlers will report to you instead of to analyzers in my department . . . through our Internet servers, of course, but with passwords and security codes to which my department will not have access."

"I'm so sorry, Mark. I didn't know – "

Clayton gestured with one hand as if he were waving off an annoying insect. "Don't feel bad about it. My department is understaffed and overwhelmed by other crucial intel. I'm happy to be divested of a drain on my resources. And don't take this personally, but despite your remarkable ability to see trees in a bamboo forest, I still think your time machine implication belongs in a supermarket tabloid instead of an intelligence report. If there's any truth to the IRF's insinuation that they can send bombs into the past, I think it's a deliberate deception."

"Time will tell."

Clayton chuckled. "Laila, I like your light-hearted manner."

"There's so much seriousness in the world already that I try not to add to it."

The corridor broadened into a dimly lit waiting room that extended beyond the building toward the helipad. Red upholstered seats lined the walls on both sides. They walked to the end where a pair of glass doors kept out the nighttime cold, and peered into the darkness outside, where all was still and silent.

"That's a good attitude to have for people in our line of work. Unfortunately, when I leave the house in the morning I leave my sense of humor behind."

She finished her coffee and dropped the Styrofoam cup into a trash can. "I'd go crazy if I did that."

Without a sound, a nearly invisible shape descended straight down from the sky and settled on the tarmac. Laila saw nothing but her reflection when she squinted through the window. She pressed her nose against the cold glass and cupped her hands alongside her head. She couldn't see anything distinct on the flight line: a slender profile that tapered toward one end. She heard a whooshing sound so slight that it reminded her of a butterfly flapping past her ear.

"What is that thing?" Clayton wanted to know.

"It's classified."

Chapter 4

A figure appeared abruptly on the other side of the door. Laila stepped back just as the glass was pulled away from her nose. She dropped her hands from the side of her head, but not before she saw a pair of deep blue eyes that sparkled like cobalt in the subdued light that emanated from the waiting room behind her. The eyes pierced hers like sharpened spears. She did her best to wipe the startled expression off her face.

The man who held the door open was grim-faced. He stood a couple of inches shy of six feet tall. He wore a black flight suit and black flying boots. Because he cradled his helmet under his right arm, Laila could see the thick thatch of blond crew-cut hair that crowned his head.

"Laila Masterson, I am Colonel Bryce Davenport. I have been assigned to take you to your connecting flight."

"Why, uh, thank you, uh, Colonel."

He held a black leather card holder in front of her face. "My ID."

Laila hardly glanced at it. "Thank you, uh, Colonel."

He stared at her with the door still held open by his right hand. "Your identification, please."

"Oh, of course. I forgot." She swung the pack off her back, then remembered that her ID card was in the pocket of her skirt for quick and easy access. She deplored wearing it on a strap around her neck as if it were a dog tag on a collar. She held the pack by the straps as the pilot examined the card.

"Thank you. If you will follow me . . . "

Laila turned to Clayton. "About the password and access codes . . . "

"I've already sent them to your email address. I attached a contact sheet with secure phone numbers for me and General Cercopley. You can call me any time, night or day, if you need assistance or information."

"Then, as they say in the insane asylum, I must be

off." She shook Clayton's hand. "I'm certain we'll be in touch."

"Good luck with the mission, whatever it is."

"Thanks, Mark."

Laila turned and walked through the open doorway as the pilot stepped aside to let her pass. The airfield was not illuminated. The aircraft showed no navigation lights, nor did any light from inside the nearly invisible craft penetrate the acrylic windows. She felt the brush of air against her face as she strode upright under the barely audible blades that whirled above her head. She redirected her course as her eyes slowly adjusted to the darkness. She passed the pilot's door and marched straight to the passenger cabin.

"I'll help you, ma'am."

"Don't bother. I can find my way." She fumbled for a moment as she searched for the inset handle, then found it and yanked open the door. Over her shoulder she called, "It's a Whispercat," as if that explained everything. She pulled the door closed behind her.

The Whispercat was a strategic reconnaissance helicopter that mimicked the stealth bomber in having rounded external surfaces and anechoic tiles that reduced the radar signature of the fuselage. Electronic noise reduction technology accounted for the almost perfect silence of the lifting and propulsion rotors. One-way darkened acrylic windows let no light escape from the interior. Most of the manual navigation was done by means of a heads-up display on a flip-down helmet visor.

Laila placed her computer pack across from her in the starboard observation seat, then got comfortable in the port observation seat. She buckled the seat belt around her computer pack. For herself she used both the seat belt and the chest harness. The interior acoustics was much like that of a recording chamber: exterior noise was inaudible, interior sound carried no echo.

She imitated a flight attendant's voice in a commercial airliner: "All personal items have been placed on the floor in front of me, my tray table is stowed, my seatback is in the upright and locked position, and my safety harness is secured."

The co-pilot glanced over a flight-suited left shoulder. With an upper lip that was not as stiff as that of the pilot, she asked, "You recognize the Whispercat?"

"Only from pictures. I've never been inside one. The Whispercat might be flown by Air Force pilots, but its design and construction were backed by the CIA. I love the whisper mode; it's better than a Bose headset. Show me what this baby can do in the air."

"We'll try." The co-pilot face was invisible inside the helmet and behind a full-face visor. "By the way, I'm Captain Danette Stackhouse."

"I'm Laila Masterson, but you already knew that. Call me Laila."

Laila received a curt nod in response. She could not see the pilot because his seat was positioned directly in front of hers. She saw his hands flipping switches on the dashboard; she had to imagine him depressing anti-torque pedals and handling the cyclic, collective, and throttle. The Whispercat lifted straight up from the ground without a lurch, with about the same thrust one would feel in an elevator. The bucket seats were fitted with hydraulic shock absorbers and anti-sway springs that steadied all but the harshest motion and sheer. She was barely able to hear the increasing pitch of the turbine.

Laila stared out the window and watched the ground recede. The Whispercat's silhouette could be spotted when the aircraft was backlit, but its smart radar-vision system predicted when this might occur, and alerted the pilot to course alternatives that would prevent or minimize optical detection. The lights of Bolling Air Force Base were bright in comparison to the dark water of the adjacent Potomac River.

The Whispercat hovered effortlessly at an altitude that Laila estimated was five hundred feet. It sideslipped westward to the middle of the river, flew upstream to the confluence of the Anacostia River, then veered northeast away from the Potomac. It stopped sharply when it reached the I-295 bridge, just short of the Washington Navy Yard. The Whispercat dropped so suddenly that Laila was lifted as far off the soft cushion as the seatbelt allowed. Her stomach continued to rise.

At an altitude of barely twenty-five feet above the water, the Whispercat executed a hovering counter-clockwise turn of 180 degrees, flew rapidly down the Anacostia, banked left onto the Potomac, then increased speed with hardly a murmur as it raced downstream toward the I-495 bridge. The sudden thrust of the turbojet engine pressed Laila deep into the cushion of the seat-back. The span above the shipping lane was tall enough to allow passage of modern naval vessels. Laila could not help but gasp as the jet-propelled Whispercat darted under the bridge at nearly two hundred knots.

As soon as the Whispercat cleared the bridge, it arced upward in a short sweeping curve that had it ascending almost immediately at an angle of seventy-five degrees. Laila gulped hard. When the Whispercat leveled out in the blink of an eye, Laila was too preoccupied with holding onto her stomach contents to look out the window.

She had barely regained her equilibrium when the Whispercat took a nosedive and gained additional speed, banking left with such centrifugal force that when she glanced out the window, she found herself looking straight down at city lights. The Whispercat rolled back to an even keel at the same time that it pulled out of the dive. Then it dropped at the exact speed that gravity exerted on a falling body. The simulated free-fall kept her floating slightly above the seat cushion.

The Whispercat came out of the dive gradually. By peering between the front seats, Laila could see out the front window. The Whispercat was fast approaching an airfield diagonally. It turned sharply before reaching the landing strip. The nose turned up as the helicopter braked to a halt less than a hundred feet in front of a darkened hangar. The Whispercat hovered inches above ground level.

The pilot's helmeted head leaned around his seat. "Satisfied?"

Laila coughed, cupped her hands over her mouth, and coughed again.

"Don't you dare vomit in my aircraft!"

Laila grappled for the inside door handle. She flipped it up and pulled back at the same time. The door slid open. She leaned outboard as far as the restraints allowed, then upchucked onto the tarmac – several times. She coughed and retched some more. Finally she generated some saliva and spit out the tiny particles that remained in her mouth.

Haltingly, "I can't think – of any – witty replies – at the moment."

The co-pilot said, "None is necessary."

"If you will slide the door closed, I will relock it."

Laila did as the pilot suggested. Immediately the Whispercat eased forward. The hangar doors opened automatically when the stealth helicopter's short-beam transmission code triggered the reception proximity signal. The inside of the hangar remained dark until the doors closed behind the aircraft. The helicopter performed a slow rotation until it completed half a circle. The landing skids touched the floor.

The cabin lights illuminated.

Laila released the buckles that pinned her and her computer to their seats. "Is this Andrews Air Force Base?"

The pilot leaned around his seat again. "How did you know?"

Laila shrugged. "You turned east off the river. Or is this Lisbon?"

The colonel chuckled. "The latitude is right, but we don't carry enough fuel to reach Spain."

Laila tugged open the door. "Is someone meeting me here? A doctor?"

"Stay in the waiting room while we shut down the aircraft."

"Will do." Laila saw the co-pilot flipping switches. The rotors had stopped spinning.

"The key code is nine-four-four-seven-seven-three-seven."

Laila rolled her eyes upward until the pupils were covered by her eyelids; only the bottom curve of her light green irises showed. She was momentarily lost in thought. "WHISPER on the telephone keypad." She opened her eyes fully and stared directly at the pilot. "Couldn't you think of anything more clever than that?"

"We're not an imaginative bunch."

Laila stepped down onto the concrete apron with her computer bag in tow. She flung the straps over her shoulders without a backward glance. She spotted a bright green light over a nearby doorway. Next to the door on one side were a long workbench and a standing tool chest; on the other side were a key pad and a drinking fountain. She rinsed out her mouth with ice cold water before entering the code number on the key pad. The door opened into a well-lighted room. She entered confidently.

A short, bearded man wearing a yamaka turned to face her. His black vest and trousers contrasted sharply with his white shirt, which was partially pulled out of his belt, making it look as if he were auditioning as a dance partner for a stage production of "Hava Nagila." He grinned broadly as he fingered the computer bag that hung over one shoulder.

Without preamble: "My name is Dr. H. Horace Leibowitz. I am the head of the Department of Linguistics at Harvard University, Professor Emeritus of the Department of Linguistics at Duke University, the leading expert in the country if not in the world on modern Semitic languages and ancient Hebrew, and the chief translator of the latest and most correct version of the Dead Sea Scrolls. I was granted sabbatical in order to accept the government assignment as official translator of historical texts. They are paying $250,000 for my indispensable skills."

"Wow. You're really into yourself. Can you fry eggs too?"

Without missing a beat: "I am the principle author

of 'Consonant Phonemes in Hebrew Past and Present,' the principle author of 'Vowel Usage in Ancient Semitic Script,' the primary autographer of 'Songs of the Arabian Nights,' the – "

"Pardon me for interrupting your resume, but take a break from Jewish folk music while I tidy up in the lady's room." She didn't know if any restrooms were located nearby, but she was willing to walk a million miles to get away from one of his smiles. "Hold the fort."

Laila walked past his fading grin. After passing through the waiting room doors she spotted a sign with arrows pointing the way to the restrooms. She relieved herself, washed her hands and face, and fretted about the scraggly locks that had escaped from her bun during the day's long travels and high-level talks. She longed for a cup of hot coffee.

She re-entered the waiting room with the apprehension that Leibowitz would restart his personal monologue.

He leered at her the way a wolf greets its food. "Are – are you my escort?"

"I certainly hope not, because I don't know where I'm going."

"I didn't catch your name."

"Laila Masterson."

"What do you do around here?"

"That's classified."

"They're paying me a quarter of a million dollars to translate some old manuscripts. They need me because I'm the best there is. The only one, really. I couldn't pass up this opportunity no matter how much the college and my students need me. They'll have to do without . . . "

The outer door opened. Colonel Davenport and Captain Stackhouse walked into waiting room with their helmets under their arms.

Davenport strode straight to Leibowitz. He towered over him as much as he towered over Laila. "Professor Hyman Leibowitz, we are here to escort you to your primary work area."

Leibowitz repeated his rote verbatim as if he had

practiced it for hours: "My name is Dr. H. Horace Leibowitz. I am the head of the Department of Linguistics
at Harvard University, Professor Emeritus of the Department of Linguistics at Duke University, the leading expert in the country if not the world on modern Semitic
languages and ancient Hebrew, and the chief translator
of the latest and most correct version of the Dead Sea
Scrolls. I was granted sabbatical in order to accept the
government assignment as official translator of historical texts. They are paying $250,000 or my indispensable
skills. I am the principle author of 'Consonant
Phonemes in Hebrew Past and Present,' the principle
author – "

Davenport assumed his strongest military restraint.
"Skip the autobiography, Professor. We have a plane to
catch." He pulled his ID card out of a zippered shirt
pocket and held it in front of Leibowitz's nose. "Please
identify yourself."

Leibowitz scratched his black beard as he stared
from Davenport to Stackhouse and back to Davenport.
"Well, I, that is, I – I have a driver's license."

"May I see it, please?"

Leibowitz dug into his back trouser pocket and
pulled out a ragged leather billfold that looked as if it
had been dragged through wet ditches in a war zone. He
fumbled his photo ID out of a credit card slot.

Davenport looked the license casually. "Confirmed.
Please follow me." When he glanced at Laila, the ends of
his lips turned up ever so slightly. "Both of you." He led
the parade out of the waiting room and along a corridor
that seemed to stretch into infinity. Laila got in line behind him. Stackhouse brought up the rear.

Leibowitz resumed his litany. "I – I – I am the principle author of 'Consonant Phonemes in Hebrew Past and
Present,' the principle author of 'Vowel Usage – "

Stackhouse interrupted. "This is a restricted quiet
zone."

Leibowitz turned his head and stared at her. "I – I
was just saying – "

"A restricted quiet zone is one where unnecessary

conversation is not permitted."

Leibowitz scowled but didn't speak.

The parade marched along a series of interconnecting and dimly lighted corridors, turning left, right, and left like mice running through a maze to find a wedge of cheese at the end. They finally emerged from a short passageway with low overhead into an anteroom that was the convergence of three passageways. They halted outside a locker room entrance that was divided in two: men on the left and women on the right.

Laila rolled her eyes upward. After a few seconds she refocused on her surroundings, then pointed to the left. "Instead of walking around in circles, why didn't we take the direct route from that corridor?"

"Very impressive, Ms. Masterson." Davenport suppressed a smirk. "The idea was to confuse you so you couldn't retrace your steps. It's a security measure."

Laila nodded. "That makes sense."

"Are – are we out of the quiet zone?"

"No!" Both Davenport and Stackhouse spoke at the same time.

Leibowitz hunkered down like a cowering dog. "I – I – I only asked."

"We have to change into high-altitude flight gear. Mr. Leibowitz will come with me. Ms. Masterson will go with Captain Stackhouse."

The foursome parted ways.

The pure ebony skin of Stackhouse's face shone brightly in the fluorescent light of the women's locker room. She placed her helmet on a wooden bench with hands that were equally as black. "I try not to be judgmental, but that Mr. Leibowitz has such an irritating personality that I don't think we'll be able to get along."

"My thoughts precisely, Captain."

"Please call me Danette."

"I will, if you'll call me Laila."

"It's a deal." Danette unzipped the front of her flight suit and pushed it down her body like a snake shedding its skin. She wore only bra, panties, and woolen socks underneath: all in matching navy blue. "You'll have to trade in your dress for G-suit, Laila. We don't have any size sixes, so just take the smallest one from the rack behind you."

Laila looked over the handful of anti-acceleration pressure suits. "Do they have any in red or green?"

"Sorry. No." Danette laughed. "They only come in basic black."

"Black is beautiful." Laila found the smallest size available, plucked it off the rack, and held it in front of her. "How do I look?"

"Black may be beautiful but you look better in that blue outfit of yours. In fact, I think you'd look better in green, to match your eyes."

Laila shrugged. "All my green ensembles are at the cleaners."

"You can't wear that skirt and blouse under the G-suit."

"No problem." Laila suddenly let out a tiny shriek.

"What is it?"

Laila stared at Danette with eyes the size of half dollars. "Omigod," she gasped. "I'm still wearing my jogging shoes." She gasped again. "I was in such a tizzy this morning that I left my dress shoes in my slicker pockets, which I left on the back seat of my car."

"Where we're going, jogging shoes will be better anyway, even if the colors don't match."

"You don't understand. I had three high-level meetings today. And I wore these jogging shoes in every one of them."

Danette laughed. "Don't worry, Laila. What's in your head is more important than what's on your feet."

Laila felt heat flush her face. There was nothing she could do about it now. She sat on a bench opposite Danette, untied her laces, and yanked the embarrassing jogging shoes off her dainty feet. She stood and pulled the blouse over her head and dropped the skirt to her ankles.

"No bra?"

"When you don't have anything larger than dimples on your chest, support isn't necessary. I've never worn a bra. I don't even own a bra."

Danette humphed. "You don't know how lucky you are. These watermelons of mine have caused more trouble than they're worth, especially when it comes to uniforms and flight suits. All they're good for is attracting looks from men who want nothing more than to see a big pair of tits."

"I've never had that problem."

"The right one gets in the way of my tennis swing: I hit it with my arm when I make low returns. And when I reach overhead for a volley or jump for a high return, they bobble and throw me off balance." Danette shook her head. "I'll trade you any day."

"Have you considered the Amazon thing?" Laila sat down and stuck her feet into the leggings of the G-suit. "These legs are tighter than pantyhose, and a lot less stretchable."

"Wait until we pressurize them."

She struggled into the leggings, yanked them up to her knees, then stood and got a grip on the collar in order to pull the one-piece suit up and over her boyish hips and flat chest. "These would be great for snowmobiling."

"Don't think they haven't been used that way."

The garment's fire retardant material was designed to protect pilots in case of a cabin fire. Insulation provided warmth at altitudes where the air was thin. Numerous pouches and patch pockets offered places to stow everything from pencils to maps to flight plans to lunch. But the primary purpose of the G-suit was to prevent its wearer from losing consciousness during high-acceleration dives and high-speed radical turns. Blackouts occurred when blood was drained from the brain and pooled in the lower parts of the body.

"Should I take a squirt before I get trapped in this thing?"

"The flight time is only an hour and a half."

"I can hold it in that long." Laila stuck her arms through the sleeves. "The top fits me like a tent."

"It'll snug up on you when we pump air into the

bladders. Besides, it's only a precaution against the loss of cabin pressure."

"I can hardly wait." After zipping up the front, Laila sat and tried to pull on her shoes. She had to pull the zipper down to her stomach in order to bend far enough to reach her feet. After her laces were neatly tied, with each bow the same size and each string the identical length, she stood and admired herself in the mirror. "These suits are so bulky that breast size doesn't matter."

"Welcome to military unisex clothing. Mine are plastered so flat that they hurt." Danette tugged on Laila's G-suit so it hung better on her tiny frame. "That'll have to do."

Laila pirouetted. "I never thought I'd have the opportunity to wear one of these." She stuffed her blouse and skirt into a pair of voluminous pockets. When she picked up her computer pack, she found that the straps were too tight to fit comfortably over the G-suit. She carried it by the top loop.

Both women exited the locker room to find the men already waiting for them: Davenport somewhat patiently, Leibowitz uncomfortably. It was obvious to Laila by the expressions on their faces that they did had not had a successful male bonding experience.

The pressure suit was so bulky on Leibowitz that it made him look like a short fat bearded gnome. Laila laughed inwardly until she realized that she must look the same way – without the beard, of course.

"This way, please." Davenport led the party to a doorway next to the locker room. He pushed open the door with his free left hand – his helmet was cradled in his right – and stepped into a hangar that held a single aircraft that looked like a giant boomerang.

"Oh, *wow*," Laila exclaimed. "The B-2 Stealth Presidential Evacuation Aircraft."

Chapter 5

Laila took a sharp intake of air and cupped her mouth with her hands. "Oh, I'm sorry." She rolled her eyes toward Leibowitz. "Is he cleared to hear that?"

Silence reigned for several seconds.

"He signed a nonrevocable nondisclosure packet that conforms with the wartime Official Secrets Act." That was Davenport's way of stating that Leibowitz held temporary clearance. He faced Leibowitz. "Captain Stackhouse will assist you in boarding."

Danette made a sweeping gesture with her right arm. Leibowitz ducked under the leading edge of the wing and stepped lightly toward the centerline staircase that led up into the belly of the fuselage; in its extended position, the staircase reminded Laila of an wasp's stinger. She started to follow Leibowitz but Davenport's firm grip on her upper arm held her back. Danette winked at Laila, then went after Leibowitz.

When Laila and Davenport were alone together, he let go of her arm. "This aircraft is a top secret Air Force project. How did you know about it?"

"Please don't take this personally, but my source is classified CIA information."

Davenport huffed. "I happen to be – " He stopped speaking abruptly. He stared hard at Laila, first at one eye then at the other. "Yes of course. You're right." He fumbled in one of the voluminous chest pockets of his pressure suit. He pulled out a small plastic vial from which he extracted a tablet about the size of a pearl. "It's anti-nausea medicine for motion sickness. Would you like one?"

With a broad smile: "You *do* care about me." She snatched the pill out of Davenport's palm and chucked it into her mouth.

"It's chewable." Davenport tipped the vial and dumped another pill onto his palm. He plopped the pill into his mouth, chewed, and swallowed.

"You too?"

"I'm not proud."

"What about Leibowitz?"

Davenport glanced at the staircase. Leibowitz and Danette had already entered the aircraft. "Let him puke."

Laila shrugged and raised her eyebrows. "It's your aircraft."

"Actually it belongs to the President. He just lets me fly it."

"Lucky you. I don't think you'd want to pay for the upkeep anyway." Laila turned and walked under the wing with her head held high. There was barely enough headroom for a person of her stature. She climbed the staircase with Davenport ducking right behind her. Danette had just finished tucking Leibowitz into the port foremost pressure seat; she buckled his seatbelt across his lap. His face projected his anxiety. For once he had no words to spout.

A movement of Danette's eyes indicated for Laila to occupy the starboard seat. Laila sat and strapped herself in without favoring Leibowitz with a glance.

The plush cabin was upholstered with light blue fabric that matched the deep-pile carpet and plastic paneling. The center aisle divided twelve passenger seats down the middle. Each seat had its own window, but the shades were pulled down and snapped in place. Restrooms and kitchen facilities occupied the rear of the spacious cabin.

Danette walked forward along a narrow aisle way between two broad computer consoles and tall storage lockers. Davenport assumed the introductory duties of an airline hostess. He glanced back and forth between Laila and Leibowitz.

"Listen up, people. Pay strict attention to what I tell you. We will be traveling at high speed and high altitude. Do not leave your seat without first asking permission. To do so, press the call button on the inboard armrest. This is for your own safety, in case we have to make sudden radical course changes. Seatbelts are mandatory but a safety harness will only become necessary if we anticipate rough passage or evasive maneuvers. To deploy the safety harness, reach over your head – " He reached over Leibowitz's black curly hair, and demonstrated. " – grab this inset handle, pull it up and over your head and down in front of you, then snap the handle around the seat belt locking mechanism."

A cross-chest harness held Leibowitz securely in place. "Hey, that's pretty neat."

"When releasing the harness buckle hold it firmly, disengage by depressing the central button, and lift it over your head." Davenport did not hold the harness firmly. The retraction spring yanked the harness buckle out of his hand.

The harness flew past Leibowitz's face and nicked the tip of his protruding proboscis. "Ouch!"

Drolly: "The retractor assembly will return the harness to the seatback. Both the seatbelt and safety harness are equipped with inertial locking mechanisms which will activate automatically upon rapid deceleration. Redundant pretensioners and webcams are designed to withstand a sudden stop from a speed of two hundred knots before assembly destruction. If the aircraft stops suddenly from a higher speed, the use of retaining systems is irrelevant.

"In case of a loss of cabin pressure, a ceiling panel will open and life-support hoses will descend onto your lap. Place the oxygen mask over your head and breathe normally. Then – and only then – plug the corrugated hose into the nozzle port on the belly button of the pressure suit. The suit will then inflate with air.

"We will be flying in stealth mode. It is crucial that we remain invisible in order to avoid detection. The window shades are closed and secured in order to prevent extraneous light from escaping the cabin. Is that understood?"

"Understood," Laila parroted.

Leibowitz was rubbing his injured nose.

"*Understood?*"

"All right, already. I understand."

"Flight time is approximately ninety minutes." Davenport winked at Laila. "Barf bags are located in the convenience cache in front of you, along with drinks and snacks. Are there any questions?"

Laila suggested lightly, "Don't forget to check for moisture in the transducer units."

Davenport's face was expressionless. "I'll do that." He turned and walked along the aisle way to the cockpit.

Leibowitz muttered under his breath: "He – he – he did that on purpose."

Laila had a head full of rejoinders but she kept them there.

In the silence that followed, Leibowitz stopped rubbing his nose and glanced around the cabin. He soon got over his snit. He examined the contents of the convenience cache by removing each item one at a time, holding it in front of his rimless glasses, then replacing it and removing another. The cache was the size of a large briefcase; it contained bottled water, canned soft drinks, candy bars, bags of dried fruit and mixed nuts, and vacuum sealed sandwich wedges.

"Now this is what I call traveling first class."

Laila stayed in stealth mode. She felt the aircraft moving ever so slightly.

He peeled open a sandwich packet, sniffed the sandwich, and squeezed the bread. "The bread isn't too stale." He took a bite. "Not bad for a prepackaged meal." He chewed silently and swallowed. "Did – did I tell you that I graduated summa cum laude?"

"I must have missed that tidbit."

Leibowitz slowly consumed the sandwich. He glanced at his watch. "After midnight. I hope they put me up in a nice hotel, with room service."

No comment.

Between bites: "What did you mean back there, about the Presidential Evacuation Aircraft? Is this a stealth bomber or what?"

Laila sighed deeply. She still didn't know what her assigned mission entailed, but she presumed that Leibowitz was a functioning member of the team with full if temporary top secret clearance. If she was going to have to work with him, the least she could do was be civil. She was cautious nonetheless. "Don't take it personally, but that information is classified."

"You heard the colonel, or pilot, or whatever he is. He said that I signed a confidentiality agreement. That means I agreed not to divulge anything I see or hear on the job. They're not paying me $250,000 because I can't be trusted with their petty secrets."

"I suppose you're right," Laila conceded.

Arrogantly: "Of course I am. So what about this plane? How can a stealth bomber be an evacuation plane?"

"This aircraft has been retrofitted as a special passenger plane for Presidential usage. It's called the B-2 PEA, pronounced bee-too'-pee." Laila giggled. "Until they officially placed the accent mark on the middle syllable, the acronym provoked a lot of jokes about wigs and urination. Anyway, the exterior is the same as the production model. From the outside, you can't distinguish this aircraft from the standard Northrop Grumman bomber.

"The interior has been modified by reconfiguring the bomb bay for passenger accommodation. Instead of bomb bay doors, the bottom of this compartment is solid except for the retracting staircase in the rear. The landing gear has been fitted with hydraulic extenders that can elevate the aircraft to enable a person to walk under the wings and fuselage without having to crawl on his belly or hands and knees."

Leibowitz laughed. "I'd rather make the President crawl."

Laila smirked but did not otherwise acknowledge Leibowitz's political quip. "As you can see, the interior provides just about every convenience. You saw the galley when you walked through it from the rear entry: pantry, refrigerator, freezer, conventional and microwave ovens, range tops, even a grill, all equipment operated electrically by a built-in generator with battery backup. It's amazing how much stuff you can install when you remove twenty-five tons of bombs."

She pointed to the twin bulkheads that straddled the forward aisle way. "Two widescreen high-definition television screens. Two computer consoles with satellite communication links and Internet access. And notice the red Presidential telephone. The B2P isn't as exclusive as Air Force One. It's an escape aircraft, not a command center. It's designed to carry the President and his primary entourage – Vice President, wives, and chief advisors – and to deliver the Presidential payload to any one of several hidden underground enclosures in the event of an attack against the Capitol."

"My tax dollars at work."

"That's one way of looking at it. A negative way. Remember that snakes and governments don't function when their head is cut off. You may not like the President or his political stances, especially those that affect you personally, but he *is* the Commander in Chief of the country's armed forces, and needs to be protected so that *he* can protect *you*."

Belligerently: "Spoken like a – a – a true if misguided patriot."

Laila sighed but did not rise to the bait.

"So how come we don't know about this plane? The public has a right to know how its tax dollars are being spent – or misspent."

"The purpose of military secrets is not to keep information from American citizens, but to keep them from enemies that would use the information against us. The number one intelligence source of America's enemies is the American media. They read our newspapers and watch our broadcasts."

"I've heard all that before."

"Don't you believe it? Or don't you want to accept it?"

"It's sounds good when you phrase it that way, but it's still a – a lame justification for keeping the taxpayers in ignorance of how their money is being spent."

Laila could see that applying reason and rationality would be no more effective with Leibowitz than it would be with a devout Muslim terrorist. Establishing a working relationship with him was certain to try her patience. She did not hear the jet engines revving, but she felt a barely perceptible lurch followed by a slight feeling of forward motion. The aircraft was underway.

"Why – why do they have to keep the plane hidden in a giant hangar, and fly late at night? This flight is disturbing my sleep cycle."

"This is a highly populated area. Spies are everywhere. Landing and taking off in the dark will help maintain the secrecy of the aircraft's movements."

Davenport's voice sounded over the public address system: "Prepare for acceleration."

"What – what was that you said about moisture in some unit?"

Laila saw an opportunity to frighten Leibowitz, so she took it. "The avionic systems are computerized, very much like the systems that maintain performance in your car. One stealth bomber crashed and was destroyed by a sensor malfunction when moisture accumulated in a transducer unit that indicated airspeed."

"How much did *that* cost the taxpayers?"

Laila answered the unasked question first. "Both pilots ejected safely. The constructive loss was close to one and a half billion dollars." She added merrily: "But the aircraft was insured."

If Leibowitz intended to remark that the aircraft was insured by American taxpayers, the sudden acceleration punched the retort out of his lungs.

Laila sank back into the cushion as if a mammoth hand had pressed hard against her sternum. She struggled to inhale. She thought for a moment that she could hear the jet engines whining dully, but quickly ascertained that the gentle whisper was made by the air circulators. She no longer cared about how ludicrous she might look in the pressure suit; she was glad that she was wearing it.

The cabin tilted upward until the floor stood on a sixty degree angle. The acceleration increased. Laila could feel her cheeks drawn back into a grimace. She wanted to scream, but every bit of air she inhaled she held on to as long as she could, before exhaling in the hope of obtaining another breath; she had none leftover for vocalization. She lost all sense of time. She was aware only of her immediate need to respire. She inhaled with difficulty; she exhaled as if she had been punched in the solar plexus. She didn't count seconds; she counted the number of breaths she took. More time passed.

The fierce acceleration finally ended so abruptly that she felt as if she had been thrust forward against the restraints by a huge wave of water striking her back. Then came a weird floating sensation that an astronaut might feel in the absence of gravity. She breathed freely, and found herself gasping.

"Wow! That was more fun than a centrifuge."

Above the susurration of the air conditioning system she perceived gagging sounds from her cabin mate. Leibowitz was reaching halfheartedly for the convenience cache. He seemed to have no strength in his arms. After a moment of concentrated effort, he managed to close one hand on the lip of the cache. He levered himself forward, reach into the cache, yanked out the barf bag, and barely got it open before his body was wracked with projectile vomiting so powerful that ejecta erupted from his nose. He upchucked sporadically for the next several minutes.

Casually: "Can't take the g's?"

Leibowitz failed to reply.

"Now you know why you got the big bucks."

Leibowitz still neglected to reply. He wretched some more, then went through several bouts of dry heaves.

Despite his arrogance, Laila couldn't help but feel sorry for him. Although, she opined, she felt sorrier for the students who had to endure his self-indulgent lectures. She pulled a napkin out of her convenience cache and handed it to him. He snapped it out of her hand without making eye contact. She popped open a can of fruit juice.

"Drink some of this. It will rehydrate you and kill the taste in your mouth."

He accepted the can. "I – I've never been airsick before."

"I'll bet you never had a takeoff like that before."

Leibowitz sipped, burped, and grabbed the barf bag again, but his stomach was already empty. After the gagging stopped, he sipped more of the juice. Finally he sealed the closure of the barf bag and returned it to the convenience cache. He leaned back in his seat. "Did I – I tell you that I translated the Dead Sea Scrolls?"

"Yes, you did."

Leibowitz kept glancing over his right shoulder but seemed reluctant to unbuckle his seat belt and make a dash for the lavatory. "They were translated in the 60's by so-called scholars, but the translations were rough and definitely second rate. Translations in the 70's and 80's were just as bad. I corrected all the errors and translated sections that had baffled previous translators."

Instead of settling in for a boring regurgitation of Leibowitz's linguistic achievements, Laila tried to redirect him into recounting some of the history of the scrolls. "What exactly are these scrolls? I know they're Biblical, so how could they possibly survive so long in open air? Wouldn't they be eaten by silverfish? Or are they copies that monks or scribes rewrote much later?"

"Oh, no, the Dead Sea Scrolls are original . . . written shortly Before the Common Era. Shortly meaning within a couple of centuries. They survived in dry desert caves near the West Bank of the Dead Sea, near the ancient settlement of Qumran, in what used to be Palestine, then Jordan, now Israel, and who knows what next."

Laila understood the unsettled nature of the territory better than he did. "Can I just have the short version?"

"The scrolls were not discovered all at once, but over a period of years from the late 40's to the mid 50's. They were written on either parchment or papyrus. The area is littered with small caves – hundreds of them, many yet undiscovered. These caves were being excavated for hoarded precious metals and Biblical artifacts, mostly ceramics. Some of the caves had been blocked up in order to conceal their contents from the Romans. Then a local antiquities collector – Muhammed edh-Dhib – literally fell through the floor of one cave into a chamber underneath. This semi-sealed chamber contained the first scrolls to be discovered. It came to be known as Cave 1.

"Altogether eleven caves were found to contain scrolls. Each cave was numbered by the order of discovery. Each one contained different documents. Cave 2 – "

"Just the CliffsNotes study guide, remember?" Laila tried to keep him on track. "What was written on these scrolls? Not just the scrolls from Cave 1, but collectively?"

"Biblical texts, the Wisdom of Sirach, Jubilees – similar to *Genesis* but more detailed – some of the Psalms, hymns, letters, Greek and Roman documents, and so on. One of them, called the Copper Scroll, lists sixty-seven other hiding places that are supposed to contain additional manuscripts that were hidden from Roman looters, as well as gold, silver, and copper. All in all, the Dead Sea Scrolls confirm that the Books of the *Bible* were not fabricated documents intended to dupe the masses, as many secular scholars believe, but ancient traditional accounts of the genesis of man, from God's creation of Adam and Eve to the conveyance of the Ten Commandments to Moses on Mount Sinai, if you believe that rot."

Laila was astonished. "What? You don't?"

"I'm a historian, not a religious nut."

"But – you're wearing a yamaka. Only observant Jews are supposed to wear that."

Leibowitz chortled. "Observant Jews and Hebrews with a bald spot." He lifted the yamaka to show the hairless circle on his scalp. "The yamaka provides good cover in more ways than one."

Laila couldn't help but snicker. Perhaps Leibowitz was human after all; or at least had a human side to his intellectual snobbery. "You had me fooled."

"For – for years now, the area where the Dead Sea

Scrolls were found has been cordoned off by the local militia to prevent looters from scavenging the caves."

Laila found an opportunity to ruffle his feathers. "A looter is a person who took something that you would have taken if you had found it first."

"Yes, well, looters always sell their loot to the highest bidder, so the stuff they steal winds up in private collections."

"What prevents museums from bidding?"

"Nothing prevents them from bidding, but they don't have the kind of money that's available to rich collectors with large disposable incomes, and who want nothing more than kitsch to display in keeping with conspicuous consumption."

"Shades of Thorsten Veblen." Laila kept needling him, and found herself enjoying it immensely. "I read recently that the president of the Independence Seaport Museum in Philadelphia was sentenced to fifteen years in prison for diverting museum funds to himself, and selling museum artifacts and keeping the money. That's similar to the case in the 1980's when it was discovered that the head curator of the Smithsonian Institution, the country's most prestigious museum, was selling museum antiquities on the black market. The items were in storage so he figured that no one would miss them.

"The National Park Service has admitted that more than three-quarters of the artifacts that they found on Park lands and used to be in their collection are unaccounted for. They were likely stolen by the Park rangers who had custody over them. It wasn't like that when Smokey the Bear was in charge.

"Then there was the situation that occurred at Philadelphia's Academy of Natural Sciences. One of the preparators wanted to examine fossils that had been stored in a metal cabinet since the turn of the twentieth century. When he pulled open the top drawer, not only were the fossils gone but so was the bottom of the drawer. It turned out that the fossils had been improperly preserved. The fossils had mostly crumbled to dust, and in the process they generated acid from the preservation solution that dissolved metal and ate through all the drawers, right to the floor beneath the bottom of the cabinet.

"Donating precious artifacts to a museum is no guarantee of either safety or preservation. Items held in private collections may be more secure because access to them is limited, and better care is taken of them. Furthermore, many private collectors allow scholars and archaeologists to examine their collections under controlled conditions. That's my point. What's your counterpoint?"

Leibowitz was momentarily speechless. "Even – even if what you say is true – "

"It is."

" – it doesn't alter the fact that more people see relics in museums than in private collections. The purpose of museums is to cater to the public and promote academic studies."

"Your first point is well taken, but I take exception to your second point. Most museums are private enterprises. They don't cater to the public as much as pander to the people in order to support themselves by charging entry fees as high as the market will allow."

Leibowitz fidgeted constantly. He stopped playing with the convenience cache and started fingering the window shade.

"A devil's advocate would point an accusing finger at such institutions as the Philadelphia Art Museum. They acquired a trove of impressionistic artwork – the largest collection of Monets in the world, plus Cezannes, Matisses, and various other artists, all of which was worth *billions* of dollars – and they acquired it by surreptitious means without paying for it. Albert Barnes collected the artworks throughout his life, then established a fund whose dividends and interest would pay for the curation of his collection and the upkeep of the mansion in which it was housed.

"His will forbade the donation of his collection to any private museum, and specifically mentioned the Philadelphia Art Museum by name. He hated the people at the art museum because they were aristocratic snobs. His will ensured that the Barnes Foundation would maintain his collection in perpetuity. Yet years after his death, a shrewd law firm and a prejudiced judge broke the ironclad will, assumed legal control of the collection, and donated the artwork to Barnes' arch enemy, the Philadelphia Art Museum. The Barnes Foundation charged no admission fee when the paintings were in their possession; the museum now rakes in millions of dollars by making people pay to see works of art that were assimilated into their collection."

Leibowitz now had a fingernail under the edge of the window shade. "Oh, sure, those things happen."

"Hyman – may I call you Hyman?"

"I prefer Dr. Leibowitz."

"Horace, then – don't take my criticism personally. Understand that I'm a government analyst. My job is to view all sides of collected information in order to obtain a balanced interpretation. I was merely posing food for thought against your thesis. Surely you know how to defend a thesis. You must have done so in order to obtain your degrees."

"I received the highest accolades ever given by the advisors and committee members who challenged my thesis for my master's degree and my dissertation for my doctorate. My research was impeccable. Both my papers – "The Evolution of the Hebrew Language from Classical to Modern," and "Alternative Translations of Archaic Biblical Hebrew Found on Inscriptions Relating to the Scriptures" – were published to nearly universal acclaim, although there were a couple of dissenters who denied my interpretations because they conflicted with their own."

"Did those studies help you gain access to the Dead Sea Scrolls?"

Leibowitz kept fingering the window shade. He was trying to peer through the space he made between the shade and the window. "Well, no, not really. I – I never got to see the actual scrolls."

"Gee, why not? I would have thought that with your

credentials . . . "

"Yes, well, the Israeli National Archives didn't see it that way. There's a great deal of competition in academia. It took me six years of correspondence and political pull just to get photocopies of the scrolls."

Laila cocked an eyebrow. "I see." His counterpoint was her initial point, but she decided not to mention that fact.

Museums were often dead ends in which items that were either donated or collected were buried in basement storage areas and never again saw the light of day. Not only did paying patrons never get to look at the items and learn about their provenance, but often neither did competing scholars or wealthy museum sponsors. Patrons of the arts need not apply. Once an important item was accessioned, the curator guarded it selfishly, sometimes obsessively.

"I wonder where we are." Leibowitz managed to peel back the side of the shade far enough that he could see through the slender opening. "It's all dark out there – "

Despite the thick pile carpet, Davenport managed to make his black leather boots clump hard enough to announce his entrance. He marched straight to Leibowitz with a gun in his hand. Leibowitz released the shade and turned his head to stare up at Davenport just as Davenport placed the barrel against his forehead and clicked the safety lock.

"What part of 'We will be flying in stealth mode' did you not understand?"

Leibowitz crossed his bulging eyes in order to focus on the gun that was pressed against his skull. "I – I – I – didn't think a short glimpse would matter – "

"It does matter Mr. Leibowitz. It matters because I specifically informed you that the window shades were to remain closed so we wouldn't give away our position by letting light leak from the cabin."

"Yes – yes, I heard what you – "

"You said you understood!"

"Yes, I did understand, but – "

Davenport cocked the hammer and pulled back the

slide. "Give me one good reason why I shouldn't blow your brains out for disobeying a direct order."

"I – I – I – I've already been paid. A quarter of a million dollars has been transferred to my account."

"This aircraft burns more than that amount in jet fuel on every flight."

Laila did a hasty calculation in her head and figured that Davenport was exaggerating – but not by much.

"I – I – But you need me to translate old Hebrew documents. You must, or the government wouldn't have paid me."

Davenport considered. He kept considering . . .

Tremulously: "I – I'm the best there is?"

He pulled the gun away from Leibowitz's forehead, pointed the barrel toward the overhead. "Mister, do you know what the penalty is for treason?"

"Treason? What do you mean, treason?"

"You're a language expert. You should know the meaning of treason."

"No, I – I know what treason is. I don't know what you mean . . . "

"Treason means betrayal. Treason means disloyalty. Treason means a criminal lack of allegiance. Treason means passing secrets to the enemy.

"Hey, I never meant to – "

"When you lifted that shade you created a condition in which this aircraft could be spotted by enemy low-light emission detectors. That is a treasonable offense."

"I – I never thought – "

"You certainly didn't." Without taking his eyes off Leibowitz: "Ms. Masterson, would you please tell Mr. Leibowitz what the penalty is for revealing state secrets to the enemy?"

Leibowitz looked at Laila with still-bulging eyes.

"In peacetime the penalty is imprisonment for life."

"And in wartime?"

Laila tilted her head and perked her eyebrows. "Execution, generally by firing squad."

"Thank you, Ms. Masterson." Davenport released the hammer and returned the slide to its normal position.

"I'm a one man firing squad, Mister, and the only reason I'm not putting a bullet into your head is because I'm afraid it might be hollow, in which case the slug would pass out the back of your skull and through the wall of this aircraft, causing sudden decompression. But I might change my mind and accept the risk. Are we clear on that, Mr. Leibowitz?"

"Well, I – "

"*Are we clear?*"

"Yes, we're – we're clear."

Davenport glared. "The next time you sign an official document, Mister, read past the dollar sign. Your confidentially packet gives the government the right to frisk your person, search your house, tap your phone, examine your records, and screw your wife. Now – " He glanced at his wristwatch. "We start our approach descent in forty-five seconds. Our parabolic curve will simulate free fall for two and a half minutes. I suggest you keep your seatbelt fastened."

Davenport turned on his heel and marched toward the cockpit with the pistol at his side. He stopped and turned. "And stop fiddling with the window shade."

Silence reigned in the cabin.

"Wow, that was pretty tense." Laila's attempt to break the tension didn't work.

Leibowitz's face mirrored pure terror. "Is that right?"

"About what? Your seatbelt?"

"About execution."

"Oh. Only in time of war."

"But we're not at war."

Laila shrugged. "I suppose it all depends on how you define war. Congress hasn't officially declared war against a particular foreign country, but the President's war on terrorism might qualify in a pinch."

Leibowitz nodded and kept on nodding. "Is that other bit true? About the confidentially packet?"

"All except screwing your wife. They need her consent for that."

Leibowitz was still nodding. He croaked, "I'm not married."

Little wonder, Laila thought. *At least his gene pool won't be propagating.*

Danette's voice sounded over the loudspeaker. "We are now commencing our descent. Please remain in your seat and keep your seatbelt fastened. Feel free to use your safety harness if the feeling of weightlessness becomes disturbing."

The nose of the aircraft gradually tilted downward. The inclination increased until Laila felt herself floating up out of her seat. The sensation was one of increasing weight loss. Not that Laila needed to go on a diet. She was fit and firm at one hundred ten pounds.

Leibowitz groaned out loud. "I – don't – like – this."

Laila pulled the tab and tightened the seatbelt around her slender waist. She knew that astronauts trained for the weightlessness of outer space by floating in a padded cabin during a parabolic curve. The experience was necessary for them, but not for her.

Leibowitz gulped at the simulated loss of gravity. He reached over his head for his safety harness. He ran his fingers across the top of the seatback until he located the inset handle. He pulled the harness up and over his head. He fumbled with the buckle in his lap. He wasn't able to make the harness buckle snap into place. He kept slamming the harness buckle against the seatbelt locking assembly.

Suddenly the seatbelt buckle released. Leibowitz called out as he floated up out of his seat, arms gyrating. As soon as he let go of the harness, the handle snapped up against his chin and then raked across his nose as it retracted into the seatback. He flailed his arms like an amateur tightrope walker who had lost his balance over Niagara Falls.

Laila would have found his antics hilarious had the situation not been so dangerous. If Leibowitz was not sitting in his seat when the aircraft straightened out and resumed its horizontal flight course, he would be slammed against the floor or whatever lay beneath him. He rose up toward the ceiling in the semblance of an epileptic fit.

Laila didn't take time to think; she just reacted instinctively. She released her seatbelt buckle. As her buttocks separated from the seat, she flailed her arms in exact imitation of Leibowitz. She stopped as soon as she realized what she was doing. She spun in the air and grabbed her seatback. Once stabilized, she reached across the aisle and grabbed the adjacent seatback, beneath Leibowitz.

One of his wildly swinging hands caught her in the face. She felt a stinging numbness, faltered, then her motherly instinct took over: she ignored the pain and went to the rescue of a man who was old enough to be her father.

She maintained her grip with one hand on the seatback. With the other hand she reached for the belt that held Leibowitz's pants in place. She managed to hold onto him for a moment before his acrobatics twisted him free. His body pirouetted near the ceiling like a drunken ballerina. He bounced lightly off the roof then descended slowly toward Laila. His mouth was agape.

Laila waited until he rotated again before getting another grip on his belt. She pulled him down backward then released her grip in order to allow his new directional momentum to propel him into his seat. After he landed she pressed her hand against his right shoulder.

She didn't feel calm but she spoke calmly nonetheless. "Fasten your seatbelt."

The circular motion of Leibowitz's arms described smaller circles as he grasped on both sides of his lap for his seatbelt straps. He made short chugging sounds which made Laila afraid that he was going to vomit again. The thought made her gag. She imagined the sickening odor.

"Stop fooling around and get your seatbelt fastened." There was more lilt in her voice than she intended.

"I – I'm – trying."

He found the metal part of the buckle but could not seem to find the insert strap. From her floating position above his head, she noticed first that his yamaka was gone and that his round bald spot glistened with sweat, which she could smell. Then she saw that the insert strap disappeared under his leg. She climbed down to the armrest, held on tight, and pulled the strap out from under him.

"Here it is."

Leibowitz held the buckle in one hand and gripped the armrest with the other as if his life depended on it. In reality, his life depended more on securing his seatbelt than gripping the armrest. "I – I can't – "

Laila held the seatbelt in front of his eyes, then lowered it until it touched the top of his hand. "Take it!"

"I – can't." He was frozen in position.

"*Take it!*"

"I – " He made a grab for it, missed, gripped the armrest, then made another grab for it. This time he caught the seatbelt but instead of inserting it, he reclaimed his grip on the armrest.

Laila put her free hand on his shoulder. "Go ahead! Do it! I'll hold you down."

Leibowitz gulped. He let go of the armrest, fumbled with the seatbelt like a child in distress, grabbed again for the armrest, then managed to insert the tab into the buckle and tighten the belt partway.

Laila tightened the seatbelt the rest of the way, then gave it a final snug that pinched Leibowitz to his seat. She realized that she was floating horizontally with her legs bent back at the knees, like a skydiver. She grabbed her own armrest, spun around, and pulled herself over her own seat. By holding onto the armrest next to the window and letting go of the other one, she gracefully rotated into a sitting position and lowered herself into her seat. She had a little difficulty in securing her seatbelt, but inserted the tab and pulled the belt tight just as the free-fall flight was ending.

She sagged into her seat just as the force of gravity resumed. The angle of the floor turned slowly upward until it was nearly parallel to the Earth's surface. Now multiple gees held her in her seat like glue, then pressed against her worse that the high gees of takeoff. She welcomed the feeling of weight until she felt her stomach sink as if it were filled with lead. Then the pressure eased. A barely audible screech was the sound of tires touching tarmac. She breathed a welcome sigh of relief.

She turned her head to look at Leibowitz. His eyes were shut tight as if from abject fear. When his lids finally rolled up, he was staring straight ahead, like scared little boy experiencing his first ride on a roller coaster.

The aircraft slowed to a halt. A moment later, a grim-faced colonel strode into the room. He glared at his passengers, both of whom were sitting quietly as if nothing were wrong.

"Welcome to Area 51."

Chapter 6

Laila never used an alarm to wake up in the morning. Due to her subconscious circadian rhythm, she had the uncanny ability to open her eyes and come to full awareness automatically at whatever time she set her internal clock. Before her feet hit the floor, she was already thinking about what she had to do that day.

This day was different. She didn't get to bed until after her normal wake-up hour. Her cell phone lay on the nightstand next to her bed, but she felt no inclination to reach for it and open the lid to check the time. She snuggled her head into the pillow for a few more minutes of slumber. She dozed off and on in the welcome darkness – for how long, she neither knew nor cared. Recollections of yesterday's memorable events flitted through her mind like wayward butterflies.

A faint tapping echoed in a hidden corner of her mind, ever so slight that she thought she must have dreamt it. Another short sequence of light taps made her think of Poe's epic poem, "The Raven": "While I nodded nearly napping, suddenly there came a tapping, as if someone gently rapping, rapping at my chamber door." Mentally she told her visitor to go away.

The rapping and tapping continued.

She sighed deeply. "The door's unlocked."

A vertical slit of illumination pierced the gloom but did not fall on Laila's face. Her sensitive nose smelled coffee. She opened her eyes and saw in the thin slice of light a bronzed hand holding a steaming Styrofoam cup.

"If that coffee's for me you'd *better* come in and give it to me."

The door opened the rest of the way. Davenport's masculine features were limned in the fluorescent lights of the corridor. He was wearing neither a flight suit nor a uniform, but was dressed casually in a loose-fitting dark blue sweat suit and white jogging shoes. "Are you decent?"

"I've been decent since the day I was born. Now get

over here and give me that coffee pronto."

Davenport strode across the dormitory room. "Why is a Type B personality giving Type A orders?"

Laila sat up in bed, let the covering sheet slide down onto her lap, puffed the purple flower-designed pillow behind her back, then swept her loose hair over her ears and behind her back. "When it comes to coffee I'm Type A all the way."

Davenport handed her the cup of steaming brew. "I'll remember that."

Sipping with satisfaction: "Boiling hot, just the way I like it."

He appeared fresh and clean shaven, as if he had just stepped out of the shower. Laila sniffed the soft scent of soap, but that could have emanated from her own body: she showered before going to bed.

"Sleep well?"

"I didn't get my nap out, as my granma used to say." She picked up her watch and focused her eyes on the crystal. "Considering I got only four hours sleep."

Davenport sat in a chair that was situated next to the bed. "You've got quite a shiner."

Laila's hand went instinctively to her face. The flesh around the left orbit was tender to the touch. Her normally pale skin tone ran from deep purple to black where Leibowitz had clouted her. "It was an accident."

"Maybe I should have shot Leibowitz when I had the means, motive, and opportunity."

"You weren't going to shoot him."

"You think so? What makes you say that?"

"You didn't have any bullets in the gun."

Davenport didn't gasp, but his hesitation and the expression on his face made it seem as if he had. "How do you know that?"

"Your pistol was an Italian made Beretta M9: a 9-millimeter sidearm that's used extensively by the U.S. Air Force, Army, and Navy. You probably selected it because you're left handed, and the safety lever is ambidextrous, plus the magazine of this particular model has a reversible release button. When you brought the gun to bear, you twisted it enough so I could see that the magazine was missing. Then you pulled back the slide. Ordinarily that would have loaded a bullet into the chamber. But since there was no magazine, pulling back the slide would have ejected a bullet if one had been pre-loaded. Ergo, you had no intention of shooting him. You just wanted to scare him."

Davenport was quiet for so long that Laila managed three quiet sips from the white lidless cup. They never took their eyes off each other.

His lips parted into a huge smile. "That was brilliant."

Laila shrugged. "I notice things."

"Now I'm really glad I picked you."

"Did *you* pick me for this assignment?"

"Yes, I did. After reading your report and your analysis of the intel, I read your dossier – "

"Has *everybody* read my dossier? What did they do, post it on the Internet?"

Now Davenport shrugged. "I had to pull a lot of strings to get it. The Air Force and the CIA don't usually share confidential information about their personnel. But General Cercopley obtained a copy and passed it along."

"And why does a pilot need to know so much about his passenger?"

Davenport pursed his lips. "In addition to being a pilot, I'm also the mission leader in charge of Project Stitch."

"So you *do* have proper clearance."

"Yes. But you were right to question my authority."

"So when do I get to read *your* dossier?"

"As soon as I introduce you to your workstation. I've already forwarded the passwords so you'll have access to the dossiers of everyone connected with the Project. I expect you to read all of them thoroughly."

Laila scrunched her face. "Why?"

"We'll discuss that later. For now, how would you like to go to breakfast?"

After a moment for contemplation: "Is this a date?"

"It is if you want it to be."

"I do."

Davenport stood to his full straight-backed height. "I'll wait in the hall while you get dressed."

"No need. I'm not shy." Laila tossed the sheet aside to reveal all of her pale blue two-piece unisex outfit. "I'm already dressed. The nurse gave me these surgical scrubs. They double as jammies and work wear, and the color even complements your jogging suit. We'll make a nice couple, Colonel Davenport."

Davenport snickered. "We're pretty informal around here. Please call me Bryce."

"I will if you'll call me Laila."

"Deal." He held out his hand, not vertical as if he was going to shake hers, but palm up.

Laila gulped down the rest of the coffee, set the cup on the nightstand, and swung her legs over the side of the bed. She slipped her tiny feet into her jogging shoes. She placed her hand in Bryce's. She pictured him bending over to kiss the top of her hand as if he were a prince and she a princess. He did not. He grasped her hand and pulled her to a standing position. Her long hair cascaded past her shoulders.

"You let your hair down," he observed.

Laila's silky tresses reached all the way to her waist. "In more ways than one." She stepped into the bathroom but did not close the door. She splashed water onto her face to wash the sleep out of her eyes: her only ablution. She patted her skin dry with a towel, grabbed her comb off the countertop, and pirouetted. "Shall we?"

Bryce led the way out of the room and along the linoleum-covered corridor. "I apologize for the sparse conditions. I'm used to living in barracks, so these dormitory rooms seem spacious and private to me."

Laila ran the comb through her hair as they strolled along the corridor. "I've slept in hotels with worse accommodations. Is this entire complex underground?"

Bryce nodded. "That's how we keep the Ruskies from knowing what's going on here. As you know, since the breakup of the USSR, we've now got three enemies with spy satellites instead of one."

"I wish Congress and the public understood the situation. Maybe then they wouldn't feel so stingy about providing more funding for intelligence gathering services."

"They believe the Soviet threat has gone away. Instead, it's tripled."

"You're preaching to the choir, as my granma used to say."

"We agree. So how is it that you know so much about handguns that you recognized the make and model of my sidearm? There's nothing in your resume about you being a small arms specialist. You're a desk jockey, not a frontline field agent."

Laila kept combing. "My daddy was a cop on the beat before he became a detective. He was a rarity among the breed: a man who was proud of his chosen occupation, and who performed his duties with an honorable code of ethics and an ingrained sense of justice. He had a low arrest record because he often made judgment calls on the spot, and let people off with a warning for breaking minor infractions. He talked to teenagers as if they were adults, yet gave them advice as if he was their father, or a Father. He believed in the basic goodness of mankind as a whole if not in certain individuals.

"Initially he was sentenced to the local highway patrol. He abhorred the job. He'd sit in his patrol car all day long then return to the station without having issued a single speeding ticket. He never even switched on his radar detector. He helped motorists in trouble, and he was always the first to arrive at an accident site. He pulled more than one person out of a flaming wreck. But he never received any commendations for his actions because he wasn't making money for the department.

"The truth of the matter is that crime doesn't pay. There's more money in traffic violations than there is in protecting citizens by arresting criminals. He got into law enforcement because he wanted to be a peacekeeper, not a legalized highway robber with a letter of marque. So he left the highway patrol to cops who didn't have a conscience. After that, most of his work involved domestic violence.

"That's where he learned how to use a gun, and how dangerous a gun can be in the hands of klutz or a cop who was anxious or scared. Not that he ever had to shoot anyone – just pulling his gun was enough to make a wife-beating husband think twice about his belligerence, and consider his option to come along quietly. The worse problem was working with cops who had never pulled a gun in anger; then when the necessity presented itself, most of them ended up shooting themselves in the leg or foot."

Bryce interrupted. "I can see where this is going – because they used a gun that didn't have a safety lock."

"Take a gold star and go to the head of the class. You'd be surprised at the number of accidental discharges that occur in the police force nationwide. If your only experience in law enforcement is handing out tickets to senior citizens, you're not mentally prepared to deal with hardcore criminals on the spur of the moment. In cases of extreme anxiety, instead of waiting until his gun is aimed at his target, an anxious cop is more likely to grip his pistol too hard when it's either still in his holster or while he's raising the barrel. The lucky ones that don't shoot themselves put a bullet in the ground in front of them.

"My daddy's department issued SIG Sauer P229's which don't have a safety lock. He put his in a drawer and bought a trusty Colt .45 automatic. The stopping power is just as good if not better, and if you really want to fire it – and have practiced your draw – you can thumb off the safety lock while you're raising the barrel."

"Your father was an exceptional man. Did he – what's his name?"

"Lyle."

"Did Lyle teach you to handle guns?"

"And how. I was just a tyke when he taught me how to shoot." She laughed. "Despite his warning, the recoil whacked the gun against my forehead and knocked me down on my back."

"That's the best way to learn. I'll bet you never did that again."

"You've got that right. Anyway, he used to take me to the firing range with him so I could test fire other makes and models. 'For self-defense,' he used to say, but secretly I think he wanted me to become a cop. I haven't fired a gun in years – since he . . . he passed away. Not in the line of duty; malignant cancer. Anyway, as you said, I'm a desk jockey, not an frontline field agent."

"I think he would have been proud of you. There are a lot of ways of making the world a safer place to live. You me and Lyle chose different ways to help make that happen."

Laila stopped combing her hair and stuck the plastic comb in a pocket of her surgical blouse.

They entered a small cafeteria that was practically empty. Midmorning was the lull between the late breakfast crowd and early lunchers. A lone black short-order cook stood idly behind the counter. She wore a starched white chef's uniform and a clear plastic shower cap.

"Good morning, Wendayne."

With a slow southern drawl: "Good marnin', Mister Bryce. Whose yer lady frien'?"

"Wendayne, this is Laila. Laila, Wendayne – the best cook this side of the Rockies."

"Ah's from Gorja, so that makes me the best cook on bofe sides."

"Don't let her hometown accent fool you. She's got a memory for facts that rivals most encyclopedias."

"Ah love to read. No boob tube for me. Nothin' but nonfiction, and that's a fact."

Laila smiled. "We could use someone like you in the CIA."

"None o' that espionage stuff fer me. I like what Ah'm doin'. Now what kin I getcha?"

Laila glanced over the menu that hung on the wall behind Wendayne. "I'm so hungry I could eat a horse, as my granma used to say. I'll have some of everything: eggs, ham, toast, home fries, oatmeal, orange juice, and coffee, black."

"Yes, ma'am. What kinda aigs you want?"

Without skipping a beat: "Chicken eggs."

Wendayne's smile was frozen on her face. After a moment: "Yes, ma'am. An' how would you like them chicken aigs cooked?"

"Sunny side up."

"Comin' right up, Miss Laila. An' fer you, Mister Bryce?"

"I don't think I can eat that much, so skip the home fries and oatmeal."

"Ah'll bring ever'thin' right over."

Bryce selected a corner table. "Don't let that fractured English fool you. It's part of her cover. She talks to her kids with perfect grammar and pronunciation, and makes sure they answer the same way, or she whacks them alongside the head with a rolled up magazine."

"They let her kids in here?"

"No. I go to her house to pick up reports. She not only cooks but she remembers everything she hears. And her listening ability is particularly astute. She can listen to multiple conversations simultaneously and separate voices from the background noise then recall the dialogue word for word and know who said what."

"So she's a snoop."

Bryce nodded. "I think of her as an ad hoc intelligence operative who's completely out of the loop. She reports only to me."

"Doesn't the base have a security staff?"

"It does. Nonetheless . . . "

"Nonetheless, you want me to perform an independent security scan."

Bryce squinted. "How did you guess?"

"I didn't *guess.* I concluded. Why else would you give me dossiers of everyone on the project?"

"You really are brilliant."

"I have my moments."

"I've noticed that. You're an aerial acrobat, too."

Now it was Laila's turn to squint. "And how would you know *that*?"

"Don't you think we have security cameras in the passenger cabin?"

"That explains a lot."

"I watched every second of your free-fall maneuvers. My heart was in my throat and not because of the aircraft's parabolic trajectory."

"You *do* care about me!"

"How would it look on my service record if I killed two of my passengers in flight?"

Laila was deflated, and her face showed it.

"I didn't mean it only that way."

Laila brightened. "Nice recovery. I'll accept it."

"I meant it." Bryce took a deep breath. "We couldn't leave the controls. Either one of us can fly the aircraft but there wasn't enough time to reach you before we had to pull out of the dive or hit the ground. All we could do was watch your antics on the screen. Let me complement you. You did a great job of getting that goofus back in his seat."

Laila shrugged. "Another useless experience."

Wendayne arrived with a large platter in each hand and silverware in her pockets. "Here ya go, folks. Napkins're in the dispenser."

"Wow, that was fast."

"Honey chile, the chickens already done laid the aigs. All I had to do was cook 'em."

"Thanks, Wendayne."

Wendayne turned away and waved her hand over her shoulder.

Conversation continued between bites and chews.

"I didn't get much to eat yesterday." Laila wasted no time in forking food into her mouth. "I suppose you'll want me to continue my outside intelligence work."

"I know it's a burden – "

"No, not at all. My boss delegated all my other responsibilities to coworkers. I'm here to focus solely on your project, or mission, or whatever you call your temporal displacement apparatus."

Bryce could not disguise his astonishment at Laila's remark. "How – how – "

"The saying is 'how now brown cow.' " Laila pooh-poohed his bewilderment by fanning her hand past her ear. "Come on, Bryce. I'm an analyst. This is what I do. Don't you think I wondered why the bigwigs paid so much attention to a report whose conclusions were so absurd? They wouldn't have bought my assumptions unless they already had confirmation.

"I have to admit, though, for a while there I thought I was being shanghaied in order to guarantee my silence. Company people disappear all the time – or so the media would have us believe. I was paranoid enough to harbor the possibility that I was about to be disappeared – especially when those stone-faced soldiers said that I wouldn't need my Company car any more, and escorted me under armed guard out of General Cercopley's office. I was *scared.*

"But once they turned me loose at Bolling Air Force Base, I began to breathe easier – although I didn't let any of my emotions show. For a while there I thought of smashing my cell phone and running."

Bryce grinned. "Where would you run?"

"Do you know why Mexico's biggest export product is Mexicans? Because most of the Rio Grande is only ankle deep. I figured I could hitch a ride to Texas and walk across the border, then ask for political asylum."

"Do you always think two steps ahead?"

Laila smirked. "Usually three. Anyway, I began to feel better after talking with Mark Clayton at Bolling. It seemed that they were really going to let me live with my knowledge. But I still had my doubts until you announced our arrival at Area 51. Then I knew for certain that my assessment was correct. What better place to build a time machine than the most secretive and most heavily guarded base in the country? A place that's so remote from civilization that it wouldn't be noticed or do appreciable damage if the machinery got out of control and caused a time-warp explosion, or some such thing.

This location is ideal."

Bryce humphed. "I'm sure that the designers and engineers that isolation is a necessary precaution although they assure me that no kind of mechanical malfunction or meltdown of critical components can cause a detonation any larger than an atom bomb." After a pause: "So, in your infinite wisdom, Miss Laila, have you guessed, or concluded, the purpose of our mission?"

"I'm afraid so." Laila's light-hearted attitude faded, and her grin turned into a grimace. "If the Muslims purport to forestall the sudden and unrestricted rise of Christianity, then your job must be to make sure that Christ gets killed."

Chapter 7

Laila pushed away her empty plate. "Wow, I'm as full as a tick, as my granma used to say."

Scraps of food adorned Bryce's plate. "Where do you put it all?"

"My granma used to say that I had a hollow leg."

"They must both be hollow." Bryce swilled the last of his coffee. "What's your take on Leibowitz?"

"I won't really know until I see his resume, but – did you pick him, too?"

"Yes, I did, but only after recommendation from an expert in his field of study."

"Then I must assume that he is what he says he is: the best at what he does. Even though you weren't going to shoot him, are you wishing that you hadn't gone for the second best?"

Bryce laughed. "The thought *has* crossed my mind. More than once since last night. But I've always found that second best doesn't always cut it. When the going gets tough I want the best support that's available. A unit with defective parts may ultimately let you down."

Laila opened her mouth to speak.

"Now don't get me wrong. I don't treat my troops like pieces of machinery. I was just making an analogy. I wouldn't fly an aircraft that wasn't fully functional. Likewise the success of a mission depends on the proficiency of the people who are conducting it whether they're pilots or logistical experts or weapons specialists or analysts – " With a nod toward Laila. " – or in this case a translator. I can't work with people who lack the skill or knowledge to perform their assigned tasks. I didn't just pluck Leibowitz out of a hat you know."

"I wasn't suggesting that you did."

"Along with my expert I read dozens of academic resumes in my search for the best translator of ancient Hebrew. They were alike in one regard: they all had chest-thumping lists of publications and personal appearances. More than one went on for page after page listing every presentation they had ever given. That's like you listing the name of every report you ever wrote along with a detailed summary or me annotating every flight I ever flew. It's not as if a presentation or personal appearance is a badge for meritorious service; it's part of their job. There wasn't a self-assured candidate in the bunch either male or female. After a while I came to believe that academia was an arcane magnet that drew only insecure emotional types into its fold."

Laila interrupted him by snickering uncontrollably at Bryce's tirade.

Bryce scowled playfully. "Okay. You laugh. But I'll bet that Leibowitz isn't much different from the other nuts in the jar. Granted that he has idiosyncrasies and character flaws – "

"*That's* an understatement."

" – but I hope that his positive qualities will eventually outweigh the negatives. I've dealt with people like him before: enlisted troops who joined the service with a bad attitude toward authority. I've turned a lot of them around by working with them. In some ways people *are* like machines. Or like a prototype aircraft with design flaws. You don't discard a plane that doesn't fly perfectly the first time you take it up into the wild blue yonder. You work out the bugs until it flies like you want it to."

"There's a lot of sense in that. Working the chiggers out of Leibowitz's ego could be an itchy chore. Could you use my help?"

"I would *love* your help. And just so you know: I didn't overreact last night – "

"This morning."

" – I was playacting. I needed to put Leibowitz in his proper place and make sure he understood the pecking order in his new hierarchy. But I wasn't lying when I said that his actions might have compromised the security of our flight. You haven't been brought fully up to speed yet because you haven't had access to DIA intel but General Cercopley has it on good authority that the Russians are selling surveillance satellite time to the IRF. Russia has three times as many dirty politicians than the Soviet Union ever had and all of them are using their newfound positions to put rubles into their pockets. If they get any worse they'll make American politicians look as innocent as Goldilocks by comparison.

"We can't afford to let the IRF get wind of what we're doing. The fate of the free world hinges on our mission. Mission Snatch, as we call it. We don't want it to turn into Mission Snafu. Now maybe you think I strong-armed Leibowitz last night – or this morning – but I treated him no differently than I've treated many other recalcitrants. When I give an order I expect it to be obeyed."

Laila flashed a mock salute. "Yes, sir."

"The same as I obey an order from my superior officers. Leibowitz may be a civilian but he took the money and signed a service contract that spelled out what is expected of him. As for his academic credentials he hasn't published as much as some of his peers but what he *has* published has always provoked controversy and negative responses. That may sound like a point against him but when you read between the lines you find that the reviewers who denigrated his work did so mostly because it contradicted their own or because it conflicted with previously conceived notions."

Laila was getting used to Bryce's run-on sentences. "In other words, he's a heretic going against convention and tradition."

"Exactly. And I have to give him credit for taking a stand that he knew would trigger a flak attack. His interpretations of symbols on the Dead Sea Scrolls went against the established grain. Derision of his translations ranged from the sublime to the absurd. Some scholars picked on trivial points – sometimes the transliteration of a single symbol – emphasized their disapproval with his novel interpretation and used that sole disagreement to denigrate his entire treatise.

"Others took exception to the overall meaning of his version of certain text blocks because it contradicted accepted wisdom that was based on their own work. These were mostly small-minded biblical scholars who couldn't accept clarification at the cost of change or admission that they were wrong. They denied his revelations purely out of envy. To give him credit he never once backed down from a position he had taken. Instead he painstakingly explained his fresh reading of the script and provided examples of similar characters in other ancient Hebrew writings."

"The proof of the pudding is in the eating, as my granma used to say."

"That's what we're going to find out. He's part of this mission because we have some biblical texts whose translation may prove crucial to its success. Attempts have been made to make sense of these documents but so far only piecemeal transliterations have been made and the results have been confusing. If Leibowitz – "

"Speaking of the devil . . . "

Bryce followed the line of Laila's gaze. Danette and Leibowitz entered the cafeteria and headed for the counter. Wendayne greeted them with an effervescent smile.

"Did you pull rank on your subordinate officer? You got me and she got stuck with him?"

Bryce smiled. "We drew cards. High card had first choice."

Deflated: "Oh."

"But I stacked the deck."

Pleased: "Oh."

Bryce placed a warm hand on Laila's. "Just in case Leibowitz doesn't work out and we have to get a replacement don't let on about the Timepiece. That's what we nonscientists call the contraption that the physicists have designated SCSC: the Synchronous Chronological Sequence Converter."

"Fancy name. Didn't your scientists ever read H. G. Wells?"

"Not so you would notice."

"Too bad." After some reflection: "With regard to Leibowitz, did you mean in case we have to go for second best?"

"Exactly. If I don't give him some basic background

information about this facility he'll be so distracted by Area 51's fictitious aura that he won't be able to concentrate on his work. You saw how he acted after our arrival last night – this morning. And don't mention my sleight of hand to Danette."

"It'll be my most cherished secret."

Danette led Leibowitz to their table. She was not smiling. They each held a tray of food that required no cooking. Danette had a huge fruit salad and a tall glass of orange juice; Leibowitz had grapefruit juice and a bagel with cream cheese.

Pleasantly: "You look like you were rode hard and put away wet, as my granma used to say."

Leibowitz was wearing the same clothes that he wore the night before, and he wore them with the same disregard for neatness. Additional wrinkles made him look even more disheveled. He clunked his tray on the table as he sat. "I – I – I can't believe this is Area 51. When can I get a tour of the place? Can I see the alien spaceship? Who do I have to see to get permission to watch the footage of the alien autopsy?"

Danette rolled her eyes as she eased into her seat. She was wearing olive drab fatigues and spit-shined jump boots. "You see what I've been going through."

"She won't tell me a thing. All she ever says is, 'That's classified.'"

Bryce took a deep breath. "Okay, Mr. Leibowitz – "

"*Doctor* Leibowitz."

"Okay, Dr. Leibowitz." Bryce did not roll his eyes or put an accent on "Dr." "I can give you a briefing about some of our work here."

"My honorific entitles me to get it straight from the big mahoff."

"I *am* the big mahoff."

"You're a pilot."

"Among other things. I'm also in command of this facility and the mission that you signed up for."

Leibowitz glowered. A long silence ensued.

"Dr. Leibowitz, I know we got off on the wrong foot last – early this morning – "

Shouting: "The wrong foot! You shoved a gun in my face."

Bryce remained calm. There was no sign of tension on his clean-shaven features. "Dr. Leibowitz in the Armed Forces everything is done for a reason. Depending upon your rank and your military specialty you may not be privileged to know that reason. Everything connected with this base and this mission is highly confidential. We traveled at night in stealth mode in order to keep the country's enemies from ascertaining our point of origin and tracking our course and determining our destination. When you let light out the window you not only demonstrated overt insubordination but you compromised the security of our flight. We could have been shot down by enemy missiles. In that case the taxpayers would have lost a valuable aircraft, two trained pilots, and a couple of VIP's one of whom undoubtedly saved your life."

Another long silence reigned.

Leibowitz cowed. He shifted his glare from Bryce to Laila. "I – I – I guess – I didn't realize – I'm sorry for the black eye."

Laila raised both hands and flapped them at Leibowitz in a gesture of disregard. "I've been slugged harder. Let bygones be bygones, as my granma used to say."

"The same goes here." Bryce made no hand movements. He sat rock-hard and straight-backed in his seat. "We've got important work to do and we can't afford to let personality differences interfere with the higher cause. So how about if we bury the hatchet as Laila's grandmother undoubted used to say and I'll give you some background history about Area 51?"

A longer silence reigned while Leibowitz contemplated the offer. "Will you tell me about the four hundred dollar hammer?"

Bryce could not conceal a snicker. "From aliens to hammers is quite a paradigm shift."

"I – I, uh, I thought that if I started with small questions, I could ask the big ones later."

Bryce shook his head. "Okay. I'll answer all your questions that fit the level of your temporary security clearance. Did you read over your contract yet?"

"I – I, uh, I haven't had time – "

"Then let me remind you that everything you see or hear or taste or touch or smell during the course of this mission is classified. You can never tell anyone about it. Ever. Understood?"

Leibowitz nodded. "I understand."

"Do you *really* understand?"

"I – I, yes, I really understand."

"Good. Now that doesn't mean that you can't discuss this mission with associated members: us and other people you'll meet. We have an open arms policy within the group. But you can*not* so much as mention this project once it's over. You can't add it to your resume. And you certainly cannot go public with it. Is *that* understood?"

"I *really* understand."

Now it was Bryce's turn to stare in silence.

Danette broke that silence. "I can tell him about the hammer."

Bryce cocked in eyebrow at her. "Go ahead."

"There never was a four hundred dollar hammer. Oh, there was a hammer all right, but it wasn't sold to the government for four hundred dollars. It was simply part of a misunderstood accounting practice. You see, the government buys tens of thousands of items from hundreds of suppliers all over the country. The volume of purchase orders is massive. Because of this high volume, the process that's used to pay for these items is the equal allocation method of accounting. Are you with me so far?"

Leibowitz nodded.

"Okay. Say the government orders several hundred items from a single supplier. In essence the supplier is a retailer that sells only to the government. You might call a supplier a gatherer. The supplier buys the items from several dozen wholesalers. The items are not delivered to the supplier all at once, but dribble in over a period of days or weeks, sometimes months. As individual items are delivered to the supplier's warehouse, the supplier repackages them and forwards the packages to the appropriate government facilities. Are you still with me?"

Leibowitz nodded again.

"Okay. The supplier has to pay the wholesaler as the items are delivered. At the same time, the supplier bills the government for part of the total purchase order. Now this is the part that is often misconstrued. The supplier doesn't perform a line item check when it bills the government; it calculates the *percentage* of fulfillment. That percentage doesn't necessarily reflect the true value of the items that were delivered. It approximates only a portion of the total purchase order. Purchase orders are dozens of pages in length. The line items on each page go from ten dollar hammers to ten *thousand* dollar electronic assemblies.

"The double-damned hammer that Congress picked on was packaged with high-cost electronic components. The supplier charged for the *number* of line items that were being crossed off the purchase order, disregarding the individual cost of each item. If a hundred items were delivered in the same package, and one ten dollar hammer was packed with ninety-nine four-hundred dollar electronic assemblies, and you divided the charges equally, you end up with a four hundred dollar hammer – approximately.

"Now, to make the situation clearer by exaggeration, suppose that hammer was stuck into a box with a $20,000 flight trainer, instead of shipping the hammer separately. If the supplier checked off two line items from several hundred, and submitted a bill for payment, you'd have a $10,000 hammer. Ten thousand and five."

Now silence reigned like evaporated water.

Suddenly Leibowitz came alive. "Hey, I never thought of it like that. It makes perfect makes sense when you put it that way."

Bryce nodded. "To everyone except John Q. Public and their elected representatives."

Laila agreed. "Congress on the half shell."

"But – but what about that two thousand dollar coffee maker."

Bryce nodded again. "It *was* a two thousand dollar coffee maker. That's where the media tricked the public into buying newspapers and listening to radio ads and watching commercials: by conjuring an image of a ten-cup household plastic coffee maker when the one under consideration was a fifty-cup commercial-grade stainless steel brewing machine built to military specifications, or milspec as we say in the Air Force."

Leibowitz was nearly speechless at these revelations. "But – but – "

Danette finished her fruit salad. "You see, plain facts can by distorted by the way they're presented."

"Or mispresented, as the case may be," Laila added.

"But – but – why doesn't Congress tell the truth of the matter?"

"Representatives don't get elected by telling the truth. They get elected by stirring voters into a frenzy with half-truths, then taking credit for fixing something that wasn't broken in the first place. They gain voter support by means of deception, illusion, and prestidigitation. The public is duped by smoke and mirrors." Laila shrugged. "What drives the world is not truth but the perception of truth."

Bryce: "That's an incredibly perceptive statement."

"I have my moments." Laila turned to Leibowitz. "I can give you a real example of gross government misspending. I had quite a quarrel about it with my immediate supervisor at the CIA."

Leibowitz's eyes expanded. "You're a spook?"

Laila nodded vigorously. "One of my official duties is haunting houses. My specialty is rattling rusty chains, but I also do manifestations by oozing ectoplasm."

Leibowitz was stunned into silence.

Bryce explained: "Ms. Masterson is here as special liaison."

"Yes, I have a reputation for special liaisons."

This time Bryce *did* roll his eyes.

"Anyway, we moved into new premises that had

more space than our previous location. My boss filled out a requisition form for new furniture that we needed to accommodate additional personnel. Coincidentally, at the same time, I was redecorating several rooms in my house, and converting one of the bedrooms to a study. One item that I remember in particular was a rolling chair without armrests, which I bought from an office store in a nearby shopping mall.

"My boss showed me the requisition form before he submitted it for approval. The same chair that I bought for my house was given on the form, but at twice the price. Worse than that, I had a sale catalogue from the store that offered a discount of one-third off the retail price – that was the amount that I paid for the chair. This meant that the government was going to pay three times the amount that I paid for the identical chair.

"Well, I tell you what: I showed that catalogue to my boss and urged him to forget buying chairs from a rip-off supplier. He could buy chairs from the local store at one-third the cost, and they would deliver them free to boot! Or he could buy three for the price of one. My boss shook his head and said he wasn't allowed to do that. All purchase requests had to be submitted to a government purchasing agent, who then put them out for bids from government sanctioned suppliers, and *only* government sanctioned suppliers. None others need apply."

Danette put in her two cents worth; or six cents worth to the government. "Once again our purchasing is hampered by Congressional mandates. Congress has ruled that no federal agency is allowed to make purchases outside the constraints of the government procurement system. Suppliers are chosen not because they offer the lowest price on brand name items, but because they meet federal guidelines with regard to the minimum wage that they pay their employees, the health and welfare benefits that those employees receive, the percentage of minorities the supplier employs, nondiscrimination regarding female employees, and numerous other criteria with regard to human rights."

Leibowitz cried angrily, "Another waste of the taxpayers' money."

"Forgiving me for intruding on this stimulating discussion but you're airing your grievances to people who can't do anything about them. If you want to try to effect positive change, send your complaints in writing to your State and federal representatives." Bryce shot a gleeful eye at each of his companions. "Now that we've filled our heads with food for thought, how about if we take that tour that Dr. Leibowitz asked for? This base is a storehouse of surprising secrets."

Chapter 8

Bryce took charge of the light brigade. Danette was tail-end Charlie. Laila and Leibowitz strode side by side between the Air Force officers. They walked along broad intersecting corridors whose walls were unadorned but were coated with beige fire-retardant resin. Cable trays that hung from the ceiling were packed with high-voltage electrical cables that were protected by metal sheathing. Separate and smaller cable trays carried color-coded multi-conductor communication cables.

"Area 51 is only marginally connected with Nellis Air Force Base which is located ninety miles southeast of here outside of Las Vegas. We rely on Nellis for supplies and logistical support but not much else because we're a separate command. We also use their airfields for non-stealth flights. We limit the amount of ground traffic between here and Nellis so as not to draw attention to the extent of our activities. Our enemies know about Area 51 of course but they don't know exactly what goes on here."

Leibowitz growled. "Neither do the American people. This place is like a black hole: billions of taxpayers' dollars go in, but no information comes out."

Laila rolled her eyes and took a deep breath, doing so quietly so as to keep a low profile. She was gleeful that Bryce and Danette had taken the lead in dealing with Leibowitz.

"That's the way it has to be in order to keep the enemy guessing about our technological progress and military developments." Bryce explained the situation as calmly as if he were speaking to a child in kindergarten.

As they approached what appeared to be a garage full of orange golf carts, he slowed his military pace to one that Laila could maintain without having to skip or run. The four-seat vehicles lacked canopies and bags of clubs, but an open rear compartment offered space for luggage.

"Where's the golf course?" Leibowitz wanted to know.

Bryce did not bother to acknowledge the rhetorical quip. He pointed to a huge diagram on the wall behind the row of carts. "You'll find a map at every intersection and charging station. The legend is located at the bottom right. The red rectangles denote surface structures. The green squares denote emergency exits; if the square has a black circle inside it that denotes an overhead hatchway otherwise the exit is a doorway. You are not to use these exits unless the evacuation klaxon sounds off; you'll know it when you hear it. The blue circles denote charging stations. Above the yellow triangle is written YOU ARE HERE. Danette?"

Danette issued folded color maps to Laila and Leibowitz.

"As you've probably guessed the majority of this facility is hidden underground. You can see that the number of surface structures is only the tip of the iceberg. The underground complex consists of corridors that connect chambers that are delineated in white."

"It looks like a maze," Leibowitz noted.

"Or a warren," Laila added.

"Unfortunately Area 51 wasn't planned by William Penn. Each new extension and chamber was created as an outgrowth from a previous location. That's why the corridors and chambers aren't formed in a grid square with blocks like Philadelphia. As you can see the underground hangars and laboratories and connecting corridors resemble a spider web instead of a planned community that's shaped geometrically or contoured for aesthetic appeal."

"A drunken spider on a bad binge, if you ask me."

Bryce winked at Laila's remark. "The flip side of the map that Danette just handed you has a bird's eye view of the entire Nevada Test Site and Training Range. Area 51 is only one of a number of areas of various shapes and sizes. Why this particular one drew more attention than the adjacent areas is anyone's guess."

"Blame the conspiracy theorists and news reporters. Once they jump on a bandwagon, they ride it till doomsday as long as it's selling copy."

"No doubt you're right." Bryce unplugged a thick cable that led from a square port on a cart to a round wall socket. "As official base personnel you now have honorary licenses to drive these Roamers as we call them. After this introductory tour you can take any one that's not in use and drive it to whatever destination you choose. Feel free to go joyriding and explore the facility whenever you need a break from your assigned duties. After you unplug the charging cable like I just did you drape it on the hanger like this. When you return the Roamer or if you park it at another charging station you plug it in to an empty wall socket. The batteries have a total drain capacity of two and a half hours. They don't drain when the motor is switched off. Danette, will you give them their badges now?"

"Here you are." Danette handed a photo name badge to Laila and one to Leibowitz. "This makes it official. Now you can go anywhere without being questioned by security personnel, except in areas that are restricted. They'll be marked with hazardous warning signs, and anyway the doors will be locked."

Leibowitz inspected the badge. "My hair is all mussed. Where did you get this picture?"

"Your hair is always mussed. That's the way you keep it. The picture is a frame capture from a surveillance camera. They're secreted throughout the facility."

"So you're surreptitiously keeping tabs on me."

"It's part of the passive internal security system," Bryce explained. "Bar code scanners in the ceiling register your badge so we can find you if you get lost."

Gruffly: "Or if I venture someplace where I'm not supposed to go."

"That too. But we regard everyone who's been given a badge to be trustworthy. Mostly – "

"Then why the tracking device?"

" – Mostly the scanners help us find you in case your presence is needed or in case of an emergency. We can go directly to your last known location if you don't call in when beeped."

"Call in on what?"

"Danette."

Danette gave each one a device that looked like a cell phone complete with call pad and screen, but with the addition of a red inset button at the top marked (DIS)CONNECT, and a blue inset button at the bottom marked CONTACTS. "Put this in your pocket. If it beeps, press the red button to open communication. The button will turn green. Press it again to close communication and it turns back to red. The blue button – "

Leibowitz cut her off in midsentence. "I hate cell phones. I don't need to call people away from my desk, and I hate interruptions when I don't want to talk."

Laila studied hers frontward and backward. "Is this the GD Encrypted Blueberry?"

Danette squinted. "How do you know that?"

"We have them in the CIA. I've never seen one, but our field agents use them all the time." To Leibowitz. "It's not a cell phone. It's a short-range comm unit: a wireless transmitter and receiver; basically a high-tech walkie-talkie." To Danette: "What's the range?"

"Five-miles through dirt and concrete; ten miles in the open air without line of sight."

"Our units have a slider on the side to increase or decrease the range. That way you can keep your transmissions close to your chest, so to speak, to reduce the possibility of unauthorized interception. Some units have a lockout feature: they won't operate unless you input a mutating algorithmic nine digit password that is downlinked from a satellite." She stuck the device in the pants pocket of her hospital scrubs. "General Dynamics also makes a unit with a self-destruct mechanism."

"You – you – you mean it explodes?"

To Leibowitz. "No. If you input the wrong password three times in a row within a five minute span, the chip is wiped clean and the unit won't operate until a new chip is installed at the factory."

Bryce humphed. "The CIA thinks of every contingency."

Leibowitz was still fumbling with his badge. "What's

this blue strip on the reverse?"

"That's a microchip radiation dosimeter in case you stray into areas where radioactivity levels are potentially dangerous after long-term exposure. Nothing for you to worry about but it's a precaution that we impose on everyone. See?" Bryce flipped over his own name badge.

Laila clipped her badge to her left breast pocket. "So the badge acts as your lost and found department."

"In a manner of speaking. Danette will drive while I continue the briefing."

Danette sat behind the orange plastic steering wheel. Bryce rode shotgun. Laila and Leibowitz took the rear bench seat. Laila pressed her body against the right panel, as far from Leibowitz as it was possible to get.

"The controls are so simple that a child can operate this vehicle." Danette demonstrated the Roamer's operation. A simple toggle switch connected and disconnected the battery to and from the electric motor. Just as in an automobile, the right pedal was for acceleration, the left pedal was the brake. The motor made a low hum when she flipped the switch. "Don't worry about breaking any speeding laws. Top speed is ten knots. That's about eleven miles per hour. The Roamer is slow off the line so it doesn't make a good drag racer – although some of our personnel have conducted themselves in a manner unbecoming to a soldier or scientist."

Bryce turned around and threw his left arm over the seatback. "There are twenty-one miles of intertwining corridors, so you can easily cruise the entire facility without charging the battery as long as you don't dawdle along the way. We've got five miles to go because Project Stitch was the last facility to be constructed. In the mean time I can take the edge off your curiosity."

Laila sat quietly. Leibowitz opened his mouth to speak but Bryce cut him off.

"To answer your first question, there are no alien spacecraft and no dissected alien bodies. There never were."

"But – but – "

"I know all about the rumors and speculations.

There's not a person in the country who doesn't. Everyone who comes to work here has heard the same urban legends. So let me give you the standard background introductory speech. Feel free to interrupt as you undoubtedly will.

"In 1947, a private pilot named Kenneth Arnold claimed to have seen a string of aerial objects that he was unable to identify near Mount Rainier in Washington State. The press described these objects as discs or saucers. This single declaration started the UFO craze. Personally I think he saw nothing more than window glare. Have you ever glanced out the side window of a car at night and seen the reflection of lights from a car on your other side? The lights appear disembodied as if they were floating at a distance and moving back and forth as the relative positions of the two vehicles changed."

Leibowitz nodded his head slowly like an automaton.

"About the same time an Air Force radar balloon deflated and crashed on a ranch near Roswell, New Mexico. Garbled news accounts confused an ordinary event by describing the deflated condition of the balloon on the ground as being shaped like a disc. The crash site later became immortalized through leading questioning and distorted promotion.

"Also about this time the Air Force was testing experimental parachute designs by dropping weighted life-sized dummies from various altitudes in order to determine their drag characteristics. These dummies were often damaged upon hard landing when the chute either failed to open or didn't drag as anticipated. The damaged and disfigured dummies were taken back to base for storage prior to repair or disposal. Passersby who briefly saw the dummies – either on the ground or on a workbench – mistook them for the bodies of dead aliens.

"These three ingredients comprised the initial recipe that grew into a modern belief system in which aliens from other planets were supposed to be studying Earth and humanity for unscrupulous purposes prior to full-

scale invasion. No doubt these beliefs originated sublim-
inally with the publication of *The War of the Worlds* in
1898 then lay dormant until the rash of space-invader
movies was released in the 1950's: *The Thing from Another World, Invasion of the Body Snatchers, It Came
from Outer Space,* and *The Day the Earth Stood Still,* to
name a few of the better flicks that stand out from a host
of B movies.

"These imaginative other-worldly concepts played on
some people's minds. Media hype exaggerated normal
events in order to pander to deluded masses and sell ad-
vertising space. The next thing you know people with
suggestive personalities were spotting flying saucers
everywhere or were having close encounters in secluded
groves and when that didn't draw enough attention they
were being abducted."

For several seconds the only sound that Laila heard
was the soft hum of the electric motor.

"It – it – it all seems to make sense when you say it
like that." He was lost in thought for a moment. His dark
eyes narrowed. "The way you make the truth sound im-
plausible by making a fabrication sound credible is a
brilliant brainwashing technique."

Bryce did not display exasperation, but Laila's intu-
itive sensitivities felt his underlying current of expression. It was time for her to join in the fracas, but
Leibowitz beat her to the punch.

"Don't you agree, Miss CIA?"

"I don't."

Leibowitz jerked his head. "I – I thought we would
see eye to eye on this. Disguising the truth with fiction
is a technique that the CIA has perfected."

"The only time we see eye to eye is when we're standing and facing each other, because we're both the same
height."

Danette concealed her smirk from Leibowitz because
he was seated directly behind her, but Laila could see
her cheeks twitching. Bryce remained stone-faced.

"And while it may be true that disseminating misinformation is in the intelligence community's bag of

tricks, I think Occam's razor is shaving a swath over your head."

"What – what – what – are you talking about?"

"Are you familiar with Occam's razor?"

"I – I, uh, that is – not exactly."

"It's a twelfth-century philosophical principle that states 'all things being equal, the simplest explanation is usually the best'. Dr. Leibowitz, you're a rational human being. You don't jump to unfounded conclusions when you decipher ancient Hebrew symbols. You study the evidence, compare known texts, make detailed analyses, and devise a script that's in context with the material and its provenience."

"Yes – yes – of course."

"Don't you ignore previous translations – preconceived notions – when you decipher text and find that your translation disagrees with previous ones?"

"Of course I do. I'm the best there is. Those other nerds – "

"Then why can't you get over your addlebrained ideas and accept the simple truth that the only aliens in this country are from across the border and not from outer space? They call me an intelligence officer in the CIA because I work with my intelligence. You should do the same."

Bryce attempted to calm her down. "Laila!"

"I don't care. Sometimes he makes me so mad that I could spit nickels, as my granma used to say."

Danette couldn't help but laugh out loud. "I agree, although my grandmother would have phrased it differently, perhaps with some big-city expletives."

"Voila!" Laila declared. "A meeting of rational minds."

Leibowitz would have taken a step backward if it wouldn't have tumbled him out of the go-cart. "I –I – I – didn't mean to offend anyone." That was the closest he could get to making an apology.

Laila glared at him, her black eye bulging and her face turning red. That was the closest she could get to accepting an apology.

Bryce humphed. "Now that we're all in like with each

other may I get back on my soapbox?"

Laila's frown turned into a pert smile. "Please do."

Leibowitz was quiet.

"Dr. Leibowitz if you look back into the history of mankind and his broad variety of belief systems you should be able to see the UFO phenomenon for what it is. Ancient cultures had entire pantheons of gods each one of which was responsible for some unexplained aspect of nature or some undesirable impulse in the conduct of man. After the mythological deities were dethroned medieval people came to believe in demons and devils and evil spirits that played havoc with human events. They invented the incubus and succubus to explain accidental pregnancies and strange liaisons. Then came ghosts and gremlins and imps and pixies and elves and hobgoblins and genies and dryads and poltergeists. And that's only counting a few of the plethora of supernatural beings that invaded European cultures.

"Embedded in man's archaic limbic system is the irrational predisposition to imagine fanciful concepts and to find more comfort in those make-believe perceptions than in reality. No one believes in leprechauns or the bogeyman anymore because people are too enlightened nowadays. The same is true for trolls and fairy godmothers. Instead the old guard has been discarded for extraterrestrial biological entities from another dimension or solar system. The collective subconscious has exchanged one impossible conviction for another one that's equally as preposterous.

"Some people – actually a lot of people – have a deep-seated need to believe in something fantastic; something that's beyond the bounds of reason. It seems to be part of human nature: an aspect of a bipartisan mind in which the emotional part subverts and overpowers the rational part. Does any of this appeal to your balanced susceptibilities?"

"I – I – I – "

Laila took the torch. "Look at it from a different perspective. Let's start with the premise that the aliens are real. Supposedly they can swoop down to Earth, flatten crops in a field to make indecipherable designs, then swoop into space without ever being seen, either visually or on radar. Does it make any sense that aliens have nothing better to do than to play gags on hard-working farmers?

"And what about abductions? How can aliens pass through solid walls, scoop people out of their beds, operate on them for hours, then put them back under their blankets, all without their spouses knowing they were gone? Supposedly the aliens insert a mind block so the victim won't remember that he's been abducted. Yet again and again and again, they somehow manage to screw up the mind block so that people *do* remember. To make matters worse, these suggestible types confuse hemorrhoids with anal probes. Then, when they go to the spot where the spaceship was supposed to have landed, there is no evidence of a touchdown – not even a field goal with flattened crops.

"In three quarters of a century since the flying saucer rage began, after thousands of reported sightings, after hundreds of supposed abductions, there's not one iota or scintilla of proof of a single solitary incident. Not one. Only lights in the sky, unsuccessful chases, and vague memories from hypnotic trances."

Leibowitz grimaced. "That's because the government covered everything up, just like you're doing now."

"Can you possibly comprehend how monumental a task it would be to cover up every alien incident that's supposed to have occurred in the last seventy-five years? Billions of dollars. Trillions. Where would the funding come from? How many people would that kind of cover up employ; people with high security clearances? Don't you think by now that some brown-nosing reporters would have gotten wind of that big a cover up? Instead, they make innuendoes and unsupported allegations with nary a fact to back up their purple prose, and a gullible public sucks up every word of their tripe. People's lives are so humdrum that they'd rather believe unsubstantiated hyperbole than the boring truth. And there's nothing as exciting as an old-fashioned conspiracy."

"As long as we're ganging up on the professor, can I join the gang?" Danette didn't wait for approval. "No matter how sophisticated alien technology is, no aircraft can break the laws of physics and aerodynamics. Yet according to accounts, they consistently ignore universal principles of acceleration and inertia with impunity. My number one complaint is that witnesses claim that UFO's travel faster than the speed of sound, yet they don't make a sonic boom like the SST when they break the sound barrier. The Mach One pressure wave is impossible to pass through quietly.

"My number two complaint is that witnesses claim that UFO's accelerate suddenly from standing still to hundreds of miles per hour. Unless the aliens are made out of metal, the G-forces on flesh would crush their internal organs and make it impossible for them to breathe.

"My number three complaint is the right-angle maneuvers that people claim to have witnessed. These people don't know anything about inertia. If you were going several hundred miles per hour and made a sharp change in direction, the sheer force would tear your body apart. Your body, your brain, and your organs would continue in the same direction when the aircraft turned. At the very least you'd have a concussion and torn connective tissues, even with a pressure suit and safety harness."

Leibowitz looked from one to the other but made no comment.

"And that's coming from an experienced pilot who's exceeded Mach Four in the atmosphere." Bryce didn't wait for Leibowitz to comment. "I have a beef against that alien autopsy movie. Think about this for a minute: the Galaxy might have as many as fifty million inhabitable planets in it. Most of those planets will have conditions that are different from Earth. Some will be hotter and some will be colder; some will be bigger and some will be smaller. Some will have different mineral compositions. A few I suppose might be Earthlike.

"But even so what are the chances that one of those planets that's light-years away has evolved a life-form that is nearly identical to what has evolved on Earth?"

The question was rhetorical but Laila answered it anyway: "Slim to none, and Slim left town."

Bryce snickered. "Correct. Now I can accept the possibility that aliens might someday visit Earth. But when they do I'll bet they won't look anything like us. The most obvious fakery in the alien autopsy movie is not that the alien on the operating table looks so different – enlarged head and bulging eyes and skinny arms and narrow chest – but that it looks so much *like* us. It's stressing the bounds of probability that an alien-grown physiology would resemble ours so closely."

Leibowitz obviously had much to think about, and he did it without murmuring a sound.

Laila: "Getting back to Occam's razor, ufologists – as UFO advocates call themselves – have repudiated a simple explanation for ordinary occurrences, and advanced a cumbersome, convoluted, incredible set of circumstances to account for the fact that no facts exist to defend badly flawed and unsustainable conceits – conceits that in some cases are the result of mental aberrations. They fancy phantoms and apparitions, then conjure justifications to explain their existence."

Bryce took back the torch. "Dr. Leibowitz, you're a reasonable person within your own field of endeavor. Try to be just as reasonable with those of us who are in other fields. What possible reason could there be to cover up an alien invasion or crash site? Think about it. If the government had intel of a potential invasion – of any kind – the first thing they would do is alert the public in order to prepare a defense and allocate money for additional defense spending.

"In the old days science fiction writers liked to exclaim that an alien visitation would throw the world into a panic – for what reason was never explained. While it's true that the Orson Welles radio broadcast of *The War of the Worlds* on Halloween night in 1938 caused a ruckus, it's also true that today people are far too sophisticated to be panic-stricken by an invasion. Look at the American response to the Japanese attack on Pearl Harbor. No one ran in aimless circles or hid in the basement. People were galvanized not only to defend their shores but to repel the invaders and plan offensive strategies to carry the war to the invaders' homelands.

"If the Creature from the Black Lagoon were to walk down the sidewalk on a populated street no one would run away screaming. Some people might gaze in awe. Others would complement the Creature on his wonderful costume. A few might ask for autographs. The fictional panic reflex is a worn out plot device that has no place in modern reality."

Bryce took a breath but did not pause long enough for Leibowitz to comment. "Before you start on the stolen alien technology kick, let me remind you that the human race has gotten along quite well for thousands of years without alien influence. We don't need to reverse engineer trade secrets from an extraterrestrial crash site; we're more than capable of inventing our own technologies. Since World War Two technological advances have increased at an exponential rate because of hard work and fundamental discoveries. Every incremental tidbit has been thoroughly documented for those who care to read it."

The minimally lighted corridor grew brighter ahead. Danette steered the Roamer into a large cul-de-sac from which a number of narrow hallways led in fan-shaped directions. She parked next to a charging station where a score of Roamers were plugged into wall sockets. She pulled down a lever on the console that put the Roamer into reverse, and backed up to the wall.

"All ashore that's going ashore."

Laila: "I thought this was the Air Force, not the Navy."

"It comes from crossbreeding. We share some of the same lingo."

Bryce stepped out of the vehicle and plugged a spare cable into the Roamer. "Dr. Leibowitz I don't expect you to be an easy customer to convince but try to keep your mind open to concrete facts. That's all I ask."

"I – I – "

"Thank you Dr. Leibowitz. Aye aye is exactly what I wanted to hear. I have a lot to show you and some of it will blow your mind but for right now I want to take you to your workstation and introduce you to your partner. Follow me please. You too Laila." He preceded them along one of the hallways.

Danette waved goodbye and started off in a different direction. "I'm not just a bus driver. I have my own work to attend to."

Bryce opened a door into a rectangular room that sported an all-around workbench, one portion of which was divided into carrels that had built-in keyboards and computer screens. Fluorescent ceiling fixtures provided stark overhead illumination.

A man in black swiveled on his chair as the trio made their entrance. He brandished a broad smile as he stood tall and firm. His black hair was parted on the left. A small black mustache masked his upper lip. His dark features implied a Slavic heritage. His only adornments that were other than black were his white toothy smile and a white priest collar.

"I've been expecting you. I am Father Nicholas Derpilbosian. My parishioners call me Father Nick, but you can call me Nick." He held out his hand.

By rote and almost verbatim: "Dr. H. Horace Leibowitz, head of the Department of Linguistics at Harvard University, Professor Emeritus of the Department of Linguistics at Duke University, the leading expert on modern Semitic languages and ancient Hebrew, and the chief translator of the latest and most correct version of the Dead Sea Scrolls."

"Laila Masterson, the small and meek." If anyone caught the allusion to Dorothy in *The Wizard of Oz*, he made no notice of it.

They shook hands all around.

Bryce indicated a sheaf of printouts that lay on a long table in the middle of the room. The paper was the size of a blueprint. "If you'll look at these, Dr. Leibowitz, you'll know why you were hired and what we want you to decipher."

Leibowitz bent over the top sheet of ancient Hebrew symbols. "Hmmnn." He ran his finger from the bottom right corner to the left along the bottom line. "I recognize some of these symbols." He continued moving his finger up the lines until he reached the top. "What is this '9 7 3' in the upper left corner?"

Nick Derpilbosian spoke softly but with precise enunciation. "It is the sequential text number. The top sheet is the nine-hundred and seventy-third text to be found in the vicinity of the Dead Sea. The sheets underneath it continue from there."

Leibowitz straightened and pinched his eyes. "There – there – are only nine hundred and seventy-*two* texts. I know because I deciphered every one of them."

Sympathetically: "Not anymore."

After a long moment of silence: "Where – where – where . . . "

"In Cave 12."

"But – but – there are only eleven caves that contained scrolls."

"Not anymore."

Chapter 9

Bryce eased the door closed to what was now being called the Scroll Room. "Can I talk you into a cup of coffee?"

"You've twisted my arm." Laila looked both ways along the seemingly endless corridor. "Which way?"

He proceeded away from the parking garage. "About a block in this direction."

"A block? As in cell block?"

Bryce snickered. "If you grew up in Philly you'd know that a block is one tenth of a mile or slightly more than five hundred feet. Willy Penn laid out the city in a grid-square pattern with the streets running north-south and east-west. Philly was the first planned urban settlement in the country, maybe in the world. If you ran once around the block you would have run four tenths of a mile. That's how we practiced for track meets."

Laila tagged along but had to hustle to maintain Bryce's normally rapid pace. "Around the block in West Virginia could have been four or five miles. You'd have been worn out before you ever got to a meet."

"Couldn't you cut through the woods?"

"You could, but you'd also have to run across fields and climb over fences that kept the livestock from wandering off and into neighboring property. Farmer's didn't take kindly to kids beating down their crops. Cattle were skittish and ran away, but I got bit by a horse once, and another time I got chased by an angry pig the size of a Volkswagen. Marybeth was taller than me so she jumped clean over the fence without ever touching the top rail. I squeezed between the two middle slats with the pig on my behind, and tore my favorite flannel shirt on a splinter. After that, we avoided that corral like the plague."

Bryce laughed out loud. "Sounds like fun to me."

"Just like a man. Or a boy."

They climbed a flight of stairs into a room that had windows on two sides and exits at either end. Outside there was nothing but desert as far as the eye could see. Neither a tree nor a blade of grass was in sight, although a few cactuses dotted the landscape and some greenery touched the hillsides in the distance.

Bryce led the way to a vending area. "This is the local snack bar. Over here are refrigerated units that serve salads sandwiches and cold drinks. Over there are the dry goods: canned soup crackers pretzels and chips. Everything is restocked on a daily basis. And here milady is a commercial grade coffee maker. Don't tell Leibowitz that it cost a gazillion dollars."

Laila was finally getting used to Bryce's method of speaking without pausing between words. "Never fear. We'd hear him for a week. Our tax dollars at work, he would say."

"It's a convenience for the civvies who have to live on base. Most of the people here are married and have families living in Las Vegas or its immediate environs. They only get to go home on weekends. The least we can do for them is provide free food and drink. It's actually more cost effective than paying for transportation to town. As you can see we're in the middle of nowhere."

Laila nodded as she took the steaming Styrofoam cup that Bryce handed to her. Looking out a window: "This must be the most remote place in the country. Like Siberia without snow."

Bryce grabbed a diet Coke, led her to a corner table, and pulled out a chair for her. "That's the whole idea. A lot of experimental testing goes on here. The prototype Timepiece was unstable and blew up on us. No one was hurt but the explosion sure scared the dickens out of us. Me included. The blast registered on seismographs all over the North American continent. We leaked a story that it was an unauthorized atom bomb test."

Laila used both hands to sweep her Rapunzel-length hair over her shoulders so it cascaded down her back. "Has that instability problem been fixed?"

"Yes that was several years ago. We've got a stable working model now. Two of them in fact. We call them Big Ben and Wristwatch. Leibowitz would call that a wasteful expenditure of taxpayers' dollars but in the military we believe in backups in case anything goes wrong."

Laila sipped her hot coffee gratefully. "Speaking of blowups, I'm sorry I blew up on Leibowitz back there, but he annoys me to no end."

Bryce humphed. "No need to apologize. He annoys me too."

"Yet I can't help but be impressed by his rock hard ego. I'd have wilted like an overripe tomato plant if I'd been sandbagged the way we ganged up on him. But he just let it all roll over him like water off a duck's back, as my granma used to say."

"I don't like babysitting someone who's twice my age but as he says ad nauseam he's the best there is."

"Judging by the way he dove into those Scrolls and identified some of the symbols right off the bat, I'm inclined to believe him. He certainly impressed Derpilbosian. On the other hand, bringing Leibowitz to Area 51 is like taking a lighted candle into a room full of gunpowder."

Bryce snickered. "Let me handle the det cord. For now – " He glanced at his watch. " – we've got a few minutes before the lunch crowd arrives and before I take you to your workstation and there is something that we have to discuss in private."

"I'm all ears."

"I think we've got a bad apple in the basket."

Laila showed no surprise. "General Cercopley intimated as much, but I didn't try to force the issue. In my job I've learned to listen, because I already know everything that I have to say. I gathered that the person in command of Project Stitch – you, as it turns out – would give me more information in that regard. What makes you think there's a leak, and do you have any prime suspects that can whittle the bushel down to a peck?"

In his seldom punctuated sentences: "To answer your second question first no. Chris Varvarelis our Chief of Security has not suggested to me that he is aware of any leakage from within the organization and I haven't presented my suspicions to him. When you don't know who to trust you call in someone from outside the inner circle."

"Me." She said it as a flat statement.

"Yes you."

Laila thought it over. "What makes you think that someone here is selling secrets to the IRF?"

"Your report. The fact that they've got a time machine."

Laila was nonplussed.

"Look at it this way. You take a mountain that no one has been able to climb. As soon as the first person makes it to the top mountaineers everywhere know it can be climbed and everyone starts climbing it. Nowadays more people climb the Matterhorn and Mount Everest than any other mountains in the world. And most of the people who climb them aren't even mountaineers. Guides lead novices to the summit as if they were trained elephants on parade or ducklings in a brood. Once unclimbable mountains are now covered with trash from high altitude picnickers."

Continuing his animal analogies: "By the same token and closer to the point as soon as the world learned that uranium was fissionable and could be made to explode the cat was out of the bag. It took only a couple of years for Russia to develop the atomic bomb.

"Once the conceptual barrier has been broken everyone jumps on the bandwagon.

"Now we have a time machine. The only people who know about it are those who've worked on its research and development. All of a sudden the IRF has one. If it were Russia or China or maybe India I could accept the idea of coincidental or parallel discovery. It's happened before. But not the IRF. They don't have the knowhow or the resources to conceive of such a device much less the technology to build one. That means that someone tipped them off and is peddling information. It wasn't the President and it wasn't Cercopley and it wasn't me. That leaves only subordinates."

"Has anyone left the project since its inception?"

"No."

"Being this close to Vegas, has anyone accumulated gambling debts?"

"Not to my knowledge." After a pause: "No one has enough time to get seriously in debt to the casinos."

"How about family members?"

"Again, not to my knowledge. Everyone who works here is well paid. Even the guards make half again as much as they'd make elsewhere. I've charged Varvarelis with maintaining an up-to-date data base of the financial activities of everyone on the base. All our people signed an agreement to waive their constitutional rights with regard to financial statements, bank accounts, credit card statements, mortgages, and other loans. We even have an on-site accountant who does their taxes for them. Nothing looks out of the ordinary. Plus Varvarelis conducts polygraph tests on everyone twice a year."

Laila pondered. "Hmmnn."

"Maybe I'm barking up the wrong tree. Maybe I'm overly suspicious. Maybe some genius Muslim physicist developed the idea independently." After a pause: "And maybe the sky is falling. The IRF is funded by third world nations. For them to build a time machine is like a sixteenth-century Polynesian islander manufacturing a pocket watch from bamboo shivers and coconut husks."

"I concede your point." Laila pondered some more. "But they are also building an atomic bomb. Or so we think."

"Anyone who can chew gum and read the Boy Scout handbook can build an atom bomb. The technology has been common knowledge for decades. As you indicated in your report they're importing pitchblende and making heavy water. Most of the bomb components they can buy from a Sears catalogue or the international marketplace courtesy of the U.S.A."

Laila kept pondering. "Does anyone here have an old allegiance to Islam? Has anyone received death threats against themselves or their families?"

Bryce shook his head. "Once again not to my knowledge. No one is supposed to know that the people who work here work here. Their official workplace is Nellis and their occupation is undisclosed. Varvarelis is good at what he does. He hasn't asked those particular questions bluntly during the polygraph tests so as not to make anyone suspicious enough to clam up before we catch him but he has routinely asked similar questions in a roundabout way. So far negative."

"Has Wendayne overheard any suspicious conversations?"

"No and she even bugged the cafeteria tables."

"I'll remember that the next time you invite me to breakfast."

Bryce made one of his very few physical gestures; he shrugged. "I'm only putting the seed in your mind. Let me know if you come up with a pearl of wisdom."

"I will."

"And keep this security check business between the two of us."

"I will."

"Don't even mention it to Varvarelis."

"I won't." After a pause: "We have a saying in the CIA that goes: Quis custodiet ipsos custodes?"

"Derpilbosian is our Latin expert. I took Spanish in high school. What does it mean?"

"Literally: Who will guard the guards themselves? Familiarly: Who watches the watchers?"

Bryce humphed. "Who watches the CIA?"

"The CIA."

"Now there's a scary thought." Bryce sipped his Coke. "Do people really 'get disappeared' in the Company?"

"Supposedly in the field. Not in the office." After a pause: "At least, not that I'm aware of."

Sarcastically: "Wonderful atmosphere to work in and I thought flying was dangerous."

"It keeps the work force on their toes."

"So does ballet, but dancers live longer."

"Really, though, the people who go missing are generally thought to have been killed or captured by the enemy; not by Company kill squads."

"Or so they say." He took another sip. "Once I get you up and running I'll brief you and Leibowitz about Project Stitch and Mission Snatch. I don't want to do it twice."

"I'm curious but I can wait."

The door opened and in walked Father Nickolas Derpilbosian.

Bryce turned to see who it was. "Speaking of the devil's advocate."

"Mind if I join you?"

"You saved my soul yesterday. What are you saving today?"

"The best part: filet of soul."

Bryce indicated a chair. To Laila: "We didn't get to do formal introductions in the Scroll room because Leibowitz got distracted by the Scrolls. Father Nick is not only a dry wit but he's our special liaison from the Vatican."

Laila was stunned. "The Vatican? How is the Vatican involved in this Project?"

"Not in the Project but in the Mission."

Father Nick sat between Bryce and Laila. "My dear, anything that threatens the livelihood of Christianity falls within the purview of the Vatican."

"But – but – how do you even know about this project? It's supposed to be top secret."

Bryce furnished the answer. "The Vatican and the American government have been working hand in hand ever since trouble started in the Middle East."

"That's quite a while. There's been trouble in the Middle East for more than two thousand years."

"Point taken. Let's say since political insurrections and terrorist eruptions that commenced after World War Two. The Vatican has a remarkable intelligence network that focuses on all things religious. After all they've got field agents in every country in Europe Africa and the Americas."

Father Nick looked askance at Bryce. "We prefer to

call them priests."

"A rose by any other name as Billy the Bard once wrote."

"As you can tell, Ms. Masterson, Colonel Davenport and I have developed a good working relationship during my residency here."

"Please call me Laila."

"Then you must call me Nick."

"Oh, I like the sound of Father Nick so much better. It sounds homey."

Father Nick bowed. "If you wish."

"So what's your role in this project, Father Nick?"

"It is through the Vatican's widespread resources that Cave 12 was discovered. Excuse me, Ms. – I mean, Laila – are you Catholic by any chance."

"I was raised as a good Southern Baptist girl."

"Just as well. God makes no distinctions. As I was saying, the Vatican has many fingers in many pies."

If Father Nick could make punning witticisms, so could Laila. "Somehow I never thought of the Vatican as a bakery, but go on."

"Touché." Father Nick did not look miffed. "The Vatican constantly measures the pulse of Catholicism in the world. It is one way of ascertaining the strengths and weaknesses of the people's faith in God. By knowing how people feel about their faith, we can cater to their needs in ways that will increase their trust in the church and their belief in the hereafter. For example, we can issue edicts to direct the focus of sermons so that they address problems that people fear the most. It is one way among others of reaching out to the people.

"As I was saying, although a priest is neither a spy nor an informant, it is part of his job to listen to the people, and not only in the confessional. The church hears a great deal of what is going on in its parishes as well as elsewhere in the world. Not only do we listen, but we have a cadre of investigators who, let us say, follow up on what they hear as it relates to Christianity."

Laila interrupted. "In other words you have field agents like the CIA."

Father Nick did not mind the interruption. "In a manner of speaking. Understand that our goals are entirely different from those of the Central Intelligence Agency. Priests are charged with the task of treating religious concerns. Our investigators scout mostly for religious artifacts, and are authorized to subsidize archaeological digs that might yield objects of a canonical or theological nature. As you may well know, the Vatican conserves a vast repository of relics and antiquities that relate to Christianity and Christian movements throughout the ages.

"The Vatican often purchases religious items at auction – but always through an anonymous bidder, I must add. Long ago we learned to our despair that wealthy collectors will bid higher for an item if they know that they are bidding against the Vatican. Outbidding the church seems to add a sense of prestige to winning.

"Our investigators also search for information as it relates to Christianity: ancient texts, papyri, manuscripts, and incunabula. The original discovery of the Dead Sea Scrolls caught us off guard, I am sad to say. The scriptures they contained were extraordinary, particularly as much of the text reflected on biblical history during its formative years. The Vatican would love to count the Scrolls among its holdings – " After a short pause: " – but I suppose that what is more important than possessing fragments of papyrus is understanding the truths that are conveyed by the ancient script that is written on that papyrus.

"To be fair, at the time of the discovery of the Scrolls, no one suspected their age or their relevance to the *Bible*. Years later, when translations corresponded to certain passages in the Holy Scriptures, the Vatican initiated a long-term search program that continues to this very day. We have never relaxed our vigil. We hired local residents to comb the area for grottoes and fissures of all sizes. Hundreds of small caves were discovered and explored, but most were empty. The few that were not empty contained physical artifacts but none that were, shall we say, spiritual in nature. Until recently, that is."

Laila sipped her coffee. "So it was your people who found the new Scrolls. I mean, old Scrolls; I mean, Scrolls that hadn't been discovered before."

"Correct."

She slowly shook her head. "It's odd that I didn't read about it in the papers."

Father Nick pursed his lips. "The Vatican does not like to advertise its achievements, especially in this time of, shall we say, intensified religious unrest. We are content to work in the background until the proper time arrives to divulge our successes."

After a moment of strained silence: "You mean, until you firmly establish that the newly discovered Scrolls confirm or validate the scriptures – without contradiction."

Father Nick glanced uncomfortably at Bryce. "That is one way of putting it."

"Forgive me for being insistent, Father Nick, but how else would you put it? The way I interpret your innuendo is that you release information when it buttresses the foundations of the Catholic church, but withhold information that shakes those same foundations lest the walls of Jericho come tumbling down."

Bryce laughed out loud. "I told you she was sharp."

"Light as a feather and sharp as a quill, as my granma used to say."

Father Nick joined in the laughter. "Now I understand why you picked her for this quest."

"Oh, so now the project and mission have become a quest. Is this like the crusade for the Holy Grail?"

Father Nick looked uncomfortable again. "Not exactly, but you are not far off the mark as it relates to chronometry."

Laila grinned. "I remember enough of my Sunday school learning to know that Christ drank from the Holy Grail at the Last Supper. Hand to mouth, so to speak. But let that go for now. What do you expect Leibowitz to find by deciphering this latest batch of Scrolls? And what affect will it have on our so-called quest?"

"I will answer your questions, but first let me give

you some context that will make my answers more meaningful. As the Good Book is written, the *Bible* represents a rough history and chronology of biblical events. Ancient chronographers did not have the benefit of an internationally accepted Gregorian calendar and quartz crystal movements. For the most part they calculated the passage of time by comparison to then-current events – wars, Egyptian dynasties, Roman rulers, and so on – none of which is known today with precision."

"I get it. It's like saying that the First Arab-Israeli War occurred during the Eisenhower administration but not specifying when within his eight-year span as President."

"Correct. The exact date of the birth of Christ and the exact date of his death are open to doubt and considerable conjecture. Modern scholars are in constant dispute over biblical interpretations – based largely on the gospel of the disciples in the New Testament – generally denoting a spread of half a decade. Isaac Newton utilized astronomical data to proclaim the date of Christ's Crucifixion as April 23 in 34 Anno Domini. Later astronomers disagreed by as much as a year.

"The place of Christ's Crucifixion is known with a fair degree of accuracy: a hill outside of Jerusalem known as Golgotha or Calvary. We can easily pinpoint the location by – as Bryce has so irreverently proposed – following the crowd. But only if we are there at the correct moment in time.

"Vatican scholars have been trying to decipher the Cave 12 Scrolls for several years. Although they have met with a modicum of success, there is much that they were unable to decipher, and more that they have disagreed upon – oftentimes violently. I am speaking of intellectual violence, not physical. As a result of these failures and differences of opinion, we facilitated Mr. Leibowitz's access to the original Dead Sea Scrolls in order to determine his expertise."

"Does he know that?" Laila wondered.

Father Nick proffered a toothless smile. "We used

somewhat devious means to protect the Vatican's name from becoming associated with the release of photocopies to his care. Because of his, shall we say, abrasive personality, we thought it best to remain anonymous lest he, shall we say, use our help as a bragging point."

Laila pulled her thumb and forefinger across her mouth. "My lips are sealed."

"Thank you. As I was saying, although many church scholars disagreed with some of Mr. Leibowitz's translations, there is much that they conceded. As it turns out, the Vatican and the DIA employ some of the same agents in the disrupted area of the Middle East."

"Isn't that an oxymoron? All of the Middle East is disrupted."

"Yes, I suppose you are correct."

Bryce interjected. "What he means is that the locals are double dipping. They get paid twice for disbursing the same information to two rich buyers."

"Pretty smart on their part."

Bryce nodded in agreement.

"Mr. Leibowitz already recognized a symbol that church scholars identified as the Son of God. He also identified certain other symbols that led church scholars to believe that the text on these Scrolls refers to the Crucifixion. References are made to stars and to phases of the moon, but beyond that our scholars were stymied about how best to interpret such astrological data. That is why Mr. Leibowitz is such an important part of this quest."

Bryce took the torch. "If the IRF doesn't know exactly when the Crucifixion occurred, the only way they can prevent it from happening is to station soldiers in the past before it happens – maybe as long as ten years prior – and let them live in the area until they track him down. Since the DIA and the Vatican both learned about the IRF plan to prevent the Crucifixion and since we both knew that the other knew we naturally joined forces. We can provide the mechanism for traveling into the past; they can provide the crucial point in time so we can arrive on site without announcing our presence in advance. Then we can foil their kidnapping plans."

Father Nick nodded stolidly. "I must say, though, that being responsible for precipitating events that clear the way for the Crucifixion is something that the Pope and I and other Vatican leaders condone with great trepidation. We acknowledge that the Crucifixion occurred because it is an historical fact. We also acknowledge that the death of Christ on the cross at the hands of the Romans was what made him a martyr. We even acknowledge that Christ's suffering can be interpreted as a brand of extreme unction. All these things must come to pass in order to preserve the very existence of Christianity. . . . "

Laila took advantage of Father Nick's long pause. "Can't you view the Crucifixion as an act that was, in some way, retroactively preordained?"

Father Nick's eyes widened. "I suppose . . . I suppose we could. But even so, it is with great anguish that we contemplate becoming a willing accessory, indeed, a prime motivating factor, to the crime of allowing the Son of God to be assassinated . . . when we appear to have it within our power to prevent his premature passing."

Chapter 10

Laila took a sip from her cup of fresh hot coffee. "Wow, talk about Hobson's choice. When it comes to either saving Christ or letting him die, the Catholic church is damned if they do and damned if they don't."

Bryce led the way along the corridor. "That's one way of putting it."

"That's two ways. " She took another sip. "I'll bet Father Nick and the Vatican say prayers and light votive candles every night, in the hope that there's a more acceptable alternative. Until yesterday morning – omigod, was it only yesterday morning? Wow. So much has happened since then. Until yesterday morning I thought the world was fairly safe. At least, our neck of the world. Now literally overnight I've learned that Armageddon might be right around the corner."

"I can't disagree with you except that I've known about it longer. Ignorance is comforting until reality punches you in the face." He extended his arm into an intersecting corridor. "The security office is this way."

They stopped in front of a solid windowless door that had the appearance of a bank safe. Bryce tapped eight digits on the doorjamb keypad. A soft click announced that the door had unlocked.

"The code number is – "

"Seven three two eight seven four eight nine."

Bryce stood like a statue and stared down at her in amazement. "How did you know that?"

"I watched." Her eyes went glassy for a moment. "SECURITY on the telephone keypad. Not very imaginative."

Bryce shook and head and grinned. "You are amazing."

"I have my moments." She pulled open the heavy door. "Shall we?"

He snickered as he followed her into a well-lit room whose walls were paved with video screens and computer consoles. The room was narrow: more like a broad hallway than a rectangular office. Personnel were absent. A door at the far end was marked LATRINE. Bryce closed the outer door behind him. He indicated a thickly padded chair at the near end, in front of a console on which a name plaque reading PRIVATE occupied one corner.

"We didn't have time to have a plaque stamped with your name but this is your personal workstation. It has a dedicated secure line to the outside world that will respond only to a code number sequence of your choosing."

Laila viewed the keyboard and multiple monitors. "How do I access the line to choose a code number?"

Bryce hesitated. Instead of making eye contact he stared at the keyboard. He kept hesitating. "Your temporary code number is two two eight."

Only a split second passed before Laila spun around, raised her left fist, and punched Bryce lightly on the chest. "BAT on the telephone keypad."

Bryce grimaced and shrugged his shoulders. "I knew I was in trouble back at Andrews when you deciphered the hangar keypad in two seconds flat."

"HEY!" The booming voice sounded like a deep peal of thunder. "Kids aren't allowed in here!"

Bryce and Laila turned and faced the approaching giant: six feet four inches tall and broad around the waist with an A-shaped torso.

"Bryce, I didn't recognize you. Who's the little girl? And what's she doing in my security shack?"

Laila held out her hand. "Laila Masterson."

The man looked thunderstruck. His jaw worked soundlessly as he collected his wits. Tentatively, as if he were reaching into a high-voltage electrical panel, he held out his right hand.

Laila grasped a hand that felt cool and clammy and as limp as cooked spaghetti. "Pleased to meet you."

"Jesus. You're no bigger than my twelve year old daughter." He gulped as his startled gaze roved down her body and lingered too long in the vicinity of her sternum. "I mean – I didn't mean – "

"You meant *taller* than your daughter."

"Yes. Yes, of course. I meant taller." He took back his hand. "I'm Chris Varvarelis, head of security." Looking at Bryce. "Why the hell didn't you warn me?"

"I figured you'd be here when we came in. Didn't the door alarm sound?"

"I didn't hear it. I was in the bathroom. Everyone else is out on patrol." Looking at Laila: "You'll have to forgive me. You caught me off guard. And you're so – so – tiny – "

"I think 'petite' is the word you're looking for Chris."

"Yes. Yes – petite."

Laila took another sip of coffee that was by now lukewarm. "I'm not sensitive about my height. Or my cup size. I'm certain that we'll make a good team. Like David and Goliath."

"Yes. Yes, like – " Varvarelis glanced at Bryce. "Is Leibowitz here, too?"

"He's translating Scrolls even as we speak."

"Oh. Oh, that's good. You'll let me know when he pinpoints the date?" To Laila: "We have a pool going. Me and the other security personnel." To Bryce: "I've got a report on that tripped pressure sensor. Mule deer tracks go right over it." To Laila: "It happens all the time but we have to check it out. We get a lot of reporters masquerading as hikers and backpackers, sometimes as mountain bikers. The area we patrol is twice the size of Delaware and nearly as large as Connecticut, so it's impossible to fence it in. People disregard the signposts all the time, then plead ignorance when we dispatch an armed patrol to threaten them with arrest for trespassing. We let them go free but we put a good scare into them first. Usually we put them in a holding tank while we run down their ID. The ones that aren't reporters are flying saucer nuts."

Bryce took the torch. "We fly experimental aircraft all the time and some of them like the stealth bomber look very much like disks or saucers when they pass overhead and block out the stars." To Varvarelis: "I've got to prepare for tonight's test flight so I'll leave you to bring Laila up to speed." To Laila: "Danette is arranging your new accommodations. The dormitory room you used last night is for transients. Now that the Project is going into high gear we're moving the whole kit and caboodle out here. No more half-hour Roamer rides." To both: "So I'll let you two get introduced." To Laila: "I'm sure you have a gazillion emails to catch up on. Call me or Danette anytime on your why-tie."

Laila nodded. "Gotcha."

The door latched in place behind him.

Laila looked way up at Varvarelis. "I hope you're a gentle giant."

Varvarelis laughed his way out of his discomfort. "The air's a little thin at my altitude so the oxygen depletion keeps me sluggish."

She dropped her empty cup into a wastepaper basket. "I'll bet you've said that a lot of times since high school."

"You know it." He glanced at the computer console. "Why don't you have a seat at your workstation, and I'll give you a briefing."

"Sounds good to me." Laila sat in the overstuffed chair. "This isn't exactly the kind of seat I'm used to."

"It's a special chair. We all use them. Watch." Varvarelis reached down along the right side of the chair and pushed down on a metal lever. The seatback folded back and a footboard rose parallel to the raised computer floor. "It's a sleep recliner."

Laila found herself lying flat on her back and looking way up at Varvarelis's grinning face. "I could get used to this."

Varvarelis pulled up on the lever and returned the chair to a sitting position. Then he knelt on one knee so that his face was even with Laila's. "Our security system is tight but we don't sit here all day and night and watch the monitors. Not unless you like wildlife and want to see mule deer, prairie dogs, coyotes, and buzzards, and the occasional roadrunner and swift fox if you're lucky."

"I could get used to that, too."

Varvarelis smiled. "You will if you're here long enough. But for us old hands – "

"You're not that old."

With a barely perceptible pause: "For us long-time hands, the animals are more of a bother than anything else, because they trigger our sensors and cause no end of fieldwork. The video cameras - " He swept his arm around the room to indicate the monitors. " – are only for nearby surveillance. No one has ever gotten that close without first being detected by our perimeter sensors."

Laila opened her mouth to speak but Varvarelis nipped her in the bud. "We also have radar antennas for flybys and skydivers. The screen is back there next to the bathroom. Oh, by the way, we're not used to having women here, and the bathroom is leftover from when this was an Air Force training center, so we don't have his and hers facilities. There's not even a lock on the door . . . "

Laila flapped her hand by way of pooh-poohing convention. "Don't worry about me. I'm not self-conscious. I'll announce my intention when I have to let some coffee out of my spigot."

Nonplussed: "Well, uh, good. That's good. Most of the time there's no one here anyway – oh, that could pose a problem if me or one of the men walks in and doesn't know you're in the bathroom."

This time she flapped her other hand. "I squirt fast so it's not likely to happen."

"Yes, uh, yes, of course. Anyway, the video footage is recorded and time-stamped, and when any one of more than a thousand detectors is tripped, a signal alarm notifies me automatically on this." He pulled a device out of a pants pocket and held it up for Laila to see. "It's a – "

"A Mini Pulse Activator, Model MPA-21-C." Laila nodded. "We use them in the CIA. Most of our equipment is supplied by General Dynamics."

"Yes. Yes, of course. Only this is the 21-A."

"I can get you a 21-C. We keep them in stock."

"Thanks. Thanks, but – "

"I'm allowed to check one out of inventory whenever

I'm on assignment. Especially *this* assignment."

He held up both hands like a cop stopping traffic. "That's okay, uh, Laila. This one works just fine. It has never failed to notify me on an intrusion. And the location is always displayed correctly on the screen."

Laila shrugged. "Just offering."

"Okay, I'll keep it in mind. Now, about your workstation. You have a dedicated line that is not interfaced with ours. Password protected. Fully encrypted. Five minute lockout." With one hand he tapped several keys; he casually dropped his other hand onto Laila's knee. "You can also patch into *our* system on monitor two."

Laila gently pushed his hand aside, then scratched the part of her knee and lower thigh on which his hand had rested.

"Did Bryce tell you that he forwarded resumes of all base personnel?"

"Yes."

"He didn't do that via open email. I created a link for you that puts you directly into our system so you can review our data files all the way back to the beginning of the Project. Resumes, polygraph tests, everything is in those files."

"Do you record personal phone calls?"

"We don't have to. Personal phone calls are not allowed. The only phones that connect us with Nellis are right here in this room. We can patch through Nellis to an outside line if we have to. *Those* calls *are* recorded."

"Automatically?"

"No. I have to switch on the recorder."

"And only you or your staff have access this room?"

"Plus Bryce and Danette."

"Does everyone have to pass through the same metal detector and x-ray machine like I did this morning?"

Varvarelis nodded. "Both entering and leaving."

"Paper documents don't show up on metal detectors or x-ray machines."

Shrugging: "We don't strip search anyone if that's what you're getting at."

"Just curious. About the security of the security. Is

there any control over personnel after they leave the base on weekends."

Varvarelis shook his head. "There's only so much we can regulate about our people. When they go home to visit their families they're pretty much on their own recognizance."

"No camcorders behind the mirrors in their bedrooms like in *1984*?"

He grinned. "No. And no thought police, either."

Laila flicked her eyebrows. "That's nice to know. I wouldn't want my thoughts to melt down the equipment."

Varvarelis squinted as if he wasn't quite certain of her meaning. He patted her gently on the leg. "Just hold that thought while I show you how to access your email. Then I'll leave you alone."

He demonstrated the keystrokes, tapped in her temporary password, and accessed the CIA server. "From here on you're on your own."

"Thanks, Chris. I can take it from here."

"I'm going out to check a faulty video feed."

Varvarelis left Laila to her own devices. She knuckled down to work. Time passed but she hardly noticed. Her concentration on the task at hand was complete. Her fingers flashed across the keyboard. Screens came and went. The data stream appeared on all four monitors until she segregated them. She worked on one screen while others downloaded data. She had a lot of catching up to do, and a lot of new information to assimilate . . .

. . . A hand touched her lightly on the shoulder. Her head jerked; her eyes snapped open. For a moment she didn't know where she was, or what she was supposed to be doing. The fluorescent ceiling lights were switched off. The only glimmer in the room emanated from computer screens and video monitors.

"Are you all right?"

"I've been better." Laila shook her head and rubbed her eyeballs with her knuckles. "But I've been a lot worse, too. Wow, I must have crashed hard."

"That's okay in your business but not in mine."

She recognized Bryce's voice, then focused on his face above her. Suddenly she realized that she was stretched out horizontally. "I must have . . . passed out."

"You fell asleep is what you did."

For the second time in a row she woke up groggy. Slowly she regained her senses, and her sense of where she was. She reached over the maroon padded arm and pulled up on the metal handle. The chair mechanism lifted her to an upright position. He long silky hair was twisted behind her. She squinted as she tried to untangle the mess.

"My hair if full of witches, as my granma used to say." She ran her fingers through her light brown tresses and managed to comb out most of the kinks. "Varvarelis was right about this chair. It's way too comfortable. I only wanted to rest my eyes for a minute, so I . . . " Laila didn't wear a watch; she used her cell phone to check the time. Her cell phone was switched off and in her minipurse in her room. " . . . What time is it?"

"Just about midnight."

"Wow. I don't know when I conked out . . . " She remembered to look at the lower right corner of one of the computer screens. "Last time check was 7:12, or thereabouts."

"You needed the rest."

"I guess so."

"Did you have many emails?"

Laila shook the cobwebs out of her head. "One hundred and twelve. I read them all but I only answered thirty-one. To answer the rest will take me a month of Sundays, as my granma used to say."

"Would you like to go for a ride?"

She looked up at him, for the first time noticing that he had changed his jogging suit for a flight uniform. "Is this another date?"

"It is if you want it to be."

"I do."

"Then it is."

Laila stood up and pushed against the chair with her

legs. It moved back easily on rollers. "Can you give me a minute to freshen up?"

"The stock answer around here is 'When you have a time machine, you can afford to take your time'."

She took two: one to squirt and another to splash water onto her face. She emerged from the latrine fresh as a daisy, although she always wondered what made daisies so fresh. Did they pinch daisies of the opposite sex?

"Feel better?"

"Much. But I could use a cup of coffee."

Bryce was dressed in a brown lightweight flight suit and black paratrooper boots. He opened the door for her. "We'll pick up some sandwiches on the way too."

In the corridor: "What kind of ride is this?"

"An airplane ride. You'll love it."

"Will I need anti-motion pills?"

"Not on this trip. We'll go slow and easy. Then we'll go fast and easy. But we'll always go easy."

"Flying slow and easy must be difficult for someone with seventy-three combat missions."

"You read my resume."

"I did."

"Don't let the statistics fool you. Most of those flights were reconnaissance missions: shooting pictures instead of bullets."

"I recognized some of those pictures. I even put them in my analysis report when I suggested that the IRF might be building a temporal displacement apparatus. I didn't know their origination."

Bryce shrugged. "Imagine my shock when I saw pictures that I had taken three years ago in your report. I always wondered what that ring structure was. I didn't recognize it even when I was transferred here to head up the experimental aircraft division and saw the full-scale version. The size threw me off."

"Don't feel bad. I didn't know what it was until the recent field reports led me to dig the pictures out of our archives.

Bryce turned into the snack bar, held the door open

for Laila, and walked straight to the sandwich counter. He grabbed a ham and cheese sandwich plus a diet Coke from the soft drink dispenser. Laila took a bacon, lettuce, and tomato wrap – the folded bread kept the contents from squishing out the sides – at least until after the first bite – and a large black coffee.

"Now I'm happy."

Again he held the door open for her. "We'll eat while we walk."

"What's the rush? We've got a time machine."

Bryce smiled. "Yes but we still have schedules."

They fell silent as they filled their mouths with food. The walk was long enough that they finished eating by the time they reached their destination: a small window-less chamber with a security locked door and a lone bench seat. Leibowitz paced back and forth in front of the seat like a caged tiger. He perked up when he saw the pair approaching.

"You didn't tell me that Leibowitz was chaperoning us," Laila whispered.

"Sorry."

"I'd rather have root canal than be cooped up with him again."

Bryce made no reply.

Leibowitz looked more disheveled than he did the last time Laila had seen him. His shirttail was pulled completely out of his pants and his vest was unbuttoned. The bags under his eyes were the size of grocery sacks.

His bleary eyes widened. "The Scrolls are amazing! Simply amazing! They recount the events leading up to the Crucifixion but not like the verses in the New Testament. There are some startling differences that I haven't figured out yet: contradictions with the written accounts of Matthew, Mark, Luke, and John. No last supper, no kissing Judas, no – "

"What about the timing? Were you able to pinpoint the day?"

"Well, not exactly."

"Or the week?"

"Not yet."

"How about the year?"

"I think so. But I'm still working on it with that bald-headed astronomer."

"Luke Kreider."

"Yes, he's the one. He had charts of the positions of the stars and the phases of the moon. But I had to get away for a while. I've been working on the Scrolls for twelve hours straight. The symbols began to blur. So I had to get away. The black pilot dragged me over here and told me to wait for you."

"The black pilot has a name. It's Danette."

"Yes, her. She said that we were going to test an experimental aircraft of some kind. Why do *I* have to go on a test flight? I'm here to translate Scrolls, not to go zipping through the air in a bungee jet. I don't have to go – "

"This is merely an introductory flight. I thought you might want to see the aircraft that we'll be flying to the Middle East after you translate all the Scrolls."

"*I'm* not going to the Middle East. I – "

"Did you read your contract like I suggested?"

"I've been too busy – "

"Then let me inform you that when you signed the contract and accepted the money you agreed to go wherever we needed your services and expertise. Eventually we will need you in the Middle East."

"But – but – but I didn't think I would – I would have to leave the country. And especially not to go to hostile territory. I – I – "

Bryce's stare was stern. "You should learn to look before you leap as Laila's grandmother undoubtedly used to say. Now come with me and I'll show you something that I promise will interest you."

"But – "

"No buts." Bryce tapped a seven digit code on the numerical keypad. He glanced at Laila.

Laila dusted breadcrumbs off her hands by swiping the hips of her hospital scrub. She returned from her faraway gaze with a questioning expression on her face. "Marsmen?"

Bryce shrugged. He opened the door and gestured for his guests pass ahead of him.

Beyond was a grated catwalk with an iron railing. The catwalk was located close to the ceiling of a huge hangar that could have fitted a zeppelin pointing in either direction. Below stood an aircraft like none that Laila had ever seen – or heard of. It measured nearly two hundred feet across, no matter which way the measurement was taken.

Leibowitz put his hands on the top rail and gripped it tightly. He slowly moved his head from side to side. "It's – it's – it's – a flying saucer."

Chapter 11

Laila was just as stunned as Leibowitz. For once her encyclopedic knowledge of top secret operations failed her. "What – what is it?" She cringed at the realization that her stuttering made her sound like Leibowitz.

"You – you – you said there weren't any flying saucers in Area 51."

"Not exactly," Bryce glowered. "I said there weren't any alien spacecraft. I didn't say anything about man-made aircraft that resemble saucers. What you see here is a prototype long-range high-altitude protracted-endurance nuclear-device delivery system: basically a bomber that can remain airborne for a number of years."

"*Years?*" Both Laila and Leibowitz shouted together.

"Yes. It's an outgrowth of experimental aircraft that have been designed and constructed in American factories and flight-tested here for reasons of security. Laila you should have some knowledge of early surveillance aircraft that were funded by the CIA."

At first Laila was so entranced by the spectacle before her that she was unable to speak. She was trying to absorb the image. The hangar ceiling was fitted with full-length rows of fluorescent fixtures whose light illuminated the vast space with incredible clarity. The fuselage, if it could be called that, was perfectly circular and unbroken by control surfaces: there were no wings, no tail, no rudder, and no ailerons. A tall bulge in the center rose twenty feet above the "roof," and appeared much like the spindle on a child's top, only fatter.

Looking down on the "saucer" from above made it difficult to gauge the thickness of the airframe, but it looked to be about twenty feet. A soft chine curved downward to a rounded outer edge. The radical hull design showed no signs of propulsion from overhead.

"I do." Laila dragged her wondering gaze from the aircraft and stared wide-eyed at Bryce. "I do."

"How much do you know?"

"When I achieved clearance for top secret sensitive

compartmented information, I made it my business to learn everything I could about CIA activities, past and present, not only out of curiosity, but to enable me to perform my intelligence duties better." She shrugged. "After the Oxcart crash, further CIA involvement in Area 51 was reduced and finally eliminated. The Air Force took over completely with the development of drones and the evolution of stealth aircraft." She shrugged again. "The public repudiates the CIA's fostered image of an intelligence gathering service. They believe that the CIA assassinates foreign leaders, engineers coups, and topples governments. While it's true that those things happen, and that the CIA supports and condones those kinds of activities, and sometimes goes as far as to fund insurgents against governments that are hostile to the United States, the CIA's role is confined to gathering intel and providing it to the armed forces, which then assume the role of executing political and military objectives. In short, the CIA learns what to do and how to do it, but the President and the Joint Chiefs determine *if* it should be done, and which branch of the military is best suited to do it."

Leibowitz closed his open jaw, then tried to formulate words. "But – but – why would the CIA – want airplanes?"

Laila glanced at Bryce.

Bryce tilted his head and raised his eyebrows. To Laila: "I'm sufficiently impressed by his performance to grant higher clearance status." To Leibowitz: "Remember that you signed a very exacting confidentiality packet so you can never reveal anything that you see or hear during this mission without explicit authority to do so."

"I – I – "

"Do you understand?"

"Yes – yes, I understand."

"Do you *really* understand?"

"Yes – yes – I really understand. Please don't put a gun to my head. I promise never to reveal anything that I see or hear."

"Good. Under present circumstances I think you've

earned the right to know more about what goes on at Area 51." To Laila: "Why don't you give the professor here some background from your end and I'll pick up from where the Air Force took over?"

"I can do that." Laila took a deep breath. To Leibowitz: "The CIA was not interested in *any* airplanes, just spy planes. For reconnaissance purposes. Think back to the Cold War and the proliferation of acronyms: MAD, DEW, and ICBM – acronyms that have largely been forgotten or never learned by today's teenagers. They're as much a part of ancient history as pinball and Pac-Man.

"DEW stood for Distant Early Warning: a line of radar stations that stretched across the Canadian tundra and were mounted on oilrig platforms along the American eastern seaboard: the most likely directions from which the Soviet Union would send bombers and ICBM's: intercontinental ballistic missiles. The U.S. prepared a massive counterattack with enough nuclear-tipped missiles to totally demolish Russia's military bases and metropolitan areas, thus ensuring Mutually Assured Destruction."

Leibowitz scowled. "That makes sense."

"The most important weapon in any war is military intelligence: not the oxymoron but the abbreviation known as intel. In accordance with the National Security Act of 1947, the Central Intelligence Agency was established to, as the name implies, gather intel. At that time the largest potential threat to the security of the United States was the Soviet Union. Russia is a vast landmass. Due to access limitations imposed by the Iron Curtain, it was practically impossible to recruit locals as informants, and even more difficult to infiltrate the country. The only way to gather intel about active missile sites and industrial expansion was from the air. This restriction led to the inception of the first spy plane, whose development program was codenamed Project Aquatone. The result was the Lockheed U-2."

"I've heard of that."

"Most people have. Most adults over the age of forty,

that is."

"Wasn't one of them shot down over Siberia."

"It was. The pilot, Gary Powers, bailed out and was captured. He spent a year and a half in Russian prison camps before he was exchanged for a KGB espionage agent. Anyway, due to its hush-hush nature, the spy plane program needed to operate from someplace that was remote and free from prying eyes. In 1955, site scouts examined Area 51 and found it ideal for their needs. The dry lake bed was the perfect landing field, the surrounding mountains created a natural barrier to intrusion, and the location was so far off the beaten track that the nearest tarred road was fifty miles away. The area could be reached only by four-wheel-drive vehicles with high ground clearance which, at that time, few civilians owned.

"The landing field was designated Groom Lake. Support facilities were constructed for base personnel, and house trailers were towed to the site to provide living accommodations for the permanent workforce. The U-2's were built in California and flown piecemeal to Area 51, where the fuselage, wings, and other components were assembled by Lockheed engineers. Civilian aircraft workers were flown into Area 51 every Monday morning, and flown back to California every Friday afternoon.

"The CIA doesn't have aeronauts, so they worked in conjunction with the Air Force, which assumed the responsibility of training the pilots, testing the planes, and flying the missions. The U-2 flew 500 miles per hour at 70,000 feet, and took photographs with a camera that was almost as big as a Volkswagen. The pictures had a ground resolution of less than five feet. Scores of U-2's were built over the years. Some have been retrofitted and are still in use today, although they quit operating out of Area 51 in 1959.

"Then came the Oxcart Program, in 1960. The Lockheed A-12 was faster and could fly higher than the U-2. Due to the configuration of the airframe, it wouldn't fit in the bay of a transport jet, so it had to be trucked to Area 51. The wings and engine nacelles were assembled on site. The A-12 became operational in 1964, but after one of them crashed under suspicious circumstances, the aircraft was scratched from the program.

"Other models and variants, particularly one known as the SR-71, hit the air in 1966. It flew strategic reconnaissance missions for a couple of years, until the entire spy plane program was phased out.

"The Air Force continued to study and develop aircraft designs with emphasis on stealth, and to build drones, bombers, and interceptors, but as I said before, the CIA was interested in gathering intelligence, not in aerial combat or bombing enemy targets.

"Afterward the CIA maintained a presence in Area 51, and kept control of the facilities, but with the advent of spy satellites, the agency left the wild blue yonder for the blackness of outer space. It was safer and more reliable to conduct black ops from orbit because satellites couldn't be shot down." She turned to Bryce. "My TS/SCI clearance doesn't give me access to subsequent Air Force secrets unless they entered the purview of CIA operations."

Bryce snickered. "You're well versed in clandestine history."

"I do my best. I know about the Flying Wing because my father was a sci-fi movie buff."

Bryce nodded.

Leibowitz grumbled. "What does that have to do with anything?"

"It was featured in the 1953 release of *The War of the Worlds*. The movie was somewhat prophetic in that the Flying Wing was used to drop an atomic bomb on the Martian invaders."

"You mean there were stealth bombers before the, uh, modern stealth bomber?"

Bryce took the torch. "Not exactly. Let me give you a little background. There are three kinds of aircraft development: conventional, unconventional, and radical. Aircraft design accelerated after World War Two. Conventional design can best be described as bigger better and faster. A good example is the B-47 Stratojet that the

Strategic Air Command employed during the Cold War. It was the aerial component of America's nuclear deterrent strategy. The other component was the nuclear submarine. Both were deployed with a nuclear arsenal that could retaliate against Soviet attack. Submarines could patrol submerged for months but aircraft could not remain airborne for more than a few hours until aerial refueling was perfected in 1954. Even then staying aloft was difficult and not fuel efficient.

"The Flying Wing was an unconventional design that originated in Nazi Germany. The Horten brothers, Reimar and Walter, completed construction of the first successful jet-propelled tailless aircraft in 1944. The advantage of the flying wing design was the lack of protruding control surfaces that reduced aerodynamic drag. The disadvantage was inherent instability. This was proven when the prototype crashed and killed its pilot. Modifications were still underway when the war ended. A pre-assembled unit was captured by U.S. military forces and smuggled out of Germany under the noses of the advancing Russian army.

"In 1947 the assembled aircraft was being flight tested at the Roswell Army Air Field when it was spotted and mistaken for a flying saucer which it closely resembled – "

"But you said a radar balloon – "

"I know what I said then. This is what I'm saying now. The radar balloon was the cover story because we didn't want the Russians to know the truth. The public had to be deceived in order to deceive the Russians who read American newspapers. I had to deceive you because I didn't know then that your participation with the project would be assured. You can take that as a compliment."

Leibowitz stared but made no comment.

"After all the press that the sighting received security was tightened and the Horten aircraft was flown only at night. The designs were turned over to Northup-Grumman because they had been experimenting with tailless aircraft since 1939 with a frustrating lack of success. A succession of so-called flying wings resulted from this collaboration including the YB-49 that was shown in *The War of the Worlds*. None of them operated with any degree of stealth. The focus was on the speed and altitude characteristics of the airframe. Technical difficulties and cost overruns eventually axed the program. Not that it was a dead-end mind you. The technology was re-utilized in later generations of similar designs such as the Northrup-Grumman B-2 Spirit that came to be known as the Stealth Bomber. So the taxpayers got their money's worth out of the research and development programs that were terminated prior to successful completion."

Leibowitz was not appeased. "So were you leveling with me about alien spacecraft?"

"Yes I was. What you see here is a radical design that is not based on alien technology."

Laila made a suggestion. "You should tell him about Project Blue Book."

Bryce squinted. "I suppose you know all about that too?"

"Oh, yes. The CIA conducted its own investigations into unidentified flying objects."

"Then why don't you tell him about both investigations: the Air Force's and the CIA's?"

"Okay." To Leibowitz: "As Bryce said earlier, the CIA gathers intel and the Air Force engages in combat. But in addition to fighting over foreign air space, the Air Force is also charged with protecting the American homeland, protectorates, and territories. When there's a threat of foreign invasion, the Air Force is mobilized in a protective capacity. In the 1940's, so many people reported UFO's that there was real concern about their origin. Their Earthly origin.

"The Air Technical Intelligence Center organized a special investigation team under the codename Project Blue Book. The CIA conducted its own investigations under the codename Ankleman. There was considerable overlap between Bluebook and Ankleman, but this overlap ensured that every base was covered – military bases as well as hypothetical bases.

"Thousands of sightings were investigated. Most were the result of over-imaginative individuals who saw uncommon shapes in common objects, or who morphed common shapes into disks. Other sightings turned out to be odd cloud formations or atmospheric disturbances that would have been ignored or merely witnessed with wonder prior to the flying saucer fad. Then there were weather balloons, low-flying aircraft seen obliquely, the planets Mercury and Venus and well-known stars seen through haze under conditions in which condensed water droplets distorted the size, shape, and color, and similar natural illusions and mirages. Newspaper hype and exaggeration stirred ingredients in a recipe for mass hysteria that fed on itself in a geometric loop. And an obsession was born.

"Even educated people were deluded by the flying saucer frenzy. Pilots chased radar blips that were nothing more than rain scatter on a screen. Law enforcement officers raced after the flashing lights of commercial aircraft close to the horizon. The streaks of meteors became contrails of alien spacecraft. Observers in low latitudes where auroras were seldom seen interpreted the colorful displays as some otherworldly invasion. Every unexplained observation of the firmament added fuel to the fire. Worst of all were outright hoaxes."

Bryce interjected: "In addition to the well-known Project Bluebook the Air Force later initiated a sister project known as UAP (Unidentified Aerial Phenomena) which was never released to the public because it's still in existence. The Air Force keeps constant tabs on any and all activity that occurs in American airspace. We're on the lookout for aliens all right but not the kind that come from Outer Space. Every intrusion is thoroughly investigated to make sure it's not a foreign aircraft bent on surveillance or attack. There's nothing in American skies that the Air Force doesn't know about."

Laila made the summation: "When all is said and done, there was no hard-fast evidence that aliens from other worlds were watching the planet or posed any threat to national security. And nothing has occurred in the decades since to change the official opinion. Or mine."

Leibowitz took a deep breath and opened his mouth to speak, but kept quiet for so long that he had to take another deep breath. "Okay, I believe you. That is, I accept your explanations for now. So what's the story with this – " he pointed down into the hangar. " – this flying saucer?"

Bryce grinned like the Cheshire cat. "This is a brain child that has been half a century in the making. It incorporates a number of radical designs none of which would work without complimentary components. I'll introduce you to the chief engineer who can take you on a quick tour before takeoff. I have christened her *Thermopylae.*"

Chapter 12

Bryce led the two-person entourage along the cat-walk and down a flight of steel grated steps to the concrete floor of the hangar. Flood lights flush-mounted in the undercarriage of the circular airframe illuminated features that couldn't be seen from above.

Most noticeable was the central pylon whose dimensions equaled those of the bulge on the rooftop. The saucer seemed to rest on this cylindrical pedestal. For balance, four sturdy outriggers in the shape of barber poles without the stripes were placed concentrically along the perimeter. These poles or legs shone like aluminum, but Laila guessed that they were made of titanium composite alloy: the strong but lightweight metal that NASA used on the space shuttles. For extra stability, four extensions or feet were splayed outward at the bottom of each leg; these feet could be retracted by means of hydraulic cylinders.

The middle of each leg was linked by means of a thick outboard shaft to a huge engine nacelle that was colorfully decorated in four likenesses, each one facing a cardinal point of the compass. Each nacelle presented one human face and three patch logos from various Air Force commands. Laila recognized Chuck Yeager and Scott Crossfield. She supposed that the other two faces were those of other early test pilots.

What appeared to be a pair of bomb bay doors were open, and airmen and women were working with a forklift and other equipment underneath them. Other bomb bay doors were sealed but were discernible by the slender lines that delineated their closures.

"Why aren't those enlisted people saluting you?" Leibowitz wanted to know.

Bryce nodded perfunctorily to the enlisted people in question. They nodded in return. "We're pretty layback around here. We all have our jobs to do and we don't need to interrupt them by following rules out of the Boy Scout handbook. We work together like a civilian corporation."

"But – but – what about the lack of respect?"

"I don't lack respect for them."

Leibowitz was nonplussed but kept his mouth shut.

Two young women dressed in utilitarian civilian garb were taking cartons off a palate jack and stacking them on the floor in the center of the pylon. They both smiled at Bryce's approach. One said, "We'll be done here in two minutes, sir."

"Take your time. Takeoff isn't for another hour. We'll take the stairs."

Bryce indicated the spiral staircase to Laila and Leibowitz. The stairs wound around the outside of the central compartment. Nine-inch risers were topped by twelve-inch treads that measured three feet in width. Laila accepted the prerogative to go first. She put her left hand on the polished plastic railing as she looked across the open center that was also bordered by four thick vertical stainless steel hydraulic cylinders. The stairs wound counterclockwise around the inside of the enclosure to a landing that was positioned in the middle of what was labeled B Deck. Bryce indicated for her to continue upward. She climbed to the upper deck, or A Deck, to what could best be described as a circular lobby from which corridors extended fanlike toward the aircraft's perimeter. The stairs continued up to another level, but Bryce motioned for her to exit.

"Danette is going through the last-minute checklist in the control cabin." He pointed to signs above the doorways. "We'll find Pat in the engineering shack."

Before they turned in the opposite direction, Laila detected movement from the stainless steel cylinder that stood next to her. She stepped back. The four cylinders were hydraulic tubes that were drawing the loaded platform up from the concrete pad to the loading deck below.

"The elevator rises to the operations deck too."

Bryce led the way along a corridor that was lined with clear acrylic partitions and doorless entrances. The compartments on either side were crammed with electrical panels, telemetry equipment, computer monitors, rows and columns of toggle switches, and banks of annunciator lights; it was much like the interior of a municipal sub-station. At the end of the corridor they walked into a similar compartment except that the outer wall was curved concave.

A tall man wearing a white lab smock over casual attire had his back toward them. He was studying printouts on a clipboard that he held in both hands. He turned around. His long face looked lugubrious until it split with a smile. "Bryce, how's it going?"

"I should be asking you that question."

"We're looking good and all systems are go. Are these our two secular consultants?"

Laila stepped forward with her right hand outstretched and placed it in Lacey's palm. "Laila Masterson."

"Pat Lacey." Angling his head: "And you must be Mr. Leibowitz."

"*Dr.* Leibowitz."

"If you say so." Lacey didn't bother to shake Leibowitz's hand. To Bryce: "If you need to help Danette with the countdown, I can give them the ten-cent tour of the misnamed *Thermopylae.*"

Bryce humphed. To Laila and Leibowitz: "We have an ongoing argument about the naming convention. Pat may be the inventor but I outrank him so I chose the name over his objection. When I was a kid I put together a model of the famous nineteenth-century clipper ship *Thermopylae.* In her day she was the fastest vessel afloat in the British tea trade with China."

"This is true, but what Bryce failed to consider is that the ship was named after a pass in Greece that became infamous during the Greco-Persian War, in 480 B.C., when King Leonidas and three hundred Spartans failed to defend the passage of the Persian army that was led by King Xerxes."

"Every battle has two sides so it could just as easily be said that the battle that was lost by the Greeks constituted a victory for the Persians."

"Except that the Greeks were the defenders and the Persians were the invaders."

Bryce shrugged. "I didn't name the vessel after the Battle of Thermopylae. I just liked the sound of the word. And this *Thermopylae* is more like a ship of the air than an aircraft."

Lacey slapped Bryce playfully on the shoulder. "He gave the model to his nephew with the proviso that he maintained visiting rights."

"Besides even though the Greeks lost the battle they eventually won the war and that's more important. Now if you will excuse me I will leave you two in the devious hands of our inventor and chief engineer."

"I'll see you post-landing," Lacey called after Bryce's retreating figure. "Our battle of *Thermopylae* is a friendly one. And even though he gives the orders he doesn't really outrank me, because I'm a civilian. How much did he tell you about the aircraft?"

"Nothing. He only revealed its existence to us a few minutes ago."

Grimacing: "That son of a gun. Left it all up to me, did he?" Lacey sighed. "Okay, then let me start by correcting a false impression that Bryce may have given you. I didn't invent the FS-1, to call it by its official designation. The plans have been on the drawing board for more than fifty years. Many drawing boards, I should say. What I did basically was to pull a lot of other people's ideas together: airframe designs, propulsion methods, even house plans for the interior layout."

"Buckminster Fuller," Leibowitz announced quietly.

"Go to the head of the class, Doctor of Philosophy."

Laila raised her eyebrows. She didn't know about Buckminster Fuller.

"Tell us more, Mr. Dr."

Leibowitz scowled but elaborated for Laila's benefit: "You're too young to remember the geodesic dome or the prefabricated dome homes. The basic dome was a sphere that was built from triangular panels that were interconnected like – like – like the honeycomb cells of a beehive. Its strength was derived from the pressure of each panel pressing against the neighboring panels." He glanced at Lacey. "Am – am – am I right?"

"You're doing just fine." To Laila: "The Roman arch operates on a similar principle."

Leibowitz scowled at the additional information. "Some were quite large – a couple of hundred a hundred feet across, and housed buildings or museums. Smaller ones were used to make houses that were light enough to be transported by helicopter – "

"I can picture it! The Air Force used them as radar domes, or radomes, to cover the dishes of the DEW line stations. Wow, I never really thought about it."

Leibowitz scowled at the interruption and kept quiet afterward.

Lacey: "Fuller engineered single family dwellings with a great room concept but the shape never caught on. The mobile home industry leaned toward the rectilinear house trailer, which could be uprooted more easily and towed from place to place. In any case, we used Fuller's curved interior layout as a model for the FS-1.

"Understand that the FS-1 was intended to be flown as a bomber with a small flight crew and a belly full of bombs. We've converted the bomb deck to living quarters and garages. The living quarters run all the way around the perimeter, so each stateroom has its own porthole. The four barrack rooms have two, but one of them doubles as a gun port for a fifty caliber machine gun for close quarter defense.

"The space between the living quarters and the core zone, as we call the center of the airframe, was compartmentalized for vehicle storage and retrofitted with lifting platforms in place of stationary bomb clamps. Because garages are rectangular and radial lines create pie slices, we converted the wedge-shaped interstices into lockers for food, supplies, ammo, and whatnot."

"War machine to peace machine," Laila opined. "Or swords into plowshares."

Lacey laughed. "The biblical connotation is appropriate under the circumstances, although we retained the chaff deployment lockers and defensive missile bays in case of aerial or surface-to-air attack.

"The airframe was fabricated from black polycarbonate: a durable shock-resistant thermoplastic resin whose rock-hardness, high tensile strength, and exceptional impact temper make it bullet- and bombproof when the gauge of the extruded sheet is thick enough."

"Like the Presidential limousine," Laila stated flatly.

"Ah, I wouldn't know about that."

"Did you have the hull material explosive tested at Harvey Point?"

"As a matter of fact, we did. How did you know . . . "

"The Harvey Point Defense Testing Facility is a CIA training and testing ground, although it's also used by the ATF and FBI in their counter-terrorism courses." To Leibowitz: "It's located outside of Elizabeth City, North Carolina, at the end of a peninsula that juts into the Albemarle Sound. Its two primary operational directives are testing the explosive resistance of newly developed materials, and testing the power of newly developed explosives."

Leibowitz made his favorite facial expression. "That – that sounds contradictory."

"In one way it is, but in another way it's complimentary. In simulated tests, the Presidential limousine has sustained multiple blasts from terrorist land mines and rocket blasts without significantly injuring the passenger."

Leibowitz was aghast. "You – you mean they blow up mines under a car with someone inside?"

"Yes, but only after it has been established that the chassis can withstand the blast. The explosions rattle windows and shake houses on stilts for twenty miles around. After all the taxpayers' money that's spent on elections, you wouldn't want the President to be killed prematurely, would you?"

"I don't know. I might make an exception with the current President."

"I didn't vote for him either." To Lacey: "The cab of the Presidential limousine is made of black polycarbonate. The windows are made of clear polycarbonate. Once when I was at Harvey Point, the explosives experts put a plaque inside the test vehicle that read "Better Living Through Chemistry."

Leibowitz humphed. "The old DuPont slogan."

Lacey laughed. "I didn't know the CIA had a sense of humor."

"You'd be surprised. Not everything in the Company is death, doom, and destruction the way Hollywood portrays it. Developing armor protection for troops in combat is a prime directive that's overlooked by the media because it doesn't sound as thrilling as clandestine operations that result in chaos in foreign countries."

"I can't disagree. Can I take it then that you have confidence in an airframe that has been harveyized, as we say?"

"Full confidence."

"Then the next thing I can tell you about is the, ah, somewhat peculiar hull configuration. Semi-saucer shapes have been around since the Hitler war."

"Bryce told us about the Horten brothers."

Lacey shook his head. "Ah, yes. They had jet engine and airframe design concepts that were way ahead of their time. It's too bad we weren't able to draft them like we did with Werner von Braun and the other German rocket scientists."

"He also told us about the Flying Wing."

"Ah, yes. That was an outgrowth of the Horton brothers semi-disk aircraft and a precursor of the B-2. The problem with the disk design has always been instability. Concurrent with the development of the various flying wing designs that led to the B-2, was research into ways to make a true disk stable without control surfaces such as elevators, rudders, and ailerons. Concepts were defeated by material deficiencies. Now that we have polycarbonate and its derivatives, we've employed an idea that was conceived long ago: the gyroscope.

"I don't need to plague you with mathematical proofs involving scalars and pseudovectors. Everyone who has ever ridden a bicycle knows how the gyroscope works. A bike that won't stand on its own when it's stationary will stay upright when it's moving. That's because the rotating wheels impart a flywheel effect: the reluctance to change direction due to the conservation of angular momentum. A child's spinning top demonstrates the same natural law.

"The gyroscopic principle has been known and understood since the early 1800's. It came into wide practical use during the Hitler war when the Sperry Company adapted the principle for shipboard use by inventing the gyrocompass. Today it's used primarily for inertial guidance systems in missiles.

"The system utilized in the FS-1 is the gyrostat. You know that a child's top starts to wobble as it winds down due to friction of the bottom point on the horizontal surface. The free end of the spindle describes a circle that's known as precession. A gyrostat stops precession by encasing the flywheel in a housing in which the top and bottom center sections are each secured in a circular frame of ball bearings. A near-frictionless condition is created by inducing spin on the frame of bearings. Once enough power is supplied to get the flywheel up to operational speed, very little additional power is needed to maintain horizontal stabilization."

Laila thought for a moment. "Are you describing something like a helicopter rotor in a sandwich?"

Lacey laughed. "I've never heard it put that way, but yes."

"Or a window fan in a wire frame so you don't get your finger cut off," Leibowitz added.

Lacey grimaced. "Not a very scientific description, but again, yes. I'll remember your comparisons when I'm allowed to write a monograph on the subject."

Leibowitz scowled. "The way the government works, that'll be next to never."

"Dr. Leibowitz!" Laila declared with mock mockery. "You're being optimistic." To Lacey: "So where is this spinning flywheel."

Lacey pointed his right index finger toward the ceiling. "About five feet over your hairy pate."

Leibowitz instinctively ducked and hunched his

shoulders. "Wha – wha – what?"

"The chamber has been sealed and evacuated to create a vacuum as another way to decrease friction. The flywheel assembly is more like a buzzsaw blade than a top with a spindle. The hole in the center measures twenty-five feet in diameter. Bordering the hole are the ball bearing frames. The droop at the extremity of the disk is measureable with a micrometer when the disk is at rest, but the disk straightens once the spin is induced. The tolerance is so fine that the chamber measures only six inches in height."

"What – what happens if the disk is fractured?"

"A good question. In engineering there is always the issue of material fatigue with age. In combat there is always the concern for damage due to, ah, combat. In essence, the combat concern is no different from damage suffered by any other aircraft. The FS-1 can be shot down. It has defensive armament as I already explained. It's greatest defense is altitude. The FS-1 was designed as a high-altitude aircraft that can fly higher than anything other than a space launch vehicle. It can defend itself from aerial attack with chaff and air-to-air missiles. Nothing is invulnerable and the FS-1 is no exception. But if it were to go operational in its bomber configuration, it would pose as much a threat to America's enemies as missile-launching submarines that rove the world's oceans. A fleet of such aircraft could roam the upper stratosphere on permanent patrol, swooping down only when it had to drop bombs on a specific target."

"But – but – but how can it stay up there so long? Does it go into orbit, or does it have helium-filled balloons?"

Lacey laughed. "That's a good segue, good doctor. The good answer is that the FS-1 is powered by a nuclear reactor."

There were two open jaws but no comments were forthcoming.

"The concept of nuclear propulsion goes back before the beginning of Area 51. The year after the Hitler war ended, Navy Captain Hyman Rickover conceived of powering submarines with nuclear reactors. In the 1940's, a reactor was the size of a small housing project. He managed to engineer a reactor that was small enough to fit into the hull of a submarine. His vision came to fruition with the launching of the *Nautilus* in 1954. The rest is history.

"After Rickover proved the feasibility of using nuclear reactors for propulsion, rocket scientists dreamed of powering spaceships the same way. These fantasies lollygagged along until the Ruskies launched Sputnik, in 1957. Then the country was thrown into a tizzy about getting into space in any way, shape, or form. A slew of projects were established to enter the space race. The proposed nuclear reactor spaceship was codenamed Project Orion.

"Area 25 was selected as the launch site. The grandiose plan called for a monster hull that towered more than a hundred and fifty feet tall. According to its proponents, the vehicle could not only fly to the Moon, but could go all the way to Mars in two months flat. This pipedream turned into a fiscal nightmare. The result was a spacecraft that never flew off the drawing board.

"In 1963, budget cuts shelved the project as far as Congress was concerned. They put all their faith in liquid fuel rockets. But the Air Force took over and the project went underground – literally. A huge tunnel complex was dug out of a mountain, and large chambers were excavated to house preliminary models. Hidden funds came from NASA, but the majority of the money was contributed by the Atomic Energy Commission, under the guise of research and development for an efficient energy-producing reactor. By similar sleight of hand and prestidigitation, the Air Force diverted funds to the project under the guise of R and D for a fuel-efficient aircraft engine.

"This so-called new project was codenamed NERVA: nuclear engine rocket vehicle application. Even Congress didn't know what it was about. Ironically, the first practical application that resulted from the project was a small-scale reactor that was used to generate electricity for the project. That enabled the project to cut back on power that was channeled through Nellis from Las Vegas."

Laila nodded and smiled. "So low electricity usage disguised the growth of the project."

"Exactly. The project seemed small to outside investigators but was growing exponentially behind subterranean doors."

Laila turned to Leibowitz: "A respectable return on the taxpayers' investment."

Leibowitz scowled.

Lacey continued: "Unfortunately, the development of a nuclear powered engine was bogged down by technical difficulties. We couldn't use jet engines on the FS-1 because they require fuel to create thrust by discharging fast moving particles through a combustion chamber. That would limit the endurance capability to the size of the fuel tank. We needed a fuelless engine, or one that didn't need to be refueled on a short-term basis. The project languished, proceeded by fits and starts throughout the decades, then was re-energized when the Space Shuttle program was terminated. Stronger materials combined with advanced nuclear propulsion technology enabled engine designers to finally achieve what they had been fantasizing about.

"With a nuclear reactor to provide power for the propulsion system, as well as for everything else in the aircraft, and a fuel cell of enriched uranium, the FS-1 has a flight duration of twenty-two years." Lacey ignored the gasps and widened eyes. "As in nuclear submarines, the actual duration is limited by food and water reserves for the crew. But we're working on a way to transfer commodities from aerial freighters and tankers. That way a female crewmember could conceive, give birth, and have her child reach voting age before the aircraft had to land."

"Wow!" Laila exclaimed. "The *Thermopylae* is better than Tom Swift's *Flying Lab*."

Chapter 13

Laila recognized Bryce's voice on the public address system: "To all personnel, all systems look good so we'll be taking off in fifteen minutes."

Lacey glanced at his watch. "Sorry, folks, but I've got to join the crew in the Bubble."

Laila cocked a thin eyebrow. "The bubble?"

"That's what we call the bulge on top of the saucer, where the redundant reactors are housed. Not that they need me up there. They have the situation well in hand. It's a matter of protocol. That's my duty station. Come with me."

Leibowitz was aghast. "I'm not going into a room with a nuclear reactor."

"I couldn't permit it anyway. What I meant was I'll escort you to the core zone and direct you to the navigating bridge."

A few seconds later they entered the circular lobby. The two civilian gals Laila had seen stowing cartons were raising the elevator and staircase into the body of the aircraft, leaving support of the aircraft on the four leg extensions. They nodded as they trundled a handcart with the last of the cartons into a side corridor.

Lacey pointed straight ahead. "You'll be guests of the flight crew." He climbed the spiral staircase to the upper level.

When Laila looked up diagonally, she noticed that the steps didn't stop at the next floor, or deck, but continued around the lead-lined containment vessel to the top of the Bubble. She turned to Leibowitz. "Let's go see our tax dollars at work."

He scowled.

Like the corridor that led to the engineering shack, this one was bordered by clear acrylic partitions that sectioned off a large compartment on either side. Computer carrels were peopled by technicians whose concentration was so intense that none looked up at Laila's and Leibowitz's passage. Laila now realized how the clear partitions imparted the impression of Buckminster Fuller's great room concept. She suspected that this was more a matter of practicality than homage to the designer. A clear view across the interior facilitated visual communication while enabling awareness of surroundings in case of trouble.

Laila stopped at the entryway to the bridge. The broad open space beyond was shaped like an orange slice. Windows curved around forty-five degrees of arc. Four seats faced the windows. Bryce and Danette occupied the center two seats; a technician sat in one of the outboard seats. Unlike a conventional aircraft, this one had no steering wheel or control pedals. Duplicate controls in front of Bryce and Danette consisted of joysticks and a vast array of toggle switches, push buttons, hand wheels, and annunciator lights below the windows, and monitor screens above the windows.

A second row of seats occupied the space behind the operators' seats: three in number and offset so that each had a clear view ahead: much in the way bowling pins were arranged. Laila held onto the entry jamb but did not enter the bridge. Leibowitz stood by her side. Nick Derpilbosian turned, put a finger to his lips, then stood up from the center rear seat and tiptoed across the soft carpet to the back of the bridge, where computer modules spread across the straight edge of the partition on both sides of the entryway.

He whispered, "They are in the final stages of countdown and should not be disturbed. We can talk quietly until the imminent takeoff announcement. Then we must buckle into the spectator seats."

Leibowitz acknowledged Father Nick's glance with an unpleasant nod.

Laila was softly voluble. "I don't know what to talk about. I'm overwhelmed. And I'm ecstatic to be here in America's most secret aircraft."

With a humph: "Another billion tax dollars wasted."

Father Nick smirked. "More like four billion, but that is neither here nor there. I believe that the crusade for worldwide peace is well worth the expenditure."

"That's because you're not paying for it."

"Perhaps."

Laila was about to ask a question when the technician rose and walked her way. He was past middle age with longish graying hair and eyes to match. He tilted his head toward Leibowitz. "I've already met the wicked witch of the west. You must be Ms. Masterson."

She nodded. "The small and meek." Again no one acknowledged her movie association, despite Kreider's specific reference to the 1939 classic.

He held out his hand. "I'm Lucius Kreider. Call me Luke."

"Laila." Kreider's handshake was firm but not crushing. "What's your part in this parade?"

Leibowitz pushed past Kreider and slunk in the farthest spectator seat.

"I've already sparred with Dr. Irascible. So far we're tied." His stout upper body shook as if a spider had crawled up his neck. "They've given me a brevet promotion to navigator. After we wind back the clock, my knowledge of calculated star positions will supposedly aid in nighttime navigation."

"You're the astronomer."

"Guilty as charged."

"What's it like back there?"

Kreider crossed his eyebrows.

"I've read your report. It was clear, concise, and scientific, but lacked the human touch."

"They don't pay me to display emotion." He leaned close and reduced the volume of his whisper. "Between you, me, and the good father here – it was a helluva rush. I've made four trips so far, to shoot star positions in order to calibrate the time clock. The transfer is disturbing – kinda like dropping down a curved track on a rollercoaster. But being there! Back in time! It was an unparalleled intellectual thrill that I wouldn't have believed possible if I hadn't plotted the star positions myself. I was *there*. Two thousand years ago! I confirmed it myself."

Kreider's whisper crescendoed toward the end of his

monologue but no one seemed to notice. He shushed himself before continuing. "By the way, where'd you get that shiner?"

Laila twisted her mouth. "From a bout with Leibowitz. He lost his balance in the Stealth. It was an accident."

"I'd like to give him a shiner, and not by accident. But I do believe the little bastard can break the time code. I didn't let on to him, but I think we've pinned down the time frame to within a couple of weeks. Certainly less than a month. Have you seen the Scrolls?"

"Only the cover sheet."

"One page has a drawing that shows the Star of Bethlehem along with some of the brighter stars that were visible from Jerusalem. The chart isn't dated because they didn't have dates back then, but he's translated parts of other pages that provide a rough time frame from Christ's birth to death. I've created a crude star chart by taking modern star positions and retrogressing their movements within the Galaxy, and by taking the contemporary star positions shown on the Scrolls and progressing them forward. Makes me feel more like an astrologer than an astronomer, but hey, it seems to be working."

Father Nick whispered, "It was the translation and representation of the Star of Bethlehem that led Vatican scholars to infer that the Scrolls constituted a biography of the Son of God that was not included in the Gospels."

"In astronomical circles, it's long been conjectured that the bright star that was observed over the manger during the nativity was a supernova. But no supernova remnants have ever been discovered that match the approximate location, so that seemed to rule it out. Other people have suggested that a planetary alignment or a comet created the bright light that led the magi to Bethlehem. Again, there's no evidence to support those suppositions. With my computer simulation I've backtracked the orbits of the planets and found that no conjunctions occurred in the decades surrounding the birth. The same goes for comets, although to be fair, comets sometimes disappear after they lose too much of their mass: swept away by the solar wind. And anyhow, ancient astronomers were too well versed in cosmological phenomena to be fooled by the presence of a short-duration comet. In addition to which, a comet was perceived as an omen of the death of a king, not the glory of the coming of the Lord."

Laila nodded. "So this is where your Chinese connection gave you some insights and got you selected for your position in the Project."

"You read my resume."

"I did my homework." Laila yawned. The lack of sleep and the change in her circadian rhythm were catching up with her: much like jet lag. "Some of it, anyway."

"Good. That saves a lot of explanation. The Chinese – "

Kreider stopped talking when the public address system squawked: "All personnel, this is your captain speaking. Takeoff is on schedule and will initiate in two minutes. Please buckle up."

Laila heard Danette's announcement in stereo: her real voice from one side and her broadcast voice over a corridor loudspeaker from the other.

"We had better sit down." Father Nick returned to his center seat.

Laila sat next to him. Kreider resumed his position to Bryce's right. They all fastened their seat belts and safety harnesses. Laila heard a faint whining sound overhead. She presumed that Danette was revving up the gyroscope. She could see out the window straight ahead by looking between Bryce and Kreider. The hangar door opened by splitting in the middle and then folding to the left and right like the corrugations of a concertina.

The outside sky was black except for pinpoints of light that twinkled in the desert heat above the distant low mountains. A faint deep-throated roar signaled an increase of power on the nuclear engines. The *Thermopylae* moved forward out of the hangar and over the apron onto the tarmac. The aircraft executed a slow left turn onto the runway, and stopped.

Danette and Bryce checked the instrument panels while Kreider idled.

"Commencing liftoff," Danette announced.

The engine roar increased slightly. The *Thermopylae* rose into the air so slightly that Laila wasn't aware of any motion at all until she noticed a change in the angle of the horizon. The aircraft continued to rise straight up for a hundred feet before a lateral component was added to the movement. Laila realized suddenly that the FS-1 flew like a Harrier jump jet, employing the technique of vertical takeoff and landing.

Both ascent and forward motion increased incrementally without intermittent jerks. The *Thermopylae* plowed upward and ahead along a gentle curve without changing the angle of the floor. Digital readouts displayed altitude, distance from start, rate of ascent, and a hundred other items that Laila couldn't begin to interpret.

The ride was smoother than one in a new elevator car. Laila ventured mentally that a marble placed on the thin-pile carpet would not have rolled farther than its own diameter. "Is it time to applaud?"

Danette glanced over her shoulder. Her face was bathed in perspiration. She returned to the controls without wiping the glistening beads off her smooth black skin.

Bryce unlocked his seat and spun it around on its swivel base. He signaled one thumb up. "The pilot is too occupied to pay attention to her guests."

"The pilot!" Leibowitz screamed. "I thought *you* were the pilot."

"What made you think that?"

"You – you – you outrank her."

Bryce stared at Leibowitz with evident disdain that lasted no more than a split second. His features softened. "Dr. Leibowitz I understand you're unfamiliar with military protocol so let me explain. Rank has two distinctions: position in the chain of command and pay grade. A colonel outranks a captain as you noted correctly. An officer's rank specifies the number of personnel under his command and is not related to her operational specialty.

"I'm in charge of everyone under my command but I don't know how to do their jobs. When I need things done I give orders to those who can do them. I piloted the aircraft that brought you here and Captain Stackhouse flew as my copilot because she had less flight time with that aircraft and was not as familiar with its flight characteristics as I am. Now the situation is reversed. Captain Stackhouse has more hours on the FS-1 flight simulator than I have because I've had administrative responsibilities with regard to this mission that have occupied much of my time."

Leibowitz nodded perfunctorily. "That – that makes sense."

"Sit back and enjoy the flight. Even though Captain Stackhouse has never flown this aircraft I have complete confidence in her abilities." Bryce spun his chair to face the control panels.

"Whoa – whoa – whoa. You just said that she had more flight time than you."

Bryce swung back to Leibowitz. "I said that she had more hours on the simulator. This is a test flight. The first test flight. What they call sea trials in the navy."

"You – you mean – this plane has never been in the air before?"

"Correct."

"You – you – you mean to take me out on an untried airplane?"

Bryce paused before replying. "I'm surprised at your attitude. I thought you would have been thrilled to participate in the *Thermopylae's* inaugural flight. Besides all the systems have been checked out on the ground and the reactor has been operational for several months." He spun back to the control panel.

Laila could not help but smile at Leibowitz's discomfort.

The flight proceeded smoothly as Danette and Bryce tested the various controls, systems, and subsystems.

They received performance reports from other areas of the aircraft. While Danette handled the flight controls, Bryce checked off a multiple-page punch list and kept notes on a clipboard. Leibowitz fidgeted uncontrollably for an hour. Laila, Kreider, and Father Nick maintained silence so as not to interfere with delicate operations.

Laila enjoyed the view through the widescreen window. She marveled at the way the aircraft rotated so that the forward view changed slowly, as the airframe turned on its horizontal axis. The engines must have been fitted with noise-reduction devices like those employed on Stealth bombers, because the occasional clatter from flipping switches generated more sound than the soft background whoosh that reminded her of the Whisper-cat.

Finally Bryce spun around and faced the three guests. "So far everything looks pretty good. We've got a few bugs to iron out but nothing too serious. Any questions before we try some radical tilting maneuvers?"

Laila raised her hand like a grade school student. "Two. The aircraft didn't have any visible wheels, nor did I see a tractor transporter, so how did the *Thermopylae* roll out of the hangar. And Pat Lavery didn't explain how the aircraft turns in the air. I didn't see any rudders. Yet we've been swinging about with hardly any centrifugal force."

"Good questions both. First the *Thermopylae* didn't roll out of the hangar. She flew in what is called pre-liftoff mode. After the gyroscope reaches operational speed microvernier thrust controls enable the pilot to tweak the engines with sufficient power to lift them off the ground." He pointed to a row of four digital screens that currently were blank. "Those readouts display ground clearance in centimeters when needed. The engines are then tilted to impart a horizontal component while automatic levelers compensate for minor variations in thrust between engines.

"Second the engines double as rudders the way they do on a motorboat. Turning the engines on their horizontal plane results in a change in the direction of the aircraft's forward motion. The turning radius is reduced by applying more thrust on the engines. Exhaust deflectors prevent damage to the pair of rear engines during straight flight. Intermittent exhaust cutouts prevent damage during a turn."

Laila imitated Leibowitz's words if not his diction and method of delivery: "That makes sense." Across Father Nick to Leibowitz: "Doesn't that make sense?"

Leibowitz scowled. "I never heard of a motorboat putting its weight on its driveshaft the way this plane rests on its engines."

Bryce rolled with the punch. "An excellent observation that shows you're paying attention to details. What looked like a cowling is a reinforced nacelle that encapsulates the engine. The weight of the aircraft is distributed along the nacelle's circular wall to the footpads extending outward from the edge of the exhaust port. The footpads spread the weight across the ground like skids on a helicopter."

Leibowitz's expression didn't change.

"Bryce." Danette motioned to him with her head. She managed a weak smile for Laila. "I'm ready for the tilt test."

Bryce nodded. To the guests: "Radical turns can be effected by reducing the gyroscope's revolutions per second so the gyroscopic effect can be overcome by decreasing thrust on the engines in the direction of the turn and increasing thrust on the engines away from the turn. This tilts the horizontal axis into the turn the way a fixed-wing or rotary aircraft banks. It's a difficult maneuver." He patted Danette on the back. "You can do it."

Danette didn't demonstrate the same degree of confidence – or *any* degree of confidence. Nonetheless, she executed the maneuver with smooth precision. Despite the tilt of the deck, centrifugal force prevented Laila from sliding in her seat. She noticed that the compass heading, whose numbers in the display panel were larger than any others, indicated that they had turned one hundred eighty degrees.

Bryce looked back. "According to the GPS we'll be

landing in thirty-two minutes." To Danette: "Good job girl. I knew you could do it."

Danette finally wiped sweat off her brow. The droplets soaked her flight-suit sleeve. "That makes one of us."

Chapter 14

When Laila got out of her new bed late in the morning she was still out of sync with the rest of the world. Her clothes and personal possessions were stacked on the counter. They made a very small pile. Rather than don her laundered street clothes, she opted for another pair of hospital scrubs. They were lightweight and comfortable and looked good with her jogging shoes. She had already gotten used to her casual uniform.

Instead of going to the security shack to work, she decided to stay in her room and use her personal computer to compose emails and reply to previously downloaded emails that needed her attention. Later she could log into the base security system and synchronize her email account to both send her replies and receive new messages. She wanted to minimize her stints with Varvarelis. As long as her room had a coffee brewer and a few packets of crackers, she could work there for days without feeling the need to leave.

The day passed with few interruptions. Her walkie-talkie was silent, but she entertained two guests. She felt keen anticipation when she heard the first barely audible knocks.

"The door's unlocked."

Wendayne Robbins slipped quietly into the room. She was wearing kitchen whites and a white mesh cap. "Miss Laila, you sho nuf look lovely in them hospital scrubs."

She masked her disappointment. "Thanks, Wendayne. And since we're alone in here there's no need to talk like an Alabamy mammy."

Wendayne laughed. "Shucks, Miss Laila. I'm so used to being in character on the job that I forget to get out of it. Prob'ly a good thing. Did you git – I mean, did you get my email?"

"I didn't. Instead of going to the office I'm working in today."

"Keeping away from the lech, huhn?"

Laila snickered. "I can handle him. So what was in your email?"

"When was a good time for a confab. When I didn't receive a reply, I figgered – I mean, I figured I stop by before the lunch crowd arrived, and pass along some gossip that I picked up in the canteen."

"Intel by any other name would smell as sweet."

Wendayne placed a paper bag on the table that Laila was using as a desk. She perched on the edge of the unmade bed. "I don't have anything earthshaking. But as I've learned in this business, sometimes the tiniest clues break the biggest cases. There's a breakfast sandwich and some crescent rolls for you. You can heat the sandwich in your microwave."

Laila removed a roll from the bag and nibbled on it. "All the comforts of home except for my cat."

"You may be home before you know it. They've pushed up the schedule because that testy translator has hit paydirt. Or so Kreider seems to think."

"You mean he may actually be worth the quarter of a mil that the taxpayers paid him."

Wendayne guffawed. "Lordy lordy lordy. You don't like him either."

"If you can't say anything nice about a person, don't say anything, as my granma used to say, so I'm keeping mum."

Wendayne guffawed again. "My granny would have used harsher words with a different meaning. She wasn't as forgiving as yours. Especially if she was wearing one of his shiners. She read her *Bible* and believed in a black eye for a black eye."

Laila grinned between nibbles.

"If you're looking for some action, Varvarelis has got a crush on you."

"I'm not looking for *his* action."

"His wife is, though. She called to complain about the lockdown. She hasn't seen him for a week, and when she called she learned that the lockdown has only been enforced for the past three days. And I didn't hear that from Varvarelis."

"You heard it from one of the female guards?"

Wendayne nodded. "She answered the phone and got an earful before she passed it along to her boss." Switching subjects: "Lavery got a speeding ticket in Vegas the day before the lockdown. He said he was eager to spend his, and I quote, 'last remaining minutes in this zip code for who knows how long,' unquote, with his family before the big trip through time."

"I can't blame him for that."

"Neither can I. I made sure I got some quality time before the lockdown."

"Wendayne!"

"I say it like it is."

"Est quod est, as the Romans used to say. It is what it is."

"Times haven't changed despite the passage." On another subject: "Walter Gouty grumbled about not being allowed time off – strange wording for a man who invented a time machine – because he wants to attend a symposium in Prague. The focus of the symposium is on quantum mechanics, particle physics, and high-speed cyclotron bombardment, which constitute the fundamental principles behind the Timepiece, so he has every reason to attend. Gouty's personal focus is on a certain female physicist named Romy Idacula, from India. As I said, he has every reason to attend. He and she have been collaborating, if you know what I mean."

"Your granma would probably have said cohabitating."

"No way. My granny would have used a four-letter word starting with eff and ending in eye en gee."

Laila snickered. "Yes, I suppose she would."

"Well, I's better practice ma Kentucky drawl an' be gittin' along so y'all kin git back to yer work."

"You're from Tennessee. I read your resume."

"Don' tell nobody, y'hear." Wendayne slipped quietly out the door.

Laila's next visitor was Luke Kreider. It was midafternoon when he brought her a vegetable platter and a tub of yogurt. He was so exuberant that as soon as he entered her room and put the food tray on the table, he threw his hands into the air and yelled, "Hallelujah."

Laila couldn't help but share his exuberance, even though she didn't know the reason for his excitement. "You're in a good mood."

"He's done it! The little bastard has done it."

Laila wasted no time in plunging into the food. "He pinpointed the date?"

"To within a week. Maybe two. But wandering for a fortnight is better than wandering for forty years the way Moses did."

"That's because he was a man and wouldn't ask for directions."

"How can you joke at a time like this, if you'll pardon the timely pun. I was so ecstatic that I almost kissed the little bastard on the bald spot under his yamaka. His interpretation of the symbols on the Cave 12 Scrolls coincided perfectly with stellar observations made by Chinese astronomers in the month of the birth of Christ. That was what I started to tell you on the *Thermopylae*. But he's gone much farther now.

"The ancient Chinese were way ahead of the rest of the world in many ways: science, invention, philosophy, social organization, and so on. There was no other civilization in the history of the world that could build a stone roadway on top of a monstrous wall that stretched for thousands of miles through untrammeled wilderness. No civilization could build such a wall today."

Laila humphed. "No doubt because of cost overruns. The Chinese didn't have to contend with unions and politicians."

Kreider did not acknowledge her insertion.

"Chinese armies were launching rockets at their enemies two millennia before the famous red glare soared over Fort McHenry. Confucius laid down his system of principles to ten times as many people as were ever aware of the writings of Socrates and Plato. And Chinese astronomers knew more about the heavens than all the ancient western civilizations put together. We just never had access to eastern cultural materials until recently, so we were basically ignorant of Chinese history and astronomical data. They recorded several supernovas – which they called 'guest stars' – that went unnoticed by western astronomers, and not only because those short-lived lights in the sky weren't visible on the European side of the planet, but because the ancient Chinese were more consistent and careful observers. Or recorders," he allowed. "This was especially true during the Han dynasty, which lasted from 206 BC to 220 AD."

Laila realized that Kreider was so enraptured by his newfound knowledge that it would be inconsiderate of her to keep interrupting him with trifling quips and flippant comments. Therefore she kept to herself her disdain of ancient western astronomers who looked up at the Big Dipper and saw a bear that they named Ursa Major. What did they inhale in those of days of antiquity?

"When President Nixon opened trade relations with the People's Republic of China in 1972, he unwittingly paved the road for cultural communication between eastern and western civilizations: a sharing of information about each other's past and historical achievements. The Chinese were content to let their history lie fallow: they were more interested in where they were going than where they had been. Despite this collective attitude of disregarding the past, long ignored Chinese texts that had been stored in stone vaults for uncounted centuries were brought to light solely because of western inquisitiveness."

Kreider neglected to mention that he was one of those prime inquisitors. As a young college student at the time of Nixon's negotiation coup, he recognized the potential benefits to astronomy that could be derived from scrutinizing ancient Chinese astrological charts and cosmological observations. His master's thesis was written with this thought in mind: "Comparison of Annotations of the Crab Nebula Supernova Observed by Arabic and Song Dynasty Astronomers in 1054 A.D."

After he earned his Bachelor of Science degree, he

pursued his Ph. D. by learning the Chinese language at the University of Peking. Years of study made him an expert at interpreting pictographic ideograms in ancient Chinese texts that related to the astrological interpretation of zodiacal phenomena as portents of evil. His dissertation ignored the spiritual fancies and noted only those astronomical events that could be corroborated by Babylonian, Greek, or Arabic observations.

His entire career then concentrated on itemizing unusual Chinese observations that could *not* be confirmed by other ancient astronomers, and searching for them in the sky using both optical and radio telescopes in his quest to add eastern knowledge to western catalogues of ancient astronomical events.

"I have found Chinese texts and charts that were so detailed that they recorded not just an anomalous event but the positions of the planets and the phases of the moon as they existed *during* the event. The Cave 12 Scrolls provide similar data as a way of establishing timeframes for biblical events before the invention of the Christian calendar. They lack the precision of ancient Chinese observations but the timeframes are closely substantiated."

Truly this was no time for jesting but for rejoicing. Munching: "So he was worth the investment after all."

"And then some. Even though he's quite enamored with himself and his ability to translate ancient Hebrew text that no one else could translate, he's worth every bit of forbearance I've had to suffer." Kreider grimaced and shook his head. "He even took the time to show me where the Vatican scholars went wrong, and why." He spread his hands. "The analogy he used was block printing compared to cursive writing.

"In block printing every letter is essentially the same and easily identifiable. In longhand, each scribe writes with a distinctive style or flow to connect one letter to the next. These differences range from ornate calligraphy to scribble to scrawl to illegible chicken scratch that doctors put on prescription forms. A tiny serif on a Hebrew character could be nothing more than an ink spot

– or it can change the meaning or context of the word. Okay, I'm exaggerating, but you get the point."

Laila nodded.

"The Dead Sea Scrolls were transcribed by individuals whose handwriting differed to a slight degree. They also made typographical errors. Leibowitz's studies found differences and similarities in the written text of the known Scrolls, which he then applied to the text on other Scrolls. That was why his translations sometimes contrasted sharply with accepted dogma. He translated portions of the Cave 12 Scrolls as if he had graduated cum laude from an Evelyn Wood fast-reading course. He put the Vatican scholars to shame.

"This isn't to say that he deciphered every passage as if it were cut from a first-grade reader, but compared to most translators of ancient Hebrew, he's a whiz kid. He's working on the last scroll now. The Scrolls he's already translated contain a rough chronology of the life of Christ from the moment of his birth to the time he became a prophet, then more detailed accounts to the year preceding his Crucifixion. Dialogues ascribed to Pontius Pilate provide an almost monthly reconstruction of Judaic events during his prefecture. Reports become weekly and finally daily when the Crucifixion became imminent."

"So he did in days what the Vatican scholars couldn't do in years."

"That's about the size of it. I just hope he completes the task before he collapses from exhaustion. The only relief he's had from the Scrolls is the *Thermopylae's* test flight and a few catnaps. He's a driven workaholic if there ever was one. I've put in a few overnighters – all astronomers do – but never two in a row. If Wendayne hadn't delivered refreshments I doubt if he would have stopped to eat."

Still munching: "Maybe we should stroll to the Scroll room and catch him when he falls."

"Not a bad idea."

Laila shoveled the remaining food into her mouth, then locked down her computer. She followed Kreider out of the room. The corridor was deserted because all personnel were working at their duty stations. Leibowitz took no notice of their presence when they entered the Scroll room. He was wearing blue hospital scrubs like Laila's, but his tousled hair ruined the effect of neatness. The grocery bags under his eyes hung halfway down his cheeks.

"Dr. Leibowitz?"

Although his computer was perched next to him, Leibowitz was furiously taking notes on a ruled legal pad. It looked like indecipherable code to Laila. He did not react to Kreider's call.

Louder: "Dr. Leibowitz."

Slowly Leibowitz turned his head. His eyes looked like road maps that were drawn with red squiggly lines. "I – I – "

Laila forced a smile on her face. "You look like something the cat dragged in, as my granma used to say."

A single nod accompanied a drawn-out squint. He dropped his pencil then rested his palms on the edge of the table. "The last Scroll is signed – by the person who claims – to be the one true disciple."

His arms were shaking with strain. He nearly fell onto the table top when his bent elbows gave way. He caught himself, managed to push up and lock his elbows, then stood upright with his hip leaning against the table edge. His expression was one of shocked disbelief.

"His name is – Judas Iscariot."

Chapter 15

There was general rejoicing among Project personnel. News of the completed translation spread at the speed of light – literally, as walkie-talkies were used to communicate the tidings, and radio waves propagate at the theoretical limit.

Father Nick was both astonished and regretful. "Of all the times to relieve myself, it had to be the very moment when Dr. Leibowitz translated the author's signature. But really, I just could not hold it in any longer."

Kreider laughed. "When you gotta go, you gotta go."

Laila shoved another forkful of spinach salad into her mouth, chewed, and swallowed. "I wish you had been there, too. Then maybe you would have caught him when he passed out."

"I barely got around the table in time to slow his fall."

"At least you prevented his head from striking the deck plates."

"Yesterday I would have said, 'Let the little bastard drop.' But after his revelation I had nothing but admiration for him. I hate to admit it, but he really is the best there is, just like he he's been telling everyone he meets."

Father Nick was eating potato soup and trying not to slurp around the chunky cubes. "Once he got into the flow of deciphering the symbols, his fascination with the text subdued some of his natural arrogance. His whole personality changed to what I would forgivingly classify as scientific curiosity. At first he demonstrated annoyance at my requests for elaboration as he ascribed English substitutes for letters and words, as if he thought that I was questioning his judgment about his facile interpretations. After a while, though, he started to express his thought processes out loud, and even condescended to explain to me how he interpreted certain symbols differently from the way our Vatican scholars interpreted them, especially when I pointed out those differences to him in a noncritical manner."

Kreider snickered. "That must have taken the patience of Job. He interprets everything as a criticism. Even compliments. On the other hand, except for a mean scowl, he lets comments go over his head like the joke about the ceiling."

"Yes, he did test my tolerance on more than one occasion. I found that by not taking his denigration personally I could maintain objectivity on the task at hand, and excuse his reprehensible behavior. I soon learned – "

Wendayne interrupted with a tray full of plates and dishes that were filled with succulent comestibles. "Here's yore steak, Mr. Luke. Medium rare jus' the way you like it. Liver and onions for Mr. Nick. And scrumptious vegetable soup for Miss Laila."

Kreider sniffed the steak with approval. "Wendy, your dinners are the highlight of my day."

"Don't you go gettin' familiar wiff me, callin' me by a pet name."

"If you didn't have a ring on your finger I'd ask you to marry me. And not just for your cooking."

"Why, Mr. Luke, if it weren't fer the ring on my finger I do believe I'd consider your proposal. An' not just so's I could cook fer you."

Everyone laughed at the banter.

Laila asked, "Will any of the others be joining us?"

"No ma'am. They got some kinda nighttime ground maneuvers they're practicin'. Hovercraft Ah think they're testin'. Dick Tracy stuff they call these toys. You'll see 'em some other time. An' Mr. Leibowitz won't be joinin' you neither, 'though I got a call from the medics that're 'tendin' him, an' they say he's gonna be a-okay. Jus' sufferin' from lack o' sleep an' dehydration an' extreme exhaustion. They got him on a saline drip, an' Ah sent over a whole pot o' hot broth an' a gallon o' sweet tea. He'll be alright. The bad news is he's just as ornery as ever. I dasn't say anything bad about that person, 'specially after what he done, but he wrinkles my fur like a cat that was rubbed backward."

The laughter was universal.

Laila said, "I couldn't have said it better myself."

Wendayne winked and returned to the kitchen.

Father Nick picked up where he left off: his supper as well as his dialogue. "As I was saying, I soon learned that what elevates Dr. Leibowitz above other translators is his talent for comprehending nuances in the ancestral Hebrew language. I do not claim to have any expertise in the Hebrew alphabets. I was not one of the Vatican paleographers who – "

"Excuse me. Paleographer?"

"Yes, my dear. Paleography is a multi-faceted discipline that incorporates all manner of studies relating to historical documents. As I think I mentioned, the Vatican possesses a vast repository of scrolls, papyri, and codices – mostly relating to ancient Christian writings – as well as a department of scholars to date and decipher them. We have one of the best equipped forensic laboratories in the world. Anyway, as I was saying – "

"Before you were so rudely interrupted."

Father Nick favored Laila with a smile. "I did not work on the translations. I was selected for this mission because, as a member of the Vatican's Committee for Historical Science, my knowledge of the life of Christ, his teachings, and the time in which he lived was my particular area of expertise. I am also conversant in Latin so I can speak with any Romans that we may encounter along the way.

"Anyway, before I so rudely interrupted myself, I was saying that Dr. Leibowitz finally came around to explaining why his translations differed from those of other scholars. I must admit that I could not apprehend the nonuniformities in the original text, but he provided analogies that made it clear as to why his translations differed from previous one. Just as certain English words have more than one meaning, so do certain Hebrew words have multiple meanings. Such words must be interpreted in relation to their context.

"He used the English word 'brig' as a crude but simple example. The word 'brig' has two meanings. It can refer either to a sailing vessel or to a military prison. The word in isolation cannot be accurately defined, or translated. The meaning of the word can be deciphered only in context with surrounding words. But the definition of the phrase 'in the brig' is also undefinable. That phrase can mean either 'onboard a sailing vessel' or 'incarcerated in a military prison.'

"The same lack of definition may be true for a complete sentence, such as one that reads 'The man is in the brig.' In this case the man may be either below deck in a sailing vessel or locked inside a military prison. Other words have more than two meanings, sometimes dozens or scores. This makes their translation all the more difficult. A person with a preconceived notion of what he wants a word or sentence to mean is placed at a disadvantage in arriving at a bona fide translation.

"This problem is exacerbated in ancestral Hebrew script for a number of reasons, not all of which I fully understand. Dr. Leibowitz bandied about such terms as niqqud (which is a system of dots that distinguish vowels from consonants, but which was not always used; or which was sometimes used in different ways depending upon the purpose of the text); meteg (which is used in biblical Hebrew to make a vowel long, but is not used in modern Hebrew); cantillation signs that dictate syntactical structure; and other strange sounding words that I cannot recall at the moment."

Kreider humphed. "Sounds worse than French. When the early Franks created words, they threw in a whole bunch of letters just for the heck of it. These letters weren't pronounced but became part of the spelling. French text is half again as long as English text."

Father Nick nodded. "In grade school I always believed that English was riddled with too many exceptions to the rules. That belief was enforced when I studied Latin, and learned how that language was so standardized by comparison. But Hebrew is worse than English – or French, for that matter – because it exists in so many forms. The ancestral forms consisted of nonstandard writing systems which Dr. Leibowitz called orthographic variants, all of which lacked case distinctions, and some of which lacked vowels. Furthermore there were lettering variants: block, cursive, and Rashi, if I remember correctly. Then there were colloquial lettering forms. . . . "

Kreider sliced his steak and placed a mushroom on every piece before forking it into his mouth. "Sounds like a big mish-mash to me. No wonder there's so much controversy over translations."

Father Nick shook his head. "I could not agree more. Dr. Leibowitz readily conceded that everything is open to interpretation. On one occasion he was befuddled by what appeared to be misplaced diacritical marks. They did not appear to belong where they were located by the characters. He was quite put out about the situation because the marks did not fit with his proposed translation. I suggested that the marks might be artifacts on the photocopy: perhaps a paper flaw or toner residue. Thinking that he had been fully briefed, I casually recommended that we look at the original Scroll to determine if the marks existed on the source material."

Kreider guffawed. "I was there. The face on Hyman Horace would have stopped a truck. When he got over standing like a statue, he asked where they were. Nick didn't bat an eye. He glanced at the Scroll number, turned to the map desk that I use for storing star charts, pulled open a drawer, removed the original Scroll that was conserved between two clear heavy-duty sheets of archival quality non-bending plastic, and laid it on the desktop. Aitch-aitch nearly had a fit when he realized he was with arm's reach of the entire set of Scrolls."

Father Nick could not help but chuckle. "His look of astonishment was precious to behold. He could not have been more ecstatic if he had seen a pot of gold at the end of a rainbow. I asked him if he would like to touch the Scroll. He promptly clasped his hands behind his back and said, 'No.' He leaned over the Scroll with his face only inches above the top plastic sheet, examined every inch, and exclaimed, 'No marks.' Then he stepped back, gazed in awe at the entire Scroll in reverence, and finally returned without a word to his translations."

"That perked the little bastard up. After that, whenever he had a question about a mark on the copy, he'd ask to see the original. I think he was making up the marks just to have an excuse to see one of the original Scrolls. But hey! If anyone deserves to handle the real McCoy, he certainly does."

Father Nick finished a chew. "Getting back to context, he explained how it was important to know whether the ancestral text told a story about a commercial sailing vessel or a naval engagement. The scenario would determine the correct usage of 'brig.' He used this same protocol on a larger scale. Having an overview of what the Scrolls were supposed to impart enabled him to choose how to interpret certain letters, words, and marks. I must admit that his finished product scans smoothly and clearly, much more so than the Vatican translations."

Wendayne arrived with another tray full of goodies. "Anyone fer more coffee?"

Laila eagerly raised her hand.

"That ain't no surprise." Wendayne filled her large-size mug from a steaming kettle. "I also got ample portions of homemade apple pie."

"Bye, bye, Miss American Pie," Kreider sang. "I'll make one slice go bye-bye."

"Me too," Laila announced.

Father Nick patted his ample midriff. "I should not, but if God is willing, so am I."

Wendayne laid down three pie plates and pushed one in front of each of the diners. "Apples is good fer you. I cut back on the sugar so's you won't hafta let yer belt out another notch."

"What do you mean, another?"

"I'm watchin yer waistline even if you ain't, Mister Nick." Wendayne grinned over her shoulder as she sashayed into the kitchen.

Father Nick glanced at his two companions. "Let us have a moment of silence, not to say a prayer but to enjoy this marvelous repast."

All three forked their pies. For a while the only sound in the canteen was the gentle whoosh of the air conditioner and the clatter of pewter on ceramic.

Laila wolfed down her pie and sipped on red hot coffee. "Father Nick."

"Yes, my dear."

"I notice things. One of the things I noticed was that you didn't seem surprised by any of Hyman's translations, even though they yielded versions of events that weren't like those in the *Bible*. At least, not like the versions that I remember reading in Baptist bible school. Why was that?"

Father Nick gulped down the last of his pie, then licked his lips and wiped them delicately with a paper napkin. He stared thoughtfully before tendering a reply. "Some of the text was familiar to me from two other sources. First, our Vatican scholars arrived at similar translations for those portions of the text on the Cave 12 Scrolls that they were able to decipher. We expected Dr. Leibowitz to clarify passages that seemed to be either vague or ambiguous. Instead he provided radical differences, in addition to which he translated other passages that seemed to us to be gibberish.

"Second, some of the text is similar to text that was found on an ancient Egyptian papyrus that was discovered in the 1970's near Beni Masah. That is, translations of the text were similar. The Beni Masah papyrus was written in an ancient form of Egyptian known as Coptic. The leather-bound codex consisted of thirty-one papyrus sheets or folios that had writing on both sides. As I explained previously, the Vatican maintains a constant vigil for ancient documents that relate to Christ and Christianity.

"Our priests, or agents, as Colonel Davenport prefers to call them, have standing high-price offers for anything canonical. Thus we were able to acquire a number of papyrus sheets from certain treasure hunters who were involved in the discovery. Unfortunately, the discoverers split the codex among themselves, and each offered the sheets in his possession to dealers in antiquities: dealers who were well known to them and who had connections with wealthy collectors of black market antiques.

"Much of the papyrus was badly deteriorated. The

sheets in the Vatican's possession were preserved in our conservation laboratory. Radiocarbon dating established an approximate year of origination of 200 Anno Domini, plus or minus fifty years. Did I mention that our forensics lab has its own carbon dating machine? The papyrus purports to be a copy of the Gospel according to Judas."

Laila gasped. "Wow. I don't remember reading any Gospel of Judas in *my* New Testament."

"No. You would not have. The Judas text has been lost to mankind for two thousand years."

Laila's eyes glazed. "What is the carbon date of the Cave 12 Scrolls?"

Kreider laughed. "You go right for the throat, don't you, girl?"

"Well?"

"Approximately 30 Anno Domini, plus or minus sixty years, which of course makes the Scrolls antecedent to the Egyptian papyrus."

"Wow. Thirty AD is the date of the Crucifixion. Are you saying . . . "

"That's what the good father is saying," Kreider supplied. "The Beni Masah codex is a copy produced by third century scribes."

"An bowdlerized copy I might add." Father Nick toyed with his fork. "You see, the Holy Scriptures had already been assembled by the third century. The basis of Christianity had been firmly established by the church. The many sects that had been vying for their version of biblical events to be canonized either amalgamated or were ousted.

"Numerous Christian writings, Acts, Epistles, and Gnostic gospels were not incorporated into the New Testament. They would only have added confusion. Other supposedly eyewitness accounts of events leading to the Crucifixion of Christ exist. Some complement the version that is accepted by the Catholic church, but others contradict it. The church needed solidarity. So they picked and chose which gospels to include in the New Testament, and which to exclude."

Kreider scoffed. "In order to create an image that was acceptable to the proletariat. Nick and I have had long conversations about the accuracy of the *Bible*. Both Testaments. The twenty-seven books of the New Testament represent less than half the books that were written by contemporary apostles, historians, and religious adherents. Each sect promoted its own version of events, but then as now, the winners are the ones who write history the way they want it to be perceived."

Father Nick pursed his lips and nodded. "Rival versions of the Crucifixion have long been known from medieval texts. Some of them were purportedly written by apostles, disciples, or converts who were not represented in the *Bible*. For example, Jesus may or may not have had a brother named James, who wrote an account of the last days of Christ. The apostle Phillip wrote gospels of which the church has a manuscript that was copied long after the event, perhaps in the 900's Anno Domini. We also have a manuscript that was putatively written by the apostle Thaddeus; and another one by James the Lesser; even one by Mary Magdalene.

"A papyrus codex that was discovered in Egypt in recent years contained a manuscript that purported to be the lost Gospel of Judas. According to this Gospel, Judas was not the betrayer of Jesus but instead was his closest companion. More than once he professed his love for Jesus. Yet that manuscript was not an original, but a copy that had been produced by scribes in the second or third century.

"The church has long acknowledged the existence of these other writings. But the truth of those writings has been repudiated. They may be forgeries, or they may be abridged or censored versions. Now we have new evidence that contradicts the commonly accepted account of the relationship between Jesus and Judas as it is written in the New Testament. And this evidence is most compelling. The Cave 12 Scrolls are not later copies, nor are they Gospels. They are in fact a diary: the original diary of Judas Iscariot, unexpurgated, and written by his own hand."

Chapter 16

Laila finally got over her jetlag and night flights. She went to bed soon after dinner with Kreider and Father Nick. This put her sleep cycle back on schedule. She awoke a five o'clock in the morning feeling refreshed and alert. She squirted, showered, dried her hair and twirled it into a bun, then donned clean hospital scrubs. She was ready for coffee.

The canteen was vacant but the coffer maker was always brewing. She poured two cups: one to drink at once, the other to sip at her workstation. She grabbed a minibox of Raison Bran to snack on dry.

The lights were dimmed in the Security Shack. Laila left them that way. She plugged her computer into the Internet connection, and began the synchronization process that would send the emails that she had written in her room, and download the activity from her last synchronization. She nibbled on her cereal while the process took place. Expecting to have the whole day to herself, instead of reading all her emails and prioritizing them for action, she read and replied to them one at a time. She had eighty-seven.

Varvarelis arrived at eight o'clock on the dot. "Whoa! The early bird gets the worm."

"But the second mouse gets the cheese, as my granma used to say."

Varvarelis laughed perfunctorily.

Laila swung her chair around. "So who won the pool?"

With a humph: "Midge Oglethorpe. I was five years off. It's not fair. I relied on my *Bible* and she used what she called women's intuition."

"Goes to show how accurate that intuition can be."

Varvarelis sat in a four-wheeled chair and rolled it next to Laila so that their arms came in contact. "What's your take on this Godforsaken plan?"

"To pre-empt the IRF?"

He nodded.

"Quite frankly, to my unimaginative mind the prospect of going back in time sounds preposterous. I can't really believe in time travel. I'm just going along with the program because that's the job that was assigned to me. But whether I believe in time travel or not doesn't alter the fact that the IRF believes in it. And so does everyone assigned to Project Stitch and Mission Snatch. So who am I to contradict all these folks?"

Varvarelis raised his eyebrows as he moved so that his shoulder rubbed Laila's. "A laissez faire kind of philosophy. I have to admit that I was pretty skeptical about it at first. We had a lot of round-robin discussions about it when the new Project was started."

Laila moved her chair a mite to break skin contact. "We?"

"The security squad. None of us could believe it either. We figured that the people who worked on the Manhattan Project must have felt the same way until they saw the first atomic bomb go off at Alamogordo."

"Have you seen the Timepiece in operation?"

He shook his head. "That's on a need to show basis, and we don't need to be shown. But with all the other crazy things that have been done around here, I'd believe anything they told me. That's how I won the pool."

"What pool was that?"

"The pool on whether the Timepiece was real or not." Leaning close to her in confidence: "I spent the winnings on a showgirl in Vegas. It was worth it."

"Easy come, easy go, as they say."

"Coming was easier than going." Varvarelis stood, stretched, and yawned. "I'd love to chitchat more but I've got my morning routine to do." He lumbered toward his workstation at the opposite end of the room. "Then I'm going out on a perimeter check with the sexy Midge."

"And I've got emails." Laila turned back to her computer. She was so intent on her work that she barely acknowledged Varvarelis's departure. With fingers flying over her keyboard, she became absorbed in her virtual world until the door opened again.

"Hey lady. How'd you like to go for another ride?"

Bryce was dressed in sweats again; gray this time.

Laila spun the chair around. "Is this another date?"

Bryce chuckled at her lighthearted game. "It is if you want it to be."

Without hesitation: "I do."

"I've got a Roamer outside. Luke is rounding up Leibowitz."

She turned her lower lip into a pout. "Is this a double date?"

"Unfortunately, yes. Are you jealous?"

"I could stand any chaperone but Hyman, the Horace of a different color."

Bryce smirked. "I'll make it up to you."

Laila started shutting down her computer. "I'll hold you to it." She unplugged her computer, slipped it into its knapsack, threw a strap over her right shoulder, and smiled. "I'm ready when you are."

They drove along underground corridors for fifteen minutes before they reached a lobby and parking area that had but a single door. Waiting for them were Luke Kreider and Leibowitz. Kreider was dressed in Bermuda shorts and a short-sleeve Hawaiian shirt that depicted green leaves intertwined with colorful tropical birds that were indigenous to the Sandwich Islands. Leibowitz was the only person who could look unkempt in hospital scrubs. His tousled hair looked as if it had been combed with an eggbeater, but Laila refrained from offering her opinion.

Kreider jerked a thumb at Leibowitz. "I found him over in D Block, gallivanting."

Leibowitz stammered, "You – you – you – said I could take a cart and go anywhere I wanted."

Bryce calmly kept his hands at his sides. "That's quite all right, Dr. Leibowitz. I'm not revoking your privileges. It's just that now that you've recovered somewhat from your translation binge I thought you'd like to see another one of Area 51's secrets. The *most* secret, in fact."

"Oh?"

"You're part of the team, and you've earned the right

to see everything."

Leibowitz didn't scowl. His face remained passive.

"Right this way." Bryce turned to the keypad and entered a numerical code. He glanced at Laila.

Her eyes were glazed for several seconds. She squinted, and her eyes glazed for several more seconds. Tentatively: "Wiggily?"

"All will be revealed."

He pushed down on a large handle and pulled the heavy, vaultlike door outward. He led the way into a utilitarian lobby in which a burly Air Force corpsman sat at a desk to the left, while a bank of monitor screens covered the opposite wall to the right. Laila watched the screen that showed Leibowitz and Kreider walking through the doorway behind her.

The guard wore a crisply starched combat uniform; his head was covered by a Blue Beret. On the desk in front of him lay an M-9 carbine with its barrel pointed toward the doorway. At his waist was a holstered M-9 pistol: the same brand of Beretta that Bryce preferred. "Good morning, sir."

"Morning, Ted. All quiet on the western front?"

The guard grinned. "Yes, sir."

Bryce placed his ID card on the scanner, then motioned for each of the others to follow suit. "It's standard security protocol. Nobody get in without a card scan. Not even me."

He tapped out another password on the inner door.

Laila's eyes glazed for so long that she had to blink. "I'm going way out on a limb, but – Skeezicks?"

"All will be revealed."

Bryce led the way again, into the inner sanctum of Project Stitch: a room the size of a basketball court. Rows of workstations and computer monitors reminded Laila of the operations room of a Shuttle launch site. Technicians were scattered throughout the complex. Several looked up, and nodded at Bryce.

Large red letters were painted in script on the back wall: "A Stitch in Time Saves Nine."

Laila smirked. "Very clever."

Bryce arched his eyebrows. "What can I tell you? Our physicists have a sense of humor."

"What – what is this place?" Leibowitz wanted to know.

"This is the secret of secrets. I don't need to remind you – "

"No, you don't."

Bryce did not favor Leibowitz with a facial expression. "This is the nerve center of a state-of-the-art subatomic particle accelerator known as a synchrotron."

"I've heard of that."

"I would tell you more about it but the man walking toward us is the one who invented it, so I'll let him do the honors. Prepare yourself for a revelation."

Over casual pale yellow shirt and black slacks the man wore a white smock whose pockets were filled with pens and instruments. The tall shock of black hair was swept back like a lion's mane; it was complimented by a handlebar mustache that attenuated to fine points about halfway between the bridge of the nose and the lobes of the ears. His fair skin contrasted sharply with his glistening hair, much like a black and white photograph.

"Walter Gouty, this is Laila Masterson and Dr. Leibowitz."

"Pleased to meet you both." His voice was deep but soft, like a base fiddle that was slightly out of tune. He shook hands first with Laila, then with Leibowitz. He indicated a conference room. "Come into my parlor, said the spider to the fly."

Over top of the doorway to his office was a mounted signboard that read: "I've got the time if you've got the place."

The first thing Laila spotted inside was a coffee maker. She went straight for it. A wooden placard on the table read, "Time is of the essence."

"Help your . . . Oh, I see you already are." Gouty laughed easily if not heartily. "Well, help yourself."

Laila was the only one who did.

Gouty sat at the head of the polished cherry table

while the others took seats on both sides. "I hardly know where to begin. Project Stitch is so hush-hush that I've never had to brief dignitaries about the work we do. General Cercopley handles all the political machinations and money laundering schemes that fund the Project. I just work here."

Laila quietly sipped her coffee.

"It's not important that you understand any of the theoretical aspects of operation, any more than it's important for you to understand the workings of the internal combustion engine in order to drive a car. But some background information might enable you to appreciate the breakthrough in fundamental temporal physics that this Project represents.

"I'll pass over the history of synchrotrons and bite right into the meat of the subject. A synchrotron is a sophisticated device for accelerating charged particles: protons and electrons. It won't accelerate neutrons because neutrons have no charge. The synchrotron works by generating a progressive magnetic field along a series of electromagnets that are synchronized in such a way that each one imparts additional energy to the particle as it passes around a torus. The result is a constant acceleration that culminates at relativistic speeds only slightly below the universal constant. Is everyone with me so far?"

Gouty continued without waiting for tardy replies. "In our universe, protons are positive and electrons are negative. These values are purely arbitrary. We could just as well create a nomenclature in which protons are negative and electrons are negative; or one is black and the other is white; or up and down; or vanilla or chocolate; or any such allusion to opposites. When protons and electrons were discovered, physicists gave them the values that they did, so we abide by those values in order to maintain conformity.

"However, it was later learned that each subatomic particle has an antiparticle. A proton has an antiproton; an electron has an antielectron; and so on. These antiparticles are called contraterrene matter. They don't exist in nature under ordinary circumstances because as soon as one meets a particle of the opposite value, the two of them annihilate each other. That means that their combined mass is converted to energy. Still with me?

"Nobel laureate Richard Feynman published a mathematical proof in which a positron – a more convenient name for an antielectron – could be regarded as an electron moving backward in time. This gave rise to a hypothetical phenomenon known as retrocausality, in which a cause is preceded by its effect when viewed from our temporal frame of reference – "

Leibowitz grumbled.

"Dr. Leibowitz, you had a comment to make?"

He scowled. "That kind of mathematics is poppycock. You only get out of math what you put into it. Like the computer term GIGO: garbage in, garbage out."

Gouty did not seem to be the least bit perturbed. "The good professor is quite right, as far as he goes. Mathematical problems that proceed on unwarranted assumptions lead to erroneous or irrational answers."

Kreider interceded. "Never let math blind you to logic. The classic mathematical absurdity is the simple formula A divided by B equals C. If A is one and B is one then C equals one. One over two equals one half. One over four equals one quarter. One over sixty equals one sixtieth. But when the formula is used in realistic terms, such as in digging a hole, it yields an answer that is nonsensical. If A is a hole, B is a digger, and C is time, the amount of time it takes a digger to dig a hole is A divided by B. Let's say that one digger can dig a hole in an hour. Two diggers can dig the hole in half that time, or thirty minutes. Four diggers can dig the hole in fifteen minutes. But sixty diggers can't dig the hole in a minute because they can't stand close enough to get their shovels on the same spot in the dirt. Nor can thirty-six hundred diggers dig the hole in a second. So a simple postulate that works mathematically yields an answer that is patently absurd."

Leibowitz glared at Kreider. "That's my point."

Gouty nodded in agreement. "The point is valid, perceptive, and well taken. The hole digger analogy is applicable with regard to Feynman's calculations. The backward flowing positron proved to be an interesting hypothetical construct but badly flawed in realistic terms. Yet it did provide food for thought, and many physicists agonized over it throughout subsequent years."

Kreider interceded again. "You should also mention that mathematics was responsible for building the A-bomb and sending man to the Moon. When it works, it works."

Laila added her two cents: "The proof of the pudding is in the eating, as my granma used to say."

"Very perceptive, your grandmother," Gouty allowed. "Physicists would be well advised to adopt her plain-language syllogisms. By the way, I spoke with Feynman about his so-called proof. He thought it was nothing more than an intellectual exercise. He was too practical a person to accept it in rationalistic terms. So while the Feynman hypothesis was acknowledged as a temporal dead end, it led to philosophical speculation that non-determinant factors might somehow affect the sequentiality of events: an unproven theorem that came to be called the 'regression of time,' or 'regressive time,' in which 'now' is considered as nothing more than a mathematical convenience."

"Be that as it may, none of the predecessors of variant chronometric theories had anything to do with the present technology. By experimentation it was learned that when alternate magnets in the synchrotron were displaced by the same amount, the resultant shift of field strength induced an oscillation in the accelerated particle that affected the coherence of its wave function. The resultant phase relationship is expressed as a complex sinusoidal wave in which a phase is followed by an antiphase. Once relativistic speeds were achieved at a certain threshold frequency, the particle disappeared. Vanished from the known universe."

Gouty did not acknowledge Leibowitz's look of surprise. "I won't bore you with quantum mechanics and relativity models because the effect is impossible to explain without a solid grounding in the underlying calculus. Indeed, we are still developing the math to correlate with the observed effects. Predictions based on formulas have met with only moderate success: close approximations at best.

"Be that as it may, what we eventually learned was that high-speed phase-shifted electrons collided with photons – which are discrete quanta of light – and swept them up like Pac-Man eating dots. Normally photons can't be accelerated. They have no charge and no mass at rest; and anyway, they're already traveling at the speed of light.

"But when photons were swallowed by a phase-shifted electron that was moving at near-relativistic speed, the photons' wave-particle duality shifted ever so slightly from particle attribute to wave attribute and vice versa. Keep in mind that mass and energy are equivalent; that is, they represent two manifestations of the same quantum in a non-simultaneous state. This alternating mass-energy state interfered with the space-time continuum in such a way that the wave attribute of the photon dragged the electron – which is nearly pure particle – along with it. In deference to Dr. Leibowitz's objection, although we tentatively established the causality of this event in mathematical terms, it wasn't until we recovered the lost electron that we actually substantiated the reality of the situation. Unfortunately, we still cannot explain the transference in mathematical terms.

"Be that as it may, it took several more years of research to ascertain the location of the lost electron after it went missing. It existed in the past until we recalled it by reverse-shifting the phases in the synchrotron. When we learned how to focus a stream of disappearing electrons from a number of surrounding discharge points into a central node, we created a bubble field in which all matter that existed concurrently within the field disappeared along with the photon-enriched electrons. We call the device a Synchronous Chronological Sequence

Converter."

Kreider took center stage. "In other words, a time machine."

Leibowitz was so flabbergasted that he was speechless. His jaw moved but no sound emerged from his throat.

"I understand that the concept is difficult to accept, but Luke here is, as Laila's grandmother would say, the proof of the pudding."

Leibowitz stared at Kreider.

Kreider nodded. "Been there, done that, but they didn't sell T-shirts. Of course, I didn't get to go back until they sent and recovered a slew of recording instruments and a whole flock of mice. Or is it a herd?"

"When they're in a corn crib it's called a nest," Laila furnished.

"Right. And I didn't go alone. I had a couple of armed Air Force chaps to keep me company; and to protect me from the local inbred rednecks while I conducted my experiments. Never saw a native. As you've noticed, Area 51 is not a nice place for human species to live."

Gouty: "Like the computer terms scuzzy and wissywig, we call the device Skeezicks for short." At Laila's raised eyebrows. "It's from a board game that I played as a kid. The good guy was Uncle Wiggily; the bad guy was the Skeezicks."

Laila tilted her head. "Which came first: the name or the acronym?"

"I suppose they were synchronized."

"Wait – wait – wait a minute . . . "

"Yes, Dr. Leibowitz."

"Do you – do you – expect me to believe – that you can travel back and forth in time?"

Gouty twisted his mustaches. "Strictly speaking, we can travel forth only after we have first traveled back, and then we can travel only to the present, but not beyond. We suspect that this is because the future doesn't exist yet, but we can only speculate. We're too new at the game to make anything but educated guesses. And for some reason, we've been unable to tweak the Skeezicks into communicating with the past more recent that one thousand sixty-one years, seventy-seven days, three hours, fourteen minutes, and nine seconds BP. That's Before Present. No matter how much power we put on the grid, we can't go back any closer than that. We don't know why.

"In science, when we observe an occurrence for which we have no explanation, we call it a natural law: like the law of gravity. Est ergo est, to paraphrase Descartes: It is, therefore it is. We suspect that the proximity restriction has something to do with paradox prevention. That means that you can't kill your mother before your own conception: an act which would prevent your birth and later existence, and therefore deny your ability to kill your mother before your own conception. In other words, it allows the universe to smooth out unlawful contraventions. But these are simply philosophical musings.

"As I have expressed ad nauseam to Bryce and General Cercopley, I firmly oppose Mission Snatch at this time – if you will pardon an overused pun – because we don't know nearly enough about the ramifications of temporal tampering, causal consequences, or effective alterations in the chronology of the time stream. Even though the purpose of the mission is to preserve the known course of events, we have no idea what accidental complications may arise from meddling with a phenomenon that we know so little about.

"We're years, perhaps decades, away from even beginning to grasp the consequences of interacting with a force of nature whose potential effects are beyond our comprehension. My colleagues, both here and abroad, are unanimous in their opinion that disrupting the consequential flow of space-time could create chaos or catastrophic – or might not, I am forced to acknowledge.

"We have no mathematics that can positively determine the outcome of temporal interference. In any case, as Dr. Leibowitz pointed out, you can't expect mathematical proofs to be meaningful in the real world unless you start with the right assumptions. Feynman told me that when he worked on the Manhattan Project, some of the physicists at White Sands, including Oppenheimer, feared that an uncontrolled nuclear chain reaction could ignite the atmosphere. The Trinity Test at Alamogordo proved that it didn't, but before that there was no way to predict the outcome of an atomic detonation.

"Now we are dealing with a realm of physics that no one knows anything about. The few successful transferences we've made are insufficient to enable us to predict the potential outcomes of extensive interaction with the past. Despite my cautious approach to this novel scientific demesne, my views have been overridden, and Mission Snatch is proceeding on schedule so that the participants can have the time of their lives, perhaps at the cost of sacrificing ours."

Despite his dire prophecies, Gouty flashed the glimmer of a grin. Laila sensed that he didn't agree with the decision to proceed, accepted philosophically that the decision was out of his hands, yet was glad in a way that was in keeping with his scientific curiosity while the responsibility of the decision rested on someone else's shoulders. He pressed a touchpad that was inlaid in the polished wood in front of him. A surface-mounted projector on the wall behind and above his head flashed an image on the opposite wall.

"This is a picture of the prototype Skeezicks which Bryce has nicknamed Wristwatch in comparison to its larger brother that he insists on calling Big Ben. Wearing spacesuits courtesy of NASA are Luke and two guards standing back to back inside the circle that's painted on the floor." Now Gouty presented a full-face grin. "We thought of painting a pentagram instead of a circle, in honor of the occult symbol that protects those within from encroaching demons that were conjured by sorcerers, but were afraid that straight strokes leading to points outside the actual perimeter might be misleading. The circular geometric construction denotes in two dimensions the boundary of the three-dimensional bubble field.

"The spacesuits were a precaution in case miscalibration or a temporary defect in the operation of the synchrotron sent the subjects to a time and place that did not contain a breathable atmosphere. The silver-colored cylinder that Luke is holding is a locator." The locator was the size of a Thermos flask. "In operation, a large bank of capacitors discharge simultaneously to produce an instantaneous bore hole through the fabric of time. The transmission distance through the temporal medium is controlled by the strength of the instantaneous power surge. The more power, the farther into the past the bore hole transmits. The bore hole closes immediately upon transmission.

"A finite amount of time is needed to recharge the capacitors. Once they are fully charged, the bore hole can be reopened and the subjects retrieved if they're standing within the periphery of the newly opened bore hole at the time of discharge.

"In theory we can keep the bore hole open all the time, but in practice the power requirements are so large that we can maintain the opening only for nanoseconds. In Luke's case, we reopened the hole at one hour intervals. If he and the guards were standing within the boundaries of the bubble field, we retrieved them. If not, we received a quantity of dirt, dust, and air, and once a jackalope that was passing through the spot, but not our subjects. We attempted subsequent retrievals at one hour intervals until they were ready to return. If the subjects wish to move about in the local time frame, they leave the locator nearby – or buried, to prevent damage or accidental movement. Each subject carries a receiver that will lead him back to the locator by following the signal that the locator emits. Any questions?"

Laila had about a thousand but didn't know how to articulate them or prioritize them. She stayed mum.

Leibowitz was aghast. "Is – is – is this all true? Or is this another flying saucer invention to trick the public and distract the media away from what you're really doing?"

"Oh, it's quite true. I daresay you'll believe it after you've seen it in operation and taken your first trip."

Kreider shuffled his feet. Bryce stared straight ahead. An uncomfortable silence ensued.

"What – what do you mean, taken my first trip?"

Gouty narrowed his eyes at both Bryce and Kreider. "Haven't you briefed him yet?"

Bryce took the bull by the horns; or in this case, the Jew by the lapels. "We were waiting for the appropriate time so to speak."

"No time like the present. Or were you going to tell him in the past?"

"He needs to know now but not until he had the need to know."

Gouty committed half a grin. "That's somewhat logical, in a reverse chronological way."

Bryce turned to Leibowitz. "Dr. Leibowitz Project Snitch is the transportation phase of Mission Snatch. Now that you have identified the week of the Crucifixion we are going back to that point in time to witness the event and make sure that it conforms to the way it is recounted in the *Bible.*"

Once again Leibowitz was speechless. Laila pondered over the issues that must be troubling him the most: either that it was possible to go back in time to watch the Crucifixion, or that *he* was to be one of the spectators.

Leibowitz satisfied her curiosity. "We – we – we! What do you mean by the pronoun we?"

"I mean that you are an integral part of this Mission. You have already proven your worth in the present and we need your language skills in the past. Your knowledge of Hebrew will enable us to communicate with the indigenous population of the ancient Middle East territory."

"I – I – I'm not going back in time. That isn't what I signed on for."

"Actually you did. Look at your contract. When you signed the nondisclosure packet and accepted payment you agreed to go anywhere any time."

"But – but – but – I thought any time meant any time *now*, like being on call to go any time, at a moment's notice. Not to go two thousand years ago."

Bryce grinned expansively at his private joke. "You thought wrong."

Chapter 17

Laila couldn't relax.

Her contemplation of future events – or more accurately, events that were about to occur two millennia in the past – was so mentally exhilarating that whenever her eyelids drooped and she lay back in her security shack recliner to catch a few minutes of shuteye, her mind raced as fast as an accelerated electron and kept her from falling asleep. Napping proved to be out of the question.

Within seconds of assuming the horizontal position, she popped up in the chair and sent another questing email. Despite the lack of an announcement tone, she immediately checked her secure email account to see if there were any replies to her previous queries. She was working in two veins: one was tasking onsite handlers to keep her informed about the Islamic Revolutionary Forces with regard to the movements of nuclear weapons, and to the final construction phase of the Temporal Displacement Apparatus; the other was accessing stored security data and law enforcement records from federal agencies, pursuant to previous activities of persons who might have compromised the secrecy of the Skeezicks (as she came to call the Timepiece; not only did she like the sound of the word, but it didn't make her think so much of a temporal prostitute). Each reply inevitably posed two or more questions that required follow-up emails.

Just as she lay back again, a tone sounded the arrival of incoming messages. This made it impossible for her to close her eyes. She sat up, clicked on the new message in her inbox, and scanned the text from one of her overseas agents. The information was – inscrutable. At least, to her. But she knew to whom it might be meaningful.

She called Walter Gouty on her walkie-talkie. "Walt. This is Laila. I just received some curious news about the IRF's TDA. I don't know what it means so I was hoping that you might have some light to shed."

"I'll help if I can."

"Well, when you had that accident with the proto-type Skeezicks, the one that blew up, did it flash like a strobe light?"

"No. There was very little illumination from the blast. The prototype didn't explode in the conventional way. It *im*ploded, although the effect is nearly the same. The im-ploding air and machine parts passed through the core of instability and out the other side. Are you thinking that the TDA may have suffered a similar fate?"

"I don't know. But I've just received a report from a handler whose local asset reported a huge ball of light at the TDA facility. Not a nuclear explosion with a mush-room cloud. Just an incredibly bright emission of radi-ant energy, like a short circuit on a mammoth scale, and a sudden gust of wind. 'Like a blaze of ball lightning' was the way the incident was described. What kind of action would generate something like that?"

Gouty was silent for a moment. A long moment. Then: "Oh, dear. Oh dear. This is bad. This is very bad."

"How bad is bad?"

Gouty was silent.

"Walt! How bad is bad."

"I must go. I must contact . . . " He disconnected.

Laila stared at her walkie-talkie as if it were turning into a serpent. She felt as if she had just taken a bite of forbidden fruit in the Garden of Eden. Or was it knowl-edge that was forbidden? "Humph." She had the feeling that all was not right in Gethsemane. She laid down the walkie-talkie, pondered for a moment, then shrugged and returned to her email screen. She accepted the fact that she was but one cog in the vast gear of Mission Snatch, and that her job right now was to collect, com-pile, and disseminate information that others in the mis-sion had the job of deciphering and acting upon. That was the manner in which any goal-oriented system worked the most effectively to achieve the desired end result.

She put aside her curiosity and concentrated on the

task at hand. Almost immediately, she started receiving follow-up emails about the TDA. There did not appear to be any massive destruction – or any destruction at all, for that matter – at the temporal displacement facility, and activity in general seemed to have crawled to a stop.

Her walkie-talkie beeped. "Laila Masterson."

"This is Bryce. I don't have time to chat because I have to get the calling tree started before we're too far out on a limb. Grab your laptop and meet me at the *Thermopylae. Now*!" He disconnected.

Laila didn't know what was going on, but one thing she learned in the intelligence business was to obey orders from a superior officer when a situation was hot. One never knew when a few minutes delay in the transmission of intel to soldiers in the field might swing the tide of battle to the side of the enemy. She unplugged her computer, closed the clamshell, shoved the laptop into her knapsack, and dashed out the door. She ran straight into Christopher Varvarelis in the hallway.

He wrapped his arms around her and rubbed his fingers along the bumpy disk protrusions of her spine as if he were strumming a guitar. "Whoa there, girl. What's the hurry?"

Laila pushed herself free. "I don't know but I have to go."

"I was going to ask if you wanted to take a break and drive the perimeter . . . "

By that time Laila was around a corner and out of his sight. She hopped onto a convenient Roamer whose seat was still warm from Varvarelis's posterior, to which she gave a moment's thought before backing, turning, and racing along the corridor to the hangar. As she approached an intersection and turned around the corner, she almost crashed sideways into another Roamer that was speeding along the straightaway. Their spinning wheels touched long enough to scrape the surface off the sidewalls and produce the scent of burning rubber.

Kreider shouted, "Park your Roamer and jump aboard with me."

Lails screeched to a halt. She switched off the motor. An instant later she was astride Kreider's Roamer riding shotgun. "What's all the hurry?"

Kreider pressed the accelerator pedal to the floor. "I was hoping you could tell me. I'm on the top branch of the calling tree. All Bryce said was to meet him at the *Thermopylae*. I made my calls to the lower limbs of the trunk and here I am."

"I can't help but think it has to do with a call I made to Gouty."

"What about?"

"Some kind of ball lightning phenomenon at the TDA."

"Ruh roh. That's bad news."

"That's what Gouty said before he hung up on me. What's it mean?"

"It means the IRF has activated their time machine. It might just be a test, but . . . "

"But what?"

"But they might have used it."

"You mean, to go into the past?"

"That's their intent. If they change anything back there – back then – we may all succumb to T.S. Eliot's prophecy in *The Hollow Men*: 'This is the way the world ends; not with a bang but a whimper.' "

"They can't have had enough time to do anything yet. I only got the message a few minutes ago, and it referred to something that happened within the last hour."

"You don't understand universal time, Laila."

"Sure I do. It's the same as Greenwich Mean Time."

"That's not the time I mean. I'm talking about time in the universal sense, as in space-time. Once the IRF left the present they have all the time in the world, or in the known universe, to do whatever they want to do in the past. If they changed something before we get there – then – to prevent it, then it has already happened, and we're history."

"Well, doesn't the fact that we're still here mean that they didn't change anything? Otherwise we would have vanished like smoke."

"Logically you may be right. But time travel is too new a concept for us to understand all its ramifications. Or *any* of its ramifications. Have you heard of the alternate universe concept?"

"No, but I have the feeling you're going to tell me about it."

Kreider concentrated on rounding a corner into another corridor. "It's a notion that science fiction writers have been describing for decades. Basically it presupposes that every turning point in history creates a fork or deviation in the time stream: one timeline or plane of existence in which, say, the Nazis were defeated (our world), and one in which they were triumphant. Or the South was victorious at Gettysburg and won the Civil War. The concept postulates the existence of an infinite number of worlds of infinite variety, each one splitting off from some pivotal point."

"Then why bother to prevent the IRF from creating a deviation if it won't affect us, but only create another timeline?"

"That's a good question. I wish I had a good answer. All I can say is that science fiction concepts don't work on mathematical principles. Just because a person with a vivid imagination spouts a far-out notion doesn't mean it's true, any more than the Moon is made of green cheese because some idiot thought it was so. It's a much a fairytale as 'Hansel and Gretel' or 'The Tortoise and the Hare.' "

" 'The Tortoise and the Hare' was a fable."

"Whatever. The point is that we have no idea how interaction with the past can affect the future – er, the present. That's why Gouty doesn't want us to go around playing God or Savior in the Christian era. Granted all we want to do is maintain the status quo by not making any changes in the past, or by not letting anyone else make changes, but to do that we need to ask the Muslims 'Quo vadis': Where are you going? It's all very complicated, and no one has any answers – especially the theoretical physicists who discussed these issues ad nauseam at the last Prague conference that Gouty and

I attended. Jesus, get me off this Latin kick."

Laila didn't know what to say, so she said nothing.

"Talk about playing with fire. We're playing with the fabric that holds the universe together: taking that fabric and folding it, tearing it, and hopefully knitting it back together. I have to tell you, Laila, what we're contemplating scares the bejesus out of me. In a scientific sense, we're like children lighting a match and wondering if the wind will blow it out or if it will cause a forest fire.

"Going back to take a few stellar observations was one thing. I was careful not to step on any bugs or cryptogrammic soil. But going back to watch Christianity either go up in flames or be extinguished is another. And I'm not even a believer. But whether you believe in God or not, you have to believe that a Christian world is better than one that's ruled by fanatical Muslim terrorists."

"In that belief, you and I are like two peas in a pod, as my granma used to say."

"Yeah, well, thanks for the company, but it doesn't make me feel any safer. Especially since I think Bryce and Nick have something up their sleeve that they're not telling us about."

Laila was surprised. "What makes you think that?"

He hunched his shoulders. "I don't know. I catch them talking sometimes, and they shut up as soon as I get close. Then they look at me as if I caught them with their hands in the cookie jar."

"I know what you mean. I have the feeling that they believe that what we're planning is a self-fulfilling prophecy; that nothing can be changed no matter what we do. Or, at least, nothing can be changed in our timeline." Laila contemplated. "Which, by the way, is a stupid idea."

"How so?"

"Well, what determines a pivotal point in history? Does a new timeline start when I change my mind and go to the market before going the hardware store instead of the other way around? Or when I reach for an apple and eat an orange instead? Or comb my hair differently?

How miniscule does an action have to be before it doesn't split the timeline?"

Kreider shrugged. "As I said, the concept is totally fictional: more of a plot device than a scientific hypothesis. All I know is that the Vatican has a lot at stake in this venture. We all do for that matter. The irony is that even though Christianity fosters a belief in the almighty and subservience to his will, Nick and the Vatican aren't content to let the chips fall where they may; or let God decide where to place his bets. Meddling with circumstances that God has supposedly foreordained goes against the very grain of their religion."

"Maybe they believe that God helps those who help themselves."

"Could be. But if we use Big Ben to rip open a huge gash in the universal fabric of space-time, instead of cutting small slits like we've been doing with the Wristwatch, we might create a tear so big that we can't sew it back together."

Laila thought of Humpty-Dumpty but didn't mention it.

"The result could be the very thing that was prophesied in Revelations: not just mankind's final battle and the end of the world as we know it, but the end of everything: Armageddon."

Chapter 18

"Looks like Nick and Leibowitz beat us to the punch." Kreider pointed with his chin toward the hangar door. "Nick is as anxious as I am, but Leibowitz is positively eager."

"Eager? He nearly had a conniption when Bryce told him that he had to go through time."

"That was at first. Like most academics, he's fearless when it comes to smiting his peers with words on paper, but cowardly when it comes to physical danger. After you left, though, it slowly dawned on him what a golden opportunity he was being given – to actually visit the timeframe that he'd spent his entire adult life studying. He had what you might call an epiphany. I assured him that the time transfer was safe because I'd done it a number of time. Now he's a changed man. He can't wait to get started on this time trek to ancient Jerusalem."

"Wow. That's quite an about face."

"Don't let his enthusiasm fool you. He's still an ass, only now he's a cooperative ass who doesn't appreciate that the road to Galilee might be the road to perdition. He has no idea what trouble we might be headed for back there – then. Or what trouble he might get us into with that arrogant attitude of his."

"I'm sure Bryce will keep him on a tight leash."

"I hope he uses a training collar and strangles the little bastard."

"Walt!"

Kreider made no apology for his dislike of Leibowitz. "In any case, now that the TDA is operational, we've got to get out of here, or get out of now, or else we might all end up vanishing like the glow of a bulb when the switch is flipped off." He stopped the roamer next to the wall. "Make no mistake about it: this trip will be scary."

Laila stepped out of the Roamer. "If I had my druthers, I'd be on my way home to set a spell with my cat."

"That makes two of us, even though I don't have a

cat."

Father Nick looked worried, perhaps troubled.

Leibowitz was bubbling over with excitement. "Can you believe this? Can you *believe* it? We're going to see the man who started Christianity, and the man who's been falsely maligned for two thousand years."

It was Laila's turn to scowl. "After being in this place for a few days I can believe anything that – "

"Excuse me, folks, but would you come this way, please?" The Air Force captain looked too young for his rank. He fatigues were clean and pressed, his combat boots were highly polished, and his blue beret was cocked at a jaunty angle; yet his face was scruffy with a dark beard that was at least two days old. "We're loading last minute materiel and leaving momentarily."

The captain's soft but firm request put a damper on conversation if not on zest and apprehension. The four civilians passed through the doorway and followed the major to the *Thermopylae's* pylon. What looked like hustle and bustle from afar looked more like pandemonium from under the airframe. Two undercarriage loading hatches were in the process of being closed. Another had its elevator platform sitting on the ground while a handful of soldiers hefted a coffin-sized crate onto it. A stream of other soldiers carried boxes into the pylon; instead of loading them on the central lift, they ran up the circular staircase, taking the steps two at a time.

After the last soldier disappeared on B Deck, the captain indicated for the civilians to follow. "Colonel Davenport has invited you to the cockpit."

Laila recalled that the cockpit was more like the wheelhouse of a naval vessel than the cramped seating arrangement that was found in combat aircraft, in which there was barely enough room to glance aside much less climb out of the seat. The foursome climbed quietly up to A Deck, then trooped along the corridor to the pilothouse.

Bryce and Danette were fiddling with the controls.

Bryce glanced around, nodded. "Take a seat people. Laila sit up here next to Danette. You can plug your computer into the wireless Internet line and download emails until we dephase."

Laila did as she was told. Emails were coming through fast and furious. There were too many to read, and no opportunity to reply, so she let them load into her laptop for later perusal.

"Hi, Laila. I'm sorry things were so hectic the last time, and we couldn't chat."

"That's okay, Danette. I understand that you were under a little pressure."

"A *little*? I was crushed. I'm not cut out to be a test pilot."

"You did just fine, even though you did look as nervous as a long-tailed cat in a room full of rocking chairs, as my granma used to say."

Danette guffawed so loud that everyone stared at her. She put her hand to her mouth. "Sorry."

Bryce slowly shook his head. "Did your grandmother write the book of hillbilly sayings?"

Laila snickered. "No, but she could have. There's a strong oral tradition where I come from."

"South Philly had an oral tradition too but it usually consisted of a string of four-letter words that were shouted in various verb forms and adjectives."

Father Nick grinned. "Perhaps we should update the New Testament with your grandmother's colloquialisms, or add them to the Hebrew Book of Proverbs."

"Solomon would turn over in his grave." Leibowitz squirmed in his back row seat. "Why are we flying instead of riding in Roamers to where the Timepiece is located?"

Kreider furnished the answer. "Because the Skeezicks is a time machine, not a space machine."

Leibowitz no longer scowled. His face donned an expression of impatient inquisitiveness.

"Walt Gouty, our past master, would have explained this to you complete with a demonstration if we didn't have to rush off like this. You see, when the Skeezicks opens a hole in the space-time continuum, it transports the subject matter to the same geographical location with respect to the point of origination. It's as if the hole is anchored by the gravitational attraction of the Earth. Why, we have no idea. But that's the way it is. Call it a natural law of the instantaneous passage through time.

"For what it's worth, Walt speculates that gravity and the moment of time transference are coupled the way magnetism and electricity are coupled. Electromagnetism is a two-fold force in which neither component exists without the other: magnetic flux generates the flow of electrons, while electricity creates a magnetic field. In a similar way, there may be some kind of interaction between gravity and time transference that binds the two components. He refers to this duality as gravitime."

"I – I – I don't – "

Kreider interrupted him by holding up his hand, palm foremost. "I'm getting there. Conjectural constructs aside, what it means is that by some law in the physical makeup of the universe, we can move through space and we can move through time, but we can't do both simultaneously. So when we pass through time we can't pass through space because it's frozen in place for the moment. In short, we're anchored to this spot on the face of the planet during our transference, so we'll appear in the past in the same location that we occupy now.

"We want to be there but not here. With regard to temporal and geospatial coordinates, we not only need to travel back to the time of the Crucifixion but to the vicinity of Jerusalem. That's about two thousand years and seven thousand miles from here, as the crow or sea gull flies along a geodesic curve." He spread his hands wide. "Thus the *Thermopylae*. We can't move the Timepiece to Israel, but we *can* move the *Thermopylae* to the time of the Crucifixion, then fly to Jerusalem."

Leibowitz nodded slowly. "That – that makes sense."

Sarcastically: "I'm glad you agree."

"I hope this isn't a one-way trip. How do we get back?" Laila wanted to know.

"The return fare of this roundtrip travel ticket is two

hundred fifty thousand dollars."

Leibowitz's eyes expanded.

"Only kidding. Bryce, is my noise bothering you?"

"Not at all. We're finished with our preflight checks. We're just waiting for Ted to close the hatches."

"Then I'll keep on enlightening the masses." To Laila and Leibowitz: "Ted Grayson was the captain who coddled us aboard. He's in charge of the Security Force: two squads of government mercenaries that will do our fighting and dirty work."

Leibowitz looked puzzled. "Why do we need so much security on an Air Force plane?"

"No, no, no, you don't understand. The Air Force Security Force is like the Army's Military Police or the Navy's Shore Patrol. They provide base security. But these guys are the Elite Guard component of the SF: equivalent to Navy Seals or Army Special Forces – tough hombres in anybody's good book. Right, Padre?"

Father Nick broke his vow of silence. "The Vatican maintains constabularies to guard the Pope and the grounds, and to handle internal security. We call them Protectors. We send them to the Air Force for training. I daresay that they utilize their military background more often than we care to admit."

"On this mission, their role is to guard us civvies from hostile intent." After a pause: "Getting back to travel visas, vis-a-vis homecoming temporal transportation, my own perambulations were done by way of the Wristwatch: a synchrotron whose diameter is large enough to create a bubble than can enclose no more than three crouching people and my photographic equipment.

"As Walt mentioned, we can't keep the portal open for more than a few nanoseconds. The first thing we'll do upon arrival is to bury a locator under the pylon. The *Thermopylae* has a built-in receiver so we can tune in on the precise location. After four days, Walt will attempt retrievals at twenty-four hour intervals. And voila! Mission accomplished and back to home sweet home the way we remember it."

"And at the same time we left it," Leibowitz added. "Amazing."

"Amazing, yes, but not at the same time."

"I – I – I thought with a time machine – "

Kreider took sadistic pleasure from interrupting Leibowitz. "You thought wrong. Theoretically – or I should say, imaginatively – it should be possible to retrieve subject matter from the same moment as insertion; or, at least, shortly after that moment. But at this stage of the learning curve, we don't know enough about the math of the phenomenon to recalculate transferences on a moving basis. By reproducing subsequent power outputs in accordance with real time, we troll instead of scroll. For now, the operation of the Timepiece requires that the passage of a day in the present corresponds to the passage of a day in the past. Some day we should be able to do as you suggest: recalibrate the reverse phase shift to retrieve subject matter at the moment of insertion, but we can't do it yet. Answer your question?"

Leibowitz nodded feebly.

"As long as we're playing q and a, I'd like to know how you concealed a synchrotron large enough to create a bubble more than two hundred feet in diameter. In what little spare time I had, I looked at satellite images of Area 51. The Wristwatch is in a building so the synchrotron isn't visible from space, but Big Ben has to be, well, huge, in order to create a portal to the past that's large enough to encompass the *Thermopylae.* No such buildings exist around here, and the synchrotron can't be underground because, the way I understand it, underground in the present is underground in the past, and you'd be sending, uh, subject matter into a densely occupied space. Isn't there some kind of rule that states that two objects can't occupy the same space at the same time?"

"Give the lady a gold star." Kreider exchanged knowing grins with Bryce. "And yes, there is such a rule. It's called the Pauli Exclusion Principle, after the formulator of the principle, Wolfgang Pauli. PEP has to do with the quantum states of subatomic particles, but the principle is just as true in the macro world we experience in every day life. For the building site of the Big Ben synchrotron we can thank the AEC.

"It's a little known fact that back in the 1950's the Atomic Energy Commission used part of Area 51 as an A-bomb test site. A-bombs were tested at different heights above ground level by detonating them on top of towers, to ascertain their relative effectiveness. After the nuclear test ban on atmospheric detonations, the project went underground – literally. During the course of a decade, more than nine hundred A-bombs were exploded in a far corner of Area 51: about a hundred of them above ground, the rest at the bottom of deep shafts and tunnels.

"One side effect of an underground blast is the creation of a subsidence crater. Laila, I'm sure you noticed that northwest of here the landscape is as pockmarked like the surface of the Moon."

"I did."

"That's because when an A-bomb is detonated underground, the surrounding rock is fused and compressed, creating a void. The column of earth and rock above the blast site collapses into void, leaving a circular pit and extruded rim wall on the surface. The construction masterminds who built Big Ben cleverly concealed the structure inside the perimeter."

Leibowitz dropped his jaw. "That – that is – that is ingenious."

"I think so, too. The focal point of the focusing nodes is the epicenter; that is, in the middle of the subsidence crater."

Laila's eyes glazed. "Wait a minute. There's no crater in the past. That means that anything sent back from the present would materialize beneath the surface."

"Give the lady another gold star." Kreider turned to Bryce. "You were right. This gal is smart." To Laila: "Matter exists everywhere on and above the surface of the planet. The difference between underground matter and above ground matter is density: rock versus air. Transferred subject matter doesn't displace preexisting material, it expels it. The expulsion of atmosphere and airborne particulate matter creates a sudden gust of expelled air. The expulsion of densely packed earth creates a bubble burst akin to an atomic detonation without radioactive fallout."

A picture was forming in Laila's mind. "So you've already hollowed out our landing zone, or time zone, or whatever you call it."

"Exactly. The bubble is globular, so Walt activated Big Ben for a test run and excavated an opening for the *Thermopylae* – which, by the way, we call a TLA, for temporal landing zone; although Walt, in his infinite wisdom and preference for scientific jargon, uses the initials SCCS, for synchronized chronological convergence sector. Even Walt doesn't know how to pronounce the acronym. Now if we can get the power grid synchronized with the previous transference coordinates – something that's never been tried before – we should materialize in a spot that's only occupied by gaseous material and a few dust motes."

Leibowitz was quick to see the light. "What – what – what do you mean, it's never been tried before?"

"I mean, dear doctor, that we've never gone back to the same moment twice. Lacking mathematical proofs, any number of consequences can occur if we arrive too early: we may be bounced back to the present courtesy of Pauli, we may merge with the topsoil and be converted to fertilizer, or Big Ben will go up in a puff of plasma or primordial matter known as ylem. I wish we had more time to experiment."

Chapter 19

By the look on his face, Leibowitz had traded his enthusiasm for apprehension.

Kreider didn't help. "Let's hope that Walt's temporal mathematics fits in with reality, and doesn't gouge an impossible hole in it like my digger analogy. We'll soon know."

"But – but – but couldn't we do a mock transference first? I mean – "

"It takes nearly a day to recharge the capacitors and realign the focusing nodes; they get knocked out of whack by the implosion of air rushing in to fill the vacuum created by the transference of subject matter. We can't wait that long. If we don't go now, we might not have another opportunity. What's worse – "

Bryce held up his hand. "Strap in. We're moving."

For the first time, Laila noticed that Bryce and Danette were each wearing a single earphone for communication purposes. This was a departure from helmets and headphones that pilots wore in conventional combat aircraft. They also wore subvocal throat microphones and oral dampeners; when their voices were transmitted, the dampener absorbed any sound that escaped from between the lips.

She fastened her seatbelt. She didn't feel any movement, but she could picture what was happening.

Danette waited a full thirty seconds after she initiated the take-off alarm so that the pylon could be retracted into the undercarriage on its telescoping tubes. Then she applied precisely enough thrust on the throttle control to lift the *Thermopylae* a few inches off the ground. She then angled and directed the nuclear engines a tad in order to apply forward motion. The hangar doors were already open. The *Thermopylae* slipped out of the hangar without a lurch, gathered speed and altitude simultaneously, and headed for the atomic bomb testing range a score of miles away.

"But – but – "

"No buts," Bryce announced.

Laila admired the clear sky. It was filled with stars whose illumination was not affected by atmospheric heat inversions. They shone bright and untwinkling, like overhead substitutes in a planetarium. She steeled herself for what she imagined was going to be a great adventure: not just the greatest adventure in her short and mundane life as a desk jockey, but the greatest adventure in the history of mankind.

Kreider eyed Leibowitz over his shoulder. "I was just funning with you, Perfessor. Walt made the hole a hundred years before our planned moment of arrival. It's barely a dimple in the ground, but enough to fit the *Thermopylae* as long as she's hovering. Can do, Danette?"

"Can do." Danette raised her voice in order to override the dampener. She was far more confident and relaxed on this flight than she had been on the previous one. "Even if I don't, we'll drop less than a hundred feet and feel a slight jar after the extender hydraulic systems absorb some of the shock."

Leibowitz looked relieved.

Bryce spun his seat to face his audience. "According to Laila's intel the IRF synchrotron is only large enough to transfer an object the size of a truck – say a deuce-and-a-half. That means limited troops and weapons. Of course they could transfer reinforcements after they re-power the TDA so as we say on a combat mission expect the unexpected."

"Will – will your troops protect us?"

"If they don't they'd better have a good reason why at their court-martial." Bryce spun back to his console.

Leibowitz looked only partly mollified.

The acceleration was so slight that Laila felt the same as if she were sitting in a tour bus on a sightseeing ride through rolling countryside, except that there were no bumps, jolts, or sudden stops. Danette attempted no radical maneuvers. The *Thermopylae* had already been put through the paces. Now the aircraft was simply being used as a transport to accomplish a task that did not require the aircraft's full capabilities: much like a racecar that was being driven to the grocery store on off-track days.

"Drives like a Mack truck," Bryce scowled over his shoulder.

"Or a jumbo commercial airliner," Danette added. "She wasn't designed for speed but for endurance and creature comforts that long-range bombers lack."

"We're carrying a few nukes just for the heck of it in Bomb Bay One but this is a defensive mission not offensive."

Through the pilothouse picture windows Laila looked for landing lights as a reference point. When none appeared, she realized that both the aircraft and the synchrotron were operating under stealth mode.

Danette and Bryce communicated in soft tones through throat mikes and earphone receivers. Laila could not hear so much as a murmur of either incoming or outgoing transmissions. Her laptop continued to download messages that she would debrief after transference, when the connection would be broken.

Danette homed in on a buried transponder whose signal registered on one of the front screens above the windows. Short-range radio transmission was used instead of landing lights so as not to attract attention from enemy spy satellites. She centered the aircraft over the radio beacon, then slowly reduced altitude until the four lateral quadrant transponders indicated that the *Thermopylae* was within the boundaries of the bubble wrap both vertically and horizontally.

"Now we wait." Bryce leaned back in his seat. His voice was calm but his manner was taut.

"What are we waiting for?" Leibowitz wanted to know.

"The okay from high command."

"But – but I thought you were in charge of this Mission."

"I have tactical control but General Cercopley has overall strategic control. Once he gives me the go ahead I take full control in the field. Until that happens we wait."

Leibowitz was persistent. "If you're *in* charge of the Mission, why aren't you *taking* charge?

Bryce spun his seat in order to confront Leibowitz face to face. He explained the situation in his best fatherly manner. "The military operates on a chain of command from the highest level down to the lowliest corpsman much like a corporation except that our business is not to sell a product or offer a service for a profit but to engage an enemy in combat whenever the top brass decides that military intervention is the only way to solve an ongoing political conflict. Let me give you an example of the way the system works because it's been working well ever since the formation of armed forces in pre-civilization days.

"Let's say for example that I'm in charge of a combat unit that consists of four platoons. I'm standing on a high hill overlooking the battlefield so I can see everything that's going on below me. I order my platoon leaders to engage the enemy on three fronts: two platoons head on and one from either side. The objective is not just to vanquish the enemy but to prevent them from overrunning my position. By watching the engagement from the hilltop I can see more than the individual soldiers can see on the battlefront because their vision is blocked by their ground-level view which is also obscured by trees and vegetation. They can see only the enemy in front of them.

"Now I notice that the platoon on the right is about to be outflanked. That means that the enemy can go around the platoon without engaging it and head straight up the hill to my command post. I order one of the frontline platoons to break off its engagement and assist the platoon on the right.

"At that moment the platoon leader of that frontline platoon might be within a hairsbreadth of overwhelming the army in front of him. He doesn't want to break off contact because he's about to win the battle. But in the big picture winning one battle is not as important as protecting my command post. If the platoon leader disobeys my order to disengage his enemy and help the platoon whose situation he can't see or appreciate then he may win his battle but my command post will be overrun and the war is lost.

"In the present situation I'm the platoon leader and General Cercopley is the mission commander. I want to proceed with this mission just as much as you do. But I don't know what Cercopley knows. He not only has my mission under his command but he has other missions that I don't know about. Perhaps he needs the *Thermopylae* for something more important than my mission or for an alternative way to accomplish the goal of this mission.

"He's also dealing with political situations that are not within my purview. He reports to the Joint Chiefs and they report to the President. Each position higher up the chain of command possesses a larger picture of worldwide events and how my mission fits into those events: political events as well as military events. It would be irresponsible for me to proceed on my mission without the authority to do so because even if I succeed I might do irreparable damage in some way that I can't imagine because of my lower viewpoint.

"Cercopley didn't authorize this mission plan without considering alternatives. As a military commander he wants to achieve his objective the simplest way possible with the minimum loss of life. The obvious solution and his first choice was a multiple-front missile strike on the enemy's nuclear weapons and time transference facilities. The President had to veto that suggestion because of its political ramifications with regard to United Nations members and worldwide public and media outcries against unauthorized aggression.

"Economic sanctions are useless because the IRF doesn't belong to any one country but operates on the fringe in a number of countries that aren't necessarily friendly with each other. Clandestine insurgent operations run in present real-time might work but would still encounter stern opposition from the United Nations and world peace organizations. Even if we had proof of the development of weapons of mass destruction a full frontal ground attack against a foreign country would be held under suspicion by the rest of the world because previous proofs have been unfounded.

"Every option has political considerations that only the President and his advisors can measure. So you see that we're not playing a game of personal domination or who can bully who; this is serious business that has to be conducted not only according to the value of ultimate achievement but to the rules of national and international politics.

"There's no room in the military for free agents. We work as a team. I expect my platoon leaders to do as they're told and Cercopley expects me to do as *I* am told. So we wait."

There was a long silence as Leibowitz digested the wealth of information. Eventually: "That – that makes sense. That makes a lot of sense."

"Furthermore unlike other missions this one has a disadvantage in that once it gets the go-ahead it can't be called off or modified because there's no communication between past and present. We can't get additional intel. We can't give feedback on our progress. We can't call for reinforcements. We're on our own and have to proceed as best we can in accordance with our operational orders."

Leibowitz nodded silently and slowly.

"When I give you or my troops an order it's not because I'm trying to exercise my authority. It's because I'm doing what I think best to ensure that the objectives of this Mission are met."

Leibowitz kept nodding.

"You've been a big help so far but the Mission is far from over. I'm counting on your cooperation and language skills to help us in the past. Can I count on you?"

"Of – of – of course."

"Good. Just keep in mind that when I give orders it's because I need something done even if my subordinates don't understand the reason why. Is that understood?"

"Understood. I – I mean, really understood."

Bryce leaned forward and patted Leibowitz on the shoulder. "I know you'll do your best."

Leibowitz kept nodding.

He was still nodding when Danette tapped the loud-speaker button, and announced, "Listen up, people. We have a go-ahead. They are engaging the synchronization sequencers as we speak. As we discussed during re-hearsal, there won't be any spatial movement during transference, but according to our local expert – " She leaned forward and winked at Luke Kreider, to her right on the other side of Bryce. " – there will be a feeling of disorientation and possibly one of nausea. Hold onto your stomachs."

Laila did her best to relax but found the anticipation was too much to bear. She steadied her laptop on the console despite Danette's instruction that they wouldn't feel any motion. She glanced at her companions-in-arms who were sharing this grand venture to yesteryear. She studied their faces. Everyone showed tenseness – except, perhaps, Father Nick. He was clutching his *Bible* to his breast as if it might be yanked away from him by a godless zealot. His eyes were closed and his lips were moving in what appeared to be silent prayer.

"Father Nick, are you praying for all of us?"

He opened his eyes and smiled softly at Laila. "I was repeating the twenty-third Psalm: 'Yea, though I walk through the valley of the shadow of death, I will fear no evil: for thou art with me; thy rod and thy staff they comfort me.' "

Kreider humphed. "At a moment like this I wish I had your faith."

"Have no cares, my son. We will prevail." Father Nick smiled more broadly as he repeated a line of dialogue that was straight out of *The Blues Brothers*: "We're on a mission from God."

Chapter 20

Laila felt an abrupt, gut-wrenching twist in the pit of her stomach, the way she remembered a steep drop on the shoot-the-chute as a preschooler. But this was no amusement park rollercoaster ride.

This was physical transcendence: a transference through the temporal barrier to the halcyon times that everyone longed for when they reminisced about the "good ole days," and unconsciously overlooked such critical truths as infant death, poor health, rampant disease, short lifespan, uncertain medical treatment, oppressive government, slavery, social inequity, class inequality, religious intolerance, and a host of other realisms that people tended to ignore or forget when they ranted about current unfavorable conditions such as unemployment, excessive taxation, child care costs, health insurance premiums, utility charges, gasoline prices, lawsuits, mental instability, unstable relationships, racial prejudice, homeless people, alternative lifestyles, and government intervention that proscribed preferred ways of life because the majority passed laws by which those in the minority were forced to live.

Some might claim that the perceived plenitude of the twenty-first century was a delusion, that enlightenment was a theoretical concept, and that the major difference between the ancient world and the modern one was merely a matter of degree.

Christians were no longer fed to lions in an arena so that bloodthirsty spectators could revel in the terror and gore of the losers. Instead, young men were drafted and sent to fight wars in foreign lands while more fortunate people sat comfortably at home in front of television sets and watched soldiers die in combat.

Slaves were no longer beaten for lack of subservience. Instead, people worked overtime in low-paying jobs in order to earn enough money to keep out of debt and not lose their houses or precious belongings. Those who didn't labor hard enough or long enough, or who weren't smart enough to learn higher-paying occupations, or who lost their jobs due to a failing economy, suffered the ignominy of welfare from which it was nearly impossible to escape.

Because of their low tax bracket, impoverished citizens who didn't fill government coffers as much as wealthy corporate barons were further penalized at the end of their lives by receiving reduced social security benefits, despite a lifetime of endeavor. They started downtrodden and they ended downtrodden.

People could not relax with mild recreational substances in the privacy of their homes without fear of prosecution and imprisonment, while those of a different bent could drink themselves to oblivion on alcohol with the government's sanction and blessing.

Debauchery was as much a part of everyday life in the present as it had ever been in the past; perhaps more so.

The list of injustices seemed as long today as it did during the height of the Roman empire.

Laila's brain seemed to have been wrenched as much as her stomach as these and other unsavory thoughts passed through her mind like fleeting images in an iconographic montage. Was modern society more enlightened than civilizations of the past, or just more technologically advanced?

Her mosaic of mental acuity faded as she became more aware of her surroundings. Bright sunshine streamed into the wheelhouse through the long row of picture windows. She gasped so hard that her first breath in the past felt like a return-to-consciousness inhalation after a long bout of mouth-to-mouth resuscitation, or perhaps like the initial breath of a newborn infant after passing through the birth canal into the world of light and confusion. She wanted to cry.

She imagined that she heard Judy Garland singing "Some*when* over the Rainbow."

She beheld vague shapes that gradually morphed into people. She heard retching that sounded like the coughing spasm of a long-time smoker. She heard a vaguely familiar voice declare, "I told you this would happen." When her eyes finally focused, she saw Bryce toss a towel onto Leibowitz's lap. The erstwhile translator promptly vomited onto the olive drab cloth.

Bryce pointed a triumphant finger at Danette. "You owe me five bucks lady."

Laila's perceptions slowly returned to normal – or what passed for normal in a world in which time travel was possible. "Wow! That sure tickles your innards."

Kreider was philosophical. "I nearly threw up the first time, too. It gets easier with repetition."

"You should know. You're our local expert."

"When you're outside without a spacesuit it takes your breath away. The expulsion of air, you know. It was less stressful in here with the hatches sealed."

"Still maintaining hover," Danette announced.

"Nice job." Bryce glanced over the controls, absorbed the information on the readouts, and checked the various monitors and computer screens. "Everything looks normal."

The captain appeared at the wheelhouse doorway. He was holding one hand to his stomach and looked a little green around the gills. "Sir?"

"Ah Ted. Come on in. Is everyone okay?"

"As far as I can tell."

"Good. You've met Laila Masterson and Dr. Leibowitz. This is my right hand man that Luke was telling you about."

The handsome young captain nodded curtly. He was the silent type.

"How about last minute supplies?"

"Everything is on board but, quite frankly, it's a mess."

Bryce held up his hand as a stop order. "Luke, what can you tell me? Should we land?"

Kreider looked out the window. "Unless there's been a pole shift, I'd say it's about two o'clock in the afternoon. I can't get a star fix till after dark so I don't know if we hit the right century much less the right day of the month.

"Understood." To Grayson: "You and the troops get some rest. Sort things out later. We've got a long flight ahead of us and we'll be landing for a photo fix along the way."

"Very good, sir."

After his departure: "He's too formal. I can't break him of that 'sir' habit." To Danette: "Take her to the top and put her on cruise control then hit the sack."

Danette's fingers played along the keyboard controls. She manipulated the joystick. "I sure wish we'd had time to test it before we left."

"We've got plenty of time now. What's the worst that can happen?"

Leibowitz demonstrated anxiety. "What – what do you mean – test?"

"We were supposed to have several more trial runs but ran out of time – literally in this case. I'm sure the autopilot will work although we have to navigate by compass."

"What's wrong with the GPS? It worked on the test flight."

Bryce kept a straight face, although it appeared to Laila that it was difficult for him to maintain. "We had satellites in the twenty-first century." He let it go at that. "Nick you'll be bunking with Luke. Dr. Leibowitz has a room to himself next to yours. Why don't you show him the way?"

Father Nick looked relieved that he wasn't sharing a room with Leibowitz. "Gladly."

"I'll take a tour of the aircraft and check on my people. Danette show Laila to her bunk as soon as you finish up here. I'll pick a technician to relieve you."

Danette nodded. "Okay."

The men filed off the bridge; Leibowitz swayed.

Danette angled the nuclear engines on their swivels. The *Thermopylae* accelerated skyward at the speed of a fast-moving elevator, while at the same time swooping eastward. "Is he really that dumb?"

"Who? Leibowitz?" Laila unplugged her laptop from the Internet connection because, as Bryce noted so succinctly, without orbiting satellites the sky was absent of transmissions on all frequencies. "If he's putting on an act he's got me fooled. He doesn't live in the real world. He lives in books and ancient manuscripts."

"Nonetheless, we wouldn't be here without him. The Vatican translators were stymied by some of the words and a lot of the usages and idioms that don't make sense unless you can relate them to the cultures in which they were written. That's what Nick Derpilbosian said, anyway. Some of the expressions were figures of speech that couldn't be translated literally because they were meant to be symbolic. The trick was in understanding the symbolism in context with contemporary religious and political agendas. Nick said that was how Leibowitz translated the other Dead Sea Scrolls to achieve a greater understanding of their meaning. The man may be an egomaniac who lacks social skills, but he's a brilliant egomaniac."

Laila lightly touched the fading purple bruise that surrounded her left eye. "He has a good right hook, too."

"I saw it on the surveillance camera."

Laila snickered. "I hope you recorded it."

"It was recorded but Bryce erased it. Anyway, I wish I could give you a for-instance that Nick passed along, but even though I attended an Episcopalian church until my parents divorced when I was ten, I have to admit that I don't remember too much of the Scriptures. I was a kid and they didn't mean much to me. I was more interested in Mother Goose and, later, Nancy Drew.

"What confused me the most about the Old Testament was the contradictory image of God. On one hand you were supposed to love Him, while on the other you were supposed to fear Him. How can you love someone you fear? God is portrayed as both benevolent and vengeful. How can a creator claim to love his children and then kill them all by destroying the world? If He's so all-powerful – omniscient, I think, is the word – couldn't he think of a more humane approach to take in solving the problem of his children going astray? The *Bible* is a litany of death and destruction and the suffering of mankind. Why did He make people suffer when He had the power to prevent it? Why did He just sit back and let it all happen? Why didn't He intervene and make life easier for children He was supposed to love?

"For that matter, why did He kick Adam and Eve out of the Garden of Eden for such a trivial offense as eating an apple? Maybe they deserved a spanking, but eternal banishment is a punishment that doesn't fit the crime. Would any self-respecting mother kick her children out of the house forever for committing what's nothing more than a misdemeanor? God must have deep-seated emotional issues if He was willing to go to such an extreme over a minor act of disobedience. Was He that shallow and insecure?

"Anyhow, Nick talked about how much of the *Bible* was not intended to be taken literally, but as parable. The Dead Sea Scrolls are the same. What the Vatican didn't know was that what they thought was another version of the Gospel according to Judas was actually a memoir of Christ's last days on Earth; last couple of years. So they interpreted a lot of the passages – those that they were able to read correctly – as allegory: Judas's way of transcribing the teachings of Christ as Christian principles.

"According to Nick, there are so many discrepancies in the canonical Gospels – those of the four major disciples: Matthew, Mark, Luke, and John – that Vatican scholars assumed that they were differently worded morality tales. They didn't get suspicious until they got back the results of the carbon-14 tests. That's when they realized how wrong they were.

Laila snickered again. "So even the Roman Catholic church has preconceived notions."

"And how! They try to gloss over biblical incongruities as mistakes that were made by later scribes who copied the original manuscripts incorrectly, or made typographical errors; maybe transcription errors is a better phrase. How else to explain the variations in the canonical accounts. Whew. I've learned more Christian history since Nick arrived than I ever remember from *Bible* school. Why, when you look at the *Bible* too closely, you get the feeling that the foundations of the church are made of wet cement."

Laila laughed out loud. "That's one of the reasons why I declined baptism."

"What!"

"Don't tell Father Nick any of this. I wouldn't want to hurt his feelings. The first time I realized that everything wasn't kosher in the world – if you'll pardon a rabbinical expression – was when I found out there wasn't any Santa Claus. Okay, you laugh. But as a child I was devastated. He was my hero! I looked forward to sitting in his lap.

"Once I accepted that my parents had been deceiving me – and that took quite a while – I began to question the validity of everything they told me. And not just my parents but every adult. That led me to question my *Bible* teachings. The older I grew, the more I began to see biblical history as absurd as a fat funny fellow in a red cloth suit climbing down a chimney of every house in the world in a single night. Talk about leaping over tall buildings in a single bound! Every page of the Old Testament was filled with situations that were equally as bizarre and impossible. I couldn't believe it. And I began to wonder how other people could believe it? Intelligent adults.

"I kept going to Sunday school (I was a prize student) but when it came time for baptism (at the age of fourteen) I demurred. I went down to the river with the preacher and the other kids, but when they waded into the water, I realized that I couldn't go through with it. My family was mortified – especially my grandfather because he was a deacon – but I stood my ground. We talked about it for years but I never gave in. Finally the issue just faded away."

Danette kept her eyes on the controls and monitors. "I've kept my lack of religious upbringing from Nick, too. There's no need to stir up bad feelings when it can be avoided. He's not pushy, anyway."

"I noticed that. I suspect that he has more faith in Christian values than in the belief system that promulgates them."

"I get that impression, too."

"So what's the game plan? Where are we? Or *when* are we? I've been so busy with my own work . . . "

"We're supposed to have arrived a few days before the Crucifixion. We don't have a time clock that works like a speedometer. Luke and Walt worked together on making correction factors based on Luke's stellar observations and Walt's power outputs. They seem confident that their calculations are fairly good. We weren't supposed to leave the landing zone, or time zone, until Luke took a star fix – so we could return to the future and try again if we arrived too early or late – but Bryce has confidence in *their* confidence. That's why he gave the order not to fly until nightfall, when we can obtain verification.

"We should have enough time to scout the area, get the lay of the land, and hopefully pick Muslim terrorists out of the crowd before they cause any trouble. Kreider has already picked a hidden location to set down; some place in the mountains where the *Thermopylae* won't be seen."

"Not Mount Ararat, I hope."

Danette laughed. "If it's a real place, I don't think anyone knows where it's located."

A technician named Rob entered the wheelhouse and announced that he was Danette's relief. By this time the *Thermopylae* had reached top altitude and was proceeding eastward at cruising speed on automatic pilot.

"Don't touch the controls," Danette warned. "If anything unusual happens, call me or Bryce." To Laila: "You can't go very far in this aircraft, and there aren't many places to hide."

"Yes, ma'am."

Danette led Laila off the bridge. "We'll have a briefing before we head out of the hills."

Their private quarters was a closet with two fold-down bunks. Laila took the bottom. She was asleep within seconds after her head touched the pillow.

Chapter 21

A vertical slash of light roused Laila from a sound sleep. Gone was the faint vibratory noise of the *Thermopylae* flying in stealth mode; it was replaced by a silence that was broken only by faint strains of music from far away, and an even fainter sound of pattering. Otherwise the aircraft merely thrummed like a disturbed hornet's nest. Partially refreshed, she opened her eyes in time to see Danette slipping out of their cubbyhole. She threw off the sheet, sat up, stuck her feet into her jogging shoes, and – still wearing hospital scrubs – followed the pilot to the wheelhouse.

As she approached the open doorway she identified the tune as one that had been recorded by the Rolling Stones: "Time Is on My Side."

The flight crew triumvirate occupied their seats: pilot, copilot, and navigator.

"Who picked the song?"

Kreider raised his left hand. "Guilty as charged."

Danette swiveled her seat. "I didn't mean to wake you."

Instead of sitting, Laila leaned forward and peered through the rain-swept windows. "How can you get a star fix and Moon phase in conditions like this? It's raining pitchforks and hoe handles, as my granma used to say."

"Bryce got ahead of the storm and landed before the sky clouded over. Luke took some snapshots just in time. Uh, no pun intended."

Bryce winked over his shoulder.

"And we do have time on our side," Kreider announced. "Although we're cutting it close. We're about four days ahead of schedule. That is, according to the little bugger who plotted our course through the black zone. God bless him; no one else will."

Each window was equipped with a centrifugal wiper that spun at high speed and whisked the dripping water off the Plexiglas. External floodlights illuminated a clearing in the middle of a dense forest of hardwoods whose leaves were whipping in the breeze like party ribbons in front of a ventilation fan.

"So where are we?" Laila wanted to know.

"I'll give you a hint. You could buy the whole place for twenty-four dollars' worth of trade goods."

"Manhattan!"

"Of course, when Peter Minuit bought the island it was only worth twenty-four dollars. It had nothing but trees on it, and the Indians already had plenty of those on the mainland. The buildings are what makes the real estate valuable today. Er, in the twenty-first century."

"So, is this Central Park?"

Bryce: "I brought her across the Upper Bay from the south-southwest and landed in the first affordable clearing. I think we're somewhere near the Federal Reserve Bank. Okay ready for takeoff? Here we go."

The *Thermopylae* lifted ever so gently. Laila detected a slight sway on the deck as the buffeting wind rocked the hull as if it were a baby's cradle.

Danette offered a few words of advice: "Increase the speed of the gyroscope in conjunction with the control jets. That will overcome the tendency to wobble."

Bryce concentrated on his flying. He flicked off the floodlights after the *Thermopylae* flew over the treetops. He gradually increased upward acceleration until the aircraft rose above the storm. Then he translated some of the lift to airspeed.

Kreider explained: "I can't get accurate readings in flight for two reasons: there's too much movement from contrary gusts, and the upward facing windows are partially obscured by condensation. That's why we had to land."

"Plot a great circle route for the hills outside of Jerusalem."

Kreider used the navigational computer to do as Bryce ordered. "It's all yours, skipper. Put her on autopilot and go to bed. Please. I'll wake you when we get there."

Laila noticed the weariness in his eyes. "You could

use forty winks."

"I could use fifty, but I'll have to settle for thirty." He missed his usual sprightly step as he ambled out of the pilothouse.

"He looks beat."

"He *is* beat." Danette didn't look a whole lot better. "He's been carrying an enormous amount of responsibility on his shoulders. Except for a few catnaps, he's hardly slept a wink since before we picked you up at Andrews. Quite frankly, we didn't expect the mission to proceed at such a fever pitch. Once Leibowitz translated the Scrolls, and you learned about the TDA going operational, we had no choice but to get out of Dodge before Dodge never existed."

Kreider shook his head. "Walt offered Godspeed, but even irrational numbers didn't help with his time travel calculations. Maybe it's more than by the grace of a monotheistic god that we made it through the temporal barrier without getting lost in the millennia." He shook his head again. "I don't like the idea of shuffling chronology until we know a hell of a lot more about the possible side effects of altering the past. But if we don't do it, the IRF will, and they don't have the best interests of the world at heart."

Laila's face was bland, or perhaps a bit pale or peaked. "It scares *me*, and I don't even understand the physics or potential conflicts. I can only see the situation from the viewpoint of a finite mind trying to comprehend infinity: it has to be impossible to create a paradox that violates the universal law of time. I know that's straight-line thinking – that time must flow like a river from source to sea – but I don't know any other way to perceive it."

"I'll trade shoes any day. And hats. A background in mathematics doesn't give you any better of an insight about contra-chronicity than you already have. Sometimes I think I'd rather be as ignorant as the huddled masses, ignore the issues at stake, and wake up one morning to find myself nonexistent. Now there's a paradox for you."

Not a snicker.

Danette winced. "Maybe we'd all be happier if, like you said earlier, we had Nick's faith."

"Yeah, well, faith doesn't keep you alive when a man-eating lion is leaping at your throat. Don't get me wrong. I like Nick. I even love him in the Roman Catholic sense. But delusion will only carry you so far. Eventually the teeth of reality bite down on your throat, and all the faith in the world won't keep you alive. That turn-the-other-cheek philosophy doesn't work against fanatics that would rather see you dead than practicing a different belief system. Talk about intolerance."

No one laughed at this sober observation.

"Did I overhear my name in vain?" Father Nick entered the pilothouse and sat in the seat that Bryce had vacated.

"Nothing personal, padre. We were just passing time – er, making small talk – by stating platitudes."

"If the Vatican did not recognize that it was not always realistic to turn the other cheek, the Pope and his advisors would not have supported this mission."

"Yeah, I'll give them credit for that. Even the church realizes that sometimes you have to do what you have to do, even if it goes against your grain. Doesn't the *Bible* say that God helps those who help themselves? Well, I guess we're helping ourselves instead of sitting back nonchalantly and waiting for the second coming."

"This is a truism."

"It's about the only catechism I remember. Most of what I know about apostolic Christianity I learned from listening to *Jesus Christ Superstar*."

"Somehow that does not surprise me."

"No offense, Padre."

"I seldom take offense. When I do, I simply turn the other cheek."

"Oh, you heard that part, too."

"My hearing is astute. It comes from years of straining my ears to hear the mumblings of otherwise good Christians in the confessional."

Laila continued to stand and stare out the window.

"Don't take this the wrong way, but going to church doesn't make you a good Christian any more than standing in a garage makes you a good auto mechanic. I've attended a number of sermons whose doctrines were forgotten as soon as the flock escaped the barn. The most worshipful bitty who uttered hosannas and amens would snipe at you as soon as the preacher left the altar."

"All too true, I am afraid."

Kreider chuckled. "You can lead a person to holy water but you can't make him drink."

Laila continued: "There was so much spiritual contention in the county where I grew up that whenever more than one person disagreed with expressed dogma, they started their own church and became proselytes for a new order. There were twenty-seven churches in a county whose population numbered all of four thousand, and that included dogs, cats, and farm animals."

"Surely you exaggerate."

"Not by much. We had churches so small that they only had one hitching post."

"Now you're on a roll."

"I'm on a baked West Virginia biscuit. The people changed churches as often as they changed their clothes. If they didn't like what the preacher had to say, they up and moved to another church that was usually within stalking distance."

"Sounds like a game of musical churches."

"It was worse. They weren't content to just listen to another preacher; they had to backbite the one they just left. Gossip flew across the pews faster than pig swill at feeding time. The family that stayed together didn't always pray together. Some families that lived under the same roof went to three different churches. Then they all came home and had dinner together as if it were the commonest thing in the world.

"When I got out of bed on Sunday morning, I never knew which church my mama would take me to. If she was sick, I went to an altogether different church with my daddy. Some days I went to two churches: a sermon with my mama and *Bible* school with my daddy. Got to be that I was on a first name basis with every preacher in the county by the time I was six; and all their kinfolk, too."

"Did you wake up with your panties in a bunch?"

"All the churches used the same hymnal so I had no trouble memorizing the songs; but the preachers created their own liturgies. As a grade-schooler I raised quite a few eyebrows when I gave the wrong response or responded out of turn. Sometimes – "

Danette couldn't hold it in any longer. She laughed so hard and so long that tears rolled down her ebony cheeks. Kreider and Father Nick were similarly affected.

"I'm being serious, people." Nonetheless, Laila cracked a smile. "Although, to be fair, the difference between Southern Baptists and Muslim terrorists is that *our* devout believers used rhetoric to convert their brethren, not explosives."

Kreider smirked. "If that's what you call old time religion, I'm all for it. Nobody gets killed in a mudslinging contest."

"A lot of people had their feelings hurt." Laila pondered for a moment. "But they had all their body parts at the end of the quarrel. A hardline Baptist might cut you to the quick but she wouldn't use a knife to do it. That certainly adds perspective to the way Islam is practiced."

Father Nick agreed. "I suppose every religion has its zealots and extremists. Islam may be the first to have *only* zealots and extremists."

"Whoa, whoa, whoa. The padre makes a slur against the dregs of humanity. I'm shocked." Kreider's face was a mixture of surprise and awe. "I'll give the Vatican credit on that score: the control they exercise over their subjects is benevolent rather than belligerent. Catholics don't sanction extreme force against dissenters."

"Thank you, Luke."

"I have nothing against organized religion. You know that. I think faith is a great thing for people to have if they need it. It's shoving faith down the throat of a person who doesn't want it that I'm against."

"Neither the Vatican nor I would disagree with you. We endorse universal tolerance."

"On the other hand, I'll bet that Leibowitz would say that the only difference between organized religion and organized crime is that religion convinces people to make payoffs by promising them an afterlife, instead of threatening them with no life after."

"It is not my place to speak for another."

"Hey, Padre. Not to change subjects but, as long as we're talking about Liebowitz and religion, what did he mean about going back to 4005 BC?" To Laila: "The old reprobate complained about his room until he saw that Nick and I were sharing one the same size. Then he made that quirky comment before he closed his door."

Father Nick nodded. "I must admit that once he got over his initial apprehension about this reversal of time, he has become somewhat tractable; not likeable, you understand, but almost tolerable."

"Coming from Nick, that says a lot."

"I might go as far as to say that he is even looking forward to it." To Laila: "He professes numerous disagreements about the veracity of the New Testament – "

"Both Testaments."

"Both Testaments, but more about the New Testament. On historical grounds rather than holy grounds."

Kreider laughed. "He thinks the New Testament was written out of whole cloth; er, whole papyrus."

"He questions every word that he did not translate personally. Then he questions the Hebrew words that were copied by later scribes, claiming that they added or subtracted passages so as to challenge the traditional view of Jesus in order to promulgate dissimilar theologies."

Laila humphed. "Sounds a lot like West Virginia churchgoers."

"There is truth in the observation that ancient religious leaders had their own agendas to promote, and that they incorporated polemical stories to support those agendas. It is also true that pre-formative Christian sects vied for dominance, each choosing which sacred tractates to incorporate in their version of the Good Book, and which ones to sanitize, suppress, or censor."

Kreider interrupted. "The only good censorship is no censorship."

"On the other hand, his view of the worth of the *Bible* and the churches that employ its allegories is far too simplistic. While it may be accurate that the world is driven not by truth but by the perception of truth, it is just as accurate that symbolism is more readily assimilated by people to whom the workings of the world are far too complex a mystery to comprehend. People with faith are people with hope. They are people who can endure the suffering of this world because of their belief in the one hereafter. It is not for me to state which beliefs are misguided. Misguidance results from the manner in which people respond to their beliefs."

The good father's eloquence was followed by an insightful moment of silence.

"Leibowitz made sense, though, when he said that every god-fearing believer in the world was a heretic to the orthodoxy of every other group." Kreider pinched his eyebrows. "Getting back to Mr. Always Right, what did he mean about 4005 BC?"

Father Nick took a deep breath. "I suppose I must repeat an oft-told historical reference that is taught in seminary school. James Ussher was a seventeenth-century bishop, biblical scholar, and staunch creationist. Using the Genesis in combination with a large number of historical texts, he constructed a precise chronology of the world from the very day of Creation. According to his calculations, working backward from the birth of Christ, the actual date of Creation was October 23, 4004 BC."

"You've got to be kidding."

Father Nick grimaced.

"Is that in the Julian calendar?"

Father Nick raised his eyebrows.

Kreider laughed out loud. "So Leibowitz wants to go back to the year before the biblical Creation to prove that Ussher was talking through his habit."

Father Nick grimaced and raised his eyebrows. "So I surmise. I suspect that he was making a little joke at the Vatican's expense. Bear in mind, however, that no one in the Roman Catholic church accepts the legitimacy of the bishop's timetable. It is one of those cumbersome quirks of Christian history that, quite frankly, is better forgotten."

"Leibowitz didn't forget it. And it doesn't require a leap of faith to assume that he's not going to forget it."

"I daresay you are correct. Yet, despite Dr. Leibowitz's antisocial behavior, he has already proven his worth on this Mission. I would go as far as to declare that he could well be perceived as our Savior's savior." Father Nick shook his head. "God works in mysterious ways, but this time He has outdone Himself."

Chapter 22

Danette's bunk was empty when Laila awoke; the pilot of the *Thermopylae* was still sitting at the controls. Laila felt completely refreshed for the first time in a week. She had even caught up on her emails before dropping off to sleep. Of course, she caught up only because it was no longer possible to download incoming mail; new messages would be stuck on the server until she returned to the twenty-first century.

She found Wendayne Robbins in the galley. She had no idea of the local time because her cell phone was in her dormitory room in Area 51, and the walkie-talkie did not display time. Nonetheless: "Good morning, Wendy. Am I early or late for a meal?"

"Honey chile, it don't make no never-mind in this outfit. They's always somebody eatin' one meal or 'nother, dependin' upon whether they's goin' on duty or comin' off. An' Ah'm always cookin'. Ah kin make you aigs iff'n you want, but I suggest you try some of ma homemade lamb stew." She placed a steaming bowl on the table, along with a hard crusty roll. "That's fer dippin'."

"I'll go with the chef's special." Laila dug into the stew with both hands: one for the roll and one for the tablespoon.

Wendayne placed a cup of hot brew in front of Laila. "That's likely the last coffee you'll git till this Mission is over."

"Thanks." Between mouthfuls: "It's so quiet in here. Where is everyone?"

"Either outside or down below gitten out supplies." Wendayne leaned close to Laila, and whispered. "Afore we left I niggled yer prime suspects fer info. Didn't git much. Varvarelis's got a honey in town, which explains why his wife complained about him not comin' home on weekends. He made a pass at me, too. Gouty don't talk much, but by teasin' him jus' right I got him to say as how he wants real bad to go to the conf'rence in Prague:

more to see his long-range girlfriend than to talk 'bout physics. That's a relationship that certainly GU: geographically undesirable. Kreider kin take it or leave it, but he was keepin' in close touch wif his wife and famb'ly till the lockdown. Can't say as I blame him fer that. I gather he's right attached to 'em an' would head straight fer home if it weren't fer his scientific curiosity."

Laila nodded but kept the spoon moving between bowl and lips when she wasn't sopping up liquid with the roll. "Don't these people talk about anything but women?"

"Sho do. The women talk about men." After a pause: "The other techies got ways or means to git info 'bout Project Stitch, an' git it off the base, but Ah'm darned if Ah kin pin any collusion on any of 'em."

"Good work, Wendayne. I'm beginning to believe that we're dealing with a case of pure coincidence. It wouldn't be the first time that a discovery was made by two people independently. Isaac Newton and Gottfried Leibniz formulated differential calculus simultaneously. Charles Darwin and Alfred Wallace separately developed theories of evolution based on natural selection."

"And Sigmund Freud and Carl Jung founded branches of psychiatry. I studied both of them as part of my undercover training. Oops! Got outa character. Ah didn't learn ever'thin' Ah know from Aunt Jemima and Colonel Sanders."

Laila snickered. "There's no one here but us grits: girls raised in the South."

"Sho nuf true."

Laila wolfed down the last of her food and drained her cup of coffee. "Thanks for the meal. Now I'd better go down below and see if I can get in the way."

"Ah'll keep ma ears open fer you."

Laila pattered down the spiral staircase. B Deck was a madhouse, or so it seemed. It looked like a full-dress rehearsal for a Hollywood biblical epic: *The Ten Commandments*, or *Ben-Hur*. All that was missing were the lions and chariots. Bryce was directing the activity with all the panache of Cecil B. DeMille. The bomb bay doors were open as crewmembers prepped the vehicles on their elevator platforms. Icy air from overhead ducts bucked the desert heat that rose into the aircraft from below.

Laila swung her arms back and forth like a Brownie waiting for the scout leader to tell her what to do. Bryce and Captain Grayson were dressed as Roman centurions. Instead of heavy coats of mail with shoulder pads and shin guards they wore thin leather breastplates that permitted more freedom of movement. They each possessed a broadsword and a wide-bladed dagger that were sheathed in scabbards at the waist. The helmets and shields looked metallic but were made of lightweight synthetic resin. The sandals were fashioned from goat hide on European lasts.

The rest of the Elite Guard were in the process of donning costumes for their various roles in the upcoming drama: as legionnaires, merchants, tradesmen, plebeians, and local peasants. Bryce noticed Laila. He broke away from Grayson and approached her with a smile on his face.

Laila let her eyes rove up and down Bryce's outfit. "Nice skirt. It shows off your legs really well."

"For your information it's a kilt."

"Does it come in size four?"

"I've got a special ensemble for you."

"I'll bet. Do I get a rubber sword, too?"

"The swords are real. We've been practicing with them for a couple of weeks. I can't claim that we're all that proficient with them but they're just for appearance anyway. For substance we're carrying sidearms tucked into the rear waistband under the woolen tunic. The outfits came from the costume department of a movie studio."

"You look good in red, but I prefer green."

"You're getting brown." Bryce led her to a locker and pulled out a stola. "You'll be masquerading as my camp follower."

Laila was not a happy camp follower. She turned out her lower lip in a pout. "Is that all I am to you?"

"When in Rome do as the Romans do. Men wear togas and women wear stolas. Try it on for size."

Laila pulled the rough cotton garment over her head. This particular model had long sleeves to protect the arms against sunburn. "It fits me like a tent."

"When you tighten the belts it should fit your form a little better. Maybe like a canvas sack."

A narrow belt was positioned under the breasts; a wider one circled the waist. "Well, it's not much better. And it doesn't match my jogging shoes."

"You'll be wearing sandals like everyone else." He handed her a pair that looked as if they had been designed for a child.

Laila slipped out of her jogging shoes and into the sandals. "What? No Vibram soles?" She shook her arms in the voluminous sleeves. "The sleeves are too big and baggy, and the material is scratchy."

"This isn't a fashion show. The rough weave accounts for the scratchiness. That's all they had in the days before polyester and we want it to pass close scrutiny. The loose clothing is an old Arab trick to allow for air flow in hot weather. We could have had the garment made out of silk but only wealthy women wore them. An officer like a centurion couldn't afford a silk stola for his women." Bryce fastened the clasps on her shoulders, the effect of which was to pull in some of the loose folds and give the appearance of pleats. "There. I want your disguise to make you unappealing so no one will look at you twice."

"Thanks a lot."

"We want to blend in not stand out. Make sure you get your shots before we leave. This world is riddled with disease. Now go outside and watch preparations. I've got work to do."

Laila tossed off a mock salute. "Yes, sir." She proceeded down the spiral staircase to the ground. The dirt was still warm, and the air was hot even in the shade of the airframe. Tall craggy peaks stood in stark relief to the north, while the other three quadrants showed rough rocky ground that a hardened twenty-first-century hiker would have found daunting.

Leibowitz and Father Nick stood out among the tool-laden technicians wearing casual apparel. Leibowitz was garbed as a well-to-do Jewish merchant with a hood in place of his yamaka. Father Nick was robed appropriately in sacerdotal vestments as a holy man. They were so engrossed in argument that they didn't notice Laila's approach. She stood aside and listened.

" – never said the *Bible* was hogwash. I said that it had to be taken with a grain of salt; maybe a bagful of sodium chloride. It's a quaint book of fairytales that were collected to keep the insecure masses from revolting. Why do you think the Romans let the people they conquered pray to their own gods instead of to those in the empire's pantheon? Because belief in a better life in the afterworld kept them in line. The deification of Christ was part of the process to ensure subservience."

"You are the ultimate cynic."

"I am the ultimate rationalist. That stupid mantra about vengeance being the province of the Lord is what the sheep bleat to the flock because they're too weak or too scared to fight for their rights."

"Is that like Jews digging their own graves and walking into Nazi ovens without putting up their fists?"

Leibowitz gasped. Laila gasped.

Behind her, Kreider gasped. He whispered in her ear, "They've been going at it hammer and tongs for the past thirty minutes."

She stared at him. He was wearing Bermuda shorts and a Hawaiian shirt. "I can't believe Father Nick would say such a thing. It's – it's so – unlike him."

"You should have heard some of the things that Leibowitz said first. Like the Old Testament had more sex, sadism, fornication, and promiscuity than a pornographic bestseller, with the licentious acts couched in euphemisms such as "knowing" this and "begetting" that. Then he carried on about how many patron saints had been sacked by the Vatican: Christopher because there was no proof that he ever lived, and the story about him carrying the Christ child across a river was probably apocryphal; George because dragons never existed; even the good padre's namesake for driving a sleigh that was pulled by eight flying reindeer. Then he started singing Tom Lehrer's sacrilegious parody, 'The Vatican Rag.'

"If I were a god-fearing man I'd have lost my temper a long time ago, and killed the son of a bitch with my bare hands, or gnawed him to death with my teeth. Nick turned his cheek for a while but then he ran out of cheeks. Leibowitz got what he deserved. Funny thing though, he shouldn't have any feelings about how Nazis persecuted Jews because he doesn't associate himself with the clan, either racially or religiously. Just goes to show how deep people are."

"And how vulnerable under the façade."

The jousters separated without spilling blood, but it was obvious that the temporary truce between them had been broken by their diametrical didacticism. They walked in opposite directions, each one stopping at the terminator beyond which the rays of the sun raised the temperature above the comfort level.

Kreider gripped Laila's arm to halt her movement. "Don't even think about interfering. Let them cool off first."

She started to make a heated comment but abruptly decided that the situation was too grim for her usual brand of quips. "Yes, I suppose you're right."

"Let them sulk in their corners for a while. Come take a look at this." Kreider led her to the perimeter where support personnel were inflating an amorphous caricature that looked like . . .

"A boat?"

Kreider shrugged. "It worked for Noah."

"But – In the desert? The nearest water is the Dead Sea, and that's twenty miles from here."

"This is a special kind of boat. It floats on air."

"Is this some esoteric technology that I don't know about? Like antigravity?"

"Nothing so unconventional. Hovercraft have been around for decades."

"Hovercraft? You mean, like the kind the Navy uses for landing craft?"

"Pretty much the same except for some mission-specific modifications and a few recent innovations. Different types are called air-cushion vehicles or ground-effect vehicles. Hovercraft is a generic term that includes them all. The Brits have been using production models to transport passengers among the British isles and across the Channel since the sixties, so they're anything but experimental. As you know, the big advantage is that they can travel over land and water equally as well, which is what makes them great for amphibious operations. You ride across a stretch of ocean and onto a beach without dockage, and make deployment without the troops getting their spit-shined boots wet. They're great for rescue work because they can travel over frozen lakes and it doesn't matter if the ice is thin.

"This particular airjeep is collapsible for ease of carriage. That's why they're inflating the pontoons. The outer material is Kevlar: bulletproof against small arms fire up to fifty caliber. It'll comfortably carry twelve soldiers and accommodate all their equipment. We've got two of them. You probably know more about their standard military apps than I do – I've only learned about their capabilities since I started working on this mission."

Kreider leaned close for confidentially. "They let me drive one. Or fly it. Or pilot it. Whatever. Turning is hard to get used to because they sideslip like crazy until you learn how to counter it, which I never did. Anyway, as you know, dual fans direct the airflow into the confined space beneath the undercarriage where it's trapped by a flexible rubber skirt. The air cushion provides lift. These airjeeps have sucker nozzles above the skirt to inhale the exhaust air from the downwash and recycle it to reduce the dust signature.

Laila nodded slowly. "When Wendayne said I'd learn about the hovercraft some other time, I didn't imagine she meant two thousand years in the past. Wow."

"This is nothing. Look what those folks over there

are uncrating." Kreider led Laila to the adjacent bomb bay. "They call it the Dick Tracy aircycle, because of its functional resemblance to the one in the comic strip."

"A one-person vehicle?"

"Two in a pinch. The Army started R and D in the fifties, but gave it up as a bad job because of their short range, loud noise, and inherent instability. The enemy could hear you coming from two countries away. But with today's compact jet engines and stealth noise-reduction technology they've come into their own. And you couldn't tip it over if you tried."

"What's the ceiling on these things?"

"The airjeep is strictly low level – say, five to six feet with an average load. But that's high enough to go over most boulder fields. Experienced pilots have flown the aircycle as high as ten thousand feet. They wouldn't let me near one, but anyhow, I wouldn't go up in an ultralight much less something that looks like a trash can on skids. Right now they're still under strict Air Force security wraps and used only in super-clandestine operations that even other military departments don't know about, but give it a few years and they'll be selling scaled-down commercial versions at the checkout counter in WalMart."

"Talk about flights of fancy."

"Kind of puts Arabian magic carpets in their place, doesn't it?"

Chapter 23

Kreider had exchanged his kaleidoscopic tropical outfit for more contemporary dress in the form of the tunic and toga that a Roman scholar would wear. The linen undergarment protected his skin from the course fabric of the outerwear. He also wore a wig of gray shoulder-length tresses. "I know that crew-cuts weren't in fashion in the first century. But I feel like a goddamned hippie in this get-up."

"Maybe you're the original trend setter." Laila adjusted the folds of her stola to fit more tightly around her slender waist. She held up two fingers in the shape of a V. "Peace."

"Don't laugh. Just remember that you're nothing more than a court courtesan who's hawking her wares."

Laila snickered. "Clever. Very clever."

"I used to get it from the kids. Now I get it from the grandkids. They're always hitting me and the missus with grade school puns and jokes. Some of them are pretty funny, actually."

"You're just a boy at heart." On another subject: "Bryce has been so busy. So what are the travel arrangements?"

"Nick and Leibowitz have been separated for obvious reasons. Nick with me in Airjeep One; you and Leibowitz in Two. Grayson will be leading the charge because I'm handling navigation." He opened the leather shoulder bag to expose the computer. "I've got all the aerial survey photos and topographic maps on the hard drive. Each airjeep has a generator for recharging batteries. Do you have your walkie-talkie?"

Laila patted her own shoulder bag. "In here with my cosmetics."

"I'm glad you requisitioned a batch of the long-range model. In case we get separated."

"Bryce is keeping me on a short leash."

"I won't be wandering far, either. I don't want to get lost in this wasteland and wilderness. I don't have a lot of faith in the Precambrian maps that Nick got from Vatican sources. He told me that they were authenticated by Jesuit archaeologists. Hell, archaeology isn't an exact science. Some academicians claim it's not a science at all, but an elaborate guessing game played by charlatans wearing blinders, like pin-the-tail-on-the-donkey. I tend to agree.

"Paleontologists are even worse. They pick up a fossil splinter about half the size of my pinky, then draw a reconstruction of a fifty-foot dinosaur based on what they believe to be a finger bone. One of them lies and the rest swear to it. That's not science; it's prestidigitation. The latest fad is painting dinosaurs with skin colors so they look like featherless parrots or kaleidoscopic canaries. Now some paleos are writing textbooks about dinosaur behavior patterns. I'm here to tell you that you can't infer good or bad manners from a pile of fossil rocks. Next thing you know, they'll be telling visitors at museum exhibits that scratch marks on bedding planes constitute proof that dinosaurs used their toenails to play the banjo, or something just as absurd."

Laila couldn't help but giggle and shake her head at Kreider's preposterous notions. "I just wish someone had invented knapsacks in the first century. I prefer to carry my pack on my back instead of over my shoulder. It distributes the weight and it doesn't swing in the way."

"They got plenty of creatures back here but no creature comforts."

"Can I use the strap as a tumpline?"

"I think the tumpline was invented by French voyageurs for the North American fur trade. It would look out of place in the Roman Empire."

"Drat."

"Oh, it looks like it's time to saddle up."

The techies backed away from the hovercraft. Enlisted personnel finished loading equipment and supplies. Costumed guards boarded by clambering over the inflated pontoons. Now Laila understood why Bryce, Grayson, and the other Elite Guards had stopped shaving several days earlier. They were growing beards to accompany their Roman costumes: to make it look as if they had been making a forced march along the Apian Way, and dry-camping without amenities in their haste to reach the area of Jewish insurrection.

Laila and Kreider went their separate ways. Laila hiked up her stola so she could climb on board. A youthful fuzzy-faced guard helped her into the rear seat next to Leibowitz. The Dead Sea Scrolls translator was silent, but his face expressed eager anticipation.

Bryce sat in front with the driver. He performed a radio check with Danette in the *Thermopylae* and with Grayson in the other airjeep. He gave the go-ahead for liftoff. The hovercraft rose slowly, like a heavy load on a hydraulic pallet jack. The engines barely hummed courtesy of stealth technology noise reduction equipment. Airjeep One pulled out from under the shade of the airframe, followed at a reasonable distance by Airjeep Two.

Leibowitz wriggled like an anxious puppy. "These things can go more than sixty miles per hour."

Laila acknowledged his information with a nod as she tightened her safety harness. She hardly noticed any movement. The airjeep rode as softly as a Rolls-Royce on hard macadam, using air as a cushion instead of leaf springs and shock absorbers. A gentle breeze wafted her long silky hair off her back. Ambient temperature rose in the sun. The desert heat was dry and not oppressive. Although the polycarbonate seat was unpadded, form-fitted contours made it not uncomfortable.

"Can you believe it? We're going to Jerusalem to witness the Crucifixion of Christ."

Laila was less passionate about their objective. "I'd feel better if we were going to save him from sacrifice instead of watching him die and rooting for it to happen. He may not be a prophet or the son of God, but he's still a fellow human being, and an innocent one at that. This isn't a movie, you know; this is real life and death."

Leibowitz sobered instantly. "I – I – I – didn't mean to sound so – bloodthirsty. I – I guess I was thinking of it as a historic event. Something that has already happened in the long-ago past. I mean, whatever is about to happen is already over, isn't it?"

"If I agreed with you we'd both be wrong. For now, this past is our present, and the future hasn't taken place yet."

"Yes, well, I – I guess that makes sense in a – a – timeless kind of way. Or does it?"

"It might make sense by and by, but right now I'm as confused as a three-legged toad, as my granma used to say."

The outskirts of Jerusalem was not a desert of shifting sand dunes, but one of dirt, rock, and low mountains whose jagged pinnacles reminded Laila of a dragon's lower jaw teeth. A vehicle that was driven on wheels or tracks would have had considerable difficulty in traversing the barren crust of baked and collapsing earth that was interspersed with declivities and narrow ravines. The airjeeps flew over the surface like low-flying aircraft – which in effect they were. Airjeeps had been considered for use in the Vietnam conflict, where they could have transported troops over delta mud flats in riverine operations; but they would have been useless for jungle deployment. The Army opted for helicopters instead, and Hueys became the iconic image of America's forgotten war.

Vegetation was sparse. Kreider picked a circuitous route around stands of trees and clumps of brush, and that approached the ancient city perpendicular to the Roman roads and mercantile trade routes, all of which were supposedly well known from historical texts and religious tracts.

Laila's apprehension was founded on Kreider's cynicism in the latter regard. At the same time, she intellectualized that an entire Roman army was no match for two squads of Elite Guards who were armed to the hilt with firearms instead of iron blades. The greatest reason for secrecy was to keep their presence unknown to the Islamic Revolutionary Forces, whose soldiers might be on the lookout for them, and consequently figure another way to alter the flow of grains from the sandglass of time. It was best not to tip their hand.

They stopped behind a low hillock. Two guards from Grayson's airjeep ran forward to reconnoiter. They scanned the land ahead through motion-steady binoculars. They reported to Grayson, who then waved his hand in the air as a signal to proceed. The airjeeps rose over the knoll and glided down a gentle slope toward a higher hill on the horizon. Miles of stone, gravel, and soft loam passed under the hovercraft as they sped to the next vantage point, then continued on to the next.

This time the advance team nodded back at Grayson, who then turned in his seat and signaled for everyone to disembark. The view over the hill was panoramic. In the near distance, a cluster of low stone buildings bordered a grove a trees that constituted a small oasis. No mosques or tall structures were in evidence. Otherwise the land was pristine except for a green plantation in the far distance.

"End of the road," Bryce announced. "From here we go on foot so shoulder your gear."

Laila and Leibowitz disembarked with the troops but stayed away from the hustle and bustle. Nick and Kreider approached and stood by their side, with Laila and Kreider standing between Nick and Leibowitz like referees at the opening round of a boxing match.

Kreider opened a metal container and commenced to distribute supplies to the civilians. "Two days' worth of MRE's: Meals, Ready to Eat, complete with a plastic spoon, packets of salt and pepper, a tiny jar of tobasco sauce, chewing gum, and, because no job is complete until the paperwork is done, a wrapper of folded TP. Use it gently."

They stowed the pre-packaged victuals in their shoulder bags.

"We had Sterno stoves in the Girl Scouts. And freeze-dried backpacking meals."

"Welcome to the first century where there's no jellied alcohol, no dehydrated food, and the local yokels don't even know that the date is 30 A.D." Next he handed out handfuls of coins. "For lodging and local delicacies. Don't spend all your money in one bazaar."

"Hey! These – these – these are real Roman coins."

"Natch. Paper money hasn't been invented yet. In fact, *paper* hasn't been invented yet. We couldn't find any counterfeit papyrus, but you can buy Roman coins by the pound on eBay. And cheap, too. These are all authentic."

"Can – can I keep the ones I don't spend?"

"Sure, but these aren't collectible grade. See how they're all worn smooth?"

The coins ranged in size from half an inch to inch and a half. They were made of copper, bronze, or silver.

"Believe it or not, these coins are worth more now than they are in the future. That is, their current purchasing power is greater what we paid for them, because the Romans minted so many and there's a glut on the market with too few collectors."

Laila examined her coins in the sunlight. "I've got one that's dated 47 B.C."

"Let me see that!" Leibowitz exclaimed, before he realized that he had fallen for a gag. He pierced Laila with a frown that slowly morphed into a grin. "Okay – okay – you got me."

Kreider stabbed Leibowitz with a finger. "Remember, oh ye of the Jewish persuasion, not to buy any pork."

Laila pulled out her walkie-talkie in order to pack the coins and MRE's. She pressed the transmission switch. "Radio check from Laila to Danette. Come in please."

Danette replied instantly, loud and clear. Laila gave her a sitrep, then disconnected.

Leibowitz frowned again. "Hey! How come I didn't get one of those?" He had left his short-range model in the future.

"I requisitioned every one we had on hand, but there wasn't enough time to order more from the manufacturer." She shrugged. "Sorry."

Bryce broke away from Captain Grayson and his two lieutenants. He approached the foursome. "We're breaking into four groups so we don't scare the natives. I want all of you with me. We'll have Jake and Tyrone as guards but we aren't expecting any trouble because the locals yield to Roman legionnaires who have totalitarian authority over the masses. We'll keep a low profile as much as we can. Each group will approach Jerusalem from a different quarter and will keep to themselves unless we need to work in coordination.

"The going will be rough until we get down from the mountain. My people are used to it but I won't push you so don't push yourself. They'll go ahead and scout the town. We'll catch up as soon as we can. Once we get the lay of the land we'll wander around town and listen to conversations: Nick to Latin and Dr. Leibowitz to Hebrew. Any questions?"

Leibowitz raised his hand but then thought better of it.

"Good. Then fall in staggered formation. Look natural as if you belong here. Try not to make eye contact with anyone we meet along the way because we don't want to encourage conversation. Only Dr. Leibowitz knows the local lingo. Don't talk among yourselves when locals are within hearing distance because we'll sound like the tower of Babel. Capiche?"

"Tempus fugit, as the Romans used to say," Father Nick commented laconically. "Time flies."

"Carpe diem," Laila added. "Seize the day."

Chapter 24

The drop off the front of the mountain was precipitous at first, but the steep angle reduced gradually until the slope was nearly horizontal with a slight downhill trend. The greatest impediment was annoying scree. Laila was forever kicking out pebbles and sharp grains of sand that caught between the soles of her feet and her sandals.

Bryce maintained a slow but steady pace that kept his squad lagging behind the three that were forging ahead and spreading outward. Shrubbery was little or no hindrance. When they descended to the tree line they lost sight of the other squads. The trees did not form a timberland of the kind that Laila was used to in West Virginia. It was more like the scrub forests found in American western States.

Her nose and throat suffered dryness from the arid atmosphere until the party descended into the more watery lowlands that surrounded Jerusalem. Flora and fauna came into existence. Tangled roots sucked water from the soil, then transported it by means of osmosis to the tree's branches and leaves, where some of it evaporated and tinged the air with moisture that alleviated the dryness in her throat and nose. She quickly emptied the canteen that she carried in her shoulder bag.

Although much of the land in what would someday be known as Israel consisted of desert, the climate improved by degrees during the labored descent. Laila detected a mild fragrance that compared favorably to that of the dust-laden, rubble-strewn flats found at higher elevations. The scent was sweet but not cloying and not nearly as strong as honeysuckle. It was more like watered down eau de cologne.

Soon she heard the chirping of birds and the buzzing of insects, although they stayed so well hidden in the sparse vegetation that she couldn't see any of them. Once she spotted a lizard on the ground as it scuttled into a hole under a boulder. Animal life was abundant but largely concealed, not as much from predators as from the common enemy: the elements.

She looked upward when she heard a faint droning sound directly overhead, much like the flutter of a hummingbird's wings.

Bryce called the procession to a halt. "Do you have a visual?"

Kreider pulled his computer out of his shoulder bag, and woke it up from sleep mode. He studied the screen. "We're on camera right now." He waved overhead, then spun the screen so that Bryce could see.

From near the back of the single file, Laila saw enough of the screen to perceive a group of hikers that were dressed exactly like themselves.

Bryce spoke into his walkie-talkie. "Signal is good. Is the town clear ahead?" He listened, then said, "Retrieve the MAV. Out." He slipped the walkie-talkie into his shoulder bag as he led the procession forward.

Leibowitz whispered. "What was that all about?"

Laila pointed at a dot that was moving across the cloudless sky. "See that bird?"

Leibowitz squinted through his spectacles. "Ye – yes."

"It's not a bird. It's a micro air vehicle, or unmanned aerial vehicle. What Bryce just called a MAV. You must have seen them in movies. They're flown remotely from a command center by someone with a joystick who's good at video games." Laila realized that her sentence structure was badly worded, but made no apology. "Anyway, it's what the military has been using to make covert observations in hostile territory where personnel insertion is too easily discovered or compromised."

"Are they the little bugs or torpedo-shaped machines that they fly around to direct missile strikes?"

"You got it. They've got some models that flap their wings to imitate birds so people pay no attention to them. Some are as small as six inches in length. The digital optics are surprisingly good. The small ones don't have much of a range because they're powered by batteries."

"Ma'am."

Laila turned around to stare at Tyrone, who was bringing up the rear. "Do I look like a ma'am to you? You make me feel old."

"Sorry, ma'am. Er – "

"Call me Laila."

"Yes – " Tyrone looked decidedly uncomfortable for a person with the body of a fullback. "The airjeep drivers are controlling the drones from a portable handset. That's another reason why they stayed behind – not just to guard the airjeeps."

"Are the images being transmitted to the *Thermopylae*?"

"Yes, ma'am. Er – yes."

Laila winked at him. To Leibowitz: "It seems as if Bryce has all his bases covered. He can use the MAV's to scout ahead and keep tabs on the other squads. He can also send the *Thermopylae* to pick us up if we get into trouble."

"I like that idea."

Abruptly, Laila stared at Leibowitz as if his face had become a Hollywood monster mask needles for facial pores and worms crawling out of the eye sockets.

"Wha – what?" Leibowitz searched his person frantically and started wiping the sleeves of his robe. "What is it? A spider? I hate spiders."

Laila remained calm. "Dr. Leibowitz, you're wearing eyeglasses."

"Yes? So?"

"Eyeglasses haven't been invented yet."

"I brought these with me."

"You don't understand. People don't wear eyeglasses in century one."

Leibowitz removed his spectacles, held them up to the light, and rubbed the lenses clean with a loose fold of material from the sleeve of his robe. "I always wear glasses. I have astigmatism."

"What she means is you'll attract attention." Bryce stepped past Laila and confronted Leibowitz. "If IRF soldiers spot you they'll know you're not from this time period and our cover will be blown. Take them off."

"But without them my vision is blurry and I get headaches."

Bryce considered. "You can wear them as long as there are no strangers in sight."

"That sounds fair."

"Tyrone, you watch him to make sure he follows orders."

"Yes, sir."

Bryce returned to the head of the column where he preceded Jake at point; he liked to lead his own squad.

Leibowitz shrugged as he looked at Laila. "That was fair." He fixed the spectacles on his narrow nose and fitted the wire temples over his ears. "That was fair."

The procession advanced into thickening woodland that provided welcome relief from the hot rays of the sun. There were no paths to follow because in those days people did not hike for fun, challenge, or inquisitive exploration, but to reach a destination by the fastest route possible. There was no reason for anyone to ascend into mountainous regions where water didn't flow, plants didn't grow, game didn't roam, and people didn't live. Cross-country travel was not on the high list of priorities for people who struggled daily to obtain food and shelter in a harsh land of Roman occupation.

Bryce took occasional sightings through his lensatic compass. He had pre-adjusted the graduated dial for magnetic declination. The magnifying lens and sight wire enabled him to maintain a straight course toward distant objects.

Leibowitz surged ahead until he was walking next to Laila. In a hushed tone: "I – I – I don't think I was fair."

"What? Fair about what?"

"A – about . . . " He hushed as soon as Father Nick peered over his shoulder.

Laila slowed her pace in order to increase the distance between them and the good father.

"I – I didn't mean the conversation to get out of hand. We were talking about Muslims. I mentioned the rising number of genetic disorders – cases of retardation and other birth defects – because their tradition of incest has led to inbreeding. He mentioned the escalation of still-births, which is a good thing. Then I mentioned how Egyptian pharaohs often suffered from mental illness for the same reason: marrying first cousins in order to keep the ruling cast in the family. Then he mentioned how insanity interfered with religious beliefs and true Christian values, making Muslims poorer than Catholics by contrast. We were agreeing until I made an offhanded comment about the Holy Ghost being a more lucrative franchise than a dead Islamic prophet. . . . "

Laila rolled her eyes. "Not a very diplomatic statement."

"I – I – I – said it without thinking."

"That's a habit with you." She realized that her voice was louder than she intended. She glanced back at Tyrone, who was close enough to hear every word of their conversation. His face remained passive. Barely audible: "My daddy always said, 'If you're right, fight; if you're wrong, admit it.' "

Leibowitz showed no expression. After several seconds he pinched his eyebrows, as if he were deep in thought. It crossed Laila's mind that he may never in his life have contemplated the possibility of being wrong in an argument, and having to apologize for his ill-tempered disposition and outspoken ignorance. Leibowitz lapsed into silence.

Soon the brigade broke into a clearing the size of a football field. A herd of domestic goats announced the invasion of their territory by bleating. Kids ran loose, but nannies and billies were tethered to posts so that their grazing range among the tall grass was restricted. A corral occupied the opposite side of the glade. A rough wooden barn and cabin were situated adjacent to each other beyond the corral. It might have been a scene out of a Western movie except that the buildings were not constructed of horizontal logs with mud chinking, but of vertical posts that were covered with goat skin. Goat skin was also used for the roof. The barn was only three-sided, like a lean-to, and lacked a manger.

In order to avoid the goats and their plops, Bryce led the column in a semicircle around the eastern perimeter of the field. The buildings were surrounded by hard-packed dirt that had been trampled flat by generations of inhabitants. No one was in sight, but the bleating soon brought a barefoot herdsman out of the adjacent woods. His only adornment was a goat skin tunic that stretched nearly to his knees. He stopped with his staff planted in the ground in front of him. A woman and two children – all similarly clad and lacking footwear – halted at the tree line. Frightened stares were frozen on all four faces.

Bryce stood at ease with his hands by his side. "Dr. Leibowitz!"

The Hebrew translator stood stock hill. He exchanged looks with Laila.

"Go ahead. Bryce wants you."

Leibowitz whipped off his spectacles. He ran his hands over his one-piece garment. "Haven't they invented pockets yet, either?" He tucked the spectacles into his shoulder bag. He cowered past Nick Varvarelis while looking askance.

Bryce glanced at the reddish sun; it hovered barely above the horizon, unobstructed by clouds or dust in the atmosphere. "Dr. Leibowitz, ask these people if we can spend the night in their barn."

Startled: "What?"

"Jerusalem is half a day's march at the rate we're moving. Ask these people if we can spend the night in their barn."

Leibowitz nodded dazedly. He took several steps forward. The herdsman shifted his gaze from the centurion with a sword to the unarmed merchant, but his expression of anxiety did not change. Leibowitz stepped closer. He spoke in ancient Hebrew. The herdsman replied in kind. An animated conversation ensued. Leibowitz spoke, gesticulated, and spoke some more. The herdsman spoke but did not gesticulate. Finally they simply stared at each other.

Leibowitz returned to Bryce's side. "I – I – I – can't

understand a word he said."

"Wasn't he speaking ancient Hebrew?"

"I think so, but – well, I think I understood some of the vocabulary – but, well, it's – it's the pronunciation I can't follow. And the grammatical structures are different. It's nothing like the way Hebrew is spoken today – I mean, in the future. His words were spoken with fricatives and sibilants that made the sentences nearly incomprehensible. It's – it's as much like spoken Hebrew as East End cockney or Irish brogue is to English. I – I – "

Bryce held up his hand for Leibowitz to stop. "I'll handle it." He approached the frightened herdsman. He pointed to himself, to Leibowitz, to his crew, and to the lean-to. He took a handful of coins from his shoulder bag, grabbed the herdsman's hand, and poured the coins into his palm.

The herdsman spoke in his guttural lingo, made a sweeping gesture toward the lean-to with his arm, and backed away.

Bryce turned to his troops. "Money talks in all languages."

Kreider humphed. "Either that or he thought that you might cut his head off if he refused you hospitality."

The herdsman and his family rushed into the cabin through a doorway that was covered by goat skin. The cabin had no windows.

The people from the future lay down their shoulder bags and made themselves comfortable on the dirt floor of the lean-to. The stink of piss and wet goat skin was pronounced, but the floor was as clean as if it had recently been swept. Any turds that the goats had dropped during their nighttime occupancy had been removed. Laila sat cross-legged.

Jake and Tyrone each carried two heavily loaded shoulder bags by crisscrossing the straps over their heads and resting the weight on their muscular backs. These bags carried amenities such as utility blankets made of heat-reflective metalized polyethylene, lightweight collapsible stoves, dry fuel tablets, emergency medical kits, spare footwear that could be carved down to size, canteens, light-emitting-diode flashlights, and extra rations. They gathered all the empty canteens, placed a sterilization pill in each one, then trooped off to the brook that Laila could hear babbling nearby.

Bryce and Kreider sequestered themselves in one corner where they spoke in soft tones and studied playbacks on the computer screen.

Leibowitz asked Bryce sheepishly, "I – I – How about if I talk with them some more, to see if I can, well, learn their pronunciation?"

"Good idea, Dr. Leibowitz. Feel free to tell them that we're headed for Jerusalem on official business but nothing more. Understand?"

"I understand. I mean, I really understand." He departed gleefully.

Laila sidled over to where Father Nick sprawled thoughtfully on the ground. "You've been awfully quiet today. Cat got your tongue, as my granma used to say?"

Father Nick was slow to reply; so slow the Laila began to wonder if he heard her question. He pulled himself upright, leaned against a post that formed a point of attachment for the goat-skin covering, stretched his legs out in front of him, and looked up as if he were seeking advice from God.

"I am so ashamed of myself. Not only am I ashamed of the things that I said, but I am ashamed that I allowed such thoughts to enter my mind." He shook his head in despondence. "Some of the things that I said to Leibowitz were – unchristian."

"Wow. Welcome to the world of normal people. All of us have bad thoughts, especially when it comes to terrorists whose sole purpose in life, it seems, is to wreak havoc on the rest of the world that dares to be different."

"But I should be above such thoughts."

"Why? Because you're a Roman Catholic priest and a high-ranking member of the Vatican? After all the catechisms and Christian study you're still mortal flesh like the rest of us. It's okay if a few impure thoughts creep into your mind. You can confess after the Mission is over, and have those adulterated judgments forgiven or exorcised. Anyway, those thoughts exist only in your head."

"God knows what I am thinking."

"Okay, but thinking thoughts is not the same as acting on them. Unless those thoughts are manifested, you haven't done anything wrong."

Father Nick cogitated long and hard. "The implications of this Mission have tainted my soul. I find the idea of interfering with the will of God so abhorrent that I am confused by the possible consequences of our contemplated actions. This wicked goal of the Islamic Revolutionary Forces cannot be allowed to succeed, and I hate them – detest them for even attempting such a foul deed. But that is no reason for grouping all Muslims together. Within their own belief system, many Muslims are decent god-fearing people, even though they call their god Allah. Most of them pray toward Mecca without any thought of harming those who pray in a different direction. They are innocent lambs being led and deceived by wolves."

Laila was insistent. "We have no argument with the lambs. They're not the ones who sponsor terrorism. That's why we don't nuke the entire Middle East. That's why we strike selectively at the individuals and terrorist cells who are guilty of committing crimes against humanity. Christian beliefs and Islamic beliefs are not very different from each other. It's the imposition of those beliefs that's insidious."

Father Nick grimaced. "I can accept your thoughts on an intellectual level, but not on an emotional level, and certainly not on a religious level. The closer we approach the denouement of this Mission, the more difficult it is for me to resolve my inner conflicts. I feel – I feel – like a bomber who has been transferred to the infantry."

"What does that mean?"

"A bomber drops his payload from the air onto people on the ground. He never sees the death and destruction that result from his handiwork. An infantryman shoots or stabs someone at close range, while looking into his victim's eyes. He *sees* the death he has caused. When we planned this Mission back in the Vatican, the outcome was a concept on imaginary paper. Now that we are closing in on the moment of ultimate infamy, I fear that we are about to see the enemy at close range – and that the enemy will pay for his lack of righteousness with death. My previous hatred of IRF terrorists who would rob Christianity of its martyr is yielding to my innate sense of – mercy."

"What about the biblical code of justice: an eye for an eye and a tooth for a tooth?"

"That is – that conflicts with the dictum that vengeance is the prerogative of the Lord."

"Yes, well, the *Bible* is full of contradictions. Both Testaments. You're enough of a biblical scholar to know that you can't interpret the *Bible* literally. You have to look at it in context with the times in which it was written, or assembled: as a collection of quaint parables, a guide for Christian principles.

"Listen to me, Nick. Early in my career with the CIA, I came to realize that I was part of a death machine. I didn't kill anyone. I didn't pull the trigger, or even load the gun. But I submitted reports that resulted in military action: actions in which foes of freedom were killed. I accepted that. I had to accept it, or get a job as a social worker and let someone else protect me and my way of life from foreign aggression.

"My daddy once grieved for months because he shot and killed a burglar who had fired at him first. It was that incident that made him realize what being a peace-keeper was all about. It was about protecting law-abiding citizens from harm. He realized that the only way to fight force was with greater force: a quality that people lacked because they weren't armed, and were therefore subject to the bidding of the criminal. His job was to be their greater force.

"Your job is similar. You provide comfort to those who need it. You protect them from their insecurities. But without belief in God to back you up, people won't have confidence in your words of solace. We're facing an adversary that wants to dominate the world through violence that's every bit as lethal as Nazism. The IRF is fighting on a smaller scale but with the same end in view. You can't placate this enemy, any more than you can placate heart disease. If the IRF destroys the foundation of your beliefs, the world of Christian principles will topple, and we'll be overrun by single-minded radicals. They don't just want to kill you and your God; they want to kill everything that you and your God stand for.

"You shouldn't have qualms about the virtue of our undertaking. You shouldn't anguish over the death of an enemy that has sworn to eradicate your way of life. You're simply swatting a mosquito that wants to suck your blood and infect you with malaria. What you feel isn't hatred but a staunch moral imperative to protect innocent bystanders from crass violations of humanitarian principles. You yourself said that we were on a mission from God. In a sense I agree. You and I and all of us here have been uniquely placed in a position to ensure that future generations won't have to suffer at the hands of organized fanaticism. In some mysterious way that none of us can fathom, this isn't a mission of cheap retribution, but one of divine intervention."

Chapter 25

Wendayne was wrong. Despite her prediction that Laila wouldn't have another cup of coffee until the Mission was over, Laila gratefully sniffed the fumes that wafted past her nostrils from the hot metal mug that Jake was holding over a Heatab. In her eagerness, she grabbed the handle of the mug before the water began to boil, and took a sip.

MRE coffee left much to be desired. The food was passable, some of it even good, but the instant coffee in the single-serving packet reminded her of the bitter brew that Starbucks served for a disproportionate amount of money: a cross between 10W40 and used crankcase oil. But, as Laila was wont to say, the first cup of coffee doesn't have to taste good, it just has to work. MRE coffee was little more than hot water with a bad attitude.

Those thoughts were four hours in the past. Fortunately for her frame of mind, Laila had had little time to dawdle over her morning sipping ritual. Events were unfolding rapidly, so she had to gulp down the poison and bid goodbye to the goat herders turned landlords. The squad was now on a forced march to Jerusalem.

"I hate lice," Leibowitz complained, as he scratched his head with all ten fingers. "I hate them."

After Leibowitz's somewhat circumpolar apology, Father Nick dared to glance in his direction, although with a certain amount of guarded circumspection. "These peasants may not possess insect eradicators, but they are abundantly hygienic. Did you see them washing their feet in the stream this morning?"

"Downstream of where they take their water from," Laila interjected.

"Sure, but upstream of the next family downstream." Leibowitz scratched some more. "Peasants always look so dirty in the movies. Their faces are smudged and their fingernails are dirty and their clothes are ragged and soiled. I have to admit that these people were clean."

"That's a standard Hollywood portrayal. They always

make poor folks look as if they lack personal sanitation, to make them appear like a lower class of people instead of just people who can't afford high-priced jewelry and designer clothing."

The closer they approached the outskirts of Jerusalem, the more of those "people" they encountered on the road. Farmers and merchants were coming from miles around in order to sell their wares in the bazaars. They kept their distance from centurion Bryce and legionnaires Jake and Tyrone, but Nick and Leibowitz did their best to mingle and chat with the locals in order to improve their language skills. Nick had the same problem as Leibowitz: people who spoke Latin did so with pronunciations and grammatical constructions that made it difficult for him to interpret their meaning. Both persisted in their linguistic endeavors, but they were a long way from proficiency when they joined the milling inhabitants in the main streets and back byways of a Semitic town that was once known as the City of David, and later as Zion.

"So many dialects," Leibowitz noted with frustration.

Townsfolk always spoke English in Hollywood epics so the audience could understand conversations that were crucial to the plot. Now, in the first century, they spoke a polyglot of languages in vernacular that had never been written in ancient texts to be studied by modern scholars.

After lodging in hostelries, the other three squads had spread out to scout the city for signs of unusual activity. None of them understood the lingo, so they merely wandered among the peasantry and did their best to interpret the meaning of ongoing events. Captain Grayson reported via walkie-talkie that people were gathering at the south end of town, enraptured by speeches from a handful of individuals who did most of the talking. He suggested the possibility that the orators might be Jesus and some of his disciples.

"Now you can get Jesus to sign the good book." Kreider raised his eyebrows at Father Nick. "An autographed copy of the *Bible* has to be worth a fortune."

Father Nick didn't reply.

Courtesy of MAV, aerial photographs were captured and displayed on Kreider's computer screen. These provided a map of the ancient city as well as close-ups of buildings and people. Bryce ordered the other squads to continue their exploration while he split his squad into three teams, each to converge on Grayson after taking a different route through town. Jake escorted Father Nick, Tyrone kept tabs on Leibowitz (who was no longer wearing his spectacles), while Bryce led his handmaiden and court astrologer.

The dirt streets were dotted with dung from pack animals that drew small carts and drays that were piled high with wares: food, tools, ceramics, and the like. But not for long: volunteers scooped up the manure and poured water over the stain.

The trio wended their way through throngs along narrow streets that separated buildings that were fashioned of stone or brick and mortar. The structures were simplistic and strictly utilitarian, without the fancy trimmings that adorned the modern city in the twenty-first century, although the occasional terrace added architectural relief. Several construction projects were in the making, and masons – minus the secret handshake – worked assiduously at their craft, while a stream of laborers toted hods that were filled with essential building materials.

The hustle and bustle of center city bazaars contrasted sharply with outlying alleyways in which passersby moved more slowly on indecipherable errands and daily tasks. No one lingered in one spot for too long except for mothers and their children. Absent were mendicants begging for alms. Everyone seemed to have a purpose – although Laila was forced to admit that she was often unable to ascertain what that purpose might be.

They entered a square whose middle consisted of a hodgepodge of rough wooden stands and rickety tables. Patrons – mostly elderly women – carried woven reed baskets in which they piled their purchases of fresh fruits and vegetables. One male vendor chastised a thickly bearded man by beating him with a stick; the man had swiped an apple.

"Humph. A thief," Kreider muttered under his breath so that only Bryce and Laila could hear him. "Didn't they used to cut off their hands in these days?"

Laila gazed long and hard at the shoplifter. He was barefoot and his cloak was in tatters: the cloth had more holes than a sieve. She whispered, "Cover me," then walked away before Bryce had time to ask what she meant. She meandered a bit before approaching the thief from the side. He was still rubbing the back of his hand where an angry welt was purpling his dark skin. He placed his other hand on the dagger that was tucked into his belt, but did not draw the weapon. He glared at the grocer.

Laila stopped by the man's side. After he noticed her presence, she spoke a few words that evoked an immediate response. He let go of the dagger and punched Laila in the face with his clenched fist. Her head rocked back. She reeled, then fell to the ground on her skinny rump. A moment later Bryce smacked the man on the back of the head with the flat of his sword. The man staggered, flung out his hands, dropped to his knees, and fell forward onto his outstretched palms next to Laila.

Kreider dashed past Bryce and knelt by Laila's side. He flung his arms around her slender shoulders. He momentarily forgot himself. "Jesus, Laila. What the hell did you say to him?"

The apple grower grinned broadly at Bryce's swift retribution. He was oblivious to languages that he didn't understand. Uniformed Romans could get away with murder in occupied Jerusalem, but seldom – perhaps never – did they stand up for everyday inequities that were committed against plebeians.

Bryce stamped his sandaled foot on the shoplifter's back, and pressed him into the ground. To Laila: "Are you okay?"

She winced when she placed her hand against her

throbbing right eye. "I'm as happy as a tick on a long-haired dog, as my granma used to say. Do I have another black eye? To match the one that Leibowitz gave me."

"Not yet but you will soon."

All eyes in the market square were upon them. Buying and selling had stopped. Except for the grocer's smile of approval, everyone else's face was blank and unreadable, so as not to draw attention from a Roman officer with a sword whose point rested on the neck of the perpetrator. It seemed as if they expected him to run the rascal through. Bryce exerted only enough pressure to keep the man on the ground from protesting.

"So what did you say to him?" Kreider still wanted to know.

"I would rather not repeat my words verbatim. Let's just say that I made a suggestion about his mother's sexual habits and proclivities. In Farsi."

Bryce nodded. "How did you know?"

She shrugged. "He looked – different."

"That was pretty clever using his own language to catch him off guard."

"I have my moments."

Kreider lifted her to her feet. To Bryce: "What say we check into a hotel with our prisoner?"

"One that takes MasterCard. I'm low on cash."

Bryce pulled the displaced terrorist to his feet, relieved him of the knife, and frisked him for other weapons. He found a rusted revolver tucked into a cummerbund. The metal plating was dirty and the inside of the barrel was choked with dirt. The gun hadn't been fired in ages, nor did the owner have any bullets.

Bryce stowed the terrorist's weapons in his shoulder bag. "Good idea. Once we're out of sight I'll get on the horn and give Grayson a sitrep especially now that we know for sure that IRF agents are here." He motioned for his prisoner to march. When he didn't move, Bryce placed the point of his sword gently against the small of his back. "We'll also conduct a little interrogation."

The prisoner was sullen as Bryce prodded him along

the narrow streets. They located a hideout a couple of blocks away. The clink of coins was the only sound that passed between Bryce and his newfound proprietor, who likely did not speak Latin.

The quarters were Spartan, consisting of nothing more than mattresses on the stone floor of an expansive room, and an urn filled with tepid water. Like a barrack or a dormitory, the lodging was intended for a large group of travelers.

"I don't suppose we could get ice for my eye."

Kreider snickered. "Sure. I'll call room service and have them send up a bottle of champagne in a bucket full of ice."

Laila plumped herself down. "This padding is fine but the covers are all whopperjawed and caperhilled, as my granma used to say." She proceeded to straighten out the horsehair blankets around her.

After Bryce spoke with Grayson: "Don't get too comfortable. I can't do this interrogation by myself."

Laila sat up with a groan. "He packs a lot more wallop than Leibowitz."

"I'm sorry Laila but we need his intel. If you can't talk it out of him I'll have to beat it out of him."

Laila nodded with her right hand over her newly blackened eye. "Okay, but please put down the sword. Let's try honey before we resort to vinegar."

"It's your call." Bryce sheathed his sword and stepped back to where Kreider was leaning quietly against a door post, keeping a lookout for trespassers.

Laila sidled over to where the prisoner crouched on his haunches. She questioned him in Farsi. He answered dourly but voluntarily. She looked up at Bryce. "He wants food and water."

Bryce proffered a single nod.

The prisoner crawled to the urn, cupped his hands, and used them as a dipper to bring water to his lips. He sucked greedily for a couple of minutes. After he had his fill and sat down, Bryce tossed a packet of MRE's onto the prisoner's lap. He immediately tore open the packet, and consumed the preserved food as if he hadn't eaten for a month.

Laila posed another question. He answered briefly between bites. The conversation went back and forth for half an hour, with the prisoner doing most of the talking. Once he got going and consumed all the food, he loosened up and became downright garrulous. Laila kept her hands on her knees but the prisoner gesticulated wildly. He seemed to be happy to cooperate. Laila had the last word, after which he cradled his head in his hands, lay back on the mattress, and closed his eyes.

"He was starving. It seems that panhandlers aren't tolerated in the city; or anywhere else for that matter. He gave me a passel of information: much more than I asked for. His name is Gamal Ibrihim Boghdadi. He was a corporal in the Islamic Special Forces – "

"Was?"

Laila nodded. "The temporal displacement apparatus delivered him and his outfit twenty-three years ago – "

"*What?*" That was Kreider.

She kept nodding. "Either the TDA was miscalibrated, or their intel about the time of the Crucifixion was in error. Boghdadi isn't a scientist, and neither was anyone else among those who survived the transference, so – "

"What do you mean, those who survived?"

Laila was patient. "The TDA was never tested. It was put into operation as soon as construction was completed and the capacitors and intertemporal amplifiers were charged. The amplifier is a component that our timepiece doesn't have. Apparently, the IRF was aware that foreign agents were watching the facility – "

"You mean agents that you assigned?" That was Bryce.

She did not mind the interruptions. "I suppose so. After I learned of the existence of what purported to be a time machine, I doubled our assets and authorized an increase in pay for local intel." She shrugged. "In a situation like this, you can't afford to be penny wise and pound foolish, as my granma used to say. It seems as if my tactic rushed the IRF into making a premature decision to launch their mission before their scientists fully understood the constraints of the unit: a military decision that contradicted scientific advice."

"They went off halfcocked, so to speak." That was Kreider again.

"And arrived with half an outfit. They packed the temporal landing zone with as many people as they could fit – "

Bryce again. "No vehicles?"

Laila shook her head. "They had the advantage of starting from a spot that was close to Jerusalem, so they figured on appropriating local transportation such as oxcarts and wagons. Anyway, so many people were crowded into the TLZ that only half of them arrived in one piece: those who were clustered closest to the globular nodal point. Those on the periphery didn't arrive intact: only those portions of their bodies that were inside the reference sphere were transferred; the parts that lay outside the reference sphere were left behind."

"Talk about a piecemeal transference." Only Kreider would make a comment like that.

Laila nodded in all seriousness. "Body parts were separated by two millennia. Special Forces personnel were grouped around the warhead and the retrieval device."

Bryce raised his eyebrows.

"Yes, a nuclear warhead. It was their backup plan, to be executed as a last recourse in case they failed in their primary mission to capture Jesus alive. In that case they were going to destroy Jerusalem and the surrounding area so the Crucifixion couldn't take place." After a pause: "Their advisors were on the outside of the circle so none of them made it through. Their supplies were also outside the inner circle. This left the Special Forces personnel on their own, without food or water. They hung around for a couple of days living on water in their canteens and emergency rations in their packs, but when they ran out of water they faced dehydration. They'd been told that it would take a week to recharge the TDA's capacitors. The facility was built at an isolated location to keep it free from prying eyes: in the middle of the desert where people didn't live because there were no oases.

"There were only twelve survivors – plus several others who lost arms or legs, but they died within hours. They dispersed in six two-man teams to search for water. They were supposed to rendezvous back at the transfer point. Boghdadi and his partner got lost in the desert. His partner died so Boghdadi took his water. Actually, he was somewhat evasive on this point, even contradictory. I wouldn't be surprised if he didn't kill his partner for his water.

"Anyway, he reached an area where he found some low-lying vegetation. Relying on his survival training, he dug a hole in the shade and placed his canteen cup in the bottom of it, then covered the cup with cloth that he tore from his uniform. During the night, dew condensed from the temperature differential and dripped into the cup: enough to enable him to reach a more thickly vegetated area. There he dug another hole until he struck groundwater – actually only little more than cool damp soil. This time he used the cloth to soak water out of the dirt. He sucked the water out of the cloth, then let the cloth soak up more water.

"This gave him the energy to keep on going. One or two days later, maybe three – he was delirious part of the time – he found a thin stream, a trickle, no more than half an inch wide. He camped there for three days until he regained his strength. He refilled his canteen. When he tried to retrace his steps, he found that the wind had wiped out his tracks. And the direction seemed wrong. He figured that he must have walked in circles in his delirium. He couldn't follow his compass because his sideways drift made a back azimuth unworkable. And he didn't see any recognizable landmarks during his travels through the desert.

"By that time his emergency rations were long gone. He followed the stream of water. Sometimes the water disappeared into the ground. They he followed the dry streambed until the water re-emerged. He ate leaves and bugs for several more days. He shot a couple of rabbits and ate them raw. Finally he reached a permanent creek which he followed to a settlement where no one spoke his language, and where no one understood his words.

"The dwellers thought he was crazy, or perhaps that he was suffering from brain fever due to his aimless wandering in the desert heat. They took pity on him. They gave him food. He stayed with them for several weeks, until a young girl complained of his attentions. He said that she was willing, but again he was evasive, and I suspect that he raped her."

Kreider humphed. "Sounds like a upstanding model citizen." Rhetorically: "Doesn't the Koran say anything about biting the hand that feeds you?"

"The elders beat him with sticks. He shot and killed two of them, supposedly in self-defense. Then he fled into the night. He reached another settlement where they didn't cotton to freeloaders. When he begged for alms, they gave him a hoe and motioned for him to work in the fields. He threw down the hoe, stole some food and clothing, and ran away. He shot game until he ran out of bullets. In another settlement he was forced to do odd jobs in return for food and shelter.

"He took up residence with a middle-aged widow whose husband had died from disease. She was the only woman who would accept him. He took over her farm and goats. I gather that she did most of the work. He picked up some of the language while they lived together. She got pregnant two years later, then died during childbirth. He sold the goats, abandoned the farm, and tramped the roads until he was arrested by a Roman army officer for stealing provisions. They kept him as a slave for the next fifteen years. He was mistreated cruelly. Eventually he escaped. He's been living hand to mouth ever since."

Kreider humphed again. "Sounds like a real hard luck story, but I don't feel the least bit sorry for him. Sponging off an old woman . . . "

"What did he say about the rest of the outfit?" Bryce

wanted to know.

Laila shook her head. "He never saw any of them again."

"What about the nuke?"

"Armed and dangerous. They rushed it into production and barely had time to assemble it before mission launch. It wasn't even code-locked. The only external mechanism was a time delay. I guess special forces personnel don't consider themselves to be expendable. They're soldiers, not fanatical suicide bombers."

"And the recall device?"

"Again, he's not a scientist, so he only knows what he heard before their hasty departure. According to the scuttlebutt, the tuning mechanism could be initiated by a push button. I gather that it wasn't just a passive locator like ours, but an activator. Apparently, every passage through time creates a permanent breach throughout the time stream, or maybe one that wears off after a while; he's not certain. Anyway, this breach leaves a scar that extends from one end to the other, connecting the past with the present like a conduit or pathway between the moment of embarkation and the moment of arrival, including all points in between. Their recall device is a temporal transmitter that homes in on the sending apparatus and triggers it for instant recall."

"Hey, wait of minute, whoa, hold the phone." Kreider stood to full attention. "Are you saying that the return transfers the target mass to the moment of origin, and not beyond?"

"That's what I gather from what he said."

"Now where did they get that kind of technology?" To Bryce: "The return mechanism of our Timepiece creates a new pathway with each operation. It doesn't work through the original pathway. A lot less power is needed if you don't have to crack a new hole in the space-time continuum and reuse the original pathway."

Bryce nodded. "Plus you can return to the precise moment of transmission as if you never left."

Kreider pinched his eyes. "A stationary transmission point instead of a mobile one that moves chronically through the time stream. Does that mean that their technology is more advanced than ours, or just divergent?"

"How could they diverge if their design is a copy of ours? They don't create they only steal."

"That's certainly something to ponder."

Laila permitted time for contemplation before returning to the subject that was immediately at hand. "Bodgdadi apologized for striking me. He also begs forgiveness. He's sorry that he ever started on this madcap adventure. He wants only one reward in exchange for his cooperation: he wants to get back to the future."

Bryce didn't hesitate: "I'll promise him that. Does he know why we're here?"

"I didn't tell him, but he must suspect that we're here to thwart the IRF's plans. He doesn't care about his mission any more. He just wants to go home and make peace with Allah. He doesn't even know what year it is. There are no calendars yet. People don't think in terms of years or hours or minutes: only months in relation to growing seasons. Otherwise time has little meaning to them. They talk about the past by referring to reigns. This is the reign of Pontius Pilate, but being Islamic, Boghdadi doesn't know what that means with respect to Jesus. He knows nothing about Christian religion or history."

Kreider humphed again. "Can't blame him for losing faith in a mission after half his life has been wasted. He looks like a lost soul. Not that I feel sorry for him. Banish the thought." To Bryce: "What say we – "

Bryce held up one hand as he answered his walkie-talkie. He listened for a moment. "What do you mean he's missing? . . . How long? . . . Let me know when he turns up. Out." He switched channels and called Grayson. "Sitrep . . . Is he all right? . . . " To Kreider: "Pull up your plotter and give me our coordinates." Into the walkie-talkie: "Don't let him out of your sight."

Kreider turned the computer screen so Bryce could see it. By means of a built-in compass and spatial movement software, the navigation plotter had been tracking their movements ever since they left the *Thermopylae*: drawing squiggly lines across a screen that was superimposed on a pre-loaded map with grid coordinates.

Bryce spoke the latitude and longitude. "Have Jake bring Nick to this location. You and your squads stick with the followers. Split them up if you need to tail more than one. Remember that they'll be under cover. Out."

Laila and Kreider looked at Bryce expectantly.

"Leibowitz snuck away from Tyrone. I'm almost inclined to proceed without him and let him become the wandering Jew." He glanced up at the ceiling. "No I can't leave a man behind no matter how much of a jerk he is." He pulled his favorite Beretta from under his belt, handed it to Laila, and jabbed a forefinger at the prisoner. "Keep an eye on him. You too Luke. Shoot him if you have to. In the leg."

Kreider drew a Glock from inside his toga. "I don't really want to use this, but I will if he gives me the least excuse."

On the way out of the door: "Give him more food when Jake arrives."

The prisoner opened his eyes at Bryce's departure, but showed no other interest in ongoing events. He closed his eyes again.

Kreider glanced at the prisoner as he knelt and steadied the Glock on his knees. "He reminds me of a scarecrow with the stuffing knocked out of him."

"He's had a hard life, but no harder than anyone else who's living at this time."

"Yeah, I sure wouldn't want to be stranded here forever. And not just because of the living conditions. I want to see my wife and family again."

"And I want to see my cat."

They lapsed into silence but not for long. Jake arrived with Father Nick in tow. The Vatican rep was in tears. His jaw moved but he was too choked up to speak. Laila glanced at Jake.

"We witnessed the abduction, ma'am. A squad of Roman soldiers escorted the designated one from the square. We were under orders not to interfere."

"You did the right thing, Jake." To Nick: "Father Nick, you knew this was going to happen. You knew that Jesus was going to be taken to Pontius Pilate. But seeing it happen – "

Several minutes passed before Father Nick was able to speak. Between tears: "You – you don't understand. It didn't – it didn't happen – the way I – expected . . . "

"There are bound to be a few differences between reality and the historical record. Word of mouth wasn't very precise – "

"It was – more than a few minor differences. We saw everything – " Father Nick choked up again. Jake held out his canteen. Father Nick took a swig, then another, then two more. He wiped his mouth of the sleeve of his toga. "We saw – "

Bryce entered the room with Leibowitz in tow. Tyrone was right behind him. Bryce held the professor by an ear the way an angry mother would haul a bad child into the house for a spanking. Leibowitz didn't seem to mind.

"Don't go wandering off again."

"I – I – I – told you, I wasn't wandering. I – I overheard some people mention Calvary, so I stopped to ask for directions. They told me how to get to the hill where the crosses were erected. It's outside of town on a grassy knoll – " He stopped as soon as he recognized the historical reference of his description. He stared at Father Nick. "What's – what's wrong with him?"

Father Nick wept. "I saw everything. I saw – "

Laila used the sleeve of her stola to wipe the tears off his cheeks. "Take a deep breath and tell us what you saw."

Slowly and haltingly, Father Nick related his story. "We met Captain Grayson in the quad where men were taking turns talking on the table of a vendor who sold tallow mixed with ashes. I wish Dr. Leibowitz was with me, because I could not understand what they were saying. The crowd was small but attentive. Some of the spokesmen attracted Captain Grayson's attention by surreptitiously waving their hands below their waists, and pointing to a hunched individual with a potbelly, a hooked nose, and a long scraggly beard, but who was otherwise baldheaded. Captain Grayson ignored them.

"After a while the preaching stopped. The crowd dispersed, but half a dozen men and four women retired to a nearby inn for a late lunch. This inn was hidden behind a garden. I asked Captain Grayson and Corporal Jake to remain on guard outside, while I entered to observe the preachers and their partially clad companions. The hunchback and a rather tall and masculine individual retreated to the back of the room. The other four engaged in raucous talk and laughter as they ate their meal, and imbibed large quantities of strong alcohol." In aside, "I sipped on a horrid mug of mead that the proprietor provided in exchange for a coin." He shuddered at the memory. "After all the food and drink were consumed, the women disrobed and allowed the men to admire their bodies and fondle their breasts.

"The two men in the back of the room engaged in passionate kissing. Three Roman soldiers entered at that point. One of the preachers called out. I caught the word Judas, whereupon the masculine man stepped away from his embrace with his partner, and proceeded to gather coins from the four male revelers. He used these coins to pay the bill.

"I approached the soldiers and apologized if my friends were making too much noise in their carousing. They stared at me but did not appear to understand my Latin accent. One of them pushed me aside. The other two strode to the back of the room, grabbed the hunchback, and dragged him out of the inn and along the street. The revelers shouted and mocked him. Judas ran after the soldiers, crying. He was knocked down by a fist, but he rose unsteadily and staggered after them, crying louder. He was – "

"He's been kidnapped!" Laila was gazing sightlessly into the distance. "They weren't Roman soldiers. They were IRF agents in disguise, and they just got away with Jesus Christ."

Chapter 26

The Mission was suddenly moving forward at warp speed.

Bryce issued orders with machinegun rapidity. He ordered one MAV to reconnoiter from the air. He ordered one airjeep to investigate the future site of the temporal displacement apparatus. He ordered one squad to take a position near Calvary. He ordered another squad to guard the roads into Jerusalem. He would have ordered Grayson to follow the fake Roman soldiers, but the worthy captain had already taken it upon himself to do just that; so he ordered him not to intercede until his arrival. He ordered Jake and Tyrone to keep a close watch on the prisoner and to follow at a discrete distance.

He gave Leibowitz a tiny green sphere that measured half the size of a pea. "I can't afford to lose you again and let you fall into enemy hands. You're the only one among us who can speak with our quarry. Keep this in your mouth and tuck it into the back of your cheek like a chipmunk. If the enemy captures you and tortures you and you can't stand the pain you bite down on it."

"Is – is – is it a painkiller?"

"Death will be instantaneous."

Leibowitz gulped – but he didn't gulp the sphere. He placed it gently on his tongue, positioned it between his teeth and his cheek, then kept his mouth shut.

"Things are happening now and they're happening fast." Bryce led his entourage to a rendezvous with Captain Grayson. "Let's double-time it."

Father Nick was despondent but he pointed the way to the quad.

Leibowitz placed a comforting hand on Father Nick's shoulder. "I – I – I'm so sorry that – that it turned out this way."

Laila also tried to soothe the good father. "It was only an innocent kiss. And it wasn't given in betrayal. You know from Judas's diary that he was Christ's greatest follower. He truly loved Jesus and his teachings."

"But not like that. Theirs was a kiss of *passion*. That's worse than the way it was written in the *Bible*."

"There's nothing wrong with that kind of relationship. Nowadays it's accepted – "

"It's accepted for mortal men and women; not for the Son of God."

"But this is Christ's worldly incarnation. That makes him subject to the desires of the flesh."

"Not . . . " Father Nick shook his head in dejection.

Laila empathized with him. Losing one's husband to such carnal desire was nothing compared to losing one's god. She also knew the lame futility of trying to argue someone out of his grief. Surcease of such sorrow could arise only from within, and only after a sufficient passage of time. Emotional wounds healed slowly.

Jerusalem in the first century was not the thriving metropolis that it had become after two thousand years of growth and urbanization. It was hardly more than a village way station that connected Rome to distant parts of its empire. It didn't take them long to catch up to Grayson's rearguard.

Grayson dropped back so he could confer with his superior officer. "They're just over the next rise. I've sent men ahead on both sides of the road so we effectively have them flanked."

"Good work. I'll go ahead with the interpreters. As soon as I stop the bogies have your men close in but don't shoot. We don't want to hit the quarry."

"Understood."

Bryce strode on with Laila, Leibowitz, and Father Nick trailing behind him. From the top of the rise they saw the three phony Roman legionnaires with Jesus in tow by means of a rope looped around his neck, and Judas bawling after them in the rear. Occasionally one of the legionnaires turned around to chase Judas away, but he was fleet of foot and always evaded the swinging sword.

The Americans were yet a hundred feet behind the Roman-garbed Muslims when one of them turned around to take another swipe at Judas, and spotted

Bryce the centurion with his followers. He called a warning to his companions. Struggling language students often declared that the greatest accomplishment of the Romans was their ability to speak Latin.

Leibowitz whispered, "That wasn't Latin. It was badly accented ancient Hebrew with glottal stops and anomalous vowel shifts."

Real legionnaires would have showed respect to a centurion the way airmen would have saluted a commanding officer. These soldiers drew their swords.

Bryce was at a disadvantage because the only foreign language he spoke was South Philly street talk. They would not have understood him if he said, "Om Cunnel Davenport. Youse guys drop yer weapons." In a low voice to Father Nick: "Now's the time to strut your stuff. Try your Latin on them and see if they understand."

Before Father Nick had time to acknowledge, Judas dashed toward Bryce and knelt on both knees in front of him. He cried and rambled in ancient Hebrew as he kissed the top of Bryce's sandaled feet.

Leibowitz whispered, "He's begging forgiveness for his sins and for the sins of his – " He glanced at Father Nick. " – his close friend."

Bryce looked down at the groveling man, then at Father Nick. "Go ahead." He gripped Judas's black curly hair, held him gently in place, then sidestepped so he had a clear path between him and his opponents.

Father Nick advanced. He spoke in a soft scholarly voice.

Despite a bleeding gash over his ribcage, Jesus remained calm and stood as tall as his short stature allowed, as if he were willing to accept any fate that the Lord had in store for him. The Muslims pinched their eyes and made threatening motions with their outthrust blades. There was no hint of comprehension.

Bryce returned their fierce Islamic glares but kept his arms at his sides. "It's your turn, Laila. Tell them that if they surrender Jesus willingly we won't hurt them. They can either go their way unmolested and live out their lives in the past or we can return them to their own time without punishment."

Laila stepped past Father Nick. She spoke to them in Farsi. Their faces expressed astonishment at hearing their native tongue. They exchanged looks with each other. The one who held the rope that was tied around the Savior's neck appeared to be the leader. He let go of the rope and advanced a single step.

In Farsi: "There is but one god. His name is Allah and Mohammad is his prophet." He charged straight at Laila.

In one fluid motion Laila drew the gun that Bryce had given to her, pulled back the slide, flipped off the safety lever, raised her arm – and barely had time to twist away from the sword tip. The blade sliced through the loose folds of her stola. In desperation she pulled the trigger without having the time or distance to lock her elbows. The recoil slammed the gun against her forehead. She reeled, felt herself caught from behind, and slid down to the ground, blinded with pain.

She didn't lose consciousness, but awareness of her surroundings was severely limited by tunnel vision and tears. She had a hazy notion that bodies lay all around her. A ghostly image that looked like Bryce pulled a bloody sword from a Muslim's abdomen. Half the skull was missing from the Muslim behind her. The one that lay writhing on the ground next to her had a small round hole in the side of his brass breastplate.

Leibowitz pulled her away from the pile of bodies. "Are – are – are you all right?"

Laila put one hand to her forehead, where a lump was already beginning to grow. "I've been better."

Bryce knelt down in front of her. "Nice shooting."

She flipped the safety lever to the locked position. "Nice stabbing."

Suddenly they were encircled by a horde of airmen dressed in various raiment. One whose name she didn't know held a sniper rifle. "I'm sorry, sir. I know you said not to shoot, but the priest was about to get run through the gut. I had a clear – "

Bryce cut him off. "You did the right thing, Tom. That shows initiative and clear thinking under fire."

Father Nick stood stock still. He was too shocked to move but not to make light of the moment. "Praise the Lord and bring the ammunition."

"All that practice in swordplay and parrying came in handy." Bryce wiped the blood off his blade by running the flat edges over the skewered Muslim's kilt. He sheathed his sword without a flourish. The Muslim that Laila shot stopped breathing.

Suddenly Leibowitz began to choke. He put his hands to his throat, gagged, and tried to split. "Colonel – Colonel Davenport." He gagged some more. "I – I – I – swallowed the pill."

Bryce placed his hands on Leibowitz's terror-stricken face, clenching the professor's bearded cheeks. He looked deep into the other man's eyes. "Did you bite down on it or did you swallow it whole?"

"I – I – I don't know. I was so scared I didn't notice. I grabbed her when she – I don't know."

"Do you feel any numbness in your fingertips? Any tingling in your hands and feet?"

Leibowitz shook both hands in the air. "No – no – no, everything feels normal."

"Then you'll be all right. The poison only works if it's released in the mouth. Stomach acid neutralizes it."

Leibowitz was so relieved that he would have collapsed if Tom hadn't caught him. Laila was aware of a great shuffling of feet and not a few knowing smirks.

"Dr. Leibowitz listen to me. You're okay and I need your help so please calm down. I need you to talk with Jesus and Judas and – " He glanced to where the pair were standing. Judas was bent over with his arms wrapped around Jesus's torso; Jesus stood upright and had one arm laid casually over Judas's shoulder. Jesus was solemn but Judas was in tears. " – tell them we're not going to hurt them. Can you do that for me? Can you tell them that we're here to help them?"

Leibowitz took a breath so deep that his chest expanded several inches. "Yes – yes – I can do that. I – I can do that."

"Jake. Tyrone. Help Dr. Leibowitz to Jesus and Judas. And see that Jesus gets medical attention for that stab wound. And a tetanus shot."

Both Jake and Tyrone said "Yes, sir" simultaneously. Tom let go of the professor as the pair led away their charge.

Bryce extracted a small cloth jewelry sack from his shoulder bag. "Anyone for trading beads?"

Some of the surrounding snickers loudened to chuckles and chortles.

"You are so bad." Laila let Kreider help her to her feet. "How could you do such a thing?"

"It kept him close to my skirt didn't it?" Getting serious: "What do we do now Nick?"

Father Nick deliberated before answering. "I am astonished by events that make it appear that *we* were the expression of God's will. According to the New Testament, Roman soldiers were supposed take Jesus before Pontius Pilate, then turn him over to King Herod, who authorized the Crucifixion. Now it seems as if the Roman soldiers were impostors who instead intended to prevent the Crucifixion from occurring by spiriting Jesus away from contention. Only part of what was written has come to pass, and that part did not occur in accordance with written accounts."

"You mean in accordance with *published* accounts." Kreider raised his voice to a whine. "You saw the apostles back at the inn. From what you told us, *they* are the ones to blame for setting these preposterous events in motion. *They* were the ones who betrayed Jesus to the Romans, not Judas." He flung his hands into the air. "Don't you get it? This is the beginning of the Christian power play. *They* orchestrated the betrayal because they wanted Jesus crucified and Judas ostracized, so the other disciples could each become the leader of their own church. Then they wrote a sensationalistic account that supported their agenda. That's why the various versions of the Crucifixion in the *Bible* differ: because the apostles didn't ever witness any Crucifixion; they made it up later because they needed a martyr to advance their cause. Then centuries later, when splinter religions abounded and Catholic leaders needed to consolidate them into one cohesive whole that granted themselves sole eternal power, they chose which canons to include in the *Bible* because they stressed the points that they wanted to make, and which ones to exclude because their viewpoints were in opposition. The apostles were like modern-day newspaper reporters, only worse. They changed the entire course of religious history by writing fictitious accounts of events that never occurred."

"But for the greater good."

"Well, I'll grant you that in retrospect. Even if they didn't practice what they preached, they created a religion of humanitarian values that's a whole lot better than Islamic intolerance and terrorism."

Silence stirred in the air. The troops in the background were silent. They were fighters, not philosophers or advisors.

Laila still held one palm against her bruised and bulging forehead. "I don't buy it. The apostles couldn't have made up such a convincing story from whole cloth. They had to start with a scrap of truth that they got from somewhere. You can't fill a sieve with water, as my granma used to say."

This last comment elicited titters from the troops who were unfamiliar with her grandmother's Appalachian aphorisms. She took the jibes with her usual good humor.

"The way it appears now, Jesus and Judas were marched off by three unidentified Roman soldiers and simply disappeared in the wilderness. That is not the stuff of which *Bible* stories are made."

Kreider humphed. "*Bible* stories are made of fluff, not stuff."

Father Nick gave Kreider a hard stare, but did not respond to the taunt.

Leibowitz made a tentative interruption. "I – I – I spoke with – with Jesus." Every living eye focused on his shocked expression. The sudden silence was deafening.

" He – he told me that he has already been tried by Pontius Pilate, and that he was released to the hands, or authority, of King Herod. Herod – Herod found him guilty of subversion, or sedition, or rabble-rousing – I'm not sure of the word – but paroled him on the promise that he stop preaching the ways of God. Jesus didn't promise, but Herod released him anyway, and told him that his parole would be revoked if he continued to agitate the masses. He – he – he's a born evangelist so I guess he couldn't stop preaching his beliefs no matter what the consequences. I – I think that if his disciples hadn't turned him over to the Muslims, Herod might have had him apprehended again, despite his initial reluctance to have Jesus crucified.

Bryce was nodding knowingly. "What do you say Nick? Do we proceed with our backup plan?"

"I knew it!" Kreider exploded. "I knew you two had something up your sleeve beside your arm."

Father Nick was less voluble and slow to reply. "O tempora, o mores, as Cicero once said. Oh what times, oh what a situation. It appears that once again it is up to us to do the work of the Lord."

"The work of the Lord! We're sure as hell not going to crucify Christ to fulfill a postdoctoral prophecy. I won't be part of it, and I don't even know the guy. I know you believe that Christ died for our sins, but he doesn't have to die yet. Salvation can come later."

"We do not have to actually crucify Christ. We only have to stage the Crucifixion."

Kreider breathed a sigh of relief. "Sure, I get it. A simulation. You don't have to do much to trick a bunch of proto-Catholics. I mean, after all, they believe in divine creation without a shred of proof. And most of these people aren't even literate so they'll be easy to fool. So what's the game plan?"

Once again Father Nick pierced Kreider with a stern look.

Bryce ignored the low-keyed contretemps. "We'll have to wing some of it so let's see how it goes."

Bryce laid out details that involved innuendo and

sleight of hand to create a plausible illusion that would be open to interpretation. The canonical apostles could fill in the blanks from their twisted imaginations, just as they must have done with the other fabulous stories that they told about Jesus: changing water to wine, healing the sick, raising the dead, and so on. Father Nick offered suggestions. Kreider agreed to take part in the performance.

Because of his local language skills, Leibowitz became the primary actor in a play that was contrived to deceive a multitude of soon-to-be believers about the death and resurrection of Jesus Christ. First, Bryce separated Jesus from Judas – who lamented horribly and volubly – and ordered the Elite Guard to escort the Savior to Calvary, where they were to prepare the setting for the first act.

Leibowitz did his best to calm down Judas with explanations. He finally convinced Judas to lead him, Bryce, Laila, Father Nick, and Kreider to the place where Judas and Jesus had rented lodgings. With Father Nick and Kreider dictating, and Leibowitz translating, Judas brought his diary up to date, then appended certain astronomical observations.

Afterward, as self-appointed town criers, Leibowitz and Father Nick paraded through Jerusalem and informed the townsfolk in ancient Hebrew and Latin that Pontius Pilate and King Herod had tried Christ again in absentia, and found him guilty of inciting revolution. They sang announcements of the imminent Crucifixion.

Citizens tagged along behind the pair like hypnotized rats or enraptured children following the Pied Piper out of Hamelin. They had no idea that they were being called to witness the greatest recorded event in the history of mankind. Bryce and Laila held Judas in the back of the growing crowd. Using his plotter, Kreider led the way to Calvary.

Once the witnesses were in place, Jesus strode confidently up the hill to where the Romans had long-ago installed a row of crucifixes on which to punish sinners, criminals, and political dissidents. Bryce sat Jesus on the ground in front of the most prominent crucifix. He bound Christ's hands behind his back and lashed the rope around the pole. The rope was loose so that Jesus was not uncomfortable. He stared at the blue sky stalwartly, expectantly, unconcernedly.

The throng watched with eager anticipation, like Roman spectators filing into the Coliseum to watch Christians get mauled by lions, although that wouldn't start happening for another fifty years.

When Laila couldn't hold Judas back any longer, he staggered up the slope with his arms outstretched, wailing at Bryce who stood guard over Jesus.

Leibowitz interpreted: "He's imploring you to crucify him on the adjacent pole. He wants to accompany Jesus to heaven."

"We'll take him with us, but he'll have to wait until our transportation arrives."

Judas got down on both knees and clung to Bryce's legs, lamenting loudly.

"For Christ's sake, will you get this crybaby out of here!"

Two airmen clad in togas pulled Judas away. Bryce stationed other airmen in strategic locations: those who were dressed as legionnaires were posted on guard against the possible infiltration of Muslims or real Roman soldiers; others who were dressed in civilian attire were charged with crowd control; some were sent as scouts to search for a suitable cave on the other side of the hill.

The late afternoon sun shone down on a long line people who were still arriving from Jerusalem to view the spectacle. The disloyal apostles were among them, hanging in the background lest they attract undue attention from faux Roman soldiers. For most of the people this was a sad and solemn occasion, but for a few it was an occasion for rejoicing. The jeering few were the howling ancestors of those who would someday point their thumbs down at gladiator games, scream for death at jousting events, cry in delight at bullfights, and shout for blood at boxing matches. The arena was different but the mindset was the same.

Vendors toting kegs of water and sacks of comestibles were the last ones to arrive. Coins changed hands among bettors.

Jesus showed signs of suffering toward sundown, partly from heat but mostly from the roughhousing that he had received from his erstwhile Muslim captors. Despite Laila's throbbing bulge, which was now half the size of a chicken egg sliced lengthwise, she approached him with a canteen full of water. She let him drink his fill, then poured the remainder over his head to keep him cool.

When the sun touched the horizon, Bryce climbed the hill and put a medical kit on the ground next to Jesus. He changed the dressing over the dagger wound that had been inflicted by the Muslims. He withdrew a large hypodermic needle from the kit, filled the syringe with saline solution, and injected the liquid into Christ's upper thigh. He used a smaller hypodermic needle to inject a long-acting anesthetic.

"That'll knock him out until morning."

In Latin and ancient Hebrew, Father Nick and Leibowitz announced that the name of the centurion who stabbed Jesus on the cross was Longinus.

The cloudless sky purpled slowly. Twinkling stars made a gradual appearance. The Moon had risen hours ago but now shed its brilliant light on an event of mythic proportions. Some of the onlookers went home to bed; the hangers-on lounged or loafed on a grassy sward long after the Moon slid below the western horizon. Most fell asleep.

Bryce waited until the cloak of darkness was total before orchestrating his next move. Silently his troops cut Jesus free and carried him over the hill to an overhanging cliff shelter, where they made him comfortable for the remainder of the night, with a suspicious Judas genuflecting by his side: first on one knee then on the other.

Civilian-clad troops aroused the nearby populace at first light. In the first century, people were not in the habit of looking up for UFO's. Bryce's Elite Guard called attention to the pair of angels that were descending from the light cloud cover. The people trembled and cowered with cries of awe.

Perhaps the most awe-stricken of the witnesses were the attending apostles, who witnessed the miracle with unbridled fear and anguish, for above the angels hovered the hand of God Himself – or perhaps it was the wrath of God who had not forsaken his earthbound son but who came in answer to his prayers. If the betrayers were about to be punished, it was too late for penitence.

Members of the Elite Guard who wore tunics and togas led the people of Jerusalem over the hill to witness the resurrection.

Two aircycles were losing altitude over the cave in which Jesus was struggling to overcome the effects of anesthesia. Over the cave entrance the guards had erected a tarp that had been cobbled together from ponchos. They threw back the tarp as the aircycles touched down and their operators cut the engines.

Father Nick and Leibowitz pointed to Captain Grayson, and spread the name of the centurion who was in command of the legionnaires who were guarding the sepulchral cave: Petronius.

Two guards in Roman uniform carried Jesus to the aircycles. They placed him upright next to the pilot in one of them. By this time Jesus was somewhat alert. He looked at the pilots in their flight gear and helmets, and – like the witnesses on the ground – saw heads surrounded by halos.

Jesus maintained his poise. He neither smiled nor showed signs of fear. He played his part without being coached, by holding his arms straight out as if he were bestowing benediction. Physically he was little more than a badly deformed gnome; spiritually he was truly the quintessence of enlightenment. Although a psychiatrist might define his mental state as a disorder that touched on psychosis, Jesus actually seemed to believe that he was the chosen Son of God. Undoubtedly the citizens of Jerusalem now agreed with him.

Judas wept in ecstasy.

The aircycles gained altitude until they were little more than dots in the sky. A squall in the upper atmospheric dispersed some of the puffy white clouds, momentarily exposing the lower hull of the *Thermopylae*. The operators guided their aircycles up and into the bomb bays. The hatches closed underneath them. Minutes later, the *Thermopylae* zoomed across the firmament and was quickly lost from sight. A hush fell over the crowd.

The normally staid troops made various remarks: "Quite a performance." "It almost had me fooled." "That's the greatest magic show I've ever seen." "Fooled them with misdirection." "That's one for Cirque du Soleil."

Laila took another painkiller. "My granma said that you can't mend a spider web, but what did she know?"

Bryce ordered the retreat of the MAV that was scouting the neighborhood. "Okay people let's tie up a few loose ends and complete this Mission so we can all go home."

The troops cheered.

He then ordered the airjeeps to meet them as they marched away from Jerusalem, not along a Roman via but by compass toward the locality where the Dead Sea Scrolls would one day be found. The clandestine part of the mission was over. If their hovercraft were spotted now, the locals would likely chalk them off as a mirage.

Judas walked compliantly. He may have lost his "close friend," but he had gained a God in heaven which he now knew must exist. They would meet again sometime, somewhere.

Bodgdadi seemed less sullen than when he had first been apprehended. His captors no longer needed his intel yet they kept him alive and did not mistreat him.

It took them five hours over rough territory to reach the cave whose position Father Nick had indicated on Kreider's computer-generated map and satellite-imaged overlays from twenty-first-century downloads. There they buried the Gospel of Judas, some of its ink still fresh on the addendum, sealed in a ceramic jar that was not to be opened for nearly two thousand years.

And there they rendezvoused with both airjeeps, which transported everyone to their penultimate destination.

"This is how I found it," stated the airjeep driver. "I didn't disturb anything, like you said."

Desiccated bones lay scattered in the sand: skulls, ribcages, thighbones, and other skeletal remains, all disarticulated in the absence of connective tissue. In the middle lay a nuclear device, and alongside it the tuner in a stainless steel container. Nearly a quarter century of desert winds had blown loose sand into the hemisphere that had been gouged out of the ground by the transference. The bomb and tuner were partially buried.

"Good work, Mitch. Let's hope the batteries are still good." Annunciator lights flickered into existence when Bryce pulled off the safety cap and flipped the arming switch. He fiddled with the electronic controls, then disabled the timing mechanism with the butt of his Beretta so Bodgdadi couldn't tamper with it. Then he signaled for Laila and the prisoner to approach.

"Tell him that he is free to go anywhere and anywhen of his choosing. If he remains with us he will be held as a prisoner of war. If he goes his own way to his own time he can rejoin his companions and make peace with his god."

Laila spoke in Farsi. To Bryce: "He said that he will go his own way. May Allah be with you."

"And with you."

Bryce took Laila by the hand and walked her out of the sphere of influence. Bodgdadi knelt by the cylindrical tuner. Without hesitation he unscrewed the cap. He looked up at the sun, then oriented himself to face the direction in which Mohammad would one day be born. He flipped the recall switch. He disappeared in an instant, accompanied by a gust of wind and the hemisphere of sand on which he had been kneeling.

Bryce smirked and raised his blond eyebrows in full awareness of what was to come. He tilted his head at Laila. "A blast from the past?"

Chapter 27

The *Thermopylae* was as quiet as a church pew on Monday morning.

After the airjeeps returned to the aircraft, Danette took off solo and headed straight for home. Field personnel took showers and collapsed in their bunks. They were exhausted. The operation of the *Thermopylae* was the responsibility of the technical team and reactor crew; they were well rested after their period of idle attendance.

Laila had not realized how tired she was until she had refused Wendayne's offer of freshly brewed coffee, and opted instead for forty or fifty winks. Now she opened her eyes to the comforting darkness of her bunkroom. She felt wonderfully revitalized. Events of the past week flashed through her waking mind in snippets that lacked chronological sequence: like the mismatched montage of a crackbrained artist.

Yet unlike a dream, somehow it all made sense – in a convoluted kind of way.

She sat up, pushed her dainty feet into her jogging shoes – right where she had placed them next to the lower bunk – and took a deep breath of recycled air. Although the stola was the height of fashion in ancient Rome, she enjoyed the casual feel of hospital scrubs. She was determined to purchase several pairs to wear around the house – perhaps even in the office.

She wiggled her fingers at the techies in their computer carrels as she skipped along the narrow corridor, following the scent of coffee to its origin.

"I see that the galley slave is still slaving in a hot galley."

Wendayne flashed a mouthful of white teeth like the Cheshire cat. "Honey chile, you sho nuf look a sight better than you did last night. Or was that this marnin'? There's no way o' tellin' in this here time machine business."

Laila leaned close. "Are you still working undercover?"

"Till the colonel tells me elsewise."

Laila gratefully grasped a cup of steaming black coffee and perched on the edge of a chair that was pulled away from the table. "The TDA recall device operates differently from the timepiece. Although . . . "

"I seen that look before."

Laila shook the cobwebs out of her head. "Oh, well. Just a thought." She slipped her coffee gratefully. "Wow. This is so much better than the sludge in the MRE's. So how are our new passengers making out. Er, I mean, how are they adjusting to, well, this?"

"They's in seventh heaven, or so they believe. Only the perfessor kin talk to 'em, so he's the one you gotta ask. He put 'em to bed in his own room. All's I know is they didn't care for the vittles I rustled up for 'em. They ate it, but I could tell by the expressions on they's faces that it definitely disagreed with 'em."

"We were so busy that I didn't have time to sample the local fare. Wow, I didn't even buy any souvenirs. Everything happened so fast. You'd think that with a time machine you could have a little time to yourself."

"Time waits fer no one, as the old sayin' goes."

Father Nick entered the room. "'To every thing there is a season, and a time to every purpose under the heaven: a time to be born, and a time to die; a time to plant, and a time to pluck up that which is planted; a time to kill, and a time to heal; a time to break down, and a time to build up; a time to weep, and a time to laugh; a time to mourn, and a time to dance; a time to cast away stones, and a time to gather stones together; a time to embrace, and a time to refrain from embracing; a time to get, and a time to lose; a time to keep, and a time to cast away; a time to rend, and a time to sew; a time to keep silence, and a time to speak; a time to love, and a time to hate; a time of war, and a time of peace.' "

Kreider was right behind him. "Sounds like Pete Seeger."

Laila couldn't help but giggle. "Luke, you're incorrigible."

Father Nick adopted an expression of mock sincerity. "It is Ecclesiastes III, chapter three, verses one through eight."

"You got it backwards, padre. Seeger's lyrics were sent back through time and plagiarized by the *Bible* compilers."

Father Nick glared, but he also winked. "Let us pray that hate and war are in abeyance, and that now – in the future – is the time for love and peace."

Wendayne: "Amen to that."

"Hallelujah," Kreider added, taking a seat. "I'll have time for love and a piece as soon as I get back to the missus."

Laila giggled again. "Is this what you call post-traumatic elation syndrome?"

"I've never heard of that one."

"I just made it up. It's the euphoria that follows a death defying experience that you somehow managed to survive: the it's-great-to-be-alive feeling."

"I'll drink to that! And the padre's got just the thing to drink it from. Show them."

Father Nick had changed back to his clerical garb. From one of his coat pockets he removed a crude and misshapen earthenware mug, gray in color. "This was, uh, left behind at the inn after the bogus Roman soldiers absconded with their prisoner. I saw him drinking from it. . . . "

Laila gasped. "You mean . . . ?"

"I did not steal it. I left some coins in its place. Strangely enough, although the pitcher in front of it contained water, the dregs at the bottom of this holy vessel were sweeter than wine." He examined the mug from all sides, top and bottom, inside and out. "Of course, I will not keep it for myself. I will donate it to the Vatican museum."

Kreider humphed. "Date testing will show it's a fake. In sequential time it's only a couple of years old."

Father Nick frowned. "I had not thought of that."

"There's a lot of things about time travel that you have to think through. Like what we just did. We didn't change the past, we just made sure the past happened the way it was supposed to happen; or the way we think it happened; or the way it was written in the good book; or the way the Christian compilers of the *Bible* wanted it to happen. Time travel is a mind bender."

"I have been thinking about what the future may bring. That is, about how future time travel may affect past events."

"You lost me on that one, padre."

"There are a great many anomalous incidents in the Scriptures that could be explained in light of visitations from the future. That is, from our present."

"For instance?"

Father Nick took a seat and pulled his prized *Bible* from another of his voluminous pockets. "The most obvious one that comes to mind is this very special aircraft in which we are flying across the heavens. It is propelled by four nuclear engines that are mounted on pylons. In the Book of Ezekiel, the author goes to great lengths to describe how he was taken up into the sky on a chariot that was flown by four cherubim, or angels. Now the ancients did not have a term for nuclear engine, would not have understood its mechanism of propulsion, and would not have been able to grasp the concept of manned flight. So Ezekiel described the aircraft in the only words that existed in his vocabulary. To the ancients, an angel was a messenger from God: a messenger that, like birds, possessed the ability to fly."

He opened his *Bible* to a passage that he had previously marked. "I will read from chapter one, starting with verse four: 'And I looked, and, behold, a whirlwind came out of the north, a great cloud, with fire infolding itself, and a brightness was around it, and out of the midst thereof as the color of amber, out of the midst of the fire. Also out of the midst thereof came the likeness of four living creatures. And this was their appearance; they had the likeness of a man. And every one had four faces, and every one had four wings. And their feet were straight feet; and the sole of their feet was like the sole of a calf's foot; and they sparkles like the color of burnished brass. And they had the hands of a man under their wings on their four sides; and they four had their faces and their wings. Their wings were joined one to another; they turned not when they went; they went every one straight forward. As for the likeness of their faces, they had the face of a man, and the face of a lion, on the right side; and they four had the face of an ox on the left side; they four also had the face of an eagle. Thus were the faces; and their wings were stretched upward; two wings of every one were joined one to another, and two covered their bodies. And they went every one straight forward: whither the spirit was to go, they went; and they turned not when they went. As for the likeness of the living creatures, their appearance was like burning coals of fire, and like the appearance of lamps: it went up and down among the living creatures; and the fire was bright, and out of the fire went forth lightning. Now as I beheld the living creatures, behold one wheel upon the earth by the living creatures, with his four faces. The appearance of the wheels and their work was like unto the color of a beryl: and they four had one likeness: and their appearance and their work was as it were a wheel in the middle of a wheel. When they went, they went upon their four sides: and they turned not when they went. As for their rings, they were so high that they were dreadful; and their rings were full of eyes round about them four. And when the living creatures went, the wheels went by them: and when the living creatures were lifted up from the earth, the wheels were lifted up.' And so on, and so on."

Father Nick closed the good book. "This could very well be a description of the *Thermopylae*, given by a person who had never seen such a craft, and whose language did not contain the words to adequately describe what he was seeing."

Kreider humphed. "What an imagination! It makes the *Bible* sound like a science fiction novel."

Father Nick could accept criticism from Kreider better than he could from Leibowitz, because his comments were lighthearted instead of flippant. "There's more."

"My mind is bent far enough already. Don't go throwing it completely out of kilter."

"Perhaps Jonah was swallowed by a submarine instead of a great fish. That would explain why he was not digested by stomach acid and was able to escape unharmed after three days in its belly. The Ark of the Covenant could have been an armored army tank that demolished the walls of Jericho by means of shells that were fired from its canon. Sodom and Gomorrah could have been destroyed by atomic bombs – "

"Okay, all right, enough already. And maybe the Pope went back to Mount Sinai and gave the Ten Commandants to Moses. I don't buy any of it, but it sure as hell beats the aliens-from-outer-space hokum, since we know that interstellar travel is impossible."

"So was time travel until it was invented," Laila interjected.

"Well, impractical then. Look, all I'm saying is that ancient writings are like statistics: they can be interpreted any way the interpreter wants to interpret them. If you want to believe that future temporanauts went, or will go, or have gone, traipsing through the past to create or mold events the way they're related in the *Bible*, I won't disabuse you. But don't you try to discombobulate my noodle any more than it already is. I've got – "

"Attention please. This is your pilot speaking." Danette's voice was melodious but firm. "We're maintaining hover in the reference sphere. Transfer will occur in five minutes. There won't be any spatial movement, but be advised that for some of you there may be undesirable side effects."

Laila caught a glimpse of Bryce hurrying to the wheelhouse.

Leibowitz popped into the galley. To Wendayne: "Quick, I need a paper bag."

"Will plastic do?" Wendayne handed him a cellophane food wrapper. "What about our guests?"

"Not a care in the world. They're sleeping like babies." He sat in an unoccupied chair across from Father Nick. "I – I – I'm sorry for what I said before. You know, about using the prophet for profit. I didn't mean to sound – crass."

Father Nick glared suspiciously, but his tone of voice leavened his expression. "I forgive you your trespasses."

"I – I – I mean – Jesus Christ is actually sleeping in my bunk. And Judas is on top. I mean, in the top bunk. They're for *real*. That's enough to unhinge any agnostic."

Father Nick nodded like the confident father figure that he was.

"But – but I – now take this in the right light – people *are* gullible. Not just Catholics, but all people. Most people. They'll believe just about anything, and the more fantastic it is, the more willing they are to believe it." To Kreider: "Am I right?"

"You're right all right."

"What I meant was, even though Jesus in the flesh doesn't look like the aristocratic Jesus in medieval paintings, those paintings were based on cultural preconceptions. The artists made Jesus look the way people expected him to look. They used facial features to portray his inner nobility, the way the apostles made up stories to demonstrate his godlike qualities. I – I still don't think he was the son of God, but he *was* – and *is* – a symbol of theological faith. A symbol that some people need. That's why the Vatican should use him to, uh, well, not use him, but promote him – advertise him – for what he symbolizes. His appearance – I mean, his second coming, not the looks of his physical body – is what is needed to renew faith in Catholicism, to restore lost beliefs, and to bring down the reign of Islamic terrorism. That's why – "

An awful wrenching motion coursed through Laila's body. Her pores dripped fluid like water being wrung out of a wet towel. She felt her eyes cross from one socket to the other. Her stomach twisted worse than the Gordian knot. Discordant images were dredged from her memory, expanded into multicolored clouds, then coalesced into meaningless patterns like a pixilated digital photograph. Her mental aberration lasted half an eternity.

How can that be, she opined: half of forever is the same as two times zero. Fleeting images appeared but disappeared before she had time to focus on them. In a time machine, shouldn't she have all the time in the world? In the universe? Or did she have no time at all? Did this second transference make her a two timer? A concurrence? A concomitance? A coinstantaneity?

She gulped, and the sentimental numbness was over. A timeless moment passed before she regained her concentration. "Wow! The repetition *was* easier."

Kreider was laconic. "Told you so."

Father Nick crossed himself. Wendayne coughed. Leibowitz didn't vomit.

"Where – where – where was I?"

"Same place you are now."

"I – I lost my train of thought."

"You didn't lose your train of thought. You lost the whole railroad."

The intercom spoke: "This is your colonel speaking. Please remain seated with your seatbelts securely fastened until the pilot taxies this baby into the hangar. I congratulate everyone for the outstanding performance of your duty to your country. I am proud of you. The next twenty-four hours will be spent in debriefing demobilizing and writing combat reports. After that I am placing all personnel on indefinite leave."

A thunderous cheer resonated throughout the normally silent airframe of the *Thermopylae*.

It took only a couple of minutes for Danette the maneuver the aircraft from the invisible transfer sphere to the hangar. "All clear."

Disembarkation commenced immediately, amid a plethora of good spirits, body hugs, and handshakes.

Wendayne threw her arms around Laila, whispered in her ear, "It's been a pleasure working with you."

Laila backed away from the embrace, her eyes glazed. "My identical thought." She remembered something that Wendayne had said – a long time ago.

Patrick Lavery waited anxiously in the hangar for the return of his expensive and experimental toy. He dashed forward as soon at the nuclear engines were switched off. The staircase was mobbed so he took the elevator up to the A Deck, where he encountered Danette, Bryce, and Laila. He expressed no curiosity about mission, whose success had already been radioed ahead. "How did she fly?"

Danette looked haggard. "Like a charm." She walked past him in a daze, totally bushed after flying solo halfway around the world. She joined the rest of the crew on the spiral staircase.

Lavery left to inspect the controls and recording instruments in the pilothouse. Varvarelis stood by the security door as crewmembers streamed past him. He made eye contact with Laila, then looked away. He followed the last crewmember through the doorway into the outer corridor, then closed the door behind him.

Bryce and Laila were the last to walk down the staircase. Walter Gouty stood stolidly on the tarmac at the edge of the airframe. Then Laila remembered something that Bryce had mentioned a long time ago.

She also recalled one of the last emails she received before delving into the past. . . .

"Cover me." Laila strode straight to Gouty and pierced him with a sharp mien. "How much does Roma Idacula know about time transference?"

Gouty's jaw dropped. His intake of breath was short but loud.

Bryce didn't have a gun on him or he might have stabbed it into Gouty's face. He took a handful of Gouty's shirtfront and cocked his left fist. "Did you put my people in harm's way?"

Gouty's mouth worked up and down like the wood jaw of a marionette. Without a ventriloquist to furnish dialogue, he was wordless. Finally he regained a bit of composure. "It's – it's not what you think."

"How much does she know!"

Gouty hunched his shoulders. "She knows all. Or nearly all. But it's not what you think."

More like a South Philly street punk than a full bird colonel: "Enlighten me before I punch your lights out.

Did you leak information to her about the Timepiece?"

Gouty gulped, and gulped again. "You've got it backwards. I obtained *my* information from *her*."

Slowly Bryce released his grip on the physicist. "Explain that."

Not quite fully composed: "The last time I saw her – Roma – she told me about a project that she was working on: a project that was based on synchrotron tests in which subatomic particles were accelerated with an induced magnetic shift that caused them to miss the intended target. She theorized that somehow the particles were converted from mass to energy, and then passed through the target without interaction. What she could not account for was what happened to the energy. According to her initial calculations, the energy increase should have been detectable, but it wasn't.

"She shared all her information with me: energy quanta, particle speed, phase shift, calculations – everything. She even made the cautious suggestion that the particles may have interfered with the space-time continuum in such a way that they created a new pathway through either space or time. That would account for the disappearance. After the conference, she went back to India to continue working on the project.

"I tried to duplicate her work. For a while we communicated via email. She complained that her funding was being cut, and that continued experimentation was being suspended due to the lack of useful results. Then the Chinese became interested in her project. Under a mutual grant process – with India providing one-quarter of the funding and China providing three-quarters – she moved to an undisclosed location in China, where she was to recreate the project and oversee a group of Chinese physicists.

"As you know, China has a greater population than the rest of the world. Their educational system of far superior to ours. In the United States, it's been estimated that ten percent of our students are honor students. By comparison of population, China has more honor students than we have students. They have brilliant physicists who are quick to grasp new concepts, and who can push those concepts to the extremes of physical reality.

"Once Roma got the new project underway, she was prevented from communicating with the outside world. She was kept incommunicado, voluntarily, just as I was. Meanwhile, I made advances that were based on her mathematics and experimentation. You see, she didn't steal anything. *She* invented the technology and discovered the underlying principle of the phenomenon of temporal transference. My work is merely an extension of hers.

"I had no idea how her project was proceeding until Miss Masterson's intelligence network uncovered information about the Time Displacement Apparatus. I can only surmise that the so-called leak originated from Roma's project. Because China has no political or territorial enemies, their security measures fall short by American standards. Their laxity was likely responsible for enabling the Islamic Revolutionary Forces to buy or steal the designs of the Chinese temporal device."

Gouty looked back and forth from Bryce to Laila to Bryce. "That's the truth."

Laila's eyes glazed. "I believe him."

Bryce was less certain. "I don't disbelieve him but I'm willing to give him the benefit of the doubt." To Gouty: "Walt, you are confined to base until your story can be corroborated."

Gouty spread his hands. "I'm already confined."

Bryce managed a weak smile. "Okay then maintain the status quo." He nodded for Laila to follow him. Inside the complex: "Would you like to see a Christian sunrise?"

"I would love to."

On the way up the stairs to the topside cafeteria: "That was really smart confronting Walt that way."

"I have my moments."

"So I've noticed." He stopped at the gazillion-dollar coffee maker. "Want a cup?"

"Maybe later."

Bryce was shocked. "That's the first time I've ever

seen you turn down coffee."

"I guess I'm coffeed out right now. This is now, isn't it? I mean, the now that we left from and not some other now in a parallel time stream?"

Bryce stared at the brightening sky outside the window. "You got me. I suppose time will tell."

"We'll know for certain by and by."

"I hope so. I admit that I don't understand everything that goes on here. I'm not a scientist I'm a soldier."

"So I've noticed."

"A soldier learns to deal with his enemy without hating him. Emotion clouds judgment." After a moment: "You handled yourself pretty well considering that you're *not* a soldier.

Laila's eyes glazed. A moment later she burst into tears. Bryce stood by helplessly while she cried her eyes out for five minutes straight. After she got her breathing rate under control, she dried her eyes on the short sleeve of her hospital scrub. "Wow. I've been holding that in for a long time. I mean – you know what I mean."

"Regrets?"

"About killing that Muslim terrorist?" Laila shook her head. "I'm a pacifist at heart, but I'm a rational pacifist. He forfeited the right of diplomacy when he tried to kill me. That's where I draw the line. A dead person isn't a pacifist; she a dead person."

"Good for you." After a consensual silence. "Do you have any idea what your face looks like?"

"The Frankenstein monster without electrodes. I saw my reflection in the restroom mirror. It could be worse. A proverb I remember from *Bible* school went, 'I wept because I had no shoes, till I met a man who had no feet.' It wasn't from the *Bible*, but the preacher used to quote it to us all the time. He told us to remember it whenever we felt sorry for ourselves. I always have."

There was another consensual silence.

"It's a nice sentiment but it's not always easy to feel that way. Four years ago my wife was killed in a helicopter crash . . . It wasn't even a combat mission . . . They blamed it on pilot error but damn it I know she was an expert pilot. . . . "

"I'm so sorry."

After a long and uncomfortable silence: "That's in the past and I've moved on. But somehow I never got back into the groove. Somehow . . . Anyway you and I have a lot of loose ends to tie up. We've got more work to do before this mission is officially over. Paperwork and such. And after the reports are written there's follow up recon, new intel to gather, analysis. . . . This job never ends. Not as long as there are terrorists in the world. Not as long as there are people who are willing to kill those who don't think the way they do. I – " Bryce faltered, fell silent, then spoke hesitantly: "I – I could use some help in this job. I could get you reassigned. We could work together . . . "

"Is this a proposal?"

Now there was a *long* silence. A yellow crescent peaked above the distant desert mountains. Sunlight bathed the sand and rocks, turning the dark surface to bright familiar ochre.

Bryce shaded his eyes from the glare. He turned his head to look down at Laila. He blinked. "It is if you want it to be."

Laila looked up into Bryce's blue eyes. She swallowed hard and took a deep breath. Then she said two words that she never thought she would say again in this context. "I do."

EPILOGUE

President Frank Marshall chatted with his staff in the Oval Office as the television crew positioned the camera and microphones. A female interne dabbed his face with white powder so as to soften the coarse shadows that were created when the stark overhead lights illuminated his wrinkles in relief. The wall-mounted video camera recorded it all.

The director held up a pair of fingers. "Two minutes, Mr. President."

Marshall nodded. The intern adjusted the red power tie that his wife insisted he wear. He seldom disapproved of her choices; nor did he disapprove now. Although the expression of the tie did not match his layback persona, he wanted to present an image of strength to help convey the harsh importance of his speech.

Mary Marshall glanced at the papers that she held in her hand. "Are you sure you don't want me to have your prepared speech put on the teleprompter? It has already been scanned."

"I'm sure, but you cue me if I get stuck."

"Okay."

"Don't worry. I've given off-the-cuff speeches before. This announcement is supposed to be impromptu, cutting unannounced into commercial television because of the late-breaking nature of the news."

"I know. I just worry that you'll forget an important point, or get the facts out of order."

He smiled. "Your job is to make sure that doesn't happen."

"Are you going to begin with 'my fellow Americans'?"

"That sounds too much like Lyndon Johnson. I'll start without the 'my'."

The director held up a single finger – not the middle digit. "One minute, Mr. President."

Marshall winked at his wife. "Thank you, Margaret," he said to the intern. He took his seat behind the Presidential desk. He displayed confidence and composure:

the personification of quiet equanimity.

The lighting engineer readjusted the angle of the floodlights and slightly reduced the intensity. The director gave him one thumb up. The room fell silent. No one coughed or cleared his throat. No shoes shuffled across the deep pile carpet. The director held up ten fingers; nine; eight; seven . . . one. When he ran out of fingers, a green annunciator light switched on.

The President's face appeared on the room's video screens. A pre-recorded message delivered the standard recitation to the viewers, and was broadcast by a number of radio stations.

"We interrupt this program for a special announcement from the President of the United States, concerning recent developments in the war against terrorism. Speaking to you live from the White House is Frank Marshall."

Like the great actor that he was, President Marshall looked directly at the camera as he spoke: "Fellow Americans and Citizens of the Free World, I bring you first-hand news about recent events that are unprecedented and Earth-shattering. As you know, for many years the Islamic Revolutionary Forces have been engaged in a campaign of terrorism against the non-Muslim world. Their goal is the extermination of free-thinking and free-believing peoples in every corner of the globe. To accomplish this sworn task they have waged a war that is not bound by political borders, that does not require the acquisition of foreign territory, that is fought without compliance with humanitarian principles, and that they swear not to end until every non-Muslim individual on the planet is either dead or has been forcibly converted to Islam. This goal is unconscionable, but it is one which the IRF has vowed to achieve."

Marshall realized that he had mixed his tenses, but there was nothing that he could do about it now. Even if his oratory contained mistakes in grammar, a homey speech was still better than one that was canned and that sounded artificial. In any case, only a self-important English professor was likely to recognize his grammatical misconstructions and call attention to them.

"Combined U.S. and NATO forces have made re-markable progress in combatting terrorist cells in Arabic-speaking nations. They have practically terminated the exportation of militants to peaceful countries. They have gone a long way toward controlling the importation of arms and ammunition that can be used against Christian and Buddhist believers.

"Recently it was learned through our intelligence-gathering services that the IRF was developing awful weapons of mass destruction. They decreased their conduct of chemical and biological warfare in order to focus on an all-out nuclear initiative, in a novel strategy to destroy Christianity by striking at the very core of western religion: the Vatican and the seat of Catholicism. Intelligence sources indicated that the IRF had secretly built plants for the extraction of uranium from pitchblende, and for the distillation of heavy water: commodities that are essential for the production of nuclear devices.

"A secret facility was constructed at an isolated desert location where nuclear devices could be assembled and launched against the heart of the Christian world. Several days ago, intelligence analysts concluded that a nuclear attack was imminent, and so advised me and the Joint Chiefs of Staff. Our military leaders asked for, and I granted, permission to prepare a pre-emptive strike against this facility before the IRF had time to implement their plan to attack the roots of Christianity.

"However, before our present ground forces could move against the assembly plant and launch site, one of the devices from the IRF's nuclear arsenal detonated prematurely. The atomic blast totally destroyed the facility and all of the surrounding support factories, as well as the personnel who were on location at the time, including a number of high-ranking IRF dignitaries and military leaders. In addition, radioactive fallout has contaminated much of the enemy-held territory, not only making it unusable and uninhabitable for years to come, but decimating the surrounding population. As the device was a particularly dirty one, we expect the fatality rate from radiation sickness to be as high as ninety-five percent over the next few weeks.

"The free peoples of the world regret this wholesale catastrophe. We take no delight that it struck the very people who swore allegiance to intolerance and terrorism. While victory in war is often perceived as the death and despoliation of the enemy, the *Bible* offers guidance that should be heeded by the disciples of Allah."

Marshall picked up the Old Testament that lay on his desk, held it so that the title on the black cover showed clearly to his viewers, and opened it to a pre-selected page.

"I would like to read a passage from the Book of Isaiah, chapter fifty-nine, verses seven and eight. 'Their feet run to evil, and they make haste to shed innocent blood: their thoughts are thoughts of iniquity; wasting and destruction are in their paths. The way of peace they know not; and there is no judgment in their goings: they have made them crooked paths: whosoever goeth therein shall not know peace.'

"Muslim terrorists have gone the way of their own choosing. Yet we, as a humanitarian nation that lives under God, mourn their passing. In this country, Muslims are permitted to follow their beliefs, but only as long as they permit others to follow their own beliefs. We do not permit the enforcement of beliefs."

Marshall put down the Old Testament and picked up the New. He turned to another preselected page. "From the New Testament I now read from the Book of Romans, chapter fourteen, verses one through four: 'As for the one who is weak in faith, welcome him, but not to quarrel over opinions. One person believes he may eat anything, while the weak person eats only vegetables. Let not the one who eats despise the one who abstains, and let not the one who abstains pass judgment on the one who eats, for God has welcomed him. Who are you to pass judgment on the servant of another? It is before his own master that he stands or falls. And he will be upheld, for the Lord is able to make him stand.' Muslim terrorists would do well to adopt this creed."

He gently closed the book. "I will now recite a passage which, because of its stupendous, indeed, supreme significance with regard to current events, I have committed to memory. It is from the last book of the New Testament, the Book of Revelation, chapter twenty-two, verse twelve: 'And, behold, I come quickly! And my reward is with me, to give every man according as his work shall be.' "

Marshall took a moment to moisten his lips. He maintained eye contact with the camera lens. "With me tonight is one who will make his own address: in behalf of all Americans, in behalf of all Citizens of the Free World, whatever their faith may be."

Now an elderly gentleman who had been standing by the sidelines stepped forward. His official regalia sharply rivaled the President's simplistic dark blue suit. Behind the gentleman stood another who wore a less glamorous robe of woven wool. And behind Him stood his proud translator.

"The Pope will now disclose a revelation that Christians everywhere have been anticipating for the past two millennia: one that will fortify the faith of the Christian world . . . "

Books by the Author

Science Fiction
A Different Universe
A Different Dimension
A Different Continuum
Entropy (a novel of conceptual breakthrough)
A Journey to the Center of the Earth
The Mold
Return to Mars
Second Coming
Silent Autumn
Subaqueous
The Time Dragons Trilogy
       A Time for Dragons
       Dragons Past
       No Future for Dragons

Sci-Fi Action/Adventure Novels
Memory Lane
Mind Set
The Peking Papers

Supernatural Horror Novel
The Lurking: Curse of the Jersey Devil

Vietnam Novel
Lonely Conflict

The Popular Dive Guide Series

Shipwrecks of Massachusetts: North
Shipwrecks of Massachusetts: South
Shipwrecks of Rhode Island and Connecticut
Shipwrecks of New York
Shipwrecks of New Jersey (1988)
Shipwrecks of New Jersey: North
Shipwrecks of New Jersey: Central
Shipwrecks of New Jersey: South
Shipwrecks of Delaware and Maryland (1990 Edition)
Shipwrecks of Delaware and Maryland (2002 Edition)
Shipwrecks of the Chesapeake Bay in Maryland Waters
Shipwrecks of Virginia
Shipwrecks of North Carolina: Diamond Shoals North
Shipwrecks of North Carolina: Hatteras Inlet South
Shipwrecks of South Carolina and Georgia

Shipwreck and Nautical History

Andrea Doria: Dive to an Era
Deep, Dark, and Dangerous: Adventures and Reflec-
    tions on the Andrea Doria
Great Lakes Shipwrecks: a Photographic Odyssey
The Fuhrer's U-boats in American Waters
Ironclad Legacy: Battles of the USS Monitor
The Kaiser's U-boats in American Waters
The Lusitania Controversies: Atrocity of War and a
    Wreck-Diving History (Book One)
The Lusitania Controversies: Dangerous Descents into
    Shipwrecks and Law (Book Two)
The Nautical Cyclopedia
Shadow Divers Exposed: the Real Saga of the U-869
Shipwreck Heresies
The Shipwreck Research Handbook
Shipwreck Sagas
Stolen Heritage: Grand Theft of the Hamilton/Scourge
Track of the Gray Wolf
Underwater Reflections
USS San Diego: the Last Armored Cruiser
Wreck Diving Adventures

Dive Training
Primary Wreck Diving Guide
Advanced Wreck Diving Guide
The Advanced Wreck Diving Handbook
Ultimate Wreck Diving Guide
The Technical Diving Handbook

Nonfiction
The Absurdity Principle
Wilderness Canoeing

Videotape or DVD
The Battle for the USS Monitor

Visit the GGP website for availability of titles:
http://www.ggentile.com